MAGNOLIA SUNSET

GISELLE CARMICHAEL

Genesis Press, Inc.

Indigo Love Stories

An imprint of Genesis Press, Inc.
Publishing Company

Genesis Press, Inc.
P.O. Box 101
Columbus, MS 39703

ISBN-13: 978-1-58571-260-1
ISBN-10: 1-58571-260-4
Manufactured in the United States of America

First Edition 2002
Second Edition 2007

Visit us at www.genesis-press.com or call at 1-888-Indigo-1

DEDICATION

Magnolia Sunset *is dedicated to the loving memory of my*
mother, Mrs. Theresa W. Dudley, *my best friend. May I*
always make you proud. Until we meet again, your loving
first born.

CHAPTER 1

She was late. The meeting at the community center began ten minutes ago and there was no way she could miss it. The meeting was too important to her. One more block and a run through the parking lot and she would be there. Anxious to make the meeting, she pressed the accelerator of her temperamental vehicle a little harder as she sped through the yellow light. For the hundredth time today, she rehearsed her speech to be presented to the board members. It had to be perfect because she knew there would be opposition. A flash of light in her rear view mirror drew her attention. Then the piercing siren demanded her attention.

"This can't be happening," Nicole Edwards wailed as she slapped the steering wheel, then pulled over to the side of the road.

As one of Biloxi's finest pulled back into traffic after giving her a ticket, Nicole wondered if the day would ever end. Fridays simply weren't meant to be like this. They were laid back winding-down days. The long workweek was all but over and the promise of a relaxing weekend loomed ahead. Since waking up Monday morning, she had been looking forward to Friday. Now it was here, and it was an absolute nightmare. She simply wished she had stayed in bed with the covers pulled up over her head. It had all begun with her turning off the alarm this morning and drifting back to sleep. By the time she awakened some fifteen minutes later, her schedule was already thrown off. And as luck would have it, her recently paid off car quit at the intersection of Pass Road and Veterans Avenue on her way to work. Fortunately, she was able to restart it and make it to work on time. She immediately telephoned the garage and made arrangements to have the car picked up. Gary, her mechanic, promised to check it out and return it to work before the school day ended. Well, of course not only was he late in delivering the car, but he hadn't discovered the problem. So once again she was behind schedule and now because of the motorcycle cop, she was even later. Finally she turned into the parking lot of the community center. She took the first parking space she saw. With ticket in hand, Nicole rushed to the designated meeting room and quietly slipped into a chair in the rear of the room.

Carmen Wells, the center's director, was at the microphone outlining her ideas for the summer program. Quite outspoken, she had the tendency to bulldoze everyone in her path, as Nicole knew from experience. Ostracized during high school, Nicole had hoped upon her return from Spelman that she and Carmen would be able to conduct themselves like adults when their paths crossed. It hadn't happened. Carmen, though successful, took great pleasure in reminding Nicole that no matter what degree she possessed, she would never be an equal.

When the time came to introduce new courses for the summer program, one parent suggested the multicultural class that had been such a success last summer. Carmen immediately disapproved with a noticeable frown as the parent spoke. Once the speaker concluded, Carmen tried to force her choice of art appreciation through the meeting, stating that she wanted to introduce the students to a little culture. When the parent, joined by others, demanded the multicultural class due to its popularity with the students, Carmen was eventually forced to concede. Not for long, however. She immediately pointed out that the instructor from last summer was no longer in the area; therefore there was no instructor for the course.

On that note, Nicole immediately introduced herself, then informed the gathering that she had been asked by the instructor to conduct the course.

If Carmen was peeved before she was now steaming. Giving Nicole the eye, Carmen thought of all the times through the years the woman had interfered with her plans. It was Nicole, who beat her grade point average all four years of high school capturing the limelight and becoming senior class valedictorian—the goal she had set for herself. She had rejoiced when Nicole left for Atlanta to attend college believing that she wouldn't return. But she had, possessing both a degree and teacher's certificate. And because of Nicole's friendship with her cousin's fiancée, Carmen had to endure her presence at social gatherings, where Nicole definitely didn't belong. Not to mention the only two men she ever truly cared for turned out to be interested in Nicole. Frank Lyons, her high school sweetheart, had humiliated her by sneaking around with the trollop, and Daryl Lanier, the man she wanted to marry, hardly knew she existed because of his infatuation with Nicole. And now here she was upsetting her plans once again.

Flashing her green eyes in agitation, she promptly lashed out at Nicole. "That may be, Ms. Edwards, but no one ran that decision by me. As the center's director I would like to introduce something more valuable to the students, like art appreciation."

"It's a summer program, Carmen. The students want to have fun, and it is quite obvious from what their parents had to say that they enjoyed the course last year. And besides, what's more valuable than learning about the various cultures which comprise our constantly changing city?" Nicole asked passionately, undaunted by Carmen's attitude.

Encouraged by murmurs of agreement, Nicole launched into outlining her ideas for the summer course. In the end she gained approval from both the attending board members and parents and returned to her chair proud of her accomplishment. At the conclusion of the meeting, she immediately made a dash for the car, knowing Carmen would be out for blood. Several blocks away she allowed herself to finally relax.

After an hour of grocery shopping she returned home to hear the faint sound of the ringing telephone coming through the door. Slipping the two plastic grocery bags onto her left arm she fumbled with her keys in her right hand. Finally mane aging to insert the key, she pushed the door open, then kicked it closed as she rushed through the living room headed for the telephone in the kitchen. With a relieved sigh she deposited the groceries onto the countertop while reaching for the telephone with her free hand.

"Hello," Nicole spoke urgently into the receiver.

"You sound out of breath," came the quick reply from Gina Lanier, Nicole's best friend. They were an odd pair. Where Nicole was petite and reserved, Gina was a five-ten statuesque, honey-brown woman who embraced life. Her romantic nature was legendary, and unfortunately for Nicole, she was always the target of her matchmaking schemes. "With any luck I've interrupted something stimulating, but knowing you it's only wishful thinking."

Nicole listened to Gina's tsking sound. "Did you call to get on my nerves or was there a purpose for the telephone call?"

"Okay, not in a joking mood, huh?" Gina replied with a hint of mirth in her voice. "Keith and I want to invite you out to dinner."

"That's a possibility. When?" Nicole asked as she unpacked groceries.

'Tonight, say about seven at The Crown Room."

The short notice of the invitation set off warnings inside Nicole's head. She had known Gina since high school and knew when her girlfriend was up to something.

"Why the sudden invitation, Gina? Shouldn't you and Keith be finalizing the details of your upcoming nuptials?"

"You are so suspicious, Nicole. I swear, you should have been a lawyer instead of a teacher," Gina responded evasively.

Nicole's audible sigh announced that she was waiting for the truth.

"All right already! Keith's college roommate has recently moved here, and he wanted to introduce you since you'll both be in the wedding."

Silent, Nicole processed Gina's words carefully, missing nothing. After a moment she said, "We could meet at the rehearsal dinner, Gina."

"Yeah, I know, but that's a month and a half away and Keith wanted to introduce him to someone nice." Gina knew her explanation was weak, and that her bright friend would not let her escape without the truth. And she was correct.

"Keith attended the Air Force Academy."

"Okay, you're right, but before you go off, give me a chance to explain," Gina hurriedly spoke.

"There's nothing to explain. He's in the military, assigned to the local base, and I'm not interested."

Frustrated, Gina forged ahead. "Nicole, for a woman who graduated from high school at sixteen, you're being ridiculous. You're intelligent enough to know that all military men are not like your father. They don't walk away from their families."

"I may be ridiculous, but it's my life—my decision. I thought you understood my feelings, Gina."

"I do, Nicole, and you have every right to them," Gina conceded, feeling guilty for making light of her friend's feelings. "Keith is a military man and you think the world of him. He wouldn't introduce you to a creep."

Anger deflated, Nicole leaned against the kitchen counter, shutting her eyes as she contemplated Gina's words. Keith Thibodeaux was a fine African-American man with honorable intentions towards her friend. He was intelligent, sensitive, and spiritual—every woman's dream. Not to mention he was six-feet-four inches of muscle and good looks. But that didn't mean his friend was of the same caliber. However, she couldn't envision Keith associating with someone of questionable character.

"Okay, I'll join you." Nicole finally broke the silence. "This guy sure better be more exciting than the new bestseller I picked up today."

Relieved by Nicole's decision, Gina rushed on, filling Nicole in on the plans for the evening. Before disconnecting from the call, Gina offered to pick Nicole up for dinner after hearing about her car trouble.

"No thanks. I prefer to take my car, just in case the prince turns out to be a frog."

"Nicole, one more thing before I hang up." There was a hesitation to Gina's voice.

"Yes?"

"Give this guy a chance. Keith considers him a real friend."

"Well, because I think so highly of Keith, I promise to be on my best behavior."

Hanging up, Nicole swiftly completed the task of storing groceries. She poured herself a glass of orange juice and took a seat at the kitchen table. Lost in thought, she traced the design of the ceramic tabletop. It had been some time since she had been on a date. Six months to be exact. Larry Douglas, the computer installer for the school's computer lab had convinced her to have lunch with him. On second thought, maybe that hadn't constituted a date. It wasn't as though men failed to approach her, quite the opposite to be exact, yet for Nicole, that period of getting to know each other was stressful. She never knew when the subject of family would rear its ugly head and ruin a perfect evening.

Nicole rose from the table while draining her glass empty. At the sink, she rinsed it out then placed it on the top rack of the dishwasher. There beside it were four other glasses. On the lower level stood four plates. Both were testimony to her solitary life. Sometimes she wondered if there would ever come a time when a full load of dishes would be the norm. At the pace her social life was going, she doubted it, but then she couldn't blame anyone for that but herself. If it were left to the women at church, the teachers she worked with, or Gina, she would be married with a house filled with children. However, the decision was hers and she had been very selective in the men she dated. If a man was interested in appearances and what others thought of him, she wasn't interested. If a man sought only to possess the package and not seek the person within, she wasn't interested. She also had no interest in a man who recited the who's who of his family tree. She knew to run from that situation. And she most definitely didn't get involved with a man in uniform. Life had taught her that most valuable lesson. So why then had she agreed to meet this bluesuiter?

She knew the reason why: because Gina had asked and she couldn't refuse her best friend anything. She was a special woman, her friend. Gina had been there for her on numerous occasions and proven her loyalty to her as a friend, even when itwasn't the most popular decision she could have made. High school for most teens could be trying and traumatic, but for Nicole it had proven to be a nightmare. Until the second semester of her freshman year when she sat down beside Gina Lanier in algebra, Nicole had been without friends: From the moment Gina introduced herself, they had bonded. Nicole was still at a loss to name what forged and held their relationship together till this day, but whatever it was, she was grateful. When rumors about her background began to circulate, she feared Gina would discontinue their friendship. She had learned during the course of their brief friendship that Gina came from a well-to-do Biloxi family. She could belong to any one of the school cliques, but bewildering to Nicole, she maintained their relationship despite the hassle it caused her. At school Gina had to contend with the nasty remarks by their classmates, and at home she dealt with her mother. Mrs. Lanier initially hadn't believed Nicole was an appropriate friend for her well-bred daughter, but in the interest of fairness, Nicole had to concede Mrs. Lanier had always treated her graciously. Today, Nicole felt like another daughter. Mrs. Lanier advised, reprimanded, and praised her, just as she did her son and daughter, for which Nicole would always be grateful.

Later in the bedroom Nicole removed the pantsuit she'd worn to work, tossing it across the bed. Standing in the open doorway of her closet she surveyed its contents. Thanks to Gina being a social butterfly and always dragging Nicole along, she had accumulated a nice collection of evening attire. Due to the mild winter, March was actually warm and humid this year. With that in mind she selected a short-sleeved, shimmering gold dress with fringe hemline. The sassy fit and just-bove-the-knee length enhanced her five-four height. The golden color complemented her rich sable complexion. She selected the gold braided sandals with heels, which had been purchased specifically for the dress. Gold teardrop earrings would be her only jewelry for the evening.

Under the warm spray of the shower she quickly washed her hair, then completed her shower with a rose-scented gel.

While skillfully applying make-up—just enough for an evening on the town—she considered a hairstyle for the evening. Deciding upon a neat sophisticated French roll, she plugged in the blow dryer. An hour later she was pleased with the results.

Back in the bedroom she slid into her dress and shoes. On the back of the bedroom door hung a full-length mirror. Pushing the door closed, she surveyed her appearance. She was pleased by what she saw and silently hoped this friend of Keith's was worth the effort. He probably wasn't, but what the devil, she didn't get invited to The Crown Room every day. Staring at her reflection a moment longer, she suddenly became apprehensive about the evening. The subject of family was bound to come up. They were meeting because of a wedding, after all, and weddings and families went hand in hand. Shaking her head miserably, Nicole tried to think of a polite way to explain being abandoned as an infant in polite conversation.

There had been such an occasion just prior to college graduation. She had been dating a young man from an Atlanta family for about a year. Devin Jamison had been her first love. She'd thought the sun rose and set by his very existence. A week prior to graduation his parents had invited her to their home for the weekend. Thinking that Devin had informed his parents about her background, Nicole was caught completely unaware when his mother asked about her parents. She had looked to Devin for an explanation, but had received only an apologetic expression. Left to fend for herself, she had promptly informed his parents about her abandonment, how she'd subsequently become a ward of the state. The look of horror and distaste which marred Mrs. Jamison's face would be forever etched in her memory. Mrs. Jamison swiftly told her in no uncertain terms that a relationship between her and their son would not be tolerated. The family had dreams of him entering politics and her questionable background could only hinder his success. She had hoped Devin would stand up and defend their relationship, but he hadn't. Nicole instead left his home wondering when she would cease being punished for something she'd had no control over.

Of course, she could lie about it and allow people to believe that her parents were dead, but that wasn't her style. She didn't run from the truth. The one time in high school that she had lied about her parental status, she had been horribly embarrassed with the truth, thanks to Carmen. Never again would she be made to feel the need to lie. People would have to accept her "as is" or not at all. And so she stood dreading the evening and speculating about the fallout effect of the truth. If the man were anything remotely similar to Keith, he would understand and not hold it against her.

"Shoot, why did I agree to this stupid dinner?" she asked aloud into the mirror. Then she promptly replied, "Because Gina asked and Keith is one of the nicest people you know." With a silent pep talk she reconstructed her confidence.

Grabbing her keys and evening purse, she left the bedroom and doubts behind.

Minutes later as she tried to start her car for the fifth time, she finally conceded that it had died. She wanted to call off the evening altogether and walked back inside her home with that intention. Then the thought of meeting this man at the upcoming wedding and the possible negative impression from her absence caused her to promptly go into action.

   Nicole entered the Imperial Palace Casino slightly late. She walked through the lobby to the bank of elevators. Stepping on board, she selected the 32nd floor. As she exited the elevator she was oblivious to the numerous male stares of appreciation and feminine stares of envy. She was greeted warmly by the young maitre d', and upon requesting Mr. Thibodeaux's table, she was escorted back. She followed the young man in an awkward path around white linen draped tables before spotting her friends near the window overlooking the Back Bay of Biloxi. Quickly noting that there were four people sitting at the table instead of three, and that the extra body was that of a woman, Nicole felt instantly like a fifth wheel. Suddenly confused, she debated between leaving before anyone one saw her or being the mature adult that she was and walking over to the table. Just as she was about to say the heck with being an adult and leave, Gina looked up and spotted her. With a vigorous wave Gina summoned her forward.

   Xavier Ramón turned his head in the direction Gina was waving and looked into the face of the most exquisite woman he had ever seen. He sure hoped this was his date for the evening. The woman sifting to his right was definitely not his type. Rising as the maitre d' escorted the woman to their table, he said a silent thank you.

"Good evening," Nicole addressed the table. As all heads turned in her direction, she was rendered speechless. The woman sitting beside Keith's friend was Carmen Wells. Obviously she had jumped to the wrong conclusion about this evening. Giving Gina a hug before taking her seat, Nicole discreetly scolded Gina for not giving notice that Carmen would be present.

"She invited herself when she discovered an available man would be present," Gina whispered back, annoyed with Carmen's presumption.

As Nicole stood beside him, Xavier inhaled the pleasant rose scent wafting from her sable brown skin. She stood just barely to his shoulders in heels. Using his professional skill, he placed her weight at one hundred twenty pounds or somewhere close. The fit of her dress made it possible to discern that she was definitely not skinny, but simply smaller than the women he usually dated. He was an old fashioned guy who enjoyed the feel of a full-bodied woman within his arms. Continuing his survey, he noted her high cheekbones and delicate, square chin. On closer observation he noted a slight cleft in the chin. A delectable mouth drew his rapt attention, as did the raven darkness of her fine straight hair. The hairstyle, however, seemed too severe for such delicate features. But what startled him most about this woman was the shape and color of her soulful eyes—almond-shaped, hinting of Asian heritage, and golden brown. She appeared young, almost too young for his taste, but when she turned the full force of her gaze upon him, it didn't matter. His heart lurched at the huskiness of her voice and the knowledge that she could spell trouble for his peace of mind.

Accepting her seat as the maitre d' assisted, two things became instantly clear to Nicole. One, Carmen resented her presence at the table. And two, Xavier Ramón was male magnetism personified. He appeared to be well over six feet tall and solidly built. The olive green suit he wore did nothing to camouflage the lean muscle mass beneath. Freshly barbered, close cut hair glistened with health. The caramel brown skin of his lean face was smooth and clear. Thick silken brows and a neatly trimmed mustache drew one's attention to his perfectly sculptured mouth. And when his steel gray eyes locked onto her, Nicole immediately felt their hypnotic pull. He captivated the table with their force and his charismatic smile. The man would be difficult to ignore. Extending her hand as they were introduced, Nicole prepared to mask her response. But at the moment of contact, an electrical current sizzled up her arm like red-hot lightning forcing her to wince.

Xavier experienced it as well. He was glad to see this cool number rattled by their electrifying chemistry. He had sensed her desire to ignore him. For what reason he wasn't sure, but the golden glow in her eyes indicated it wasn't going to happen. She was keenly aware of him now.

"It's a pleasure to meet you, Nicole," Xavier said without releasing her hand. His commanding voice was as smooth as aged brandy and just as potent "I've heard so much about you that I feel as though I already know you." He flashed his roguish smile for sheer effect and was delighted by Nicole's breathless response.

She knew her eyes were glowing golden, communicating her captivation with this man, but she was unable to rein in her response.

"Nice to meet you too, Xavier."

She didn't dare say more. She couldn't think with the electrical current running from her fingers through her arm, then straight for the brain. Placing her freed hand finally into her lap, she gave him a faint smile.

"So we meet again, Nicole." Carmen's high-pitched voice drew everyone's attention. Her smile was saccharine sweet, but her eyes were sheer hostility.

"It appears so"

Carmen didn't waste any time making it perfectly clear that she was staking a claim to Xavier Ramón. She slipped her arm through his familiarly and flashed her high wattage smile, ignoring Nicole completely.

For an exhausting hour Carmen monopolized the entire conversation. She spoke of her travels to Europe and shopping sprees in New York, of political fund raisers and Mardi Gras balls. Any subject that reminded Nicole of Carmen's social standing was up for discussion.

On several attempts Keith tried unsuccessfully to take command of the conversation. For an intelligent woman, Carmen could behave quite childishly at times. At one point she actually recited every reason why she was any man's best catch, beginning with her family lineage and concluding with her family's wealth and the advantages it could offer the right man. She has no shame, Nicole thought to herself, and Xavier Ramón must be an idiot. He disgustingly hung on to Carmen's every word. Maybe he wasn't as together as Keith.

Initially she'd thought he might prove her theory about military men wrong, but watching the interplay between him and Carmen fortified her belief. It was clear he wasn't interested in a woman of substance, but a pretty face, for Carmen held his undivided attention. And she made it obvious she wanted the man.

"I've never been out with one of Keith's officer friends," Carmen purred in her annoying voice. "Are you a prosecutor in the Judge Advocate's Office like Keith? And what did you say your rank was again?"

If you're waiting on this officer friend to ask you out, you never will, Xavier thought "I'm a major, but no I'm not a prosecutor," Xavier answered with a forced, smile thinking about the woman sitting silently to his left. He had been keenly aware of Nicole all through dinner and more so now over coffee. The vibes generated said she didn't care for Carmen and liked him even less. Every attempt he'd made at conversation, on those few occasions when Carmen allowed someone else to speak, had been aborted by her curt responses. Unable to sit there any longer without looking at her, Xavier turned the full force of his gaze upon her.

Nicole knew the moment that he did. Helpless, her eyes rose slowly from her cup of coffee to be captured by the gray magnetism of his. Unsure of the game he was playing, she tried for a stern glare.

Carmen was quite aware that she had lost Xavier's attention. All evening he had been pretending to listen to her, but she could tell by his sly glances in Nicole's direction that it was she he was concentrating on. Motivated by her love for Daryl and her deep resentment of Nicole, Carmen set out to remind Nicole of her place in society. She didn't deserve respectable men like Daryl and Xavier, and the sooner she realized that, the sooner she would end things with Daryl. And so with that in mind she set out to eliminate the competition.

"Xavier, is your father a military man as well?" Carmen asked, stealing a glance at Nicole.

"Actually no."

"May I ask what he does?"

For the briefest of moments Xavier and Keith's eyes collided. Carmen, desperate for a kill, missed the exchange, but not Nicole. She sensed there would be more to the answer than what Xavier would actually reveal. She was right, for Xavier offered no great detail. We share a love for the law. He's happy. That's all that matters."

"Of course, but there's nothing wrong with being financially secure," Carmen spoke smugly. "My father founded the first African-American bank and insurance company here on the coast." She beamed with pride.

Keith, who was truly sick of his cousin, added, "I believe he and my mother founded the bank and insurance company, Carmen."

"Well of course, Keith, that's what I meant."

Keith and Gina shared one of those silent exchanges between lovers. He knew what Gina was thinking because it was his thought as well, so he tried to steer the conversation in a different direction, but was interrupted by Xavier.

"Nicole, you've been quiet this evening. Are we boring you?" he asked, probing the depths of her golden brown eyes for the truth.

"No, just taking it all in," she lied.

Smiling a knowing smile as she spoke the words, he arched his left brow like a parent challenging a guilty child for the truth. "Are you following in the footsteps of your parents?"

Nicole's heart stilled, then slowly began pumping once more. She'd known the moment was coming because Carmen had set the stage, yet she was thrown off balance when Xavier asked the question. Thinking quickly, she offered another curt response.

"No." *Now move on to another subject.*

The abrupt reply wasn't lost on Xavier. He read the fear momentarily visible within her eyes and could have sworn that for a moment there she had actually stopped breathing. He presumed the subject of her family wasn't one of her favorite topics either. As he watched her trying not to squirm, he wondered what secret she was hiding. He wouldn't push. He would respect her privacy because he understood the need.

"Nicole, I swear you can be so rude at times. Can't you see the man is interested in you? Just tell him that you were abandoned as an infant and raised in foster homes," Carmen reprimanded with false indifference.

The conversation at the table immediately ceased. It was several tense heartbeats before Keith and Gina both launched into chastising Carmen for *her* rudeness. Nicole recognized it for what it was. A challenge and a reminder that men like Xavier always chose women like Carmen. Nicole had heard plenty of nasty comments through the years that she was good enough to sneak around with, but never acceptable to take home. And so Carmen had politely, although childishly, reminded her that Xavier might sleep with her, but he would marry a woman like Carmen, socially acceptable.

Xavier sat quietly watching the display of emotion appear in Nicole's eyes, then disappear. He, too, recognized Carmen's words for what they were—an ambush. Continuing to observe Nicole as she squared her shoulders and raised her regal head a notch higher, Xavier knew in that single moment that she was a fighter and someone he wanted to know better.

With an unwavering stare Nicole nailed Carmen to her chair. However, tempering her response, she simply said, "Xavier, it appears Carmen has answered your question. I'm sure that if there is anything else you wish to know about me, Carmen will be more than happy to supply the details."

Keith jumped in before Nicole could say more and Carmen could reply. The night had been a disaster. He wished he hadn't let it slip that they were meeting Xavier for dinner. He had really hoped his friend and Nicole would hit it off, but they hadn't said more than five words to each other, once again because of Carmen. She was his cousin and he loved her, but she was one self-centered, spiteful, materialistic woman. The last thing Xavier needed was a woman like that in his life.

"Nicole, I apologize for my cousin's rudeness. Believe me, we were raised better than that," Keith commented, shooting daggers at Carmen.

Unfazed, Carmen pressed further. "Oh, be quiet Keith! I was merely trying to help Xavier understand why everyone was discussing family except Nicole. Didn't you see the curious expression on his face every time she responded with a one-word answer? How was the poor man to know she didn't have parents to follow? It's not like Nicole was going to provide the information," Carmen stated flippantly, scoring a bulls-eye.

Busted, Xavier was forced to dig himself out of the hole Carmen had dug for him.

"I have to admit I was curious, Nicole. When I tried to move the conversation in your direction, you cut me off," Xavier voiced openly and honestly. He hoped his words weren't as offensive as Carmen's were, but he couldn't lie now. He knew Nicole would be able to sense the truth.

The moment Xavier began to speak Nicole felt Gina's hand searching, then claiming her own, which were clinched tightly within her lap. The loving touch was just what she needed at the moment She glanced at her friend and the man she was due to marry and said a silent prayer for their happiness. They were both good people. Fortified by their love, she faced Xavier and Carmen.

"It's really all right, Keith. Yes, it's true, Xavier; I don't have a family. I was raised by the State of Mississippi after my mother abandoned me as an infant. My heritage is questionable, yet all indications are that I'm half Vietnamese and half African-American. And with that said, I believe I'm going to call it an evening." Nicole rose from the table.

Gina knew how painful it was for Nicole to bare her soul to complete strangers and reached out to halt her friend's escape. She couldn't let her go home like this.

"You might not have parents, Nicole, but you most definitely have a sister for life," Gina declared lovingly.

Nicole squeezed Gina's hand affectionately and flashed a genuine smile for the first time that evening. "That I know."

Gina continued to hold Nicole's hand. "Did you drive tonight?"

"No. My car wouldn't start. I guess it finally died on me. I'll take care of it tomorrow," Nicole commented, unconcerned.

"Since you don't have your car, come dancing with us at the Officers' Club, then we'll take you home later." Gina rushed on, sensing Nicole's rejection of the idea.

The only place Nicole wanted to go was home. This had been the longest day and evening in history and she was ready to put an end to it.

"No thanks. I'm sure Carmen and Xavier would love to join you." She made a point to sound sweet and uncaring.

Xavier missed the exchange between the two women. He was still processing the news of Nicole's abandonment. Never in his wildest dreams would he believe this gorgeous slip of a woman had been abandoned as an infant. What kind of woman carried a child for nine months only to abandon it? *The same type who place a price on a child.* She had been hurt. He saw it within her eyes. Soulful eyes his grandmother would have called them, eyes that had seen too much. In that instant he wanted to be the one who lifted the veil of sadness from them.

Only now realizing that Nicole was leaving and that she planned to call a cab, Xavier seized the opportunity. He desperately wanted to get to know this young woman. Something about her called to him and he was driven to answer.

"There's no need for a cab. I would be pleased to escort you home."

Nicole glanced back over her shoulder trying to gauge his sincerity. What she saw reflected within his eyes was more than sincerity, and it frightened her.

"I appreciate the offer, but I don't want to spoil your evening."

"You heard the lady. Let's go dancing," Carmen demanded, grabbing onto Xavier's arm.

Very gently Xavier extracted his arm. Saying goodnight to

Carmen and promising to speak with Keith tomorrow, he kissed

Gina goodnight warmly. With a guiding hand to the small of

Nicole's rigid back, he steered them towards the exit.

Clearing the doorway, Nicole pulled up short, then proceeded to encourage him to join the others.

"Major Ramón, there is no need for you to cut your evening short."

"Humor me, please." The sincerity within his eyes finally made her comply.

"All right, Major Ramón, I accept your offer."

CHAPTER 2

Side by side Nicole Edwards and Xavier Ramón walked out into the well-lit parking deck of the casino. The thick muggy air immediately cloaked them in a blanket of intimacy. Both were highly aware of the person beside them, but neither spoke a word. To distract her attention from Xavier, Nicole tried to guess which vehicle belonged to the man. Something large, yet stylish and most definitely powerful she guessed. He was a tall man requiring plenty of leg—room, so no small sedan for him. As they continued to walk in silence, Nicole instantly realized how safe she felt beside him. His military training was evident in his continual scanning of their surroundings as they walked through the parking deck. She wondered what he did in the Air Force, knowing that whatever it was, he was excellent at it

Feeling Nicole observing him, Xavier returned her open stare, smiling slightly as she quickly whipped her head around to face forward. He decided it was going to be tough getting to know this young woman. But, nothing got his juices to flowing like a good challenge, and Nicole Edwards would definitely be a challenge. Funny, he had never been attracted to younger women. One or two years younger was the limit. But there was something about Nicole which sparked his interest. He wondered how old she actually was. He knew Keith was thirty-five, like himself, and that Gina was younger than he was, but how much younger he wasn't sure.

"Here we are," Xavier announced as they came to a black Lincoln Navigator.

Smiling, Nicole silently congratulated herself on pegging Xavier correctly. The dark, sleek, and powerful vehicle complemented his personality.

As Xavier unlocked the doors automatically with the remote, Nicole contemplated how to gracefully maneuver herself onto the elevated seat. Xavier sensed her problem and came to the rescue. Opening the door for Nicole, he graciously assisted her onto the buffer-soft leather seat with a "watch your head" as his hands enclosed her waist and lifted.

Securing her seatbelt, Nicole acknowledged that under normal circumstances they would probably be friends, but at the moment, there were too many obstacles in the way. For starters, he was a major in the United States Air Force—a definite no-no, and lastly, her parentless background. She had been quite conscious of Xavier's silent pondering at her announcement. It had disturbed him deeply. No doubt he pitied her, or then again, maybe he was thanking the Lord it wasn't him. Anyway, if it hadn't been for Carmen's *helpfulness,* or his ultimate bust, he wouldn't have graciously offered her a ride home. She understood the workings of a guilty conscience.

Nicole supplied her address and directions to her home once he too was secured inside the vehicle. Then she sat back quietly, waiting for this night to end.

"You're not far from me," Xavier commented before starting the engine. He waited for the logical question about exactly where he lived, but it didn't come and he didn't volunteer the information. This woman was making it painfully clear that she wanted nothing to do with him beyond a ride home. Deciding that was okay with him, Xavier switched on the radio, searching for the "Beat of the Bay." As the Mobile radio station played the latest hit, he maneuvered out of the parking space.

Nicole knew she was being rude and petty when she didn't follow up with the polite question, but she didn't care. Why should she make small talk with a man who was only being nice to her because of his guilty conscience? It wasn't like they had anything in common other than Gina and Keith. And conversation would only lead to more probing questions. She would leave things as they were.

Nicole folded her arms across her chest as they rode silently down Highway 90. She lost herself in the view. The moon reflecting off the calm water illuminated the night. Even at this late hour people could be seen walking along the beach or sitting on the boardwalk benches. Watching the numerous couples snuggled together, Nicole longed to experience that kind of love. Was it possible that one day she too could find that special someone who wouldn't care that she didn't have a family name or heritage to pass on? Someone who could simply appreciate her and unconditionally love the woman she was. Maybe, but she wouldn't get her hopes up, because she had already experienced a lifetime of disappointment Glancing over at Xavier she knew not to place her hopes and dreams on him.

Xavier couldn't stand the silence. He also couldn't stand Nicole's obvious dislike of him. Had he imagined their initial response to each other? *No.* He was certain she'd experienced the intense attraction just as he. Why then, was she finding it so easy to ignore him?

"Nicole, I never meant to offend you when I inquired about your parents."

Drawn from the view outside the window Nicole studied the man to her left. "I know you didn't, Major."

"If that's true, why the silent treatment?"

"Was there something you wanted to discuss?" she asked flippantly.

"No, Ms. Edwards, nothing in particular, just the customary polite conversation between new acquaintances. For instance, what do you do for a living?"

Sensing that the man wouldn't give up, Nicole relented, giving Xavier her undivided attention. "I'm a second grade teacher."

"You're a teacher?" Xavier exclaimed, shocked. "No teacher I ever had looked like you."

Despite herself, Nicole laughed. The sound of her husky laughter delighted Xavier. He recalled being stunned by the alto resonance of her voice earlier. It too didn't seem fitting for such a young woman.

"Poor Xavier. I bet they all had warts on their chins and flying broomsticks in the closet."

"Okay, so they weren't witches, but they weren't stunning like you."

He chanced a glance in her direction at the next red light. Now that she had relaxed and was talking she appeared more beautiful than before.

"Trust me, my second graders don't think I'm anything special."

"You're wrong. I bet there is some young boy in your class crazy in love with you." Xavier joined Nicole in laughter, liking the sound of their mingled voices.

"You sound like someone who knows."

"There *was* Miss Jackson, my first grade teacher. Now that I think about it, she wasn't actually all that special, but to a young impressionable male mind she was everything."

Laughing softly, Nicole turned her head toward Xavier. She was beginning to see him in a new light. "You're a romantic, Major Ramón.

Xavier quickly glanced at her. "Does that surprise you?"

"I don't know you well enough to be surprised."

"We can remedy that quickly. Ask me anything."

"Okay, what's your military duty?"

"I'm commander of the security forces squadron," he stated proudly.

"You're a cop?" Nicole blurted. "I should have known. You exude power and authority, and you're very aware of your surroundings."

"Actually we're called force protectors these days. I hope those qualities aren't negatives in your book."

"No, of course not. Just the opposite actually?

They rode in silence for two blocks. "Where do you teach?" Xavier asked, turning the questioning back onto Nicole.

"Biloxi Christian Academy. This is my second year teaching."

"Oh no, I don't believe this," Xavier laughed. "You're Miss Edwards. My son can't stop talking about you."

"Your son?" Nicole stared, confused. Gina hadn't mentioned a child or a wife.

Seeing her confusion Xavier explained. "My son is Ryan Ramón. He's in Mrs. Collins' second grade classroom.

"Ryan is your son?

"So you do know him?"

"Yes, I do. Mrs. Collins and I share activities sometimes. Gina told me that you only recently arrived in Biloxi."

"That's true. I was on a temporary duty assignment. My housekeeper, Rosa Gomez enrolled him three months ago."

"Oh, I see. So it's just the three of you." She attempted to mask her interest with a statement, yet waited with eager anticipation for his response.

Just the three of us," he gave her a teasing smirk. "His mother and I are divorced, Nicole."

"I wasn't fishing for information, Major," Nicole lied.

"Sure you were Nicole," Xavier replied with a teasing smile. "Now what you choose to do with that bit of information is left completely up to you." The comment was as suggestive as his roguish smile.

"Major, I can assure you that I don't plan on doing anything with the information. For the record, there will be no involvement outside of friendship between us, despite our friends' best efforts."

"No?" Xavier quipped with his hypnotic gray gaze locked on to her.

Fighting the effect, Nicole replied, "No! You're in the military."

The bitterness of her tone as she stated those last words wasn't lost on Xavier. Being his direct self, he asked the next question without hesitation. "Some guy in uniform left you?"

The hard glare Nicole cast his way was one of sheer hostility. He had definitely hit a raw nerve. "Look, Major Ramón, I've answered one too many personal questions tonight. You don't get in my business and I won't get in yours."

"I hear you," Xavier replied thoughtfully. "Nicole, I would be a liar if I said I wasn't curious about your obvious avoidance in discussing family."

"You should talk. I didn't hear you answer Carmen's question when she inquired about *your* family."

The lady was sharp. He would have to remember this if he intended to pursue a relationship with her. Ignoring her comment he continued, "My interest in you was more than mere curiosity. It was sincere, and besides, when we shook hands our awareness of each other was electrifying."

"Are you always this direct, Major?"

"It's the only way I know how to be. It keeps down confusion. Listen Nicole, I like you and I want to see more of you." *No! No! No!* Nicole screamed silently to herself. She couldn't get involved with this man. She knew first hand what men in uniform were like and so she steered clear of them. Only her connection with Gina and Keith had brought her into contact with the military.

Pulling into Nicole's driveway Xavier killed the engine. He faced her head on giving her his undivided attention. He was attracted to her and in that brief moment wanted her.

"I think you're a nice man, Major Ramón, but I can't get involved with you."

"Does it have anything to do with your calling me *Major?* What? You have to keep reminding yourself that I'm in the military to fight the attraction?"

Nicole couldn't respond because he had guessed correctly. Was he that intuitive or was she just that obvious?

"Plain and simple, I don't date men in uniform."

"Not yet you don't."

CHAPTER 3

With her brain stuck on Xavier's last words Nicole closed the door behind him after they entered her home. She deposited her purse on the end table where she'd left the lamp on. Offering Xavier a seat, she took her time facing him. She needlessly tested the soil of the ivy sitting on the table and stalled for time. At last turning to Xavier who sat casually in a wing-back Queen Anne chair, she found herself suddenly nervous. What in the world had possessed her to invite this man into her home for coffee? Her original thought was simply to be polite——thank him for the ride home, but now looking at him lounging casually in the chair, she wondered if she were playing with fire. One look into those steel gray eyes and she could feel herself being drawn to him. Fighting the force she made herself head for the kitchen.

"Why don't you relax while I start the coffee." She flashed Xavier a nervous smile walking past him into the kitchen.

"This is a nice subdivision you're in. I even like the name, Magnolia Sunset," Xavier commented, trying to delay her exit.

"Thank you." She paused, turning back around to face him. "Gina was the real estate broker for the development. When she showed me this area I fell in love with it. The numerous magnolias give the area a quaint, homey feeling. I knew immediately this was where I wanted to live."

"I see why," he said as Nicole headed towards the kitchen once again.

From inside she yelled back, "The remote for the television should be in there somewhere."

"Thanks, but I prefer to talk with you," came the response from the doorway of the kitchen.

Nicole was startled by his sudden appearance and could only stare. He was more than handsome Nicole noted. Simply put, he was the epitome of maleness: tall, lean, and muscled. She studied his handsome face, his neatly trimmed mustache which appeared just as silky and smooth as his brows. She suddenly wondered how it would feel to be kissed by him. Would the hairs of his mustache tickle or enhance the sensual experience? Shyly dropping her head at the thought and the sudden realization that she had been openly admiring the man while he watched, Nicole somehow managed to start the coffee maker.

Task eventually completed and under better control of her emotions, she spun around to face Xavier, who still remained standing in the doorway. They stared at each other. Not a word was spoken, yet so much was communicated.

Finally breaking eye contact, Nicole smiled shyly. "I'm going to change clothes while the coffee brews. Make yourself comfortable."

Xavier returned to the living room pacing. He tried to take his mind off the beautiful woman with the golden brown eyes, who had looked at him with such longing. As he calmed down he began to examine Nicole's home. It was too small for his liking, but for a single woman it was ideal. The living room opened up into the dining area. Both were decorated in shades of blue, beige, and white. Large floor-to-ceiling windows adorned the front of the house, which no doubt offered plenty of light during the day. More floor-to-ceiling windows walled the dining room. The windows were dressed in lacy floral white curtains with tie backs, then allowed to billow freely onto the natural stained hardwood floors. Tasteful Queen Anne furnishings filled both rooms. The blue sofa and loveseat were covered in the same miniature plaid pattern, as were the dining room chairs. Two beige chairs, one high back and one not, were placed strategically in the living room.

As he sat in the chair by the bookcase, he counted six plants in this room alone, and judging by their healthy appearance, Nicole had a green thumb. He recognized some as standard household plants, but then there were several new to him. Beside the chair in which he was sitting was a tote bag with what appeared to be the start of an afghan.

A picture of Nicole was beginning to take shape within his mind. The abandoned little girl was creating the home she'd never had. It was warm and bright—filled with loving touches. It was in stark contrast to his more masculine taste. He liked it though, and was beginning to like the woman who owned it even more.

Nicole changed clothes quickly in the bedroom, then sat down on the bed trying to bring her thoughts together. She knew without a doubt that she was headed for trouble with this man, but nonetheless decided to proceed with caution. She could do that. A platonic relationship with Xavier would be easy to maintain, as long as she focused on the single fact that he was military.

Who was she kidding? The mere sight of the man made her forget her very name, his career, and her resolve. She warned herself not to be taken in by a handsome face and magnetic eyes. The man was far worldlier than she. If she became involved with him, he would destroy her, because she would be helpless to protect her very heart and soul from him. Already she had been caught perusing his incredible body. He knew she found him absolutely captivating. He was probably in the living room now trying to formulate a plan to get her into bed. Then once she had been conquered, he would move on to the next available woman without a moment's thought

Going to the mirror she studied the reflection, trying to see what Xavier saw when he looked at her. Was it an attractive intelligent woman worthy of love and respect or a woman with no more value than one night in bed? His wandering military nature probably wouldn't allow for a more substantial relationship. Not a man like him—no way. He no doubt enjoyed a variety of female companions. Wasn't his divorced status proof of that? Surely no sane woman would divorce a man like him willingly. He no doubt didn't want his former wife or their marriage. Reluctantly, she conceded that he at least wanted his child. Maybe he wasn't all bad. She decided to give him the benefit of the doubt and rose from the bed. At the bedroom door she took a fortifying breath before returning to the living room.

Xavier was overcome by Nicole's youthful appearance when she entered the living room. She looked criminally young, dressed in well-worn faded jeans and Spelman sweatshirt, not to mention sock-clad feet. The swinging ponytail dancing down her back didn't help matters much either. He barely noticed the fine silk texture of her lightly waved dark hair, so disconcerted by the transformation. He was suddenly uncomfortable. Reaching out as she walked past him smiling, Xavier caught her arm, halting her steps. He stared into her puzzled face and was once again stunned by the contact.

"This isn't the transformation I was expecting. Just how old are you?" His voice had taken on a hard, accusatory tone.

Nicole returned his hard glare, not missing the change in his voice, or the hint of something dubious. She was angered by his tone, and started to say something cutting, but didn't when she saw the beginning of a frown and stress wrinkles across his brow.

"I'm twenty-five—quite legal."

"Just barely," he bellowed. "There's a ten-year age difference between us. Hell, I command troops your age." He abruptly released her arm and turned his head to stare off into space.

Nicole felt set adrift by his sudden withdrawal. Apparently he, too, found it easy to walk away from her—the story of her life. It hurt more than she wanted to admit. Telling herself that her response was ridiculous, she walked on into the kitchen alert for the sound of the front door closing. She didn't want a relationship with this man, so what difference did their ages make?

Reluctantly, Nicole admitted that there was something developing between them. And if she had any common sense at all, she would be just as upset as Xavier was. She of all people knew firsthand that military men were wanderers. Sure they spoke of love, marriage, and had families, but they also cheated and abandoned those families. She couldn't allow

herself to be fooled by a pair of magnetic gray eyes or a titi-
lating smile.

Thinking of Keith, Nicole had to revise her statement. He
didn't fit into that category of military men. He was devoted
to Gina and their life together. He had proven his love over
the course of their relationship. She knew he would never
walk away from Gina or his responsibility. But what about the
man who remained in her living room. Would he lie, cheat,
or walk away from her without a backward glance? She didn't
know and didn't want to be placed in a position to find out
She would stick to her guns and refuse to go out with him.

"Nicole, I'm sorry for the outburst," Xavier apologized
from the doorway. He had removed his coat and tie. "I just
didn't realize that Gina was that much younger than Keith."

Startled once again by his appearance, Nicole glanced in
his direction. She admired the casual way he looked standing
in her kitchen doorway. He seemed very much a part of the
space. She especially liked the sight of his hairy forearms
visible now that he'd folded his sleeves back. The fine hairs
prompted her to wonder about his chest and legs. The unexpected thought caused her a moment of discomfort. She
shouldn't be thinking such things. However, being honest,
Nicole realized that she liked everything about this man
except his career choice. Seizing that point as a weapon to
combat the feelings churning within, she faced him head on.

"Don't apologize. You were absolutely correct. I'm too
young and you're too old to be starting something. So let's just
nip this *whatever it is* in the bud right now. I'll say thanks for
the ride home, and you say goodnight. We part as acquaintances and exchange friendly greetings when our paths cross.

No big deal!' She raised her cleft chin in defiance as Xavier came to stand before her. "And by the way, Gina is twenty-seven."

Closely watching Nicole as she tried to convince herself of what she spoke, Xavier realized that even though their reasons were different, she was just as frightened by what was transpiring between them as he. Staring down into her upturned face, he placed a long tapered finger on the cleft of her chin. Then he smiled that roguish smile which was fast becoming familiar to Nicole.

"Which one of us are you trying to convince with that pile of manure?"

Despite the implication of the question, she laughed and silently admitted to trying to convince herself. The truth reflected across her face drew Xavier's comment.

"That's what I thought. Let's get a couple of things out in the open. Yes, the ten-year age difference between us makes me a little uncomfortable. However, the idea of never seeing you again, hearing your rich laughter, or staring into those stunning golden eyes of yours causes me a great deal more distress than the age factor. And as for *your* fears, the air force *is* my career and a way of life for me. Allow me to introduce you to my world."

"I don't know, Xavier."

He saw as well as heard the fear and longing in her unsure response. Cupping her delicate face within his safe hands, he tried to reassure her. "I'm not him, Nicole. I wouldn't deliberately hurt you."

"Not deliberately I'm sure, but you would hurt me." It was inevitable. Just as it was inevitable that this feeling for him would blossom with the more time they shared.

At the table Xavier enjoyed watching the efficiency of Nicole moving around her kitchen. She was obviously quite skilled at cooking if her homemade apple pie was any indication. He had devoured two large slices with a scoop of vanilla ice cream on each. The food, coffee, and conversation had been extremely enjoyable. Intimacy was what he missed in his life. After the divorce he had vowed never to allow any woman that close again, and up until tonight he hadn't Yet, with little effort this woman had slipped behind his walls of self-preservation, making it difficult to ignore her.

Nonetheless, he had no illusions about falling in love, getting married, or beginning a family. He had taken that journey once and discovered just how treacherous it could be. Besides, he didn't believe marriage was what Nicole was seeking, at least not with someone in the military. They would enjoy this relationship as long as it lasted in whatever form it took shape. When it ended, they would both walk away with cherished memories and, he hoped, a friend for life.

He wanted to solve the mystery of Nicole Edwards more than anything else. So much about her piqued his curiosity. Her tragic childhood, which she skillfully avoided discussing, obviously held many secrets as to the woman she had become. Her heritage was another source of interest He found himself wondering about the two people who had created the lovely woman sitting across from him. Who were they? How did they meet? Did they love each other? What happened to that love? And how could they abandon their child? He knew he wasn't the first to ponder those questions. He was sure Nicole had recited them numerous times throughout her brief life. The mere thought pained him. No child should have to question being loved.

The other intriguing fad about Nicole, which puzzled him, was her blatant disdain for the military. Sure people didn't always agree with the military mission, but they usually respected the men and women carrying out the orders. And to be honest, he believed Nicole was one of them. So who was responsible for such a deeply ingrained bitterness? He couldn't bring himself to say hatred, because if that were true, then he and Nicole might never have a chance.

"Where does a woman your age learn to bake like this?" he asked, pushing his empty plate aside.

Nicole accepted his hearty appetite and question as a compliment. She took pride in her culinary skills and was always pleased when someone enjoyed her efforts.

"My foster mother started me baking at an early age. I remember being about three when she gave me my first ball of dough to knead—I've been hooked ever since." She smiled thoughtfully.

The reflective expression wasn't lost on Xavier, or the love with which she mentioned her foster mother. It was so hard for him to comprehend someone not wanting or loving this woman. She would make any parent proud, yet hers would never know what treasure they had discarded.

"Is it difficult for you to discuss, Nicole?"

"My being abandoned or my foster mother?" she asked quietly with a lift of her chin.

"I guess both, but I'll settle for you telling me about your foster mother."

Laying her fork aside, Nicole sat back in her chair smiling wistfully.

"You can't talk about Lillian without discussing Ronald. The Edwards took me in as an infant. They were my parents for six years. I couldn't have been happier or more loved than during that time."

"You carry their name. Were you the only child they took in?"

"Yes, I do, and no, my brother Jon was there when I arrived."

"I didn't realize you had a brother," Xavier commented, sitting straighter.

Nicole shook her head as she sipped her coffee. Replacing the mug on the table, she explained.

"My brother in here, Xavier." She indicated her heart with a finger,. "But not my biological brother. Jon is white, but we couldn't be any closer than if we had been born of the same womb. I know it may sound strange, but, you see the Edwardses were an interracial couple. Lillian was black and Ronald white. He couldn't have children so they decided to become foster parents. Jon's parents were killed in a car accident while driving through the state. No family came forward to claim him, so the Edwards took him in and healed his young heart. Me, I was in need of a home, and not easily placed, so once again the Edwards came to the rescue."

Silently surveying her unique features, Xavier listened to the unspoken hurt and sense of loss. "I don't understand. Why were you difficult to place?"

Smiling a rather sad smile as she met Xavier's questioning gaze, Nicole knew it was difficult for others to understand her plight in life, yet Xavier was inquiring with an honesty she found refreshing.

Xavier, when accepting foster children into the home, or adopting children, people generally like a little history on the child. Outside of my ethnic make-up, there was nothing. I remember when I was seven a couple came to meet me. They were considering me for adoption, and I was so excited. I remember being on my best behavior. I wanted to go home with these people so badly. However, after discovering, I was abandoned with no family history, the husband convinced his wife to leave me. They were in the hallway arguing, and I heard him say they couldn't be sure of what they were getting if they chose me. After that incident, I never got my hopes up about being adopted because I knew it wouldn't happen."

Unconsciously, Xavier had taken Nicole's left hand within his right, squeezing lightly as she spoke. During the last hour he had allowed himself closer to this woman than any since the divorce. It frightened him, yet excited him as well. Maybe the wounds were finally healing.

Nicole knew that she liked this man. It would be so easy for her to open her heart and allow Xavier Ramón inside into that place she kept locked away and protected from all the pain and disappointment of love. But the fact remained that Xavier Ramón was in the military and not to be trusted one hundred percent, at least not with her heart. Therefore, she would keep her emotions under control and her distance from the major.

"He was right you know. I don't know my family's medical history. Who knows what terrible gene I could be carrying?"

For several long minutes nothing was said. Xavier and Nicole merely sat quietly lost in their own thoughts. Then it happened. That magnetism that had startled them earlier in the evening was back. The air around them became charged with energy as their mutual awareness sparked to life once again. Xavier continued to hold her hand. He caressed it tenderly within his own much larger hand. It was warm and soft, delicate and so feminine, like the rest of her. The rich sable coloring of her skin was flawless and such a contrast against his own more golden. He admired the contrast, as he did the woman. Making the conscious decision to become involved in this woman's life, Xavier gazed into her frightened eyes. He could tell she was ready to bolt away from the table and his life, and he knew that was not what he wanted.

"She left a letter behind."

"Who left a letter, Nicole? he asked startled by the suddenness of her speaking.

"My mother."

"Tell me about it," His voice had dropped an octave, sending a delicious current of warm sensuality down Nicole's spine as his hypnotic gray eyes locked onto her.

Entranced by their powerful pull, Nicole didn't register his request for a moment.

"The letter, oh yeah. It contained nothing earth-shattering, just my first name and date of birth. She made mention of loving me and being sorry." Nicole's voice took on a disbelieving tone.

"Nicole, she could have been a young girl in trouble who did what she felt was best for her child," Xavier added softly, hoping to ease some of the hurt locked inside Nicole.

"You know, after the fall of Saigon, many Vietnamese refugees coming to the United States migrated to coastal areas for the fishing industry. Many times were met with prejudice and hostility. But their community was strong, and like the African, they persevered."

"You believe your mother was one of them?"

"No. Not originally anyway. The authorities were able to discover that a Vietnamese woman was brought into a Jackson hospital after giving birth at home. While the doctor searched for an interpreter, the woman and her child disappeared. The date of the incident matches the date of birth mentioned in the letter."

"Nicole, do you realize that your mother left the hospital *with* you? She had no intentions of abandoning you, so something awful must have contributed to her making that decision."

"That may be true, but it doesn't change the fact that she left me." Nicole's voice hardened, not giving an inch.

"The Edwardses tried to adopt us, but Ronald was diagnosed with heart disease," Nicole informed Xavier, picking up her story where she left off. "His condition deteriorated quickly. After his death there was no way the system was going to allow Lillian to adopt us. We were eventually taken from her and separated," she concluded, drawing an unseen pattern on the table.

"Have you been in touch with her or Jon since then?"

"Lillian died a month before my eighteenth birthday, and yes, I would see her every now and then. It was against policy, but she always managed to find me." She finally stopped drawing to meet his attentive regard. "Jon and I will always be close; he's my brother. He lives in Atlanta. You've probably heard of him, Jon W. Edwards, author of..."

"*Lost in the System,*" Xavier supplied. "Pretty impressive, his novel. It was on the bestsellers list for a year. I know it was fiction, but I realize *now* that a portion of it was based on your lives."

"Writing became a way of escaping the system for Jon. I'm proud of him." She smiled truly for the first time since revealing her history.

"You should be. You should also be very proud of yourself, lady. You've made a success of your life."

Humbly, Nicole accepted the compliment, returning Xavier's contagious smile. She realized that they had spent the last hour dissecting her past and had yet to delve into his. Getting up from the table, she removed their plates, then returned with the coffeepot to replenish their cups. After returning the pot to the burner, she returned to her seat, eyeing Xavier expectantly.

"It's your turn, Major. I'd like to hear all about you and your military endeavors."

CHAPTER 4

"There really isn't much to tell," Xavier answered evasively. He too hated discussing family, especially his own. It wasn't that he had grown up in an unloving household. To the contrary actually. Raymond and Helena Ramón were exemplary parents. Their three children had never experienced one moment of doubt where their love was concerned. All three had attended the best of schools and were high achievers. His reluctance in discussing his family was not due to lack of affection, but the family's prominent position in New Orleans society. The Ramón name carried great privileges and opportunities, yet he had chosen his own path.

He was proud of his career choice. It had been all that he'd expected it would be. However, he never could have imagined the toll military life could take on a marriage. But then, he would never be sure whether it was his military career or his wife's greed which was truly responsible for the destruction of his marriage. And hence his dilemma.

He had vowed after Monique walked out on him and their three-day-old son, that he would never disclose the truth about his family again. He would never place such temptation before another woman. He'd also vowed never to love another woman so completely that her rejection could destroy him. Monique had almost succeeded in doing so, yet he had found the strength, or maybe it was his love for his son, to pull himself back together. Ryan had become his entire world and he needed *no* woman to make him complete.

Not until now did he actually think of a relationship with a woman. Sure, he had been with women since Monique. He was a man with needs like all others, but never had his heart entered into the relationship. He had been careful in his selection of the women with whom he shared a bed. They too had been looking only for the company and comfort of the opposite sex—nothing more. But, with Nicole it would be different, and he really had to decide whether or not he wanted to be that close with a woman again. Not to mention all the baggage Nicole brought with her. Could she love him despite the military career, or would it drive her away.

On the other hand, because of her abandonment, she would probably make an excellent mother for Ryan. She of all people knew what it was like to grow up without a mother. She longed to experience family. He could offer the respectability of his family name, the money and position which would make people forget about her past. Those things created a tantalizing package, reason enough for a woman to want a man. He quickly decided he didn't know Nicole that well to reveal all that about himself, and he felt like a hypocrite, because he was sure Nicole had revealed far more of herself than usual—all because he had asked.

"Of course there's something more to tell. How you decided upon the air force, the birth of your son," Nicole suggested, not to be put off.

"Don't do your teacher routine on me, Ms. Edwards." Xavier laughed dryly. His steel gray eyes were reflective as he came to the conclusion that he was immensely enjoying the evening.

"All right, I always dreamed of going into the air force. I was appointed to the Air Force Academy straight out of high school. I majored in criminal justice. For a while I considered being a lawyer, then decided against it. Security forces is where I wanted to be, and I have enjoyed every moment of it. We do so much more than general policing. The young men and women I command are on the front lines each and every day. They are the base's first defense. It's my responsibility to make sure that they're trained and capable of fulfilling the miss ion."

Nicole heard the pride in his voice. He obviously loved his career choice and was no doubt excellent at it.

"You already know that we're forever moving or being deployed around the world. We get to see many great places, but we also miss a great deal at home."

"Have the frequent movements been difficult on Ryan?" Nicole asked safely, not daring to ask the question which was truly on her mind.

"I don't believe so. You know how resilient children are. Everything is a new adventure for them. Plus, we've been blessed with Rosa. Without her love and support I couldn't do the job I love with a peace of mind. Ryan comes first in my life and always will."

"Where was Ryan born?"

Instantly Xavier's face hardened as his steel gray eyes bore into her. Nicole's heart ceased to beat as the silence between them stretched on. This was definitely unwelcome territory and realizing her mistake, she tried graciously to step out the quagmire.

"How many foreign countries have you visited? I would really like to hear about them all," she rambled on.

Aware of what Nicole was doing, Xavier tried to relax. He knew she had no way of knowing Ryan's birth was a difficult subject for him. He had pried into her life unconscionably tonight, and therefore fair was fair. He tried his winning smile as a way of lightening the mood; it failed. Nicole was withdrawing and he didn't want that—not now.

"It's okay, Nicole. I know you're curious about Ryan's mother. It just caught me a little off guard, that's all."

"I wasn't trying to pry this time, Xavier. I know better than anyone does that there are certain areas of our life that are off limits. I can respect that."

He appreciated her allowing him his privacy, but she of all people had a right to expect candor from him. Unfortunately, he had come across too many women who were bold in their questioning about his missing spouse, demanding to know the intimate details of their marriage, and her current whereabouts. Nicole hadn't done that. She hadn't played any of the mating games he had become accustomed to maneuvering. With great consideration, he acknowledged he would have to give a little of himself to experience the inner beauty of this amazing young woman.

"Ryan was born in England. His mother and I divorced soon after he was born. She like you, didn't care for the military lifestyle."

"No, not like me." Nicole shook her head vigorously. "I'm single no husband to love or child who needs me. She was a wife and mother—the military lifestyle shouldn't have mattered. She had a family who loved her and needed her. You did love her?"

Lost within the golden hue of Nicole's eyes, Xavier wasn't sure anymore. Never once had he seen the purity of love within Monique's eyes as he was now seeing within Nicole's. Even in such a short spell of time, he could see that she honestly cared for him and felt his sense of loss after Monique's departure. If he were capable of loving again, he could very easily see it happening with this woman.

"Yes, Nicole, I *did* love her."

"Well then, if that were true, it should have negated her dislike for the military lifestyle. She had the most important of things—your love."

Just hearing Nicole put to words what he too felt, Xavier couldn't suppress his next words, no matter how he hated to hear them.

"She didn't want Ryan, Nicole."

Nicole heard the words and immediately disliked the woman without knowing her story. In her book there was absolutely no excuse for a mother to desert her child.

At the sound of his broken voice, Nicole covered his hand with her own, offering comfort. "It was her loss. Ryan is a delightful child. You've done an excellent job of rearing him."

She was so close, and her words were so desperately welcomed. They were genuine and kind, and spoken from the heart. She made him feel good about himself and the choices he had made. Wanting to express what he was feeling, Xavier raised her hand, kissing it lightly. She was sweet and caring, and for a brief moment he thought of never letting her go.

"You're good for my self-esteem." He gave her the now familiar smile.

Nicole was dazed by the brief kiss and struggled to regain her balance. Recognizing the smile for being natural and not some contrived move, she allowed herself to enjoy the view. However, uncomfortable with the closeness, she tried to remove her hand, but was halted from doing so by the strength of Xavier's clasp.

"Don't pull away just yet. This is nice." He indicated their clasped hands with a gentle shake.

Nicole didn't know how to read the sudden change in mood. His piercing gray eyes were making her uneasy, not to mention that peck. It was brief and innocent, but nonetheless potent. Major Xavier Ramón was causing feelings inside her to blossom. It was too soon for such feelings, she kept trying to remind herself, but as Xavier's thumb stroked the backside of her hand, Nicole knew she was losing the battle.

Her heart was beating a hundred miles a minute and she was suddenly unbearably warm. She needed to put some distance between herself and Xavier. But the look in his expressive eyes caused her to rethink her position. Through his telling eyes, she saw Xavier open himself to her. He wasn't all trusting, but just the same he was trying. She couldn't ask for more.

"Hold tight if you need." The alto resonance of her voice purred with a sensuality made for starting fires. Nicole quickly cleared her throat as she stole a glance at

Xavier. She noticed his dark gray eyes were smoldering. Not wanting to encourage him any further, she continued to ask questions.

"I'm always curious about people's families. Do you have brothers and sisters?" The heat this man was generating with the mere stroke of his thumb was enough to send her up in flames if she wasn't careful. Trying to formulate other questions in the hope of channeling her thoughts away from the sexuality of the man, Nicole failed to notice Xavier's hesitation.

I can understand your curiosity. I have an older sister, Michele, and a younger brother, Drew. Before you ask, no, they are not in the military. Next question."

At the front door Nicole and Xavier stood face to face. The evening had been salvaged and had exceeded both their expectations. This was the moment of awkwardness Nicole dreaded. A part of her expected Xavier to ask to see her again, then another part of herself prayed he didn't. She feared opening her heart to him any further than she already had. So, she waited to see how the evening would play out.

Xavier too contemplated the best way to end the night. If he were without responsibilities at home, he would have chosen to spend the night getting to know this lovely young woman better. But his son was home, and that's where he belonged. So he instead leaned forward kissing Nicole's cheek lightly. With sheer will and determination, he refrained from stealing a kiss from her sweet lips, though he desperately wanted to experience the full taste and shape of her succulent mouth.

Nicole was mesmerized by the raw hunger visible in Xavier's gray eyes as he drew away—a hunger which surprisingly reflected her own. He was tall, handsome, and all male, a definite threat to her peace of mind and well being. Hampered by fear and doubt, she would do the only thing that she could: maintain her distance.

"It was a pleasure meeting you, Nicole. I enjoyed the evening greatly. Maybe we can get together again for possibly dinner and a movie."

Nicole lowered her head briefly while trying to sort out her thoughts. She liked this man, and dinner and a movie sounded completely innocent. Yet the energy passing between them was too volatile to be considered innocent. She raised her head, and searched his handsome brown face and did what needed to be done.

"I'm sorry, but I can't.

CHAPTER 5

Saturday morning Nicole abandoned her attempt at sleep. Her brain just wouldn't shut off. It was too preoccupied with thoughts of the gray-eyed man with whom she had shared the previous evening. Now here she was at six o'clock on a Saturday morning wide-awake. She had never discussed her past with anyone so openly as she had done last evening. And why had she disclosed the details of her life so completely? She wasn't certain of the answer, but only knew that some part of her wanted to be honest with him. His interest had been genuine—not simple morbid curiosity. She had to respect his direct approach. Then again, maybe Carmen's putting him on the spot had been the catalyst. Whatever his reason for asking, she respected it.

Rolling onto her left side and looking at the dawn light spilling through the slats of the mini blinds, Nicole had a disturbing thought. What if after a night of reflection Xavier decided he didn't want to see her again? It had happened before with far fewer details of her life being revealed. Maybe she shouldn't have been as honest as she had.

She thought about his disclosure of his brief marriage and realized that she had definitely misjudged him. He had obviously loved this woman deeply; otherwise she wouldn't have been able to hurt him so severely. It was possible that he still loved her. She *had* given birth to his only child. That in itself reserved a special place for her in his life, regardless of the fact that she didn't want the responsibility of raising that child. At least she had left him in the loving hands of his father.

Over a meager breakfast of toast and juice, Nicole allowed her thoughts to roam, wondering again about the woman who shared Xavier's name. Was she tall and voluptuous like Carmen, with the right family name behind her? To be loved by a man with Xavier's strong character she would have to be a special woman. To be honest, Xavier with his devastating masculine good looks could have his choice of women. He was male perfection, and the fact that she was keenly aware of every detail of his person frightened her immensely. It wasn't conceivable that a man like Xavier Ramón would actually be attracted to a throwaway like herself.

There was nothing special or endearing about her. She looked like no one and had no family to offer a dedicated family man. Last night while he talked, she had once again discovered the look of familial pride. Even though he didn't go into great detail about his family in New Orleans, she still was able to paint a picture of a close knit family who took pride in each other's accomplishments. She'd learned of his brother and sister, and that his parents had been married for thirty-eight years. According to Xavier, they were just as much in love today as the day they met. The picture he'd painted of the perfect family left Nicole envious. It also left her empty, because she knew there was no place for her within a family like his.

Displeased with her bout of self-pity she cleared away her breakfast dishes. Needing something to lift her spirits, she decided baking something special for her Sunday school class would do the trick. A quick inventory of her cupboards yielded all the necessary ingredients for cup cakes. So for the next couple of hours Nicole prepared cup cakes and a batch of chocolate chip cookies.

Just as she was cleaning up the last of the mess, her doorbell rang. She dried her hands on the dishcloth while running to answer the door. Half expecting it to be Xavier, Nicole was relieved to see it was Gina. She wasn't strong enough at the moment to resist Xavier. Opening the door Nicole greeted her friend.

"Hey, what has you out and about before noon?"

"Hi yourself. I wanted to hear what happened after you and Xavier left last night." Wearing a denim skirt and pullover sweater, Gina swept past Nicole. Her shoulder-length auburn hair was worn in a fashionable bob that framed a beautiful round face with chocolate brown eyes.

Nicole closed the door and followed Gina back towards the kitchen. She waited while Gina sampled a cookie before speaking.

"Those are sinful, Nicole," Gina replied, savoring each bite.

Laughing lightly, Nicole grabbed one herself, enjoying her friends vivaciousness. It was always contagious and uplifting. "What makes you think something happened last night?" she asked before biting into her own cookie.

"The fact that I was worried about you last night and had Keith drive me over to check on you, and to my surprise, Xavier's vehicle was parked in the driveway." Gina's raised eyebrows implied she was waiting on the details.

"What did you expect the man to do, slow down and tell me to jump?"

"Of course not, smart mouth, but his Navigator was still parked there two hours later."

"My God Gina, didn't you have something better to do than drive by my house all night?" Nicole replied, dodging Gina's reason for being there.

Giving her friend the once-over with a critical eye, Gina could tell something had transpired last night. Nicole wouldn't meet her eyes, and when she did, she looked like a child with a secret to tell. "Spill it because I'm not leaving until you give me the details," Gina sassed, plopping down in a chair with a purpose.

Nicole's whole face glowed with the memories of last night. "Okay, here's the deal." Nicole swiftly began filling her friend in on the evening.

"You told him what?" Gina asked not believing her ears.

"You heard me. I told Xavier I couldn't go out with him."

"Didn't you just say you found him to be nice, attractive, and a great listener?"

"Yes, you did," Nicole commented beginning to pace the length of the kitchen. "But..."

"No buts, Nicole," Gina interrupted. "The man wants to see you again. He didn't run because he discovered you were raised in the foster care system."

"No, he didn't run, but I saw his expression at dinner. He was surprised, Gina, and though I believe his interest in me was sincere, I can't be for certain."

"No one in a relationship can be sure of anything. But we have to be willing to trust, Nicole."

"Get real, Gina, I can only trust him just so much." Nicole's expression hinted at annoyance.

Exasperated and tired of Nicole's pacing, Gina rose from her seat and stood in Nicole's path. "What's really preventing you from pursuing this relationship, Nicole?"

Nicole shook her head troubled. She exhaled a breath, then collapsed into the chair Gina had vacated. "He comes from a close knit family with brothers and sisters, and loving parents. I can't compete with that"

Gina grabbed Nicole's shoulders, giving her a shake. "Compete. What are you talking about? You don't have to compete with his family."

"I have nothing to offer him, Gina!"

"You have so many wonderful qualities, Nicole. His just knowing you is worthwhile."

Nicole was humbled by her friend's devotion. She smiled weakly before speaking. "Gina, Xavier's career and his family are extremely important to him. He's not going to risk losing them for me. He shouldn't have to."

"Nicole, do you know how ridiculous your thinking is? Xavier doesn't have to choose anything. if he decides that he wants to pursue a relationship with you, he can. Wanting you has nothing to do with his career or his family. Why do you believe he will be forced to choose?"

Thinking back to another man and another time, Nicole told Gina about Devin.

Gina couldn't believe this. As long as she had known Nicole, this was the first she had heard about her break up with Devin. "Why didn't you tell me about this before? I thought you and Devin just drifted apart like a lot of college relationships."

"I was embarrassed. I was so foolish to believe love and marriage were mine to have. It's not, Gina, and I know and accept that now. That's why I can't get involved with Xavier, because if it comes down to them or me, I'll lose, Gina. I'll lose more than Xavier. I'll lose my very soul, because that man possesses the ability to make me forget everything and everyone. When I was with him last night, I had to keep reminding myself that he was in the military and would probably leave me too. No, it's best to avoid the entire situation."

Gina's expression was one of disbelief. "How can you think so little of yourself, Nicole? Is this what being abandoned has done to you—made you feel undeserving of love? You can't go through life running away from involvement. You're a flesh-and-blood woman who needs and deserves to be loved. There's someone out there for you. It may even be one Major Xavier Ramón. You're rejecting him before he has a chance to reject you. It's early, give this relationship a chance and see where it leads."

"I don't know, Gina. I'm afraid to hope."

"Don't hope, Nicole. Just take it one step at a time, one day at a time. Promise me that you'll at least think about what I've said."

With a nod of her head, Nicole agreed.

Yet each time Xavier called, Nicole allowed the answering machine to pick up. She didn't trust herself to refuse him again.

Two weeks later Nicole still had no answer for the dilemma in which she found herself. She thought of Xavier and the evening they shared often. Distance wasn't solving anything. It only served to make her speculate about the what ifs. She was honest enough with herself to admit to wanting to see him again. Maybe Gina was right about taking it one day at a time.

Little did Nicole know that the opportunity to put those words to the test would be the very next day. She was standing on the school's front porch while waiting for each parent to retrieve his or her child, when her attention was drawn to a figure to the left. Turning her head in that direction, she immediately recognized Xavier. Dressed in blue jeans and squadron T-shirt, he looked good. She smiled shyly as their eyes met before being forced to glance away as another parent approached to claim her child. Just as she was about to turn facing him once more, Mrs. Collin's class exited the building. Standing beside her, Mrs. Collins immediately pointed out Xavier as he approached.

"That's a fine man there," she whispered. "Girl, if I weren't married I'd have to chase the brother down." She laughed good-naturedly.

Nicole merely smiled, trying not to look obvious as Xavier finally made it to the porch.

He called Ryan to his side while approaching both women.

"Good afternoon, ladies." He greeted them both, but only had eyes for Nicole. She looked beautiful dressed in a simple floral dress which stopped mid-calf—hiding the beautiful legs he remembered.

"Mr. Ramón—Major Ramón," the women chorused. Then as fortune would have it, Mrs. Collins excused herself to speak to another parent, leaving Nicole and Xavier alone as Ryan stood off to the side chatting with a classmate.

"So I'm still Major Ramón, am I?" Xavier smiled teasingly at Nicole.

"How are you?" Nicole asked, trying to appear calm.

"Better now that I've seen you. I've thought of you often."

"I've thought of you too, Xavier." Nicole smiled brightly as Xavier registered that she had used his first name.

"Does your calling me Xavier have anything to do with your changing your mind about dinner?"

Releasing a deep breath, Nicole answered, "Look, Xavier, I really enjoyed the evening we shared together. It was nice to have the attention of a handsome man, but I'm not looking for anything serious."

Though not the response he was looking for, Xavier knew there was room for maneuvering. Turning his high wattage smile onto Nicole as he gazed into her golden brown eyes, he replied, "Well I don't believe a book review and signing in Mobile on Sunday would be too serious."

She'd been played. This wasn't a chance meeting. He had an agenda. She narrowed her eyes at Xavier and called him on his duplicity. "You deceived me."

"No, I didn't," he defended, smiling this time with definite roguish intent. "You wanted to see me as badly as I have wanted to see you. I can see it in your eyes," he taunted. "And you also want to join me on Sunday. Gina told me you're a bookworm, so the signing would definitely be to your liking. Come on, Nic, say you will come. Gina and Keith are both attending."

With him looking at her like that she could almost agree to just about anything. Instead of responding right away, she glanced around to see if anyone was watching them. They weren't, so she focused back on Xavier, arching a sculptured brow.

"Nic? No one calls me that." It was the look that sent terror through her second grade class. However, receiving Xavier's wide toothy smile she realized it wasn't having the same effect on him.

"Good, I rather enjoy being the sole owner of the privilege. Say yes, and no more teacher's dirty looks."

"Yes."

By one o'clock Sunday afternoon she was dressed in a pair of lavender slacks and matching short sleeve sweater with white lace collar. On her feet she wore brown pumps with medium-sized heels. She recalled Xavier's considerable height advantage and wanted to at least gain a couple of inches. Checking her appearance in the mirror, she tried to calm her runaway nerves. She reminded herself while French braiding her hair that this wasn't a date. It was just a group of friends getting together for the day. *Sure it was.* She could lie to herself all that she wanted, but that wouldn't change the fact that Xavier affected her like no man before. Finally pleased with her hair, she grabbed her purse to wait in the living room for their arrival.

Exactly at one-thirty her doorbell rang. Opening the door, she was once again struck numb by Xavier's handsomeness, as his bright smiled greeted her. She stepped aside to allow him to enter her home. So transfixed by the sight of him in dark blue slacks and an ecru pullover sweater which molded to the muscular walls of his chest, Nicole nearly failed to notice Gina and Keith waiting in the Ford Expedition. Regaining her composure, she went to the door and waved before ducking back inside for her purse. Xavier now stood beside the table which contained her purse. She picked it up while meeting his expectant expression. Nicole was sure she wore the identical expression of "What do we do now?" on her very own face. As though reading her mind he took a step towards her and planted a quick kiss on her cheek.

"I'm glad you're joining us today. It wouldn't have been the same without you," Xavier murmured, separating from their embrace.

His words, though simple, were meaningful and appreciated. "Thank you for the invitation."

Xavier led the way to Keith's Ford Expedition and opened the passenger door on the driver's side for Nicole. He would ride up front with Keith. He smiled wickedly into her twinkling eyes as she swept by him, taking a seat beside Gina. Settled, Nicole greeted her friends who appeared quite interested in what was transpiring between her and Xavier.

The ride into Mobile was filled with companionable conversation and laughter. The women listened as the men recounted tales of their days at the academy. Their closeness was evident in the good-natured ribbing they exchanged. During one exaggerated story, Nicole and Gina exchanged glances, smiling at the absurdity of their story. By the time they arrived in Mobile everyone was in a jovial mood.

The book review was for the up-and-coming young writer Curtis Winslow. His first book had captured the publishing world's attention, and his second was on its way to being a bestseller as well. His books dealt with relationship issues found in the African-American community.

The lecture area of the Barnes and Nobles was filled to capacity. Several people were forced to stand in the rear of the designated area due to limited availability of seating. Thankful that they had arrived early, the foursome had seats on the second row. The tight fit of the chairs caused extreme closeness among the crowd. Xavier and Nicole practically shared the same space. The constant contact and sharing of body heat reawakened the awareness between them. Neither commented nor tried to avoid the contact. In actuality the closeness of the other was rather comforting.

Nearing the end of his lecture, Curtis Winslow spoke of entering relationships with excess baggage. His words hit home with several people in the audience, Xavier and Nicole included.

"So many times when we begin new relationships, we do so with excess baggage dragging behind us. I'm talking about that heavy, bog-you-down baggage, which interferes with us getting on with our lives. That baggage we insist upon dragging from one relationship to another, then wonder why each new relationship fails. What I want to express here tonight is that we are all human, and as such we make mistakes. Learn from those mistakes and press on. Don't continue to blame yourself about bad choices. And whatever you do, don't punish your new partner for past wrongs. And definitely don't automatically assume they too will do the same as your last partner. That weight is too heavy for an innocent body to carry around. So ladies and gentlemen, take that baggage and place it in the rear of the closet and close the door on the past. Go to your new partner with a clean slate and get on with your life."

There were heads shaking in confirmation of his words throughout the crowd. He had the room captivated and worked up into a frenzy. His perfectly modulated voice punctuated each point of his book and caused everyone to seriously listen to the message he was delivering.

As for Xavier and Nicole, each felt as though Curtis Winslow was speaking to them. They were each carrying excess baggage which needed to be placed in the rear of that closet he spoke of. Overall, Mr. Winslow had given them both something to consider.

After the lecture and book signing they milled around in the bookstore. Xavier was checking out the fiction section when he came upon *Lost* in the *System*. He had checked a copy out at the library when it initially was released, but now knowing the relationship between the author and Nicole, he wanted to read it again. Hopefully this time he would gain more than the joy of reading a good novel. He hoped to gain insight into the world that Nicole had been reared in.

Nicole was browsing through the cooking section when Xavier walked up behind her holding a copy of Jon's book.

"Do you think if I purchase this book you could arrange to have it autographed?"

She glanced over her shoulder taking the book from his hand. Instantly recognizing Jon's book, she smiled brightly. "I believe that can be arranged, but I thought you had read it."

"I have, but I checked it out at the base library. Now that I know who the author is I want to own a copy."

Nicole heard what Xavier said, but the little she knew of him indicated a more meaningful reason for the purchase.

"Hoping to delve into my psyche?"

Xavier was silent for a moment, stunned by Nicole's intuitiveness. Was he that transparent or was she that perceptive? "We're friends, and as such I would like to gain a greater understanding of the world you grew up in. And I hope you will take the same interest in the career I love."

"Of course I wilt."

For a moment Nicole and Xavier forgot they were in the middle of a busy bookstore. Something beautiful had just transpired between them. There was this connection and energy surging between them. Although their friendship was brief, they cared enough to explore the other's world and make an attempt to understand the importance of that world in developing the person they knew.

Nicole had never experienced that depth of interest from the opposite sex. The less they knew of her sordid background the better. True, she hadn't shared the intimate details of her life as she had with Xavier that night, but enough so that she could be understood. In exchange for her openness, she had been rewarded by their nonchalant "it's in the past—get over it" reply. Xavier's willingness to explore her world of the foster care system meant more to her than she could express.

"Nicole, I just realized something. You and Jon carry the same surname. How is that possible? I know you were abandoned and taken in by the Edwardses as an infant and were given their name, but you said Jon's parents were killed in a car accident Shouldn't he carry his parents' name?"

With a smile that could only be described as sad, Nicole briefly glanced away before refocusing on Xavier's face. "When Ronald died and Lillian wasn't allowed to adopt us or to be our foster mother, Jon was eventually adopted. Gerald Edwards was Ronald's oldest brother. He and his wife Patsy knew how much Ronald had loved Jon, so on his death and Lillian's denial, they filed for adoption. The whole process took about a year, and during that time Jon's life was thrown into turmoil. Some of that comes out through the main character in the book. But in the end it all worked out for the best"

"That's wonderful, but Ronald loved you both. Why didn't they adopt you as well?"

"For one thing Gerald and Patsy didn't approve of Ronald's marriage to Lillian, and for another, their only son was killed in Vietnam. To have me around would have been a constant reminder of his death. The wounds of that war were still fresh back then. Therefore, they understandably didn't want me." She tossed her head nonchalantly now, but the rejection as a child had hurt Nicole deeply. "I will say this on their behalf though. They allowed Jon and me to remain close. At eleven he couldn't have forced the issue, so for that I'm grateful."

Xavier allowed the subject to drop. It was obvious Nicole had dealt with the rejection in her own way. Nonetheless, it cut deeply to know that people could be so cruel to a defenseless child. Offering comfort and support the only way he knew how, Xavier grasped Nicole's hands, bringing them to his lips for a kiss.

From across the bookstore that day Gina and Keith had watched the exchange between their friends. They had speculated about the budding relationship and vowed to offer it a boost. And so for the following two weeks they did just that Wherever Nicole was, Xavier materialized and vice versa. It was all made to appear quite innocent, but Nicole and Xavier had their suspicions.

So was the case the second week of April when Nicole was summoned to Gina's home. It was near two o'clock in the afternoon and Nicole was preparing for a jog along the beach. Dressed in royal blue sports bra and matching jogging shorts, she was just about to walk out the door when the telephone rang. Answering quickly she listened as Gina launched into her performance.

"Hey girl, I need you over at my place right away," Gina spoke as a way of introduction.

"What's happening at your place?"

"I'm trying to select a fabric to re-upholster Keith's furniture so that it doesn't clash with mine, and I need your help.

Although Nicole had become quite suspicious of her best friend lately, the desperation in Gina's voice seemed sincere. "Gina, you have excellent taste. You don't need me to select fabric. That should be something you and Keith share together."

Exasperated, Gina sighed for effect. "Nicole, if the man had good taste I wouldn't be re-upholstering his furniture, now would I?"

Nicole could only laugh. "I guess not. Okay, I'll run over. In thirty minutes I should be knocking on your door."

"Thirty minutes? Are you actually planning on running over here?" Gina asked, astonished. She knew Nicole jogged for fitness, but to run over slightly three miles was beyond her comprehension. She didn't believe in running anywhere. Why did people think the car was invented?

"Yes, I'm running over there. I was just headed out for a jog along the beach when you called, so instead of the beach I'll simply run to your place."

"You are crazy, you know that?" Gina laughed softly. "By the time you get here you'll be all hot and sweaty."

That last sentence caught Nicole's attention. "So what? You've seen me hot and sweaty before." After a pregnant pause, Nicole asked, "Gina it will be just the two of us, right?"

"Right," Gina responded. "Anyway, bring a change of clothes. You can shower and change here. I'll order take-out."

Conceding the point and knowing that she would definitely be ready for a shower, Nicole confirmed she would see her in a few minutes. She placed the phone back in its cradle and headed for the bedroom. There she grabbed her backpack from the rear of the closet and stuffed it with the necessary items.

Thirty minutes later she turned onto Sycamore Drive, conscious of only her breathing and Gina's house at the end of the block. The sweatband around her head was damp with perspiration, as was the cotton lining of her sports bra. Her thighs burned, due to the increased pace of her last mile. She could think of nothing else, as a trickle of sweat charted a path between her breasts, but the feel of a refreshing shower. With that thought in the forefront of her mind, she barely heard the horn blowing behind her. She glanced to the left and immediately recognized the black Navigator as Xavier's. She watched its progression down Sycamore and finally into Gina's driveway. The passenger door swung open and Keith stepped out, waving in her direction. Then Xavier emerged from the driver's side to stand at the rear of the vehicle waiting for her.

Nicole felt her anger rise. Gina was once again manipulating these chance meetings with Xavier. Granted, with each meeting their attraction grew stronger. Today proved to be no different, as she allowed her eyes to take in his casual appearance. Dressed in black well-filling jeans and a canary yellow T-shirt, Xavier looked as devastatingly handsome as always. In a completely masculine move, he propped his left leg on the rear bumper of the vehicle, causing the denim fabric of his jeans to tighten in strategic areas. The movement nearly caused Nicole to lose her stride. She regrouped and immediately became self-conscious of her own appearance.

Slowing her pace to a brisk walk two houses away from Gina's, Nicole took the opportunity to stretch out her muscles and cool down. She utilized her wristbands to mop the perspiration from her face. She raked a hand over her head, releasing the band holding her ponytail, before smoothing and gathering the tresses once again. Conceding the fact that she could do nothing about her sweat-dampened clothes, she finally joined Xavier at the rear of his vehicle.

From the moment he'd turned onto Sycamore and spotted Nicole jogging to the right of the road, he knew they had been manipulated. But the sight of Nicole's beautiful brown legs and her tight round behind encased in running attire instantly replaced the short-lived thought He had slowed his speed to enjoy the rear view of her long ponytail swish ing from side to side down her back. The motion was like a beacon drawing the eyes to her firm derriere. The woman was a hazard and shouldn't be allowed on the road.

Now standing at the rear of his vehicle, he appreciated the view from the front. Nicole's legs were long, lean, and well shaped. The muscle tone was evident in her loose runner's stride and flat abdomen. The blue sports bra she wore afforded him the best view yet of Nicole's shapely breasts. They were high and pleasingly full for such a petite woman. The slight bounce fired his blood as he thought of their lushness. Sensing tightness in the lower region of his body, he straightened his stance trying to calm his blood. As Nicole neared, he found humor in her attempt to right her appearance. The woman obviously had no idea the effect her sweat-glistening body was having on him.

"Surprise, meeting you here," Nicole joked, finally standing face to face with Xavier.

"I bet," he voiced in a disbelieving tone. They both broke into laughter.

"You would think they could be a little more subtle."

"Why bother? You and I would recognize a set-up no matter how they tried to whitewash it," he replied.

"True, but I don't know what they expect to achieve with these games."

"Don't you?"

When Nicole failed to respond to his question, but focused on his lips, it was all Xavier could do not to sweep her up into his arms and kiss her. But knowing Nicole was trying to ignore the chemistry between them, he instead threw his arm around her shoulders giving them a squeeze, before escorting her inside.

They caught a brief glimpse of Gina and Keith rushing back to their sitting places, as they approached the front door. Exchanging glances, they realized that they must have been under surveillance.

"Hi," Nicole called as she entered Gina's home.

"Hey girl, I see you made it," Gina murmured, innocently pretending to be absorbed in fabric swatches.

Nicole caught Xavier's eye as they both fought to conceal their smiles. She approached Gina who sat on the floor in front of the coffee table. Leaning over her shoulder close to her ear, she whispered, "Don't think we don't know what you two are up to."

"Is it working?" Gina responded, unfazed.

"You were at the window. You tell me," Nicole sassed, excusing herself to the shower.

"Okay, so we were spying. Shoot me, why don't you," Gina threw out, unrepentant for her meddling or spying. Her comment drew the men's attention. Ignoring them, she continued to search through the numerous samples.

Keith and Xavier sat side by side on the sofa, pretending not to know what the conversation was about. Keith knew if he directly approached Xavier about Nicole's virtues, his friend would reject the idea, but subtle little pushes in her direction just might work.

Xavier didn't voice his thoughts because he didn't want to give Keith anymore incentive. The moment he showed true interest in Nicole, his friend would be reciting the woman's virtues and he wasn't quite ready for that. He wanted to enjoy this new friendship without the hassle of expectations.

Nicole stepped from the shower and dried her body off quickly. Just the idea of Xavier being in the same house as she while undressed, caused the butterflies to dance in the pit of her stomach. The sight of him made her heart race. And the sound of his voice stirred her insides. She could easily allow herself to be drawn in by those wondrous feelings, but experience had taught her to be more cautious.

Returning to the living room after donning a red cap-sleeve sundress, Nicole was surprised to find only Xavier. He still sat on the sofa, but now the television was on. As she sealed beside him noticing the television, she got the distinct impression that he hadn't been paying attention to the program.

"Are you interested in reducing the cellulite in your thighs?"

Xavier's startled gaze settled on Nicole's teasing face. "When did you sit down?" He had been so focused on the image of Nicole nude down the hallway, that he had failed to hear her leave the bathroom. Just knowing she was one door away had him aroused and hungry for a taste of her. Only now processing her words he turned back around and focused on the television program. When he realized he had been watching an infomercial on a miracle cellulite cream, he threw his head back and released that rich baritone laugh Nicole had come to love.

Sobering some, he looked deeply into her eyes as his thumb caressed her lips thoughtfully. "Damn woman, you take the most erotic shower."

Nicole lost herself inside his smoldering gray eyes. Her lips trembled under the caress, then widened into a teasing smile upon hearing his cryptic words. "Care to elaborate?"

"Not a chance."

"Okay, maybe you'll answer this question then."

"Shoot."

"Where are Gina and Keith?"

"They went to pick up Chinese."

"And conveniently left us alone in this big house."

"Seems like it." Xavier nodded his head thoughtfully, then broke out into another bout of laughter. "Don't look so shocked, Nicole. You know those two won't stop at anything."

"I know," Nicole conceded.

The sudden deflated tone wasn't lost on Xavier. He studied her troubled face for a moment before voicing his question.

"What do you want, Nicole?" His voice had taken on a seriousness that was reflected within his piercing gray eyes.

Hearing the concern in his voice, Nicole gave voice to what she had been struggling to ignore. "I want these feelings to go away, and I wish our friends would stop manipulating these chance encounters."

Just as Xavier was about to reply, Gina and Keith returned. The subject would have to be dealt with at a later date.

CHAPTER 6

Later would prove to be a week from their encounter at Gina's home. Xavier had telephoned on Wednesday to invite her to his place for a backyard cookout. Nicole was noticeably hesitant in accepting the invitation. She knew they both had ventured into an area they weren't quite prepared to deal with at the moment However, Xavier was not to be put—off, and in the end Nicole relented, accepting the invitation for Saturday evening.

A quick shower and change of clothes—denim skort and yellow tank top with brown strappy flat sandals, and she was just about ready for the cookout. Standing before the mirror she once again French braided her hair. With light make-up and spritz of White Diamonds she declared herself ready.

Back in the kitchen Nicole examined the product of her nervous energy. The countertop contained several dishes ranging from side dishes to desserts. She hoped Xavier wouldn't mind her contributing to the cookout, but she had been so nervous about the evening that she had to do something to stay busy. Utilizing her skills learned as a waitress during college, she skillfully balanced dishes on her arm and in her hands as she carried them out to her vehicle. A hearty quick start-up and she was off. Following Xavier's direction, she took Pass Road into the base. She supplied her name as instructed and was immediately given directions and waved through by the immaculate gate guard. A few short minutes later, she pulled up in front of Xavier's base quarters recognizing both vehicles in the driveway. She examined the replicated red brick homes which lined both sides of the quiet, tree-shrouded street They were each alike, yet the residents through their landscaped yards created individuality. It was a nice community. Focusing on the house where Xavier dwelled, Nicole suddenly realized that she was nervous. She took a deep breath before exiting the car. From the passenger door, she removed her dishes then took the walkway to the front door.

Just as she approached the door, it swung open as Xavier stepped out to greet her. He looked good dressed in jeans and an oversized shirt. Long, slightly bowed legs were encased snugly in denim, drawing her admiring glance. Her heart immediately began tap dancing within her chest Nicole returned his warm welcoming smile, glad that she had accepted the invitation. She had missed the sound of his voice and the sight of his handsome face.

"There you are. I was beginning to think you had changed your mind," Xavier spoke excitedly. "What's all this?" he asked, relieving Nicole of dishes.

"Just a little something I whipped up."

"A little something? Did you forget you were the guest?"

"No, I didn't. Let's just say I had energy to burn, so I put it to good use. I hope you don't mind." She looked at Xavier, worried.

"Are you kidding? The way you cook? I can hardly wait to sample."

With that he led the way into the kitchen and showed Nicole where to deposit her load. He placed those dishes which required cooling into the refrigerator, then turned back to his guest. He was pleased beyond words that she hadn't reneged on her acceptance. With a guiding hand, he led Nicole out onto the patio and to his other guests.

"Look who I found."

Gina and Keith, dressed ridiculously alike in khaki shorts and matching green shirts, reclined on chaise lounges overlooking the peaceful waters of Biloxi's Back Bay. At the sound of Xavier's deep baritone, Gina looked up, noting the sudden joy and relaxation in his expression. She also noticed her friend's brilliant golden eyes alight with something new. Could it be that Keith's plan stood an actual chance of working? Studying the two people standing a breath apart and the stupid, yet pleased expressions mirrored in their faces, she decided that it most certainly did. Nicole's usually unapproachable demeanor was gone. In its place was the warm loving woman she had known for years. She silently watched as Xavier, with a light touch to Nicole's back, led her over to greet Rosa. Any other time her girlfriend would have skillfully positioned herself out of reach, but not this evening, Instead, she looked sweetly up into his attentive gray eyes, smiling. Unbeknownst to him, Xavier had accomplished something no other man had—the beginning of trust.

"Hello Rosa, it's good seeing you again."

"It's good to see you as well, Ms. Edwards," the salt and pepper-haired Latino woman spoke. Her motherly smile was warm and welcoming. Glancing at the couple before her, she recognized the beginning of something special. She was pleased for the major because he was such a good man.

He deserved the love of a good woman, and her instincts told her that Ms. Edwards was just that.

"Nicole, please." As Rosa nodded her acquiescence, Nicole was startled by the boisterous yelling of her name.

"Ms. Ed. . .wards," screamed a running blur in blue. Ryan Ramón was thrilled to see his favorite teacher in the whole world with his dad. How many times had he dreamed that the two would marry and they would become a family? He flung his arms open wide as he ran a little faster.

Nicole squatted down on her haunches to receive the hug she knew would be offered. Now knowing something of Ryan's history, she understood his need for her attention and reassurance. Rosa, closer to his grandmother's age, was thought of as just that, but by virtue of her single status and being closer to his father's age, she was seen as an object of hope. Suddenly reluctant about coming today, she would make sure not to doing anything to give him false hope. She squeezed Ryan's little body tightly, then withdrew for a moment as she studied the handsome face glowing with adoration, knowing there could be no wishful thinking on the little one's part. She wouldn't be responsible for putting the hurt in his warm brown eyes.

Xavier wasn't surprised by his son's exuberant welcoming of Nicole. He had expected it, yet had hoped he had been wrong about his son's fascination with Ms. Edwards, but he hadn't. Maybe this wasn't such a good idea. He didn't want Ryan getting the wrong idea about him and Nicole. He liked the lady immensely and wanted a relationship, but was by no means considering anything permanent. There was nothing wrong with a man and woman being friends, or maybe more than friends. However, Ryan was too young to understand the concept.

As he stood watching the warm embrace shared between his son and the woman he had gotten to know over the past month, Xavier noticed the slight change in Nicole. What was it? Did Ryan's exuberance bother her? Maybe the lady wasn't who she had presented herself to be. She had seemed genuinely interested in Ryan's well being during the times they had shared previously. Had his judgment been impaired once again by another pretty face? Anger suddenly clouded his features as he pulled his son out of Nicole's embrace.

Startled by the sudden withdrawal of the warm small body from her arms, Nicole stared into Xavier's dark gray brooding eyes. What had she done? Maybe Xavier didn't appreciate her affection towards his son. She wasn't his mother and maybe her response had been too personal. Whatever the reason for his displeasure she was sure she would find out soon enough.

"Whoa partner; give the lady a chance to settle in. She'll be here all evening." He spoke to Ryan, but cast a speculative glance at Nicole. He waited as his son trotted back off to the tent he had assembled in the backyard earlier. Then he turned his attention to Nicole. He grasped her upper arm and steered her to the picnic table laden with food. The ever-present sensation associated with the feel of Nicole's flesh was ignored, as he pulled her closer to his side. With their backs to the others he demanded an explanation for her displeasure.

"What's going on, Nicole?"

Not knowing what he was referring to, Nicole followed his lead in keeping her back to the others. She had hoped for a pleasant evening, but it appeared that wasn't going to be the case. "I don't understand the question."

Undaunted by her wide-eyed, innocent stare, Xavier explained. "For the past month you have appeared to be concerned for my son, always assuring me of how well I was rearing him. But a moment ago you went all stiff like a board when he hugged you, and I want to know why. My son has so much love to give, and I will not tolerate another uncaring woman hurting him."

Angered now herself, Nicole's eyes darkened. "Who do you think you are accusing? I am not your ex-wife, Xavier Ramón. And I would never deliberately set out to hurt any child. My concern was genuine then, as it was a moment ago when I realized that Ryan viewed me as a substitute for his mother. Being a child he would automatically begin having fantasies of the three of us becoming a family."

"A family! You've got to be kidding," He bit the words off in disbelief. "Don't you think you've jumped the gun here?"

The sarcasm in Xavier's voice sliced through Nicole like a knife. Telling herself that Xavier hadn't meant to hurt her deliberately, she tried to ignore the pain centered in her chest. She wanted to ask why the idea was so unthinkable, but wasn't sure she could tolerate the truth. Instead she weakly voiced, "I was worried for his sake. That was the expression you saw." Filled with hurt once again for obviously not measuring up, she glanced out over the water, fighting the burning sensation in her throat. She hadn't cried in years and refused to now. It didn't matter how this man felt about her because she had no designs on a romantic involvement. "I think I should go."

The moment the thoughtless words had flown from his mouth, Xavier wanted to call them back, but it was too late. The pain and damage had been done. He had mistaken Nicole's concern for something less than honorable, and now had insulted her unmercifully. Why did he continue to judge all women based on one?

"Nicole I didn't mean that the way it sounded. I just meant…" Xavier didn't know what he meant. He only knew he didn't like the dejected expression clouding Nicole's features. Without concern for the others he lightly touched her face forcing her to look at him. "Please don't go. This evening is not taking shape the way I had envisioned. Nicole, you are a lovely young woman, I only meant to say I've done the marriage thing and I don't plan on repeating the mistake. Any man would be honored to have you as his wife."

Any man but you. it hurt and she didn't understand why. She and Xavier had only met recently and she possessed no ideas about marriage, but the cutting words stung nonetheless. Forced to meet his eyes, Nicole heard the words spoken quickly and with honesty. She couldn't fault Xavier for stating what she already knew. Marriage and love weren't for her. She received love from her adoring students and that was enough. Besides, what did she know about love anyway? She would probably make some man an awful wife, and God knows she didn't have a clue about being a mother. With all that said in silence, it still didn't salve the hurt. "I understand—you were only looking out for the welfare of your son." She did understand more than Xavier knew.

Keith took a great interest in the activity he saw at the picnic table. He knew Xavier's mannerisms and recognized the moment he became angry. What had happened? He had been watching the exchange between Nicole and Ryan. It was beautiful and filled with unconditional love. Both were in desperate need and seemingly had discovered it within each other. So what had angered Xavier?

Concerned, but trying not to alert Gina to the scene at the table, he pushed his wire rimmed glasses up on his nose, watching surreptitiously. He knew Xavier could be cruel and thoughtless at times where women were concerned. Never intentionally, but always as a defense mechanism. However, Nicole wasn't like those women. She was vastly inexperienced in the dating game, and her self-confidence wasn't as sound as she tried to pretend. Only those close to her knew this. One harsh, thoughtless word from Xavier could ruin a chance at happiness for them both. Nicole didn't trust easily and a man in uniform even less. He prayed Xavier wouldn't damage the fragile trust, which obviously existed between them for Nicole to be here today. If he did, it would be a long road to regaining it. However, taking note of Xavier's uncharacteristic public display of affection, Keith thought maybe there was hope.

Rosa and Ryan retired to the house a short while later, leaving the couples enjoying the quiet evening. It had progressed nicely. The food had been delicious and the company warm and gracious. The evening had been so different from their first when Carmen had monopolized the entire conversation. Glancing at his guests, Xavier was pleased with the outcome of the evening, all but for Nicole. Where she talked and laughed on cue, the golden hue of her eyes had not returned. Nor had her trust in him, and he was disappointed, If she were one of his troops, he would never have been so callous with his words. He prided himself on building self-esteem and confidence in the people he commanded. Nicole should have been no different. He knew of her life, and the feeling of rejection she endured as a child, and yet he too had rejected her in a sense. However, no one watching her would know she had been hurt. He now realized how good she was at concealing her emotions. He didn't like it. He wanted to know when she hurt, when she was happy, what she thought, and dreamed.

Nicole met Xavier's thoughtful gaze. He had been watching her off and on all evening. She had tried to present a carefree attitude, but obviously failed. No one noticed except for him. She didn't want the man to recognize her weakness. She didn't want nor need pity. She had made it this far in life alone, and she would make the next twenty-five plus years as well. Lifting her proud chin, she met his stare head-on, silently conveying the message that he was of no great importance to her.

The message was received loud and clear from across the patio. It didn't set well with Xavier. He didn't want marriage and he wouldn't lead Nicole to believe otherwise, but in the same breath, he didn't want to lose her as a friend or possible lover. They were adults, he more than she, and they were quite capable of conducting an honest adult relationship without the hassle or complications caused by love.

He was attracted to her, and the intensity of that attraction surprised him. Not since Monique had he felt so drawn to a woman. All during the evening he had been keenly aware of her moving throughout the yard. With his eyes closed he could distinguish her scent from all the others. The chemistry between them was that strong. Suddenly turning to face Nicole, he knew she felt it as well. It was in the now golden brown eyes. He wanted her. The thought had been needling him since their initial meeting. So much so, that his mind conjured up images of her beside him in bed last night, under the warm spray of the shower this morning, and now in the fire of his belly. Damn all the reasons he probably shouldn't pursue her—age difference, her aversion to the military, and her ability to get closer to him than any other woman—he meant to have her.

Her wide golden brown eyes registered his resolve and she knew she was in danger. In danger of losing her peace of mind, and her body and soul to a man that would never love her. She wasn't ready for this and would have to steer clear of the man.

"Nicole, I hear you're going to be teaching at the community center this summer," Keith spoke, interrupting Nicole's musing.

"Yes, I am. Did Gina tell you?"

"No, it was actually Carmen."

"Yeah? Well I'm sure she told you she isn't happy about the decision."

With a slight shake of his head Keith replied, "She didn't mention it."

"I'm surprised she missed an opportunity to badmouth me," Nicole commented, dumbfounded.

"Nicole, Carmen is jealous of you. She always has been, and that Frank Lyons incident only made matters worse," Keith added, trying to defend his cousin.

From the sidelines Xavier listened to the exchange. He knew Keith was correct in his assessment of Carmen. She was jealous of Nicole. But who was this guy Frank?

"Who's Frank Lyons, and what's he to you?" Xavier asked with a nod of his head in Nicole's direction.

Nicole glanced across the patio to where he sat, trying to gauge his guarded expression. What must he be thinking? Probably what everyone else thought at the time.

"Frank Lyons was Carmen's boyfriend in high school, captain of the football team and every mother's hope for her daughter. He was failing calculus miserably and was close to failing the senior year. He asked me to tutor him and I agreed. But one day while we were studying he asked me out on a date. I didn't know whether to take him seriously or not, but anyway I said no. The next thing I know Frank was telling lies about me and why we were meeting."

"Let me guess. It wasn't for *hitting* the books," Xavier growled out

"No. The rumors started flying and I was caught in the middle. Carmen accused me of trying to seduce her boyfriend away from her. At that age I didn't have the first clue about seduction. I was too focused on finishing school so I could get on with my life."

After a pause and Nicole didn't continue speaking, Xavier knew there was more. He wasn't sure he wanted to hear it, but he needed to hear it, for it too would enlighten him about this woman he admired. "What happened, Nicole?"

She glanced first at Xavier, then Keith, and finally at Gina, who barely met her eyes. Taking a deep breath she forged ahead. "Some of the parents tried to have me expelled from school when they got wind of the rumors. I was labeled a bad influence on the nice girls from respectable families."

"My mother was leading the way," Gina said softly while looking at Nicole.

"Gina, that was a long time ago. Your mother has more than made up for that incident. I've forgiven her. She treats me like one her children."

"I know, Nicole, but it never should have happened. She wouldn't listen to me. No, she listened to Carmen's mother. The lies that woman created about you were unforgivable, and my mother believed her over me."

"Gina, just be thankful that you have a mother to be concerned. Don't judge her too harshly because everything that she did was out of love for you."

This woman amazed him. Here she was divulging a past injustice done to her, and now she sat defending one of the participants. She knew the true meaning of a parent's love and recognized the limitless boundaries it would go to protect. She was an extraordinary young woman.

"Nicole is right, sweetheart. Your mother is great and she loves you. I know all mothers and daughters have issues, but this one you should forget," Keith suggested lovingly.

Outnumbered, Gina conceded the point. "Okay, you're both right, but Nicole never should have had to experience such loathing."

The memory prompted a shiver to race down Nicole's spine, causing her to tremble. She recovered quickly, but not quick enough, for Xavier saw it and moved immediately to her side. Placing an arm around her shoulders he drew Nicole near. At the moment he didn't care what Gina and Keith thought, he only wanted to be there for Nicole. "Are you okay?"

"Yes, I'm fine," she whispered, looking into his eyes.

"Bad memory?"

"Yeah, but it turned out okay. Frank came forward and told the truth; however, it still didn't change some people's opinion of me."

"You mean Carmen."

With a shaky smile Nicole nodded yes. How could she explain to anyone how the ordeal had affected her. Even after the truth came forth, people still gave her speculative glances, teachers, parents, and students alike. There were no loving arms offering her comfort at the end of the day, no words of love and faith in her spoken. Just a foster mother who kept telling her *it better not be true."*

CHAPTER 7

Side by side Nicole and Xavier waved good-bye to Gina and Keith. Xavier had asked her to stay behind so that he could speak with her in private. The time had come to apologize and clear the air between them. He valued their newfound friendship and didn't want to lose it. Being completely honest he didn't want to lose Nicole. He was attracted to her and wanted her like a man wants a woman. But knowing if he pushed too hard Nicole would retreat, he decided to allow her to set the pace.

Nicole followed Xavier into the backyard. She was nervous and unsure of what he had in mind. Several bamboo torches illuminated the dark space creating a realm of intimacy. It was in this atmosphere that they now found themselves alone. There were two chaise lounges, a bench, and two chairs scattered around the patio. Nicole elected to sit in one of the chairs as Xavier settled onto a chaise.

Several minutes ticked by without a word being spoken. For right now words weren't important. They both sat quietly enjoying the gentle breeze off the bay and the chirping of the crickets. Nicole closed her eyes and listened to the night activity. The lapping water, and the occasional sound of fish breaking the surface soothed her nerves. Her rapid pulse was now slowing back to normal, allowing for rational thought.

She had to get out of there. "I really should be going now. Thank you for a lovely evening." Nicole never looked at him directly while she spoke, just somewhere in his general vicinity. Standing, she attempted to walk past Xavier but was halted as his hand whipped out, hauling her into him. She lost her footing under the force, landing half on the chaise and half across his solid chest. As she met his dark smoldering eyes, fear and anticipation warred for dominance inside her body.

With their faces so close together, Xavier could see the fear in Nicole's wide-eyed stare. Yet deep inside, he knew it wasn't him she feared, but the uncontrollable chemistry sparking between them. "I owe you an apology for earlier. My words were cruel and thoughtless, and you didn't deserve to be hurt like that."

Nicole could hear the sincerity in his voice. Searching his eyes for signs of deceit and discovering none, she released her anxiety. "Apology accepted."

"Nicole, I care about you and value our friendship. But I would be a liar if I said I wasn't attracted to you." He released his hold on her hand as he swept a loose strand of hair away from her face. "The other day over at Gina's you admitted to having feelings for me."

With her eyes downcast, Nicole didn't speak right away. Instead, she toyed with the tail of his shirt. "it's true, and the more I see you, the stronger the feeling intensifies."

"So why not go with what we're feeling and see where it leads us?" he asked, tilting her chin up so that she faced him.

"Because for right now I'm enjoying our friendship just the way it is. It's actually quite nice."

With great exaggeration, Xavier rolled his eyes at the sound of those words.

"Stop it," Nicole laughed, swatting his chest playfully as his rich laughter filled the air. "I know that's not what you wanted to hear. Don't you think I see the heat in your eyes when you look at me?" She traced his brows while her eyes roamed the surface of his face. "Neither one of us is ready to cross that line. You have issues of trust, and me, I have issues with your being in the military."

"I thought we agreed to explore each other's world?"

"We did, and I'm willing, but I'd like to keep this relationship friendly."

Xavier stilled her nervous hand which had resumed toying with his shirt. Bringing it to his lips, he kissed it lightly. "Thank you for your honesty. And you've raised some serious issues that do need to be addressed. So we both do a little work on ourselves and see what happens." Swinging his legs around, he stood, bringing Nicole with him. He suggested they return inside. Before doing so, he methodically moved around the yard dousing each flaming torch. When the last flame was extinguished, he reached for Nicole's small hand, leading them inside the house. On crossing the kitchen threshold they were greeted by the pleasantly cool interior and the aroma of backyard grilling. The silence and vacancy of the living room indicated that Rosa and Ryan had turned in for the evening. Xavier suggested they sample Nicole's banana pudding, then excused himself to the kitchen. Nicole was left alone in the living room. She took the opportunity to examine Xavier's home. There was much that could be learned about a person by studying their living space. Taking the time now, since she wasn't given the opportunity upon arrival, she absorbed a feel for the room.

The large spacious area was decorated in multi shades of brown, beige, and indigo. The occasional splash of burnt sienna added vibrancy. It was too dark for Nicole's liking, but fit Xavier's no nonsense personality perfectly. Rich overstuffed brown leather furniture created a comfortable seating arrangement. The sectional sofa focused on the large screen television placed against the far wall. Wraparound windows occupied each corner and were covered with beige linen vertical blinds. A massive solid wood, five-shelf, German cabinet sat on a wall leading into the hallway. Sparkling crystal decanters and glassware occupied the center glass-encased shelf. Another glass door up top displayed what she recognized as English Wedgwood China. The fine bone vase and fruit bowl with its distinctive Windsor blue pattern gleamed under the display light. The lower shelves were laden with military history books.

Nicole paused before a grouping of four unique paintings. Admiring the bold black, gold, and red metallic paint depicting ancient Egypt, she was captivated by the beauty. The delicate artwork was painted on what appeared to be some type of pale yellow material. She would ask Xavier about it when he returned. She admired all the odd collectibles from around the world. His home was reflective of his military years of travel. She thought it exciting to visit foreign countries that most people only dreamed of visiting. Nicole decided that the military wasn't all bad, and that Xavier and Ryan probably had wonderful memories.

Xavier returned, carrying a gold serving tray with black embossing of the Great Pyramids. Another treasure of his travels abroad. Black glass bowls containing banana pudding sat in the middle of the tray, surrounded by napkins and spoons. Nicole rushed to clear an area of the coffee table. Placing the floral centerpiece of silk ivy on the wood and wrought iron end table, she admired its beauty. Actually Xavier's home was quite nice, just dark.

Nicole took a seat on the sofa thinking about the books she'd read on the colors of the zodiac. She herself was a Pisces, ruled by Neptune. Her home no doubt was decorated in the various shades of the ocean. Piecing together what she knew of Xavier and the colors he'd chosen, she would venture a guess that he was Capricorn—protective, practical, and methodically cautious. What she didn't want to acknowledge was the fact that they were romantically compatible. The thought caused her to doubt the wisdom of their delicate friendship.

"I hope I didn't keep you waiting out here too long," Xavier spoke as he placed the tray in the space Nicole had made. He joined her on the sofa.

Still contemplating the power of the zodiac as Xavier sat down beside her, grazing her knee with his own, Nicole nervously tucked a ribbon of hair behind her ear.

"Not at all. It gave me the opportunity to marvel over the treasures of your journeys." Her eyes glowed brightly with excitement. "You have some fascinating pieces."

She rose from the sofa, walking around the coffee table back to the grouping of four. "These paintings are exquisite. What type of surface are they painted on?"

Pleased by Nicole's enthusiasm for his collective treasures, he too walked over to the grouping. Laying his hands on her slight shoulders he rested his chin atop her head. He just couldn't seem to keep his hands off her tonight. He wasn't sure if it was the rose scent clinging to her skin, or the enticing velvet softness of it which kept inviting his touch. His large strong hands moved in slow, massaging motion, as he focused his attention onto the paintings.

"I picked these up in a little market in Saudi Arabia. The surface is actually a plant called papyrus. It's quite delicate to the touch. The quality of the work is excellent."

Nicole heard what Xavier said, but could barely concentrate on his words. The magical warmth he was stirring inside her with his gentle caressing was clouding her mind and making coherent thought almost impossible.

Unaware of Nicole's state of distraction, Xavier continued telling her about his visit to the Middle East. It was only when he opened a glass door to the cabinet, retrieving a black and gold pyramid, that Nicole managed to focus once again on the conversation. The absence of his touch allowed her brain to function properly. "Oh, Xavier it's gorgeous!"

"I thought so too when I came upon it." His gray eyes beamed with pride and pleasure that Nicole found it just as precious. "You know people believe the Pyramids hold special powers."

Surprised by the comment or maybe it was the reverence in his voice she heard, Nicole's eyes swung immediately to him.

"Come on, don't look so surprised. I may be military, but I too believe in the spiritual," he chuckled self-consciously.

Analyzing the play of emotions within his eyes and on his face Nicole recognized his discomfort with his sensitivity. He was so accustomed to being a leader and protector, that he sometimes forgot to allow the human, more spiritual side of him to show through. The sweet vulnerability warmed her heart and found a resting-place inside of it. Tenderly she reached up, placing a hand to his cheek. "Don't be ashamed to show your human side. It above everything else is what makes you special. I sensed you possessed a good heart and loving spirit, and now you just confirmed it. You're an amazing *person,* Major Ramón."

He held her hand pressed against his face with his own. For several minutes they remained standing, just staring into each other's eyes. Then Xavier caressed Nicole's slightly parted lips with the thumb of his free hand. Repeatedly he outlined the shape of her lips, before boldly dipping his thumb through the slight opening. Instinctively, Nicole's tongue reached out to greet the intruder. Her eyes darkened as her heart raced away and Xavier released a deep agonizing moan. Their energy was powerful enough to charge the room. When they were both on the verge of crossing the line, Nicole removed her hand and walked back toward the sofa. Looking for her purse, she prepared to leave.

"I'm going home," she blurted. "I'm sorry, you must think I'm some type of tease. I say I want us to simply be friends, then a mere touch has me ready to forget everything." She was rambling while searching for her purse. Never once did she dare look at him.

"Of course I don't think you're a tease," Xavier hurriedly spoke while running a hand over his face. "You're just stronger than I am." When she continued to search for her purse he caught her arm, halting her escape. "Hey, wait a minute, Nic. There's no reason for you to leave."

Ashamed of her behavior, Nicole couldn't bring herself to face Xavier. She could hear the ugly words rumored about her during high school. The last thing she wanted was for Xavier to believe she was an easy woman. "Please don't think badly of me," she mumbled, trying to extract herself from his hold.

"Nicole, look at me, sweetheart. I'm not like those people from your past. Baby, it's normal to have these feelings."

Her head shot up. "How did you know that's what I was thinking?"

"Because I saw the shame in your eyes. You exhibit this persona of strength and confidence—an I-don't-care-what-people-think attitude—but in actuality you're quite vulnerable to people's opinion of you.

"You don't understand how careful I must be at all times. People have always expected so little of me. I constantly have to prove myself better than most"

"Baby, you don't have to prove anything. You are one class act, Nicole Edwards, and don't you allow anyone to make you believe otherwise." He drew her against his chest, rubbing her back soothingly. Feeling the tension slowly leave her body, he tilted her chin up so that she faced him. "Besides, you can't leave now."

"Why not?"

"You haven't eaten your dessert."

Later at home, Nicole curled up inside her lonely bed, contemplating all that had occurred this day. She had ridden on a wave of emotions from start to finish. Intelligent enough to know that you couldn't run from the truth, she wouldn't do so now. She was extremely attracted to Xavier and acknowledged the fact. A part of her wanted to take that blind leap of faith and explore those blossoming feelings, but her practical nature wouldn't allow it.

Nicole smiled in the dark as she recalled Xavier's reaction to her reference to their friendship. She realized the platonic boundaries were difficult for Xavier to handle, but what surprised her most was the fact that he was willing to accept them. There were plenty of women out there who would be more than willing to satisfy his needs. Rolling over onto her back, she contemplated the meaning of his actions.

Frustrated, Xavier tossed and turned in bed. He ached for Nicole, but knew he would have to wait for her to accept what he felt was inevitable. Their chemistry was too strong to be ignored. But she was right; they both had issues to resolve. Nicole had pinpointed his correctly; however, he felt hers was much more complicated than a mere aversion to his career.

Something far deeper forced her to keep him at arm's length. She claimed she wasn't looking for a serious relationship, which of course suited him just fine, since he wasn't interested in anything permanent. But he did care for her. If he wasn't careful he could find himself right back where he started—hooked on a woman that could turn his world completely upside down. That caused him a moment's pause. Exhausted from the hours of contemplating, he finally drifted off to sleep. But his last conscious thought was of how he couldn't wait to see Nicole again.

CHAPTER 8

Angry, Nicole slammed the door to her home, then kicked it for added measure. This had been one heck of week and it wasn't over yet. She threw her purse and tote bag containing her school materials onto the floor by the chair. Stepping out of her shoes, she proceeded into the kitchen barefoot. She yanked open the refrigerator door and grabbed a bottled water. Still standing in the open door, she allowed the cold air to cool her heated flesh. A long drink from the bottle pooled in the pit of her stomach heavily. Finally closing the refrigerator door, she retraced her steps back into the living room, where she collapsed onto the sofa. She threw her feet up and rehashed the events of the week.

Monday she hadn't arrived home until after seven o'clock. There had been a teacher's conference followed by the last PTA meeting of the year. Carmen had shown up to discuss the upcoming summer events for the community center. She'd handed out fliers outlining the activities to be offered at the center. Noticeably last on the list was Nicole's cultural class. Nicole didn't really care where it was positioned, just as long as it was listed. Knowing she would have to deal with Carmen one on one the following evening at the community center, she'd hoped to make a quick escape.

And was she ever correct about Carmen, except the confrontation was immediate. Not even Nicole could have imagined the scene that would unfold after all the legitimate issues had been decided. As the meeting ended Nicole was halted from escaping by one of the parents who wanted to offer her services to Nicole for the summer. Her eagerness to assist was welcomed, as was her friendliness. Then Carmen appeared on scene. Rude as usual, she didn't wait until their conversation ended before she began speaking. With her back to the parent, she started in on Nicole.

Not in the mood for one of her public scenes, Nicole quickly assembled her belongings and proceeded out of the nearest exit. Walking straight to her vehicle, she knew she wasn't alone. Carmen's heel tapping was close behind as she eventually made it to the car. She ignored Carmen calling her name as she unlocked the door. Just as she was about to pull the door open, Carmen leaned her body against the door, holding it close.

"Oh no, you don't! You won't escape me this time, Nicole. For once you're going to hear me out," Carmen raged.

"Carmen, please go back inside. I don't want to do this," Nicole stated calmly.

"Who cares what you want, Nicole? You're going to stand right here and hear me out" Carmen pointed to the ground for emphasis.

Annoyed, Nicole replied, "Whatever it is, please say it so I can go home."

"All right, I will," Carmen sassed, flipping her hair over her shoulder. "I hear that you and the major have been seeing quite a bit of each other. During this time together did Xavier happen to mention that he comes from a very prominent New Orleans family?"

Surprised by the news, Nicole tried to appear unfazed, but something must have given her away because Carmen laughed mockingly.

"No, the good major didn't tell you? I wonder why Nicole?"

"Carmen, get out of my way." Nicole snatched on the car door, trying to budge her out of the way.

"He didn't tell you because you aren't important to him. You're his walk on the wild side. Once he's had his fill of you, he'll toss you away, just like your dear mother."

"Why are you telling me this, because it sure isn't out of the goodness of your heart?" Snapping her finger, then pointing in Carmen's direction, Nicole continued her thought "I know, maybe you're upset because the man left with me. Poor abandoned Nicole left with the man you wanted."

"He may have left with you Nicole, but you sure as hell can't keep him. He'll grow tired of your classless behind."

Taking a step closer, so that they were mere inches apart, Nicole looked deeply into Carmen's eyes. "That may be, but while he's growing tired, you'll still be at home alone."

That had taken place the night before and this night it had been Carmen who drew blood. Tonight was the final fitting for the bridesmaid dresses, and Nicole couldn't let Gina down. She'd made it a point to be early. She had hoped to be fitted and gone by the time the others arrived. She'd almost made it too, but just as she pushed the dressing room door closed, Carmen entered, carrying her dress. The two women eyed each other for several heated moments. Nicole elected to walk past without a word. Just as she entered the boutique common area, Carmen's words stopped her cold.

"Nicole, I may be at home, but I'm never alone; I have a family who loves me. What will you have once Xavier grows tired of his temporary entertainment?"

Nothing and Nicole knew it. That's why she was fighting so hard to keep their relationship platonic. She knew that once she crossed that line and entered into a intimate relationship with Xavier, he would inevitably leave her behind with only a broken heart to show for their relationship. So without a word, she'd raised her chin and straightened her shoulders as she walked out the door without responding.

Now she was angry with herself for not standing up to Carmen. And she was upset with Xavier for not having called this evening as was the norm since the night of the cookout. Maybe he was bored with her already. She was so worked up she had to struggle to keep tears at bay. What was wrong with her? For years she had managed her emotions with no problem, but it seemed the more she allowed Xavier past her defenses, the more susceptible she became to people's hurtful words.

Nicole was tired of all the second-guessing. She finally managed to pick herself up from the sofa and drag into the bathroom where she stripped away her clothes. A long soak in the tub would help ease the tension. The numerous candles spaced around in the bathroom were each lit. The CD player on the vanity was switched on. Next, she turned on the faucet, adding bath crystals. Finally submerging herself into the scented bubbles, Nicole turned off the faucet, then sat back and allowed the smooth sounds of Jill Scott to transport her to another time and place.

The intrusive sound of the telephone interrupted her journey. She thought to ignore it, then considered it might be Xavier. Extracting herself from the soothing water, she wrapped a towel around herself as she answered the portable phone on the vanity, then worked herself into a robe.

"Hello."

"Hey Nicky," came the familiar voice.

It was Jon. It always amazed Nicole how he seemed to sense when she needed him. "Hi yourself. How were England and the book signing?"

"England was great and the book signing was fantastic. You know, Nicky, it still surprises me that I get paid for doing what I enjoy."

"Well, just be thankful."

He sobered, hearing something she wasn't saying. "How are you doing, kiddo?"

"I'm doing well."

"Nicky, since when have you and I not been able to talk?"

"I can't pull anything over on you, can I?" she laughed.

"No, you can't, so fill me in."

For the next hour Nicole and Jon shared the details of their lives. Nicole discussed Xavier, not leaving anything out, and expressing the hope that they would like each other when and if they met. Then they reminisced about their time together as brother and sister, and made plans to visit during the summer. Before ending their conversation, Jon informed Nicole of his recent engagement. The sudden announcement caught her completely off guard. The world as she knew it was changing. She was happy for him, of course, and said all the appropriate words, but the very thought left her feeling replaced within his life.

"Nicky, you know this doesn't change anything between us. You're my sister and I love you. When can you come to Atlanta and meet Kimberly?"

Feeling selfish and ashamed, Nicole cheered up. "Gina's wedding is next weekend, and I'm teaching a summer program. Let's plan for Labor Day weekend. The coast will be so congested with visitors trying to squeeze the last drop of sunshine out of summer that a trip to Atlanta would be perfect."

"Sounds great, I'll be looking forward to seeing you. By the way bring Xavier," he invited as an afterthought.

Nicole would definitely have to think about that. "Jon, does Kimberly know about me?"

"She knows," he stated matter-of-factly. "Hey, what about Xavier? I don't want any surprises." Jon laughed mischievously.

"He knows my history too, and about my brother."

"Nicky, do you really like this guy? Maybe even love him just a little?" He really didn't need an answer for he could hear it in her voice, and the fact that she had confided her childhood spoke volumes. Not to mention this guy was in the military and she was actually seeing him. Maybe he was the one for his sister. She was due a little love and happiness. He prayed this man was sincere in his interest

"Not all relationships are about love, Jon."

"If they're not then they should be."

"Oh, please! Are you telling me that every woman you became involved with, you loved her?" When there was no response she commented, "That's what I thought. Besides, Xavier and I are just friends, like I said."

"Only because you're trying to ignore what's right before your face."

"And what exactly would that be, oh wise one?"

"That you have strong feelings for this man. Stronger than any before. But because of your twisted thinking, you're settling for a friendship rather than a genuine relationship. Tell me if I'm wrong," he challenged Nicole, who remained silent on the other end.

The ringing doorbell saved Nicole from responding. She made her way to the door with phone in hand and looked through the peephole. Pleasantly surprised to see Xavier on her doorstep, she said good-bye to Jon, then proceeded to open the door. She was dressed in a silk robe and therefore positioned herself discreetly behind the door. The security bolt was disengaged as Xavier was allowed to enter. He breezed through carrying take-out and headed for the dining room. Nicole checked the belt on her robe, then followed behind Xavier.

"Hi. What's all this?" She indicated the plastic white bag containing numerous Styrofoam cartons.

Nonchalantly glancing up as he deposited his load onto the table, Xavier didn't answer right away. He was momentarily rendered speechless by the sight of Nicole wrapped in silk. His heart rate escalated as he realized she didn't have on a bra. The shape and size of her nipples were clearly displayed, as they had pebbled under the friction of the silk fabric. And the gentle sway of her breast beckoned to him each time she moved. Breathing deeply in an effort to clear his head, he inhaled her scent. She smelled good; looked even better. He allowed himself a bold leisurely glance down the length of her body before finally answering her question.

"Dinner."

The simple word was all he could manage at the time. He was too busy fighting his weakness to touch her. In his mind he could see himself lowering his head for a kiss, then wrapping his arms around Nicole, drawing her flush against him. With his tongue he would taste her, and with his hands he would discover whether she was bare beneath the robe. Though he wanted nothing more than to continue the fantasy, Xavier was forced to shake it off. He was long and hard with desire, but this wasn't his reason for being there tonight.

Nicole was uncomfortable standing before Xavier in only a robe and nothing underneath. There was no way she could carry on an intelligent conversation half-naked, and especially not after the thorough examination he had given her. She finally glanced in his direction and noticed his obvious state of arousal. Slowly she raised her eyes, but immediately wished that she hadn't. Xavier's roguish gray eyes watched her watching him with interest. She excused herself rushing from the room embarrassed.

"I'm going to get dressed," she mumbled, running as fast as she dared.

Laughter erupted behind her. Xavier was enchanted by her innocent nature. It was real and unrehearsed. He had already guessed that she wasn't very sexually experienced. The thought actually pleased him. He wasn't the type of man to sleep with every woman who came along and he was sure Nicole was just as selective in men. But more and more he was beginning to wonder if there had been anyone. If the answer was no, as he suspected, then he knew he would have to take precious care with her emotions when the time came.

With that thought tucked away for the moment, he set about fulfilling his plan. From the large bag he retrieved a white linen tablecloth, china, and crystal. Candle holders and candles soon followed, as did silverware. Not to be forgotten were the matching linen napkins. Before Nicole returned to the room, he wanted to have the dining room all set. He worked skillfully and with military precision.

By the time Nicole returned to the living room the lights were out. Following the candlelight and aroma of mouth-watering food, she was stunned by what greeted her. Candles flickered on the table, which had been set beautifully with china and crystal. They had to be Xavier's. She moved further into the room, drawing his complete attention.

From the sideboard, Xavier glanced over his shoulder beaming with happiness. He had accomplished his mission in record time and was proud of the finished product. However, the moment he saw Nicole standing there dressed in a gold silk lounge ensemble, he lost his train of thought. All he could do was devour Nicole's loveliness. The thin spaghetti-strapped top revealed her smooth sable shoulders and showcased the elegance of her graceful neck. The blousing satin pants skimmed her round hips and swung seductively with each step that brought her closer. The satin golden mules on her feet completed the outfit. She stole his breath away with her beauty.

He met her midway into the dining room and captured her hand with his own. Slowly he turned her around. He allowed himself a leisurely view. When she completed the revolution he kissed her lightly on the lips. That was all he dared do.

Xavier finally spoke. "I'm not sure which one of us has received the best surprise." The awe within his eyes conveyed his sincerity.

Slightly embarrassed, yet pleased by his response and rattled by that peck, Nicole moved past him to examine the table. He had outdone himself. She was genuinely touched by the thoughtfulness. She couldn't remember the last time that someone had made her feel special. Still admiring his handiwork, she responded, "Hands down, I received the best surprise."

The compliment pleased Xavier immensely. He had wanted to do something special for Nicole to let her know his interest in her extended beyond desire. She did so much for everyone else without thinking of herself. She was a devoted teacher and involved citizen. Tonight he planned on pampering her for a change. "Come on, have a seat before dinner gets cold."

At the table Xavier offered a prayer of thanks. Nicole was pleased with the spiritual layers she was discovering buried beneath Xavier's strong masculine exterior.

"Everything looks absolutely wonderful, but you didn't have to go to such trouble," she said while salivating over the golden fried chicken, collard greens, macaroni and cheese, and steaming corn bread.

"It was no trouble. I thought you could use a little pampering."

"Pampering. I don't believe I've ever been pampered," she commented with a smile spreading across her face. She could get used to this.

"Well, then it was past time, wasn't it? You know you don't take proper care of yourself, Nicole."

Her eyes flashed golden, challenging his observation. "Yes, I do."

"Okay then. Tell me the last time you had a decent meal. It wasn't Sunday because you had a can of soup while talking to me on the telephone. Monday was sandwich night, and Tuesday was rabbit food."

"So tonight you wanted to make sure I ate a balanced meal?" she voiced humbly.

"That and the fact that I missed you terribly. You're such a busy lady that a guy has to force his way into your hectic schedule. I hope when school is out for the summer that you have more time for your friends." He opened the bottle of sparkling white grape juice, filling two glasses. Placing one before Nicole, he raised his for a toast. "To the beginning of a wonderful friendship."

Nicole took a sip, sealing his toast. "I hope I'm not being too nosy, but do you not drink alcohol? I've noticed the times we've been together that you drank tea."

"Of course you aren't being nosy," he laughed. "You're correct in your observation, but it's a personal choice, not a health issue."

"I wasn't implying it was," she rushed on, suddenly embarrassed.

Reaching out to cover her hand, Xavier shook his head in understanding. "I know that, Nic. What's your excuse?"

"The same as yours. I didn't like how foolish my friends in college behaved while drinking. I like being in control."

"Oh, please don't tell me you're a control freak," his deep baritone rumbled teasingly.

Forgetting the manners that had been drilled into her as a child, Nicole pointed her fork at Xavier. "Let's not go there, Major Ramón. I don't command a squadron of people."

"No, you just boss a classroom of second graders."

Their laughter dispelled the usual quietness of Nicole's home. She couldn't remember when she had last entertained at home. Gina visited often, but was more like family than guest. And Xavier, what did she call him? Guest sounded so impersonal, and friend didn't began to scratch the surface of her feelings. Admiring his good looks as he ate heartily, she instantly knew what she would like to call him—husband. The unexpected thought caused her to choke on her food. Coughing and sputtering, she reached for her glass of juice.

Nicole's coughing spell had Xavier out of his seat in a flash. "Are you all right?" he asked.

"Fine," she weakly replied.

Later after dinner Nicole and Xavier sat companionably on the sofa watching the late night news. They had cleared the table together and washed the dishes. Xavier inquired about her day and she told him about the scene with Carmen at the boutique, yet avoided in-depth details. When he offered to speak with Carmen about this unfounded jealously, Nicole declined the intervention, informing him that she fought her own battles. With her appetite sated and she completely relaxed, her eyelids grew heavy. Scooting down into the sofa, she accepted Xavier's shoulder as he tapped it in invitation to make herself comfortable.

A wave of contentment washed over Xavier as Nicole snuggled against him. It felt natural, right, and as it should be. He inhaled the familiar rose scent of her dark tresses as his heart beat a little faster. Burying his fingers into the back of her head, he gently massaged the scalp. The familiar braid drew his curiosity. He began releasing it. Once it was free, he ran his fingers through the long mass, surprised by its volume.

"Why did you do that?" Nicole sat up alarmed, grabbing her hair. She had drifted to that in-between state of sleep and consciousness before his action registered.

Startled by the reaction, Xavier also sat up, watching her. He realized that she was angry and upset, but for the life of him he couldn't imagine why. "I wanted to see you with your hair free. If you're not wearing that braid, you've got it in that awful French roll."

Offended, Nicole rose from the sofa, planting her hands on her hips. She glared at him as the firestorm inside swelled. "Well, if my appearance is that dissatisfying, why don't you find someone who pleases you." Her eyes glowed golden with anger.

"Stop being silly, Nicole."

"Oh, so now I'm being silly. I suppose because I'm ten years younger than you, I'm behaving immaturely."

"No, you're behaving like a person avoiding an issue. This conversation in itself is simply a smokescreen to avoid the real issue." He too now stood. His eyes were intent as they tried to discern what was actually transpiring. "That's it, isn't it?" he asked as a thought came to mind.

Agitated, yet trying to act calm, she responded nonchalantly, "I don't know what *it* is." She shrugged her shoulders with indifference.

Xavier stared at her strangely for several quiet moments. It was as though he was seeing her for the very first time. "My God, I thought you were beautiful before, but with that head of hair cascading down your back, you're absolutely breathtaking. And that's what you're trying to hide."

Nicole wanted to bask in the compliment, because she knew Xavier meant it as such. But his words also confirmed what she had been made to believe. "Mrs. Scott was right," Nicole commented, a little saddened.

"Right about what? And who the hell is Mrs. Scott?"

Glancing up at Xavier who stood directly in front of her, she sighed. "She was my last foster mother. Surprisingly, I lived with her for two years. She was a stern woman. A throwback to a different time and era, when woman were prim and proper ladies. In her eyesight there was always something wrong with me. My friends, my clothes, or my hair. She told me men would never take me seriously because they couldn't see me for all the hair. She said they liked pretty things, and that's all I would ever be to a man. But if I wanted to be respected and taken seriously, I should always wear my hair bound or up like hers. But instead, I cut it short right before high school graduation." Shaking her head as the memory returned, Nicole laughed sadly. "Boy, what a mistake. Mrs. Scott hit the roof. She railed that loose women wore their hair short, and that a woman's hair was her crown and glory. So as you can see, I haven't cut it since."

"No, you've just bound it up trying to hide your beauty." Angry at a woman he didn't even know, Xavier couldn't believe an adult would tell an already insecure child something like that The woman obviously had no business being a foster parent "And how do you know she was right?"

"Because you focused on this immediately," she tugged on a strand of hair for emphasis.

"That woman really did a number on your self esteem." Shaking his head in disgust, Xavier cupped Nicole's face between his hands. "Sweetheart, the woman fed you a line of bull. Yes, men appreciate looking at a beautiful woman, but we also appreciate an intelligent mind, an honest soul, and a warm, giving heart. You have all three in abundance. However, Nicole, you also possess an exotic beauty that no braid or upswept hairstyle is going to hide. You could be bald, woman, and men would notice you."

Nicole was deeply moved by Xavier's words. Her heart was full and begged to be set free to express itself. Backing out of his embrace, however, she struggled to contain her feelings. This man was doing a number of his own on her willpower.

Not to be put off again, Xavier grabbed her hand before she could escape to regroup. "You're not running from *this* again. Gently, yet determined, he drew her into his arms. "Tonight you're going to acknowledge what you're feeling." Xavier lowered his mouth to Nicole's trembling lips. He bathed them lazily with his tongue before gently tugging on her lower lip. On her startled gasp he forced her lips apart, tasting her with his tongue. He mapped every ridge of her mouth as he sought her tongue in a game of search and seizure. Capturing his prey, he stroked masterfully to bring them both pleasure. By the time he pulled away, Nicole was clinging to the front of his shirt with her eyes closed and her head thrown back. She opened her eyes slowly. Angered by her weakness, she stormed across the room, hanging her head low.

"Please don't do that again."

Exasperated, Xavier inhaled deeply, calming his emotions. "Don't try and deny you didn't enjoy it, because I was the guy you were clinging to." His words rushed out fast and harsh.

"I wouldn't do that."

"Then why are you fighting this so hard?"

"Because by becoming involved with you, I have to be willing to accept the consequences. And Xavier, I assure you there will be heavy consequences to pay for being with you both physically and emotionally."

"We're both adults here. But more importantly we're friends who care about each other, and I'll accept whatever you're willing to give. Only you can determine if the benefits outweigh your perceived consequences. Because in all honesty I can only see the benefits of a relationship."

Finally turning around to face him, Nicole shook her head in disbelief. Did he not hear what he was saying? "You're not looking for a relationship. A relationship stands the probability of leading to a commitment"

It was Xavier's turn to be disgusted with himself. Monique had destroyed his belief in love and marriage. Nicole deserved far more than what he could give her. Sure, he could sweet-talk her and swear undying love, but that wasn't the type of man he was. He was honest and wouldn't lead Nicole to believe he was looking for a lifetime commitment. "I believed in love once, and it bit me in the butt. So I'm honest about what I want out of life. I want you, Nicole, and I'm not ashamed to admit that to you, but in the same breath, I can't promise you that I'll ever want a lifetime commitment. I've been down that treacherous road and lost. I don't plan on repeating that mistake. But what I can promise you besides my friendship, is honesty, respect, and loyalty. And please don't think this is simply about sex, because I can get that anywhere. What I want most from you is the intimacy a man and woman share. I believe I've found that with you."

Nicole also cherished the intimacy. She felt safe physically and spiritually with Xavier. He listened to her thoughts and took them seriously. He acknowledged she was a person, and not a side show exhibit. He asked honest, intelligent questions about her background in an attempt to understand who she was. So many others only wanted the juicy details to feed the gossip mill. Safeguarded within his strong protective nature, she could lose sight of everything and fall head-long in love with him. It was that consequence which held her back.

But maybe it didn't matter, she finally concluded. Sometimes people had to settle for what was offered and make the most of it. Xavier was a good family man who would respect her. He would be there when she needed him and give her the space to be herself. She could channel any feelings of love that might occur to Ryan. In him she recognized a kindred spirit. He too hungered for a mother's love. She could be there for him and his father. Perhaps overall it was better than being alone.

"What about you?" Xavier asked.

"What about me?" Nicole replied defensively as she raised her chin in defiance.

"You aren't looking for a commitment either," he challenged, unaware of how deeply Nicole desired to be loved by the right man.

She met his intense gaze. "I have no misguided notions of love and marriage. I too enjoy the intimacy we've discovered with each other. But the possible consequences keep holding me back."

Xavier admired Nicole's strength and determination in resisting the chemistry between them. However, being the more mature and experienced one, he knew it couldn't be ignored indefinitely. And so he would wait, because Nicole was well worth the wait. In all honesty, if he were capable of loving another woman, he could easily imagine it being Nicole. She was everything a man wanted in a wife.

And then his beeper went off, ending the conversation for the moment. "I better check that," he said, removing his beeper from his belt. Reading the number on his beeper, he went into the kitchen to phone the squadron. After a brief conversation he told the person on the other end that he would be there shortly. He hated to leave Nicole right now, but duty called.

"I'm sorry, sweetheart, but I have to go to the squadron. My troops have had an altercation with one of the socially elite of the community who was driving under the influence."

Relieved that their conversation was momentarily on hold, Nicole came to stand before him. "I know you have responsibilities. Do you get beeped like this often?" she asked.

"Often isn't the correct word. How many times in one night is more like it," he supplied, wrapping his arms around her waist Before Nicole could draw away, he secured her cleft chin between his thumb and index finger. He drew her mouth to his. He didn't have time for the thorough kiss he wanted, but instead planted a sweet peck which would keep her warm and wondering all night.

Twenty minutes later Major Xavier Ramón strolled into his squadron and was immediately brought up to date on the situation. It seemed the mayor's teenage son was stopped at the main gate and found to be intoxicated. All the proper procedures had been followed in dealing with a DUI, but since the suspect was the mayor's son, Xavier had come in personally to handle notification. Dialing up his superior and apprising him of the situation, he informed him of how he would like to resolve the situation. Thankful that his superior agreed, Major Ramón then dialed the mayor personally to tell him about his son's detainment. He was pleased that the mayor supported his actions. His son would be processed like any other citizen and released into his father's custody.

An hour later the mayor had picked up his son and thanked Major Ramón for the professional manner in which he handled the situation. The men shook hands in mutual respect. It was now a quarter to midnight and Xavier was missing Nicole like crazy. What was happening to him? He remembered the days, just months ago to be specific, when his career and his son were all he needed to feel complete. Since meeting Nicole, however, he'd come to realize that there was more to life. Still convinced that marriage wasn't in his future, he nevertheless wanted her beside him.

He turned out the lights and left his office. He paused at the front desk to speak with the desk sergeant on duty. "Before I head home, is there anything going on that I need to know about?"

"Yes sir," the young staff sergeant replied while keeping an ear tuned in to the radio he monitored. It was his responsibility to monitor all radio transmissions and dispatch patrols where needed. Giving his full attention to the commander, he informed him of a domestic assault in military housing.

Back in his car Xavier's mind returned to the domestic assault call. He had stuck around until the suspect was brought in and charged. He had spoken with the young troop's first sergeant, then left the situation in his capable hands. He was thankful his marriage hadn't come to such violence. He didn't believe violence had a place within a marriage, and he absolutely despised the name-calling. Monique had been notorious for vulgar outbursts.

On the drive back home he recalled their initial meeting at his first assignment. She was the daughter of a retired chief master sergeant, and sexy as could be. Her thick red hair was cut short and sassy. He had been drawn to her swaying hips on the dance floor of the local hangout She had pretended not to notice him, which only encouraged him to pursue her harder. They played the usual mating games, with Monique using her feminine wiles to bend Xavier to her will. And like a sap, he'd fulfilled her every whim. He wondered now how he could have been so duped by her. So absorbed in thought, Xavier hadn't realized he had made it home. The awareness of his lack of attention frightened him. Shutting off the engine, he headed inside trying to dislodge the memory of his ex-wife.

By the time he was settled under the covers, he was more confused than ever. He had been completely wrong about Monique, and attracted to all the wrong attributes. He couldn't afford to make the same mistake with Nicole because it just wasn't himself to consider. Ryan was infatuated with the lovely Ms. Edwards and it was his responsibility as his father to shelter him from being hurt. With Nicole he was taking his time discovering the woman inside. But all indicators pointed to her being a class act. Of course, Friday at the squadron picnic would be an excellent time to observe her in action. She would be around people her age, but more importantly, men her age. If she was remotely like his ex-wife, she wouldn't be able to resist the temptation. Finally exhausted by the hours of contemplation, he gave himself over to sleep.

CHAPTER 9

The telephone was ringing. Stepping out of the shower Nicole reached for the towel on the vanity. Haphazardly wrapping it around herself, she ran back into the bedroom.

"No, Gina, you haven't forgotten anything. And yes, Gina, it's going to be beautiful," Nicole's annoyed voice greeted her caller.

"I take it Gina has a case of wedding jitters," Xavier responded, laughing.

Surprised that it was Xavier calling instead of her best friend, Nicole tightened her grip on the towel. "Xavier, I'm sorry, I thought it was Gina placing one more wedding jitters call."

"No problem. I really should be the one apologizing for calling you so early, but I wanted to catch you before you left for work."

Nicole eased down onto the bed making herself comfortable. "You have my attention."

"I need a date for the evening, and I would appreciate it if you would accompany me."

"This evening?"

"Yes. Look, I know it's short notice, but my superior was supposed to be attending this dinner hosted by the Chamber of Commerce.

Nicole supplied the logical conclusion. "And something has come up and you have been asked to fill his place."

Laughing softly, he mumbled, "You've got it! I believe his actual words were, "An opportunity to succeed."

"Oh, please!" Nicole laughed along with him "Well, Major Ramón you have yourself a date. How could I hinder your opportunity to succeed?"

Relieved, Xavier filled her in on the details. It was a black tie affair on board the Starship Cruise Dinner Yacht. All the local dignitaries would be there.

"I'll pick you up at seven."

"I'll be ready."

"Nic?" His rich baritone voice caressed the nickname.

"Yes," she answered slightly breathless.

"Thanks, sweetheart. I really appreciate it."

"That's what friends are for."

"I know, but you and I both know that we're beyond mere friendship."

Xavier hung up the telephone before Nicole could respond. She was left to ponder his words all day. Cursing with frustration, she practically sprang from the bed as she made her way back into the bathroom. Wasn't it enough that he had deprived her of sleep last night with that chaste kiss? Did he also have to ruin her day at work? Realizing that she was going to be late for work if she didn't get moving, Nicole attempted to tuck thoughts of Xavier to the rear of her mind.

At six forty-five that evening, Nicole studied her reflection in the mirror. She wore a red sequined, haltered gown, which highlighted her rich sable skin. The dress complemented her petite figure in an elegant fashion. She checked her hair, not completely comfortable with the thick mass of waves worn free and flowing tonight. But Xavier's comment and the several heated conversations she and Gina had about her hairstyle had provoked her to make a change. She actually liked it She had in the past before Mrs. Scott had persuaded her against it

Xavier arrived promptly at seven. Opening the door to him, Nicole was unprepared for the roguish devil that greeted her. He was tall, dark, and handsome dressed in a tailored fit, black tuxedo. His golden brown skin possessed a deep healthy glow. His smile was broad and sure. There was a hint of *something* Nicole couldn't place her finger on, which made him appear different tonight. She made eye contact and instantly knew what it was. His smoldering gray gaze projected the confidence of a victor.

Xavier took his time savoring Nicole's beauty. She was picture perfect standing in the doorway dressed in red. The haltered gown accentuated her high round breasts and narrow waistline. The flare of her hips was alluring as the sequined fabric swept over them. And the red color highlighted her exotic beauty. But what stole his breath away was the sight of her dark waves worn free and loose. Erotic images flashed through his mind as he read what was in her eyes. She was his woman. They would share their lives as well as their bodies in companionable bliss. Silently he vowed to never give her a reason to regret her decision.

"You've decided to stop resisting."

Swallowing the lump in her parched throat, Nicole looked him squarely in the eyes. "Yes, I have."

Xavier moved away from the doorway. He swept Nicole up into his arms loving the feel of her against him. He claimed her scarlet lips hungrily. Pleased when she opened to receive him, he swept his tongue inside, trying to drink her in. His heart beat rapidly within his chest as he kissed her. For a moment he simply listened to their mutual ragged breaths.

"Thank you," he finally managed to say.

With her eyes closed, because she was too weakened from the kiss to open them, she responded. "For what?"

"For trusting me with your emotions."

"I take full responsibility for my own emotions," she stated firmly, pulling away slightly to stand in the circle of his arms. "So don't worry about hurting me when you feel the need to move on," Nicole managed to say without losing her nerve.

Xavier had known she would eventually come to him, but he never imagined she would come with her soul bare. She'd made it perfectly clear that she wasn't looking for a commitment, and that suited him just fine. Being in the military he was always moving and didn't want the responsibility of trying to end a relationship when he got permanent change of station orders. Nicole had just made things easy. Maybe too easy. Why would a young, intelligent, beautiful woman settle for half a relationship when she could have it all? Looking into her vulnerable golden eyes he suddenly had his answer. Nicole didn't believe in love. She had never had it; therefore she didn't believe love was hers to have. She was settling for the next best thing. The thought made him sad and angry with himself because he didn't have it to give. Monique had destroyed his chance at love, and in a sense he was doing the same to Nicole. If he didn't agree to this arrangement, there was a chance that she would find the man who could love her. She deserved to be loved.

"Nicole, are you sure about this?"

"Of course I am." "Nicole, I can't love you."

"I don't recall asking for your love, Xavier."

"No, you didn't," Xavier sighed, rubbing his chin thoughtfully against her head as he pulled her back against him. He would have to be a damn fool to turn this woman away. He couldn't deny he wanted her, but it was more than that She was smart, witty, and caring to a fault. She was loyal to her friends and spoke the truth when they needed to hear it. She was all those things and so much more and just the type of woman a man married. He kept coming back to that same conclusion. But it wasn't meant for him to be that man.

Without a word Xavier tugged her chin up, zeroing in on her mouth. At first the kiss was sweet and gentle. Then somewhere in between Nicole's sigh and his swollen flesh pressing against Nicole's warm belly, it changed. Finally coming up for air, he separated their mouths, questioning the wisdom of his decision. He was as sexually excited as one of his young troops. Maybe he had been out-mastered.

Nicole was thinking the same thing. Never had a kiss affected her so completely. Her toes tingled, her pulse raced, and her flesh where they touched burned for more. She was in trouble. She had entered a pact with the devil. If just a kiss left her reeling, then making love would be her downfall. There was no way in heaven she could stop herself from falling in love with this man. Deciding she didn't want to stop the wondrous experience unfolding, Nicole silently accepted full responsibility for her broken heart.

Nicole and Xavier were having a wonderful time. The scrumptious meal had been served while the yacht cruised the coastline. Big band tunes played quietly in the background, not hindering table conversation. Couples now crowded the dance floor while others strolled along up top on the deck. That's where Xavier and Nicole now found themselves. They had occupied a table off to the side, out of the way of strollers. A warm gentle breeze chased away the oppressive heat. The coastline was all lit up as the yacht cruised along, providing a breathtaking view for its passengers.

"Tonight was wonderful, Xavier. Thank you for inviting me." Nicole turned to him pleased.

"It did turn out to be quite enjoyable." Xavier brought Nicole's hand to his lips for a kiss. Then covering her hand with his own, he simply stared at her. "You're positively glowing tonight. I thought I was going to have to deck the city councilman back there."

Nicole laughed with delight. She was unaware of the effect it was having on Xavier. "I think he eventually realized it. He was only being friendly."

"Friendly? Is that what you call his eyes glued to you?"

"Now Major, you're sounding like a jealous man," Nicole teased.

"Damn straight," Xavier stated unequivocally as he pulled Nicole from her seat "Come here, let's go stand by the railing and catch a better breeze."

In the circle of Xavier's arms as the yacht cruised smoothly through the water, Nicole was at peace. The sky was littered with stars and the moon reflected off the water. It was a perfect evening for romance. She buried deeper into Xavier's arms and wished they could stay like this forever.

A female voice interrupted their tranquil moment. "Finally. I've been trying to speak with you all evening, Xavier."

Nicole and Xavier turned in the direction of the voice. A pretty woman dressed in a bronze beaded gown walked in their direction. Her smile was friendly as she stuck out her hand to Nicole. "Hi, I'm Major Lydia Hightower."

"Hello, I'm Nicole Edwards."

"It's a pleasure to finally meet you, Nicole. My friend here speaks highly of you," Lydia smiled.

Glancing over her shoulder at Xavier, Nicole was surprised that he had even mentioned her to his friend. The idea that he had pleased her.

"Enough sucking up to my lady, Lydia, I know when you want something." Xavier smiled knowingly at the tall thin woman.

Nicole remained in Xavier's embrace while the two discussed an issue. From the conversation she surmised that Lydia worked in the legal department with Keith. She too was a prosecutor. As their conversation wore on, Nicole found herself studying the woman's features. She was tall, about five ten, and thin with a reddish brown skin tone. Her raven black hair was course and straight. She wore it in a short straight edge bob, level with her chin. She wore no jewelry, just a wide gold wedding band.

As their conversation drew to a close, Lydia apologized to Nicole for interrupting their evening. "I guess you have realized that we military types are always on duty," she joked.

Nicole returned her smile commenting, "Yes, I have." She paused thoughtfully then forged ahead. "Lydia, I hope I'm not being offensive, but what nationality are you?"

The woman returned Nicole's curious stare, recognizing Nicole's own unique features. Smiling with understanding she shook her head no. "Of course you aren't. Most people assume I'm a Mexican American, but I'm actually of the Seminole tribe."

"Ah, warriors of the seven year war."

"You're familiar with my people's history," Lydia responded with pride.

"Some of it. What I've read is quite impressive," Nicole conveyed honestly. "Lydia, I'll be conducting a multicultural course at the community center during the summer. I'm searching for speakers and I would be honored if you would agree to spend a day with the class teaching about your people. I'm looking for speakers to bring clothing, artwork, stories, and games to share. Do you think you would be interested?"

Lydia's faced glowed with the possibilities. Sharing her people's history was a mission of hers. "I would love to, Nicole. I'm a member of the Native American Committee on base. During Native American Month we put on presentations just like what you're asking for." She opened her purse and retrieved a white business card. She passed it to Nicole. "My numbers are on there. Give me a call with a date and time, and I'll be there in traditional dress."

"Oh that's wonderful, thank you." Nicole beamed with pleasure. Her summer course was going to be a great success.

"You really made Lydia's day," Xavier informed Nicole later as they sat at the kitchen table drinking coffee.

"If I can assemble more enthusiastic presenters like Lydia, my summer program is going to be fabulous." Her eyes danced with excitement.

Xavier reached for Nicole's hand as he rose from his chair. "Thanks to you Ms. Edwards, this evening was fabulous. But it's late and I know you have school tomorrow, so I'm going to head on home."

At the door, Nicole didn't resist when Xavier took her into his arms. She stood on tip-toes returning his kiss. "Drive carefully," she said, stepping back.

"I will, and don't forget the picnic tomorrow."

"I won't," she called out to him as he eased out the door.

CHAPTER 10

The base marina was the perfect location for a squadron picnic. The day was Mississippi hot with plenty of sunshine, but under the Spanish moss-covered oak trees shade was plentiful. A refreshing breeze was blowing off the water of Biloxi's Back Bay, helping to minimize the heat. The main outdoor pavilion was where all the food was spread out. Nicole had taken her contributions by Gina's place on the way to work. Now they both carried covered dishes to add to the feast.

Nicole was dressed in a yellow floral sundress. The style was simple, yet flattering. She had agonized over what to wear and was pleased with the choice. It was her desire to make Xavier proud to be with her. She had even worn her hair to his liking. It was free and unbound.

Nervous about coming today, she was pleased to have accompanied Keith and Gina. This would be her first time amongst Xavier's troops and it helped to have friends close by. From behind dark-colored shades she scanned the crowd of people, searching for Xavier, but didn't see him. She knew that Ryan had been invited to a swimming party and wouldn't be attending. Disappointed, she continued to the pavilion beside Gina and Keith, taking in her surroundings. People of all ages were in attendance. Children climbed over playground equipment. A game of volleyball entertained both men and women. The football was being tossed around by a group of guys, while others participated in a game of old fashioned horseshoes. A circle of men stood by the grill laughing boisterously. Keith headed in that direction. Nicole and Gina were left on their own. They continued to the pavilion where the majority of the wives and girlfriends were busy preparing or serving food. The new arrivals were warmly received by the women who reflected all racial groups and ethnic backgrounds. They were immediately offered cold beverages and relieved of their contributions.

A pretty Latino woman with a contagious smile welcomed them to the smorgasbord of food. Conversation flourished around them as children darted gaily in and out of the circle of women. Nicole was recognized from school by one of the women and swept up into a conversations. She was actually having a very good time. The women were warm and unpretentious, and she felt very comfortable amongst them. As she glanced around she noticed several children of mixed heritage running about and realized that this could have been her life. Shaking off the thought she tuned back to the current conversation.

The Latino woman urged them to get something to eat and Nicole and Gina each took a plate. As they approached the hamburger and hot dog laden grill, Nicole caught sight of Xavier emerging from a military police vehicle. Dressed in camouflage battle dress uniform, he was the epitome of the modern day warrior. The navy beret tilted to the side added to the mystique. His black boots were laced tight and shined to a high gloss. This was her first time seeing him in uniform and he cut a fine military figure, if she had to say so herself. Thankful for the dark shades she wore, she allowed her eyes to feast undetected, or so she thought.

"Is it the hamburgers causing you to drool like a baby or Major Ramón over there?" Gina whispered, nodding her head in Xavier's direction. She was delighted by the budding romance and couldn't help laughing.

"Was I that obvious?"

"Only to me because I know you're smitten with the guy." Nicole glanced over her right shoulder to meet Gina's teasing eyes. Her face was expressionless. "I never said that."

"You didn't have to. That dopey in awe expression you're wearing says it all."

The two women burst into girlish laughter. It drew Xavier's immediate attention.

He too wore dark shades to shield his eyes, but Nicole knew the moment he saw her. That gray-eyed magnetism he possessed was in full force, drawing her to his presence. Her body tingled with the awareness that he was watching her and was pleased by what he saw. She bit her lip to keep from smiling her pleasure on seeing him.

Finally, there she was, Xavier exulted silently. She had been on his mind all morning. It had been impossible to work. He had typed and retyped a report three times before finally giving in to defeat. Nicole was all he could concentrate on at the moment. With each passing day she piqued his interest more. Even though his heart rate kicked into overdrive, he presented the picture of calm as he stood watching her. He wanted to march directly to where she stood and sweep her up into his arms, but he didn't. Instead he would take the long approach.

Closing his car door, Xavier headed toward the in progress volleyball game and stood on the sidelines watching. From there he meandered to the horseshoe area and offered his observation. He stopped to talk along the way with his senior personnel. Finally he made his way toward the pavilion of women. He greeted each woman by name, complimenting her efforts and inquiring about her family. Despite his short time in the squadron he had come to know some of the women quite well. Jennifer Melendez was the mother hen of the bunch. She made sure that each wife was taken care of during her husband's deployment. Xavier found her to be a definite asset to his military family. Rupert, her husband, was a lucky man.

Xavier decided to wait in the pavilion amongst the other women for Nicole and Gina to arrive. He would personally introduce Nicole so there was no confusion about her place in his life. It was his desire to see her embraced by his military family and included in upcoming squadron functions.

From his vantage point under the pavilion he kept a discreet eye on Nicole. She looked fantastic. It was obvious to Xavier that she had intended for the sundress to be nondescript and innocent, but up against her sable brown skin, the yellow dress was striking. Not to mention the way the fabric flowed sensually over her hips with each step she took. There was no taming her beauty. The woman could drape herself in a sheet and still turn heads. His troop's admiring glances confirmed his assessment of the situation. The woman was a knockout.

Surprisingly though, he wasn't jealous at all of the attention Nicole was receiving as she strolled past his men. She spoke in a friendly fashion, smiled pleasantly, and carried herself with grace and poise. Not once did she flirt or sway her hips seductively before his men. She didn't try to test her sexual appeal by seeing how many heads she could turn. She was so unlike his ex-wife and he was extremely proud of the fact. She had even worn her hair loose to his liking— most definitely he wanted her on his arm.

Nicole removed her sunglasses on their approach back to the pavilion. She wanted to be able to see Xavier unfiltered. As she grew closer she tried to present a calm, carefree appearance. She glanced casually in Xavier's direction before sliding onto the wooden picnic bench beside Gina. The pull of his magnetic eyes demanded attention. When he finally moved in their direction, blocking out the sun before them, Nicole was left with no choice but to acknowledge his presence.

Still protected behind the dark shades, he flashed that roguish smile Nicole had come to love. He dutifully introduced both Gina and Nicole to the squadron wives. Many of the women recognized Gina as Major Thibodeaux's fiancée and commented about the upcoming nuptials. Nicole was welcomed as the lady in Xavier's life and immediately inducted into the family. The gracious acceptance caused Xavier to breathe a little easier. He had been afraid someone would put him on the spot about Nicole's age, but it hadn't happened. In all honesty, Nicole carried herself with the maturity of a much older woman. No doubt a result of her difficult childhood.

Jennifer insisted that Xavier eat as well. He took a plate as instructed and proceeded down the food laden tables making selections, then headed to the grill. There he spoke to the squadron members cooking. He also took the opportunity to steal a couple of minutes with Keith.

"So, my man, things must be going pretty well between you and Nicole," Keith observed.

Xavier glanced back in Nicole's direction. He admired her ability to fit right in with the other women. He didn't have to work to entertain her, or hold her hand through the afternoon. She possessed an independent nature and the makings of a good military spouse. *Damn, where had that thought come from?* "Yeah, good," he declared, distracted.

"I'm happy for you both. She's a sensational lady and deserves the love of a good man."

In one fluid movement, Xavier removed his sunglasses, arching a dark brow at Keith. "Who mentioned love?"

Tired of Xavier's old song, Keith commented, "Let it go, man. You chose to love the wrong woman, that's all. Don't hold all women responsible for what Monique did to you and Ryan. If you've noticed, Nicole is nothing like Monique."

"I've noticed and I know you're right, but once bitten, twice shy."

Keith placed an understanding hand on Xavier's shoulder. "I understand—I really do, but don't miss out on a good woman while trying to protect your heart."

"You're right, Nicole is a nice lady, but like I've told you before, I'm not looking for anything permanent. But a steady woman at my side during my time here I couldn't ask for better than Nicole. I have to tell you, man, I enjoy being with this woman."

"That's a good sign, brother. Just remember the heart doesn't always listen to the head."

"Now don't go making more out of that statement than what was intended," Xavier warned Keith. "But I have to say that I'm really pleased with the way things are going. You know I was a little reluctant about a relationship with someone ten years younger than me. However, Nicole is so levelheaded and mature that I actually forget her age."

Keith listened to his friend's words but paid closer attention to his expressive gray eyes. During their friendship he had always been able to read Xavier's sincerity through his eyes, and when he spoke of Nicole he was sincere. The lady was making an impression. "That's right, Nicole graduated high school at sixteen. I forget she's two years younger than Gina. You mentioned her childhood. How much has she discussed?"

Xavier recalled their conversation. "More than enough— more than any child should have to experience. She's a strong lady—a fighter."

Keith acknowledged Xavier's words by nodding his head in confirmation. "You're right about that. From what Gina has told me, school was a nightmare for Nicole. Carmen no doubt played a definite role in her misery."

"How can people be so cruel and judgmental? She was a kid alone in the world trying to make it. They had parents to rely upon and she had the state. It's amazing she survived the system. You're always hearing about children falling through the cracks."

The two men didn't speak for a moment as both were lost in thought. They each had wonderful loving parents who'd provided them with fairy tale childhoods. They both had taken a great deal for granted in life. Xavier made a mental note to telephone his parents later in the evening. Keith decided a visit would be better.

By the time the two men returned to the pavilion with their plates, Nicole had finished eating and was now holding a baby. The young mother sitting at the table had been trying to feed herself while balancing a fussy infant. Nicole had quickly offered to hold the child while she ate. The tender scene caught Xavier off guard. He halted in his tracks watching the ease with which she fed and cooed to the baby. He instantly remembered Ryan at that stage with no mother to love him. The pain ripped across his heart.

After a moment of regrouping, he finally eased down beside Nicole with his plate. As he did, she glanced up, meeting his eyes. Her concerned frown indicated that she had glimpsed his pain. She reached out and tenderly touched his cheek with the back of her hand. He smiled weakly, trying to convince her that he was all right, yet knew that this scene would be with him tonight as he tried to sleep.

A minute or two later, the little girl squealed with delight as Nicole blew kisses on her belly. Observing the interplay, his heart fluttered to life with something new. A feeling he wasn't prepared to acknowledge engulfed him. As he watched Nicole and the baby once more, he found himself playing the "what if" game. What if it had been Nicole he married instead of Monique? Would she have wanted his child? Would she be around to raise it with him, or would she too have walked away? He dismissed the thought, unable to imagine Nicole ever walking away from her child. He couldn't honestly picture her walking away from a commitment either. Smiling as the tiny bundle took interest in her gold hoop earrings, Xavier took a deep breath, trying to calm this new feeling.

"You're a natural," he found himself saying.

The pained expression on Nicole's face instantly made him regret his words. Her golden brown eyes darkened immediately, and he knew he had somehow hurt her unintentionally. However, before he could make amends he was notified of a house fire on base. Switching gears into a military mode, he and his senior staff took off running for his parked car. With lights flashing and sirens blaring, he sped to work.

Nicole couldn't believe Xavier would be so cruel. How could he say something like that to her? How could she possibly be a natural at mothering when she had no mother? Was he taking his pain and disappointment in Monique out on her? She wouldn't stand for it, and as soon as she got the opportunity she would tell him so in no uncertain terms. Nicole was drawn from her musing by the escalation of chatter. It took only a moment to piece the conversation together.

"That's another missed meal," one of the wives was saying, referring to Xavier's untouched plate.

"Does it happen often?" Nicole found herself asking.

"When your husband is a military cop you're thankful if you actually get to see them at any event, squadron or otherwise. Something always happens to draw them away. An emergency, special event, visiting dignitaries, inspections, or heaven forbid, a natural disaster. They are usually the first and last on scene, and if you ask me, the community doesn't appreciate them enough. But you just stick around and you'll see what we're talking about."

"Spoken like a true cop's wife," Nicole added, drawing everyone's laughter. Despite their jokes and funny stories, she realized that there was a great deal of frustration and disappointment among the spouses. However, she also recognized pride in these women. They supported their husbands by taking care of home, allowing them to concentrate solely on the job. These women were a special bunch. They allowed her an inside view into their military families, thus dispelling her preconceived opinions.

The military members themselves had done a great deal today to change her opinion of military life. The men she had observed today were dedicated family men. They spent just as much time as their wives running behind children. What amazed Nicole most was the men's attentiveness to their wives. All during the afternoon one husband or another was sliding by to check on his wife—making sure she was okay. And the family-like atmosphere amongst the squadron was like nothing she had ever witnessed before. It was a special bond, and today she had been a part of it.

Thinking now of Xavier, she knew he wouldn't deliberately hurt her. She had over-reacted to a sensitive subject. Maybe it was possible to be a good mother despite not having one. If so, she would have Lillian and Mrs. Lanierto thank. She would also have to apologize to Xavier for being so touchy.

It was eight o'clock and Nicole had been home for hours. There had been no word from Xavier, and so she planned to call him later with an apology. She really had enjoyed the afternoon amongst his squadron. She had learned so much about him from the spouses. He was a caring man, which she already knew, but the stories the wives told of his checking on sick loved ones, or on them while their husbands were deployed truly emphasized the fact. His people were his family and as such he cared about their lives.

She was curled up on the sofa reading the latest best-seller when she heard a car pull into the driveway. Peeking out, she recognized Xavier's vehicle. By the time he made it to the door she was holding it open. She read the hesitation in his eyes. Before he could apologize for something that wasn't his fault, she threw herself into his arms apologizing.

"I'm sorry for getting angry with you earlier. I know you didn't intend to hurt me."

Afraid to return the embrace because his uniform was filthy and filled with the scent of smoke, Xavier tried to ease Nicole away. "Baby, I'm dirty and sweaty. I smell like smoke, Nic"

Unfazed by his comment, Nicole drew Xavier into the house closing the door behind him. "I don't care about a little dirt or smoke. I hurt you this afternoon and I am really sorry."

"I believe I should be the one apologizing even though I have to admit I'm not sure what I said to anger you."

"Have you had anything to eat?" Nicole asked changing the subject.

Only now giving into the dictates of his stomach, Xavier acknowledged that he was hungry. "No, I haven't and I'm starving."

Without hesitation Nicole led the way into the bathroom. Handing Xavier a washcloth and towel, she instructed him to wash his face and hands. In the kitchen she set about warming a plate of leftovers. She removed pinto beans, fried corn, smothered pork chops, and tap water cornbread from the refrigerator. They were leftovers from her contribution to the church dinner on Saturday. In no time at all she set a steaming plate of mouth-watering food before him. A glass of iced tea finished off the meal.

Xavier had removed his shirt. He now sat at the table in his black T-shirt and uniform pants. He had never felt so cared for by a woman other than his mother or Rosa. Nicole had a way of making him feel special—cherished. He hadn't experienced that with Monique. It had always been he who had done the giving. It was nice to have a little attention showered on him.

"Baby, maybe you should just wrap this up and let me take it home. I must smell *awful.*"

"You smell like a man who's been working. Shut up and eat," Nicole ordered, taking the seat across from him. She too had a glass of tea even though she hadn't taken a sip.

She quietly watched as Xavier tore into his food. It gave her pleasure to do something nice for him.

"Back to the original subject," she began, drawing his attention away from his plate. "What you said wasn't intentionally malicious, and I later realized that. Xavier, I question whether I'll be a good mother, or if I'll ever get the opportunity. Outside of Lillian, I didn't have a mother. I guess the little I do know about mothering was learned from her and Mrs. Lanier. Once Gina's mother accepted me into her life, she hovered and fussed over me just like one of her own. Your statement just caught me off guard. I'm so used to fielding criticism that my defense system kicked in automatically. Please accept my apology."

Xavier was humbled by Nicole's disclosure. It was true he hadn't meant to insult her, but her explanation made perfect sense from her point of view. "Nicole, did you ever consider that maybe your lack of a mother has given you the ability to be a better mother? You know what it is to grow up without a mother's love. You know what it is to want that special attention, a kiss, a hug, or a pat on the head for an accomplishment. You'll take all the negatives of your life and create positives for your children. I have no doubt in my mind that any children fortunate enough to call you Mom will be loved."

His words brought a bright smile to her face, as well as tears to her eyes. "You're going to make me cry," she sniffed, swatting at his arm. "I hate appearing weak."

"Don't I know. I can still visualize your stunned expression when I assisted you onto the front seat of my vehicle." They shared a laugh. "Not to mention the arm twisting it took for you to accept the ride home in the first place." He reached out, holding onto her free hand, then brought it to his lips for his kiss. "Nicole, no one who knows you considers you weak. Lady, what you have done with your life requires strength and determination. A couple of tears won't change their opinion."

"You're right and a little dirt and smoke don't change the fact that you're one terrific man."

"You think so?" Xavier asked in his most seductive voice.

"Most definitely, and I'm not alone. The spouses all think you're pretty terrific as well."

Xavier continued to his eat his meal while Nicole relayed the details of her conversations with the spouses. It made him feel proud that the women thought so highly of him after such a short time on station. It validated his belief that it was important to make the wives feel a part of their husband's careers. He was a firm believer in a happy home making a happy troop.

"I really enjoyed myself today. It gave me a new insight into military life. The men and women I met weren't anything like I had imagined they would be."

"Nicole, I know I asked this question before, and I understand if you aren't willing to answer now..."

She supplied the answer to his question. "My father was the military man who left me. I told you my mother left behind a letter. In it she mentioned that my father was in the air force and that he abandoned her. So...she discarded me on the steps of a church and walked away."

This time when Nicole spoke of her parents, it was a little easier and less painful. She attributed the fact to Xavier's presence in her life, in just a short time, he had filled some of the emptiness inside her. "I allowed myself to paint all men in uniform as womanizers and unscrupulous. It was foolish and today I got a lesson in reality. Thank you for inviting me"

"It was my pleasure and thanks for sharing." Xavier too was less lonely since meeting Nicole. She was only a phone call away, and just the sound of her mellow alto voice could make him feel ten feet tall. Every man wanted to be special in some woman's life, and up until Nicole, he hadn't experienced that feeling. It was nice.

"Mmm, that was one fine meal!" Xavier exclaimed, leaning back in his chair. "It's my turn to feed you next."

Feeling carefree and mischievous, Nicole asked, "Oh, you're cooking?" Her golden brown eyes twinkled with devilment. I can't wait to see you in a little apron."

Xavier felt better than he had in months. The meal, conversation, and company were all excellent, and for once he decided to relax and enjoy life. Taking Nicole up on her taunt, he responded. "Well, Ms. Edwards, since the only *cooking* I do is in the bedroom, *you* just may get to see me in that apron." He winked and smiled roguishly across the table.

At the moment Nicole could think of far worse things than seeing Xavier's tall lean body in only an apron. Embarrassing herself with the thought, she retreated from her musings only to discover Xavier watching. She read the wicked gleam in his eyes, knowing immediately that he knew what she had been doing.

"Liked what you saw, did you?" His baritone voice stimulated her senses.

Her breasts tingled and something stirred in the pit of her stomach. She hadn't experienced feelings like this before. The youthful giddiness and sweaty palms that she recalled from days with Devin were nothing compared to what this man was causing her to feel.

I believe I'll keep that little tidbit of information to myself." She scrunched up her nose childishly.

As Nicole approached the end of the table to clear away Xavier's plate, she was roughly drawn down across his thighs. His large hand buried itself within her mass of hair, anchoring her head in place as his mouth sought hers. Xavier captured her soft lips in a kiss hot enough to burn the house down. With his teeth he tortured her full lower lip. With his tongue he ravaged the sweet interior of Nicole's mouth. After a while his lips captured her tongue inviting it to explore with his.

No invitation was necessary, for Nicole was just as ravenous for a taste of him. Her warm teasing tongue fluttered around, tracing the shape of his mouth before sampling deeply. She wrapped her arms around his neck, securing herself in place, as she gave herself over to the sensation ebbing inside. Her breasts ached, and so she pressed herself against Xavier's chest to ease the pain.

Xavier's hands were everywhere all at once. He wanted to bury himself so deep inside Nicole at the moment until he hurt with need. Pressing her buttocks down upon his aroused flesh made matters worse. He shoved his long-forgotten plate out of the way, as he laid Nicole across the table for better access. *That noise? What is it?* It was a moment before Xavier recognized the sound as his beeper. Swearing, he tore himself away from Nicole.

"One of these days I'm going to get rid of this damn thing," he promised, checking the readout. It was the squadron. Breathing heavily with his head pressed against Nicole's, he kissed her temple. "I'm sorry I have to check in."

Flustered by the interruption, Nicole merely nodded her head in understanding. Mercy, what had nearly happened? she asked herself while Xavier used the telephone. She wasn't a child. She knew the answer. She and Xavier had come close to making love on the kitchen table. She should feel ashamed, shouldn't she? Maybe so, but she wasn't.

She looked to where Xavier stood talking on the telephone. He communicated verbally with his mouth, yet visually he sent smoldering messages of passion. Nicole freely welcomed his attention. She approached where he stood talking. On raised toes, she kissed the side of his cheek, then down lower to his chin. She assaulted his earlobe next, then the column of his throat. All this was done while her breasts grazed against his body.

Xavier was losing the ability or the willingness to concentrate. Nicole was driving him absolutely crazy with that mouth of hers, and if her soft firm breasts pressed into his chest one more time, he would be forced to say the hell with the phone call. In an attempt to concentrate on the call he closed his eyes, then realized he had made a grave mistake. Behind closed lids, the sensations were ten times more stimulating. Just as he was about to tell the young sergeant he would have to call back later, the man wrapped up his call, finally. With eager anticipation Xavier disconnected from the call. He clasped the back of Nicole's head and brought her mouth back to his.

Their passion was once again ignited. With his back to the kitchen wall Xavier swept Nicole up into his arms by the hips, then turned pinning her against the wall. The position afforded him easier access to her mouth; not to mention the pleasure of having her long shapely legs wrapped around his waist. His right hand ventured under the hem of the sundress caressing an exposed thigh. Then the beeper went off again.

"Shoot!" It was Nicole's turn to swear.

"Not exactly the word I would have used, but close enough," Xavier managed to say before crumbling into a fit of laughter. Nicole looked so cute frustrated. He was glad to know he wasn't the only one in an aroused state.

This time the call was urgent. He would have to return to the unit and take care of an issue. At the door he thanked Nicole for dinner and *dessert,* drawing a shy laugh from her. "I really mean it, Nic. Thank you for making me feel special."

With a light peck she replied, "That's because you are."

CHAPTER 11

It had been a week since the day of the picnic and the events of that night. Xavier had been forced to settle for the memories rather than the pleasure of Nicole's company since he was sent to San Antonio that following Saturday for a conference. How many times had he replayed that night over in his mind? He still couldn't believe the fiery nature of their chemistry. Yeah, he knew from the moment they touched that they would be good together, but nothing had prepared him for such fireworks. And to think they had only participated in heavy petting. Lord, what would making love to Nicole be like? Just the thought of the possibility had him squirming under the covers. Unable to lie in bed any longer, he kicked the covers back and made a beeline for the shower. Since that night he had grown quite accustomed to cold showers.

Toweling off afterwards, he checked the time, realizing how late it was. It was an hour past noon. He had driven straight through yesterday after the conference's closure. He couldn't miss this wedding and that was all there was to it. Keith and he had been best friends since their first year at the academy. Keith had been with him when he met Monique; he had also been the person he called when she placed demands on the divorce. They were actually a great deal closer than he and his brother. He was sure it was due to their shared love of the military. Anyway, Keith and Gina were making a commitment to each other today and he planned to be at his friend's side.

Nicole would be there also. The thought brought him a great deal of pleasure. He had missed her more than he ever imagined he would. Was it an omen that he and the maid of honor had hit it off so splendidly? Could there be more good things yet to come? Reprimanding himself for thinking so far into the future, he told himself to take it one day at a time.

He still couldn't bring himself to believe that she could have responded so amorously with just anyone. There were too many little nuances about her, which led him to believe that her experiences with men were limited. Did he dare believe it possible that they were actually nonexistent? And did he want the responsibility of schooling a young innocent? Definitely not, he thought possessively, not if Nicole planned on sharing her knowledge with some other man later. Suddenly angry for caring so deeply, his ardor died. He would be damned if he would allow some twenty-five-year-old girl to make him behave like an infatuated teenager. He would have to make more of an effort to listen to his head rather than his softening heart.

It was all Nicole could do to keep from calling Xavier. She had missed him terribly this past week and was eager to hear his voice. Just knowing that she would see him later at the church was the only thing keeping her from placing that call. That and the fact that she was due over at Mrs. Lanier's. Today was Gina's day and she was thrilled to be sharing her best friend's happiness. She left the bedroom carrying the garment bag containing her dress and shoes. In the leather tote she slung over her shoulder she carried all her other necessary items for the big event. She was excited for Gina and a little jealous too. Gina had been blessed with the love of family and now she was about to be blessed with the love of a good man. Nicole would settle for just a fraction of her friend's good fortune.

Nicole left the house before she gave in to depression. She took Highway 90 going east into Ocean Springs. The Laniers had moved to the quiet neighboring city a little after the casinos opened. Mr. Lanier had predicted Biloxi would become congested, and he had been right. These days, a drive that used to take fifteen minutes at the most now took anywhere from forty minutes to an hour. Arriving at the Lanier home several minutes later, she felt rejuvenated again. The sight of the large four-bedroom brick home always made her feet good. It was filled with so much love and laughter. As always, Mrs. Lanier was at the front door waiting for her. That was one of the little things, which always made Nicole feel like one of the children. She was so protective. She also possessed this uncanny sixth sense which told her the precise moment one of them arrived. Nicole grabbed her purse, but left everything for the wedding inside her vehicle, because she would be following the Laniers over to the church later. As she met Gina's mother, who resembled Diahann Carroll in appearance and poise, she kissed her on the cheek.

"How are you, Mrs. Lanier?"

I'm so happy, baby, I could cry. Now you come on in here. I was about to serve lunch. Then we can get prepared for the festivities later."

Nicole followed Mrs. Lanier through the formal living room into the great room where the family was assembled. She greeted Mr. Lanier in the same fashion as she had his wife. Daryl Lanier, Gina's younger brother, tried unsuccessfully for a kiss as well. Nicole maneuvered just out of his grasp with a laugh. It was an old game they had participated in since school.

"Hi Daryl, I see you haven't changed one bit.." She smiled brightly, happy to see him. It had been several months since he had been home. He lived in Birmingham where he was a resident at UAB, the University of Alabama at Birmingham Hospital. Daryl was quite handsome and the spitting image of his father. Tall with roasted chestnut skin, brown intelligent eyes and prominent masculine features, Daryl was every woman's dream man. And he knew it. The women in town lined up for a smidgen of his attention, all but Nicole. To her he was family.

"You're looking beautiful as ever," Daryl complimented Nicole after a roguish perusal. He wished Nicole would see him as a man and not family as she always made a point of reminding him. He was Gina's brother, not hers, and he was a man, not some infatuated boy. Tonight he would get Nicole to see him as such—the man for her.

Something was different about Daryl this time, Nicole noted. It was in his eyes, the way they scanned her body. She was suddenly uncomfortable with the game they played. Daryl was a terrific man, but there would never be anything more between them than friendship and a brotherly love. She decided to make a quick exit before he could say anything more.

To Mrs. Lanier she inquired, "Is Gina in her old room?"

"She's been there all morning, Nicole. I believe my girl is actually nervous." She laughed happily.

"I don't know why. She's marrying the best man around." Suddenly appearing in the doorway, Gina caught everyone off guard. "I'm surprised at you, Nicole. I expected you to say the second best."

Confused, Mrs. Lanier knew she was missing out on some vital information. "Do tell, Nicole. Who is the best?" Her golden brown faced tinged red with interest.

Nicole said nothing, just stared at Gina admonishingly. Knowing her friend so well, she realized Gina was about to reveal the details of her new relationship. "Don't you dare," Nicole warned.

Unfazed and enjoying the twinkle in Nicole's eyes, Gina blabbed. "Oh, just a particular Major Ramón!" she screamed as Nicole sent a throw pillow from the sofa soaring.

"Well now, that is interesting," Mrs. Lanier spoke up as her sharp mind began plotting. Major Ramón—best man—and little Nicole, maid of honor—were an item. "Good for you, Nicole. Maybe with a little prodding this won't be the last wedding I organize."

Nicole and Gina rolled their eyes in unison as Mrs. Lanier rambled on. They rushed from the room and vanished down the hallway laughing loudly.

Daryl sat beside his father digesting the new information. So Nicole was following in Gina's footsteps. She too was interested in some blue-suiter. Wasn't that the way? You spend your entire life trying to get a woman to notice you, and just when your dream is within reach, some outsider shows up to ruin everything. Refusing to go down without a fight, Daryl mentally prepared for tonight's showdown.

The base chapel was filling up quickly. Every pew was crammed with well-wishers. Nicole knocked lightly on the dressing area door. She was dressed and ready for the big event. Checking her reflection in the hallway mirror, she was more than pleased with her appearance. The stunning royal blue maid of honor dress she and Gina had selected was perfect. It highlighted her best features. The off the shoulder style gave her a regal appearance. The low cut bodice accentuated just the right amount of cleavage, and the cinched waist and straight long skirt showcased her narrow waistline. The mini detachable train enhanced the simple beauty of the dress, creating a stunning design.

Nicole had expertly applied her make-up to complement the dress. Her long dark hair was a mass of loose curls. The front had been gathered high atop her head by a shimmering, studded clip. The back hung loose and springy. In her ears she wore diamond studs.

With her matching silk gloves in hand she slowly opened the door to the dressing room. Before her stood the most gorgeous bride she had ever seen. Gina looked as though she should be gracing the cover of a bridal magazine. Her traditional white gown was a creation of silk and lace. Layers of sheer lace formed the billowing skirt of her dress, making one think of Cinderella. She was absolutely breathtaking with her auburn hair piled artfully atop her head. Her honey brown face was skillfully made up to accentuate her beautiful brown eyes, and to-die-for cheekbones. Nicole stood for several minutes in awe of her best friend before being able to speak.

"You are...stunning. Keith isn't going to be able to take his eyes off you."

Gina felt beautiful as she stood before her best friend since high school. She was so happy and wanted the same for Nicole. "You look pretty darn good yourself, girlfriend. Xavier's tongue is going to hit the floor when you walk down that aisle."

The two women were silent as they clasped hands lovingly. No words were needed for they possessed the ability to communicate silently as sisters often do. They each recognized that their relationship was about to change, but also knew that they would always be a part of the other's life. As teens Gina had always spoken of this day. She'd known exactly what she wanted and had followed through on her dream. Nicole had never dared to dream of a wedding day. instead she had always enjoyed being a part of Gina's dream, and so today she got to live it out.

Mrs. Lanier knocked on the door before coming in. She studied the two women before her and beamed with pride. Her girls had done her proud. She walked over to where they both stood, giving them each a hug. "I'm so proud of you both. You're beautiful women with loving spirits, and any man should consider himself blessed to have your love."

Mrs. Lanier's words meant so much to Nicole considering their initial meeting. Brought to tears by the loving words, she excused herself, leaving mother and daughter alone. This was their special time and she didn't belong there.

Out in the hallway she headed toward the wedding party. It was near show time. Searching the hallway as she went along, she saw no sign of Xavier. Surely he had arrived back in town for the wedding. Gina hadn't mentioned his absence. She was anxious to see him after their last encounter. He had phoned her that Saturday from San Antonio explaining his sudden departure, yet she hadn't heard from him since. She had actually lain awake last night expecting him to call once he returned home. He hadn't done that, and he hadn't called this morning. Was it possible after being away that he had rethought their agreement? Did her behavior Friday night appall him? She was suddenly nervous and anxious all at the same time. She needed to see Xavier. At the sound of the organist, Nicole ran, taking her place behind the bridesmaids. She passed Carmen on the way and was given the royal snub.

The inside of the chapel was a bouquet of fragrances. Flowers were decoratively strewn throughout the church. Each pew had a bouquet and streamers. The bridesmaids held bouquets of springtime flowers in various shades of yellow and the occasional sprig of blue. A white runner led the way to the altar, which was bathed in candlelight. The organist began the processional music. The doors of the church were thrown open and the wedding party slowly marched in. Carmen and a groomsman walked down the aisle first. The lighter shade of blue the bridesmaids wore complemented Nicole's dress; the style wasn't as flattering on all the women. Carmen, however, was as striking as always. As she neared the altar she flashed a winning smile in what appeared to be Xavier's direction before taking her place on the bride's side.

Xavier hardly noticed Carmen. His mind and eyes were focused and waiting on one woman. He had missed Nicole and could barely wait to see her. During the drive over to the church, he had thought long and hard about his earlier decision. it was a sound decision to take it one day at a time. He and Nicole had established an agreement between them that was mutually satisfying. They would share their day-to-day lives with each other, filling some of the empti-ness they both felt. Ryan would have the love and attention of a good woman. All in all, it was an ideal situation.

It was Nicole's turn down the aisle. She was so nervous and it wasn't even her wedding. Glancing back over her shoulder, she blew Gina a kiss, then marched slowly down the aisle. The oohs and ahs she received on entering were startling—she wasn't the bride. Nonetheless, she was a magnificent sight to behold. Midway to the altar she got her first glimpse of Xavier dressed in a black tuxedo. Memories of their night on the cruise came to mind. He was a welcome sight for her lonely eyes. Smiling brightly, she was pleased to finally see him. He looked absolutely wonderful. He didn't return her smile she noted, but stood staring as she marched down the aisle. The familiar gray eyes had darkened with appreciation and what she believed to be passion. Yeah, he was happy to see her too.

Xavier was more than happy to see Nicole. He was in a state of awe. He had never seen her look more beautiful. She was poise and grace personified in the royal blue gown, which fit her like a glove. The sophisticated style was simple, yet stunning, and Nicole carried it off with regality befitting a queen. His pulse quickened as his eyes greedily devoured the sight of her. Her brilliant smile went straight to his heart. She too had missed him.

Keith chanced a glance at his best man just as Nicole began her entrance. What he saw registered on Xavier's face was love. Whether his friend was ready to admit it or not, he had definitely given his heart to the lady coming down the aisle. Pleased with the relationship between these two special people, he whispered over his shoulder, "She's beautiful, isn't she?"

Xavier watched Nicole take her place, then turn facing him and Keith smiling. He whispered back, "Breathtaking."

Keith wasn't the only one aware of the sparks flying between the maid of honor and best man. Standing just one body over from Xavier, Darryl watched the exchange with great interest. It was obvious that the two were smitten with each other. He couldn't fault the brother for trying, but he didn't have to make it easy for him either. He focused on Nicole, watching her through loving eyes. She was stunning and all he wanted in a woman. This was his last chance to win her heart. Last Christmas he had tried subtle ways to indicate his true feelings for her. A slow dance at a Christmas party had been just the beginning. They shopped, dined, went to the movies, and popped popcorn in front of the fireplace. He had given her a gold heart pendant as a gift, expressing that he loved her. Nicole in return had whispered, "I love you too, baby brother." With those words she had effectively killed the moment. So today he was determined to give it one last chance. Before the evening was over Nicole would know his true feelings.

From her vantage point in line, Carmen had a bird's eye view of both men salivating over Nicole. Xavier was too good for the likes of Nicole, yet now that Daryl was home, she was welcome to him. Daryl, on the other hand, was the man she had fallen in love with last Christmas and he was off limits to Nicole. She had waited anxiously for his return home to launch her attack on his male senses. She was determined Nicole wouldn't get Daryl.

She recalled Daryl's interest in Nicole last Christmas at his parents' party. Yet when Nicole showed no more interest in him than that of a sister, she had stepped in to lift his spirits. They had danced the night away. He had been attentive to her needs and interested in what she had to say. They had taken a late night stroll around the neighborhood, leaving the party behind. Daryi had kissed her lightly on the lips promising to call the next week for dinner. She had fallen hopelessly in love with him that night. And so she'd waited for his call. Not until she'd spotted him and Nicole across the room in a restaurant where she was dining, did she stop waiting. But that was then. Tonight she intended to regain Daryl's interest and win his love. She had lost Frank to Nicole, but she refused to lose Daryl without a fight.

Then the wedding march began and all rose to greet the bride. Gina, dressed angelically in white, walked down the aisle on her father's arm. She was truly a vision of loveliness with eyes only for her groom. As she reached her mother who stood weeping, Gina paused, giving her a kiss, then continued marching to the altar and Keith. Finally standing before God and witnesses, she smiled timidly from under her veil at her husband-to-be. She had never been so happy.

The wedding had gone off without a hitch. Everyone had assembled for the customary wedding photos. Nicole and Xavier had taken a picture with the happy couple. During the photographs, Xavier had cuddled close to Nicole, whispering in her ear.

"You're not supposed to upstage the bride."

His right hand had been placed gently against her hip, and memories from their last encounter caused the touch to singe. His warm breath against her sensitive flesh stirred the already fluttering butterflies. In no time at all this man had made her a wanton woman. Just as she was about to comment, the photographer had yelled *cheese*.

Nicole sat alone at a corner table in the grand ballroom at the Beau Rivage Resort. She didn't know what had become of Xavier. After the photographs he had excused himself and disappeared. She watched as Keith and Gina shared their first dance as husband and wife. They were in their own private paradise. Nicole was so absorbed by their love that she didn't hear Daryl slide into the chair next to her. Scooting closer, he draped himself over the back of her chair giving Nicole a light peck on the neck.

"You look absolutely beautiful."

"Thank you."

"Dance with me," he said, rising from his chair.

Nicole accepted Daryl's outstretched hand as she had done numerous times before. She allowed herself to be drawn into the circle of his arms. They swayed to the slow tune, with Nicole thinking nothing of Daryl pulling her closer. Not until he began nibbling at her earlobe did she realize that this dance was indeed different.

"What do you think you're doing?" Nicole asked agitatedly while discreetly shoving Daryl back.

"Trying to show the woman I love what it could be like between us," Daryl declared with such feeling that Nicole openly gaped in bewilderment.

"Daryl, we're the best of friends, but nothing more."

"That's only because you refuse to see what's in front of you."

Nicole eased out of his arms and walked away. She was confused and needed a moment to think. Solitude was what she desired. Seeking refuge on the balcony, she was pleased to discover it empty. Maybe she could decide what to do about Daryl. And then there was Xavier. It had been a blessing that he wasn't around to witness Daryl's little show. With Xavier's inability to trust, Nicole knew he would no doubt jump to the worst possible conclusion. It would be unfortunate for their agreement to end because of a misunderstanding.

Daryl was not to be put off. He followed Nicole out onto the balcony to finish what he had started. The sooner he got the words out, the sooner Nicole would realize the life they could have together. He spied her in a dark corner alone. It was a good sign.

"Nicole, please hear me out."

Nicole jumped with alarm at Daryl's sudden appearance. "No Daryl, leave it alone, please." She tried to step around him, but was halted when his hand shot out to stop her escape.

Daryl almost backed down when he stared down into Nicole's troubled face. He sensed that this could possibly be the last opportunity to convince her of his love and held on a little tighter. "Nicole, I would never hurt you. You know that, don't you?"

"Yes." Her response came out weak and whispery.

"Good. Nicole, there's no easy way to say this, so here I go. I'm in love with you. I have been for sometime now. I know you see me as a brother, and for awhile that was okay, but not anymore. What I feel for you has nothing to do with brotherly love. I want to give you my name and make a life together. We can have the family you've always wanted but were too afraid to hope for. With me, you'll never have to fear being alone again."

God, why couldn't she love this man? Nicole silently asked. Truly touched by Daryl's words, Nicole wished the outcome could be different. She adored this man, but as a brother. She didn't want to be responsible for hurting him.

As she met his pleading brown eyes, a lone tear escaped. Swiping at it, she chose her words carefully.

"What you say about me being afraid is true, but I'm not so afraid that I would use my friend as a means not to be alone. I respect and love you, and want to see you with a woman who returns your affection. But that woman isn't me, Daryl."

Not ready to accept defeat, Daryl clasped Nicole's face between his hands bringing, his lips down to meet hers. The kiss was intended to be gentle and persuasive but ended up one of desperation and frustration. Breathless, Daryl finally broke off the kiss, resting his head against Nicole's. Stroking her hair lovingly, he acknowledged defeat.

"You didn't feel anything, did you?"

Nicole stared at the base of his throat because she couldn't look him in the eyes. She didn't want to hurt him, yet knew she had to be truthful.

"No, I didn't."

"He'll leave you just like your old man left your mother." The angry words flew out low and menacing, before Daryl could halt their escape. He hadn't meant to turn this into an ugly scene.

Nicole was shocked by the revolting words. She stepped out of his embrace.

"Gina told you about my parents?" Nicole's voice heightened in anger. She couldn't believe her friend would reveal such private information. "Answer me, Daryl," she yelled.

Only now realizing what he had done, Daryl felt awful. He was destroying a wonderful relationship all because he had taken it upon himself to fall in love with his sister's best friend. Nicole didn't deserve the pain he had caused. "I'm sorry, Nicole, please forgive me."

"You haven't answered my question Daryl."

Suddenly nervous because he knew this could possibly be the end of their relationship, and also because he knew there would be hell to pay when Gina discovered what he had done, Daryl tried to rectify the situation.

"No, she didn't tell me. I heard her and mother talking one night in her bedroom years ago. I eavesdropped on the conversation. I'm really sorry, Nicole."

With the confession and apology Nicole was no longer angry. She just felt a sense of loss for something they'd once shared. Turning away from Daryl, she looked out over the city of Biloxi. From this vantage point she could see all up and down the coast. Slightly to the right she could see the Ocean Springs Bridge in the up position. On hearing retreating footsteps, she exhaled a breath. Maybe in time she and Daryl could recapture the friendship they'd once shared. She hoped so anyway.

Alone on the balcony Nicole recalled his angry words and acknowledged the truth within them. Xavier probably would leave her after his two-year tour. It would hurt and a part of her would leave with him, but at least she would have the memories.

From her position behind the potted palm near the doorway, Carmen had watched the exchange between Daryl and Nicole. Unfortunately, she couldn't hear what was being said, but who needed sound to interpret that kiss? She had seen enough. This was the last time Nicole would interfere in her life. Anxious to leave the balcony, she failed to see Xavier, who also had watched the young couple from a secluded position.

Xavier had returned to the festivities just in time to witness Daryl's peck on the neck. He halted in his steps and found a place to blend in unnoticed. Watching further as this new guy wrapped his arms around Nicole possessively and began nibbling on her earlobe, Xavier damned her to hell. He should have known she was no better than Monique. Hell, she was young and beautiful. Why in the world would she settle for an agreement instead of a genuine relationship? His instincts told him to just turn around and leave the ballroom. Yet Nicole's subsequent retreat out onto the patio made him pause. He waited to see if the young man would follow. And when he did, so did he. Who was this guy? Had he and Nicole been seeing each other behind his back? Did she respond as hungrily to his kisses as she had his the Friday before last?

Hardly, if that poor guy's miserable expression was any indication after the kiss he laid on Nicole. Maneuvering himself to a better position where he could hear what was being said, Xavier stood in the darkened shadow listening to Nicole and Daryl's exchange. The moment she mentioned Gina, he knew who Daryl was and could guess what had happened. Young brothers were always falling for their sister's girlfriends. A sigh of relief escaped. He had misjudged Nicole once again. She hadn't been manipulating him while she strung some other man along. She had been trying to outmaneuver unwanted advances from someone she considered a brother. After Daryl returned inside, Xavier moved out of the shadow toward Nicole.

At the sound of footsteps Nicole's head whipped around. She visibly relaxed on seeing Xavier. She waited patiently for him to come to her, even though her first instinct was to run across the floor and sling herself into his arms.

"Hi. What happened to you after the wedding?" Nicole asked, taking Xavier's hands.

"I ran over to the squadron to check up on things."

"You're always on duty aren't you, Major?"

"Not tonight, baby," he whispered low and seductively. "Tonight I'm all yours."

The change in the timbre of his voice had the desired effect. Nicole was rejuvenated with energy and a desire to be alone with him. "I missed you," she whispered.

"Not half as much as I've missed you." He kissed her forehead lovingly before leading her back inside. He decided to wait until they were alone to ask her about Daryl. In the ballroom bodies twirled around the dance floor. On seeing Keith and Gina in the center of the action, Xavier led Nicole out onto the floor. She still wore the royal blue dress, but had removed the detachable train. She was gorgeous and Xavier couldn't wait to wrap his arms around her.

As they took up position alongside the bride and groom, Whitney Houston's "You Give Good Love" began to play. Xavier drew Nicole into his arms and into a world where only they existed. He liked the way her rose-scented head tucked neatly under his chin as they danced. Their movements together were sure and smooth. His mind instantly conjured up images of their moving this smoothly under the sheets. At the stir of nature, he quickly channeled his thoughts onto something safe. The last thing Nicole needed was for him to become aroused in the middle of the dance floor.

Despite their adherence to dancing etiquette, there was no doubt in anyone's mind that the young couple was falling in love. The energy they seemed to generate on the dance floor radiated throughout the room. People's eyes were repeatedly drawn to the maid of honor and best man swaying to the music. They were in a world of their own.

Keith and Gina shared a knowing glance as they watched their best friends dancing to the music. Whether or not Xavier and Nicole were willing to acknowledge their feelings for each other, Keith and Gina recognized them for what they were.

Later that night back at Nicole's home, Xavier stood in the kitchen doorway watching her prepare their coffee. She had removed the gown. In its place she wore another silk lounger. It too was in royal blue and she looked just as lovely. As he watched her move around the room he was reminded of their last encounter. A smile broke out across his face as he recalled Nicole's frustration at the interfering beeper. He laughed drawing her attention.

"What's so amusing?" Nicole's expression was coy, because she knew exactly what he was thinking.

Walking toward her, Xavier enfolded her within his arms. He kissed her temple sweetly, remembering her passion. "If the walls in this room could talk," he murmured while his large hands palmed her hips, then ran the length of her thighs.

Nicole squirmed within Xavier's hands. His mere touch could set her blood to boiling. She didn't quite understand what it was about this man that made her blossom. "If you don't stop that, there really will be something to tell."

Xavier looked down into Nicole's upturned face, realizing that he hadn't tasted her lips today. With a determined move he corrected the minor oversight. The kiss began playful and sweet. Then Nicole nipped his lower lip and his restraint dissolved. His large brown hand clasped the back of her head, bringing her mouth closer to his. His tongue made love to her sweet mouth for several heated moments before he was forced to come up for air. "God, Nicole we have got to stop doing this. I'm only human, baby. I want you so bad I hurt," his frustrated words rushed out.

Nicole clasped Xavier's face within her own hands bringing his lips back to hers. She kissed him soundly before finally releasing him. "And I want you." Her smile was purely sexual.

"Our time is coming, sweetheart."

Nicole moved out of his arms before the time became right now. She retrieved two cups from the cabinet and spoons from the silverware drawer. She asked Xavier to bring the coffeepot over to the table while she sliced the lemon pound cake. As she placed the servings on the table, Xavier came up behind her, placing his arms around her waist. Kissing her temple, he inquired about Daryl.

"The guy out on the balcony was Gina's brother, wasn't he?"

Nicole whipped around in alarm. Staring at Xavier's hard-to-read expression, she tried to gauge his emotions. She didn't know how much he had seen, but with her luck, he probably had seen it all. "Yes, but it's not what you think," she rushed to explain.

Eager to quell Nicole's fears, Xavier silenced her lips with a finger, followed by a quick kiss. "I know what happened, Nicole. I finally figured it out. You know I'm a younger brother myself. I remember making a fool of myself a time or two over my sister's friends."

"I'm so relieved that you understand. The last thing I wanted was for this incident to come between us." She placed her hand against his chest, smiling weakly as she looked into his knowing eyes. "I hurt him with my rejection, and he in turn said something to hurt me." Remembering those words, Nicole eased out of Xavier's arms. She busied herself with arranging the table while warding off the tears which threatened.

Xavier recalled their exchange, knowing what Nicole was referring to. Wishing he could alleviate Nicole's fears but knowing he couldn't guarantee anything at the moment, he too eased away. He took his usual seat, feeling the need to share some of himself with Nicole.

He began speaking, drawing Nicole's attention. "Monique married me to leave home. She hated the small town her father retired in and felt she deserved bigger and better. She said she would have married any man to escape that town."

"I'm sure she didn't mean for it to sound like that. She loved you." Nicole couldn't stand to think someone could be so cold and heartless. The woman definitely hadn't deserved Xavier.

Xavier met Nicole's sympathetic eyes. He was astonished by her capacity to love. And she did love him, he realized. The truth was in the depths of her golden brown eyes. It had happened suddenly, and she was unsure of him; but nonetheless it had happened. He wouldn't push the issue because they had a great deal to learn about each other, and he was in no position to be discussing the *I* word.

"She meant them, Nicole. From the very beginning she used me. She played me from start to finish."

"Her loss is my gain," Nicole declared vehemently.

Xavier studied Nicole in silence for several minutes. His fingers traced the delicate bone structure of her face. She was spiritually even more beautiful than her physical self. "I want to be able to give you what you want and need, Nicole. But until I have dealt with my own personal issues, I can't offer you false hope. I can say that the more time I spend in your company, the less hold these fears possess. There are days when I can actually visualize a future with you; then other days I find myself backtracking, questioning every move. For now, I'm pleased with the current state of our arrangement and would like to enjoy it. I feel like we've known each other for years, rather than months."

Nicole smiled understandingly. She had watched the emotional play within his expressive eyes. She heard his confusion, but also an acceptance. Was it possible for him to let down his protective guard and allow this relationship to develop into the wonderful love she knew it could be? She surely hoped so.

"I feel the same way. The other night when we were in here on the..."

"...table making out like teenagers," he finished with a wicked grin.

"Exactly. It felt so right. Like we had been together forever."

"Maybe we have," Xavier stated.

"That's your spiritual side exposing itself again," she teased.

"I thought you said you liked my spiritual side." Xavier's voice became low and seductive once again.

"Amongst other things."

"Well do tell."

"Daddy, it's Carmen."

"Hi baby girl. How was your cousin Keith's wedding?"

"It was beautiful of course, but Daddy that's not why I'm calling. I know you're aren't feeling well, but this really couldn't wait."

"You know I always have time for you. Now tell Daddy what has you all agitated.

"Daddy, I need a big favor from you."

"Just name it sweetheart and it's yours."

And so she did, knowing that her father wouldn't deny her anything.

CHAPTER 12

It was the last day of school for teachers, and Nicole was in room 6 packing class material for the summer. Just as she was sealing her last box with tape the silence was interrupted by the intercom. Going to the pad on the wall, she depressed the button to respond to the page.

"Yes, I'm still here," Nicole quickly answered.

"Before you leave, please come by Principal Dailey's office," the office secretary instructed.

"I'll be there in a moment," Nicole responded, distracted. She released the button unable to imagine why she was being summoned.

As she paced the floor of the classroom, Nicole tried to think of what could be wrong. The school year had been a success. Her students had mastered the required course work with flying colors. The majority of them were already performing on a third grade level or higher. Taking stock of those facts and her exceptional evaluation, she convinced herself that she was allowing her imagination to run wild.

With purse in hand and the last box to be loaded into the car, Nicole made her way to the principal's office. She deposited the box just outside the closed door then knocked before sticking her head in. She and Principal Dailey shared a mentoring relationship and so she moved into the office comfortably.

"You wanted to see me?" Nicole asked, closing the door behind her.

The red-haired woman with streaks of gray framing her long thin face could barely meet Nicole's unsuspecting eyes.

They shared a relationship she was extremely proud of. Nicole was her shining star and the best find yet. She possessed the remarkable talent of reaching the most challenged student. She could take a failing student and lead him back to the path of success. Her tutoring skills were in high demand by the upper classmen and their parents. Those abilities made the task at hand painfully difficult. She didn't understand the reasoning and had pursued the issue with the superintendent But his firm, no-nonsense tone let her know he meant business, and the inevitable task had to be performed.

"Yes Nicole, come on in," Principal Dailey invited, minus the usual warmth to her voice.

Picking up on the difference, Nicole knew that she should now be worried. She took one of the chairs usually reserved for visiting parents and waited for the news she knew would change her life.

"Nicole, as you know money is tight everywhere, and school systems aren't exempt. The superintendent informed me that we are going to be forced to consolidate classes in an effort to save money. And in doing so we are unfortunately forced to cut one of our teachers."

Nicole didn't need to hear any more. She knew that teacher was she. She was the last hired and no doubt the first to be released. They didn't have any teachers who were near retirement, so she was it.

"I'm sorry, but we're not going to be able to renew your contract," Principal Dailey was saying when Nicole tuned back into the conversation. Opening a file on her desk, she retrieved a sheet of paper, extending it to Nicole. "I've taken the liberty of writing you a letter of recommendation."

"Did you know about this?" Nicole ignored the offered letter.

"Not until this morning when the superintendent expressed the paperwork over."

"Doesn't this seem rather sudden?" Nicole asked dazed by the turn of events.

"Yes, it does. That's why I telephoned the superintendent this morning." Principal Daily replied with frustration.

"What did he have to say?

"Exactly what I've told you. Money is tight, and school systems are looking to cut expenses any way they can."

"But surely my salary can't make that much difference," Nicole commented bewildered.

"I don't have the answers, Nicole." Principal Dailey raised her hands in a helpless gesture. "You have to know how difficult this is for me." Her eyes pleaded for understanding. She offered the letter of recommendation once more.

This time Nicole grasped the letter. "I know this wasn't easy for you. Thanks for the recommendation." Believing there was nothing left to discuss, she rose to leave.

"I've inquired about available positions in the local school districts." Principal Daily spoke halting her departure. "All have openings and are anxious to hire qualified teachers. You shouldn't have any problem securing another position."

The news was welcomed and helped to alleviate some of her fear. She had savings, but as a product of the foster care system, she didn't dare touch that money unless she absolutely had to. There was no family to fall back on.

Two weeks later the fear had set in. Nicole had been up and down the Mississippi coast searching for one of those so-called available positions. She had been from Moss Point to Bay St. Louis in search of a position. Each district said basically the same thing—no position available. Each had politely taken her application and credentials with a promise to call should the situation change. But knowing there would be new graduates competing for teaching positions, Nicole now feared the new school year would begin without her having a position.

Nervous and unable to sleep due to her unemployed status, she decided upon a run. Dressing in running attire, Nicole locked her home, then jumped into the car and headed for the beach. It was an early work week morning and the beach would be deserted. After parking her vehicle she went through her warm-up routine. Then just as the sky turned pink and turquoise, she took off at a moderate pace. While she jogged her mind was free to roam. Thinking about her options, she reluctantly admitted to there being only one. It was time to stop running in circles and take control of her life. By the time she completed the run she was indeed more relaxed.

Xavier had just arrived at work. It was a little after seven o'clock and he was working on his first cup of coffee. Opened and unopened mail was scattered before him. Sipping his coffee he thought of Nicole and how happy she made him. Just as he was about to pick up the telephone to give her a good morning call, it rang. Then it rang again. He assumed his secretary hadn't arrived yet, and so he answered the telephone himself.

"Major Ramón speaking."

"Xavier, it's Gina. Are you aware Biloxi Christian released Nicole?"

Not believing his ears, Xavier asked her to repeat herself.

"I said Nicole's teaching contract wasn't renewed for next year."

Unable to believe he was only now hearing this, Xavier was livid. "Did Nicole tell you? How long have you known?" He was afraid he was unable to disguise his anger.

"No, she didn't. I stopped off at the red roof McDonalds on Highway 90 and ran into a friend who teaches at the academy with Nicole. She inquired about Nicole and wanted to know if she had found another position. It seems she was released the last day of school. Imagine my surprise and disappointment."

"I understand your disappointment," Xavier replied. He recalled the evenings he and Nicole had shared. His gut instinct had told him something was going on with her. But each time he'd questioned Nicole about it, she'd replied everything was okay. She had lied to him.

"Gina, I'm headed over there now. I'll call you..." He didn't get the chance to finish.

"You'll do no such thing," Gina interrupted. "Keith and I are headed over ourselves. Meet you in a few."

Fifteen minutes later Nicole opened the front door to the threesome. From the expression on their faces she knew something had happened. Xavier and Keith were both in uniform so her immediate concern was for Ryan.

"Is Ryan hurt?" she asked with fear in her eyes. A nervous hand ran through her hair while she waited for them to enter.

Xavier promptly relieved her fears. "Ryan is all right, sweetheart."

With a hand on her heaving chest she said, "Thank God." Then searching each face as her guests took up positions in her living room, Nicole grew inpatient. Gina chose the chair by the bookcase, Keith the sofa. Xavier chose to remain standing in the middle of the room, glaring. His expression indicated that she was the cause of the long faces. Not one to run from a fight, Nicole jumped right in.

"Is someone going to tell me what the devil is going on?" she asked angrily.

Xavier was the one to respond. He met her anger. "That's a very good question. How about I ask you the same thing, and please don't lie to me again."

"Lie to you?"

At first Nicole was confused and angry so she returned his glare. As he slipped his hands into his pockets, rocking back on his heels staring at her, it came to her. They had somehow found out that she'd lost her job. Not wanting to drag them into her mess she told them just that.

"Look, guys, this has nothing to do with you."

"Like hell it doesn't," Xavier shouted. "You lost your job and you didn't tell anyone? My God, why would you keep this to yourself?"

"Because it's my business, Xavier."

Xavier was taken aback by the coldness of her words. He could only stare at her. "Are we not in a relationship?"

"We...," Nicole pointed at him then herself, "have an agreement."

From the chair Gina asked curiously, "What agreement?" Both Nicole and Xavier chose to ignore her as they continued to face off. Then on second thought, Xavier grabbed Nicole by the arm, dragging her into the kitchen for privacy. "Excuse us."

"Hey, no fair Xavier. I'm the one who told you in the first place," Gina yelled out to Xavier's retreating back. Secretly she was delighted to see the flash of protectiveness in his eyes. Nicole deserved the love of a good man and she believed the major was just that man.

Xavier didn't release Nicole until he was completely in the kitchen. Picking up their conversation where they left off, he faced her once again.

"To hell with that agreement, Nicole. What's between us goes deeper than that." Xavier thumped his heart. "I care about you, lady, and I expect to be included in every aspect of your life."

Nicole was touched by Xavier's sincere words. The fight went out of her. She stared at him, dumbfounded by the confession. "You really do care," she repeated as an affirmation.

Xavier closed the space between them, drawing Nicole into his arms. He rubbed her back as she hung onto him tightly. "Tell me why you didn't confide in me, Nic."

With her cheek pressed against the wall of his chest, Nicole tried to explain. "With this agreement between us it's like saying you want to be close, but not that close. I never thought you would be interested in my life beyond the boundaries of our agreement." She leaned back so that she could see his eyes. "You have to understand something. When you've lived the life I have you learn to depend on only yourself."

He still didn't completely understand Nicole's logic, but he was willing to concede the point because somewhere in her battered life it made sense. "Hear me clearly, Ms. Edwards. If it concerns you in any shape, form, or fashion, I wish to know about it from *you*. Are we clear on this matter?" He tilted Nicole's cleft chin up as he stared into her apologetic brown eyes.

"Very clear, Major."

Later at the kitchen table Gina explained how she'd found out about her layoff. "Gloria Newman was concerned about you and asked if you had found another position."

Nicole could only smile as she listened. "Gloria isn't concerned about me. Don't get me wrong, she's a nice lady, but our favorite science teacher is a gossip. Believe me, her interest was in being the first with the information."

"Maybe so, but I'm glad she told me." Gina looked at Nicole accusingly. Her big brown eyes held disappointment.

Nicole admitted to herself that she had handled the situation improperly. She apologized to them all, then proceeded to inform them of her notification.

"Despite what Principal Dailey said, it appears that all the positions have been taken. I've been from district to district with no success." She paused, thinking about the past two weeks. "You know, I was instructed to contact one principal about setting up an interview. I was told that the school would have two available positions. One teacher was retiring and another had decided to stay home with her newborn."

"Well, that's great. You made the interview right?" Gina asked hopeful.

"Now that's where the problem comes in," Nicole commented, pointing her finger for emphasis. "The moment I showed up and introduced myself it was as though the positions disappeared. The principal said the board was misinformed. You know, if I was paranoid, I would swear someone has blackballed me."

Keith had been quiet through the discussion. Now he stared at Nicole, absorbing her words. He pushed his glasses up onto his nose while his highly intelligent mind clicked away. A similar incident came to mind, stirring his curiosity.

"There is one option," Nicole informed the group.

"What's that, Nic?" "Atlanta."

"Atlanta!" Gina exclaimed.

"Hear me out," Nicole interjected before Gina went off on a tangent. "A friend of Jon's is a superintendent of a private school in Atlanta. He has been trying to persuade me to work for him. He said he would make a position for me anytime I wanted to come work for him."

"I bet he did." Xavier's voice escalated accusingly. He had never once imagined he would be the one left behind when the relationship ended. It wasn't the best of feelings and he regretted placing Nicole in this position. He now possessed a better understanding of her abandonment, because that's exactly how he felt about her announcement.

"He's a nice man, Xavier."

"And you're a beautiful woman, Nicole."

Gina, pleased with what she was witnessing, glanced over at Keith, only to discover him daydreaming.

Keith pushed away from the table. He needed an answer to the numerous questions running through his mind.

"Gina, I just remembered an appointment I can't miss."

Surprised by the abrupt announcement, three pairs of eyes stared at him.

"Now?" Gina asked.

"I'm sorry, sweetheart. But if you want to make that little getaway next week, I suggest we leave right now," he replied consulting his watch.

"Getaway? Didn't you people just return from your honeymoon?" Nicole asked, amused.

"We had such a fabulous time we thought we would drag it out a little bit longer." Gina too stood. She gave Nicole a hug. "We'll talk later."

Keith pulled into the community center parking lot and was pleased to see Carmen's car. He locked his vehicle then went in search of his cousin. As he knocked on the closed office door, he mentally prepared for the encounter.

"Come in," Carmen's high-pitched voice drawled.

"Hi cousin." Keith entered casually. Eyeing his cousin dressed smartly in a blue designer suit, Keith thought she looked stunning. She was intelligent and capable of being a nice woman, but something about her personality just couldn't allow the goodness inside to show.

"Welcome home." She came from behind the desk to give him a hug. "How were the islands?"

"Great."

The brevity of the response caught Carmen's attention. "What's going on, Keith?" Carmen feigned innocence.

"That's what I would like to know."

"Well, obviously you've got something on your mind."

He folded his arms across his broad chest while locking gazes with his cousin. "Did you know Nicole was released from Biloxi Christian?"

"Why should I care?" Carmen began walking around the room repositioning items.

"Circumstances are similar to what happened to that cone tractor who dumped you a few years back."

Carmen spun around angrily. "He did not dump me. I dumped him."

"Is that why you asked your father to have him black-balled in the local area? The poor guy couldn't get a bid on a job anywhere."

"He deserved what he got." She stood glaring at him.

Keith closed the distance between them. "Does Nicole deserve what you've done to her?"

"I don't know what you're talking about." She turned around, giving him her back.

"Xavier really cares about Nicole, Carmen. I'm sorry he wasn't interested in you."

"I don't give a damn about Xavier. She can have him, but she will never take Daryl from me." She was now facing him with fire in her eyes.

"This is about Daryl?" Keith was confused. Then he recalled the occasions he had witnessed Carmen in Daryl's presence. She *was* a different woman around him. She was actually softer, likable. So that was it. Carmen was in love with Daryl and she somehow felt Nicole was a threat. "Nicole isn't interested in Daryl, Carmen. She's involved with Xavier and appears quite happy."

"Are you sure? I saw them kissing at your reception."

"I don't know anything about a kiss, but I do know Daryl left for Birmingham the very next day. His mother was worried that something was wrong. Maybe what you saw didn't actually turn out the way Daryl wanted." Placing both hands on her shoulders, Keith gently stroked them "Listen, I just left Nicole's place this morning. She's very upset about losing her job, and Xavier is right by her side to comfort her. There's nothing going on between Nicole and Daryl."

Carmen returned to her chair behind the desk. "I just wanted her out of my life. I'm tired of men tripping over me to get to Nicole. They take one look at her exotic features and that hair hanging down her back, and go chasing behind her."

"That's not Nicole's fault. She's a beautiful woman and a really nice person if you give her a chance."

"That may be, but as long as that woman is around, Daryl won't notice me."

"I think you're wrong. I also think you're being unfair to Nicole. She isn't responsible for Daryl's feelings. Hasn't she had enough hardship in her life?"

"Don't try to make me feel guilty because Nicole was abandoned. I'm not responsible for her crummy life."

"No, you're not; but you are accountable for your actions." There was an ominous tone to his voice.

"Do I hear a threat in there?" Carmen asked, arching her brows.

Keith advanced in her direction with such intensity, that Carmen pushed away from the desk, startled. He placed both hands firmly on the desktop as he leaned in closer. There was a menacing look in his eyes.

"You better believe it. Call off your father and I won't tell my new brother-in law about your involvement in Nicole's dismissal."

Carmen knew her cousin well. She knew that he wasn't one to make threats. So this uncharacteristic behavior was to be taken seriously.

Keith sighed. He was sorry the situation had deteriorated to a threat. But unfortunately, sometimes that was the only way to get Carmen's attention. He straightened to his full height. Pushing up his glasses, he reached for the telephone, then held it out for Carmen.

CHAPTER 13

The summer program kicked off fabulously. Nicole had been miraculously reinstated at the academy and with that worry behind her, she went about fine-tuning her curriculum. She wanted the students to get all they could from the summer course. Her room had been decorated to represent the various cultures located on the Mississippi Gulf Coast. Each week she invited people from the local community to speak to her class on Friday. The speakers brought art, clothing, games, stories, and a wide variety of cultural items from their homeland.

The success of her class caught the attention of the local newspaper. A reporter came out to observe the class, then to interview the students as well as Nicole. On meeting her, the question of her heritage came up. Up until meeting Xavier, she had been reluctant to discuss herself. However, Xavier had explained that by trying to hide her abandonment, she allowed it to become a greater issue than it actually was. So with that in mind she told her story to the reporter, who in turn treated it with sensitivity, and focused on the course, as he should. Xavier had been right.

He had also been right in requesting that she experience military life beside him. So much of what she believed was based on what she knew of her father and the rambunctious young airmen she avoided. However, since meeting Xavier, she had come to know a different aspect of the military community. She had met families who were sharing the military experience together. They loved and supported each other in every way. She respected the men and women who placed their lives on the line each day, and the spouses who took care of home in their absence. She especially respected Xavier for taking both of his commitments, his son and his squadron, so seriously. It was a delicate balancing act, but he managed both just fine. She had come to realize that the men and women of his unit were a part of his family as well. There were times when he saw more of them than he did his own son or her, which didn't always sit well with him, but was unavoidable.

The last week had been one of those times. She and Xavier had been looking forward to finally being able to spend quality time together. However, the military had a different idea. Due to an unexpected inspection, she and Xavier had only spoken to each other briefly, and had seen each other even less. He was focused on the mission and promised to make it up to her later. The time he did manage to squeeze out of his busy schedule was spent with his son. Nicole couldn't complain about that. It was as it should be. She herself had spent many hours entertaining Ryan in his father's absence. She hoped her presence had been comforting to them both.

Thursday night, after she'd spent the week alone, the telephone began ringing as she crawled into bed. She glanced at the clock and became alarmed because it was after eleven. Only bad news arrived so late. Hesitantly she picked up the receiver.

"Hello."

"Hi, Nic. I know it's late, baby, but I just needed to hear your voice," came Xavier's exhausted baritone.

Relieved that it wasn't bad news, just a late night call from the man in her life, Nicole smiled as the richness of his voice caressed her ear. "It's good to hear your voice as well. You sound exhausted."

As always, her concern for his welfare made him feel important in her life. It was nice to have someone who cared. "It's been a long two weeks, but we placed the inspectors on a plane this afternoon."

"Is that your way of telling me that I may actually get to see you this weekend?"

"I wish that were the case, baby."

"I hear a but coming," Nicole mumbled, disappointed.

"Would you believe I've been asked to instruct a course at Maxwell?"

"How wonderful," Nicole replied proudly. "I'm sure you'll do well. Have you done this before?"

"Once while overseas."

"Is this one of those opportunities to succeed?"

He laughed as she knew he would. "You've got it, but I'm actually looking forward to it. The only drawback is you and Ryan. It's a month long course, and I'll miss you both terribly."

"A month?" Nicole half-shouted. "When do you leave?"

"Actually they want me there tomorrow. The current instructor has an ailing family member and needs to leave right away. We'll spend a day going over the course curriculum, then come Monday morning the class is all mine."

"What are Ryan and I suppose to do while you're away?" She knew she was whining, but didn't care. She would miss him.

"I tell you what. We could take turns visiting on the weekends. That is, if your car is up to the long drive."

"My car is running perfectly. The mechanic replaced a couple of parts and it has been running smoothly ever since."

"Glad to hear it. Now, like I was saying, You and Ryan could come up there one weekend, and I down here the next. There's a great deal of history in Montgomery. I'm sure we could find some interesting things to do."

Liking the sound of that, she agreed to his suggestion. "Is there anything I can do around here while you're away?"

"Just take care of my son, baby. He's the most important person in my life."

His words weren't meant to hurt, but they did. She knew he loved his son fiercely, but it would have been nice to know she was important to him as well. "I know he is."

There was a change in her voice that Xavier immediately picked up on. He knew Nicole had no way of knowing how he was beginning to feel about her. "Nic, I didn't mean that the way it sounded."

"Hey, I know you care about me," she commented as convincingly as possible.

There was a long pause while he wrestled with how to respond and how much to say. "Nicole, I haven't allowed another woman into my life since my marriage ended. That makes you very important to me, sweetheart."

Not sure how to respond to those words Nicole chose not to comment directly. "I'll take care of us both," she promised.

Over alternating weekends Ryan, Nicole, and Xavier managed to squeeze time in for each other. It helped the separation go a little easier. Ryan and Nicole really got closer during those drives up to Montgomery. For a youngster, Ryan was quite articulate. He and Nicole shared personal secrets that only two people who grew up without a mother would understand. Their bond was obvious to Xavier each time he was around the pair. His son seemed to blossom under Nicole's attention and love. That something new and different inside of him also blossomed into something beautiful.

He had one more week of class. Well, actually four more days. Friday morning he would be headed back to Biloxi and Nicole. The time away had allowed him to view their relationship clearly and analyze his feelings. He still didn't believe marriage was in his future, but when he truly thought about their so—called agreement, he recognized that it had always been far more than that. In the beginning it had been a mutual attraction. But that had grown into a caring friendship, and now he saw the possibilities of it becoming much more. When he returned home on Friday, he and Nicole would have a long talk. It was time to lay his cards on the table.

Monday morning after spending the weekend in Montgomery with Ryan and Xavier, Nicole awakened with a new attitude. She would make the most of her current situation and leave the future to take care of itself. Determined, she threw herself back into teaching at the community center although the summer program would soon be ending. It had been a great success. She was proud to see her ideas materialize. Consulting her organizer she noted an interview with a potential guest speaker was scheduled for Friday. Mrs. Nguyen, a local Vietnamese artist, had agreed to the interview. She would be the last scheduled guest of the summer.

Nicole had spotted Mrs. Nguyen's work while strolling through the Ocean Springs Annual Arts and Craft Show. An assortment of artists as well as storeowners displayed their talents and wares to the local community. It was always a big event during the summer, drawing large crowds. The quaint, tree-shrouded streets of downtown Ocean Springs were reminiscent of a bygone era. Though the city was gradually growing, it still maintained its small town feel. Friendly faces smiled and greeted you along the way. This was Nicole's third time attending the event and each year it got better and drew larger crowds.

Thursday afternoon before heading home, Nicole busied herself straightening the chairs and returning misplaced materials. She checked her lesson plan for Friday and assembled the necessary materials. Just as she was about to grab her purse and head home for the day, the door to her classroom swung open. Glancing up as a petite Asian woman with a stylish haircut, and floral blue and white sundress entered, Nicole closed the drawer containing her handbag. She quickly rose to greet her visitor. Obviously this had to be Mrs. Nguyen. It appeared as though her assistant had gotten the interview date confused. No problem, she decided. She would conduct the interview today, then be free to head on home early tomorrow. Actually it was a better idea because Xavier would be returning.

"Hello, you must be Mrs. Nguyen." Nicole greeted the silent woman by extending her hand. "It's a pleasure to finally meet you. I spotted your work at the crafts fair and thought it was magnificent. I read your bio and was tremendously impressed. Your personal history was one I wanted my students to hear firsthand. I hope you didn't mind me asking your assistant to request an interview," Nicole rambled on.

The woman didn't respond, nor did she except Nicole's hand. She studied Nicole with great interest. Her eyes were keen in their observation as she slowly scrutinized the young woman. She wrung her hands nervously as though trying to decide what to say. Then as Nicole continued talking, she finally interrupted.

"I'm not Mrs. Nguyen."

"You're not?" Nicole responded, confused. "Oh, forgive me for assuming and running my mouth." She smiled at the woman, only now becoming aware of her curious examination. "May I ask who you are then?"

The woman's face crumpled as she returned Nicole's piercing gaze. Her lips trembled as her eyes filled with tears. In a surprisingly strong voice the woman began to speak.

"My name is Linn Walker. I read about your class in the paper. When I saw your picture I couldn't believe I had finally found you."

Something inside Nicole shifted. She knew her life was about to change, but she wasn't quite sure how. As Linn spoke and Nicole digested her words, her pulse increased. Her ears were ringing so loud that she couldn't be sure what she was hearing.

"What do you mean, you finally found me?"[7]

"I'm...your...mother, Nicole."

Shaking her head no, Nicole backpedaled away, then began pacing the room. She suddenly halted, turning to face Linn. "You're wrong. I don't have a mother." Her voice wasn't as strong as she would have liked, but at least she had managed to control the trembling she was experiencing inside.

Linn approached her daughter gingerly. She could see the fear and anger in Nicole's eyes. She had to reach her before Nicole closed the door on her emotions. "Yes, you do. I gave birth to you twenty-five years ago. I was unable to provide a safe home for you so I left you on the steps of the Catholic Church. I enclosed a letter giving your name, birth date, and a brief explanation."

"Doesn't mean anything. You could have gotten that information from a file or something."

"You know that's not true, Nicole. I know it's a shock, daughter."

"Don't call me that," Nicole growled out angrily.

Linn ignored Nicole's expected anger. "You are my daughter, Nicole. I named you after your father Nicholas because you were born with his golden brown eyes. Of course you have his skin color and that chin." She smiled as a memory resurfaced. "I was fascinated by your father's dimpled chin, and then you were born with it." She smiled again before shaking the memory away. "But your face is mine," she said in awe. She saw so much of herself in her daughter.

"That doesn't prove a thing."

"Maybe, maybe not, but how about the mole on your left hip and breast." She smiled as Nicole's hand flew to cover her left breast. She watched her daughter's face as acceptance slowly took hold, and she knew the moment anger took control.

Tears blurred Nicole's vision as the truth of this woman's words took root. She fought to focus on the face she had always dreamed of seeing as a child. Studying the thin, angular face she began to see herself. This woman *was* her mother. Her brain was reluctant to accept the truth, but her heart knew it to be so. A part of her, the abandoned child, wanted to rush into the woman's waiting arms. However, the woman in her wanted to scream, rant, and rave. Somehow, she wasn't sure how exactly, she managed to quell the anger. When she spoke, the words came out controlled, though scathing.

"No, you're not my mother. You're just the woman who gave birth to me. You see Mrs. Walker, a mother doesn't abandon her child on a doorstep like forgotten trash."

"You were never trash to me, Nicole. You were my baby girl. I did what I felt was best for you."

That phrase immediately brought back memories of Mrs. Scott forcing her desires and opinions onto Nicole. She was always doing "what was best" for her. It seemed everyone who caused her pain did so with her best interest in mind. The concept caused her to unleash years of anger. She rounded on Linn with widened eyes and a raised voice.

"How dare you make it sound like you did me a favor? You did what was best for *you*. You got rid of your dirty little secret and went on with your life. *I* paid for your sin, *Mother*," Nicole screamed, thumping her chest. "*I* paid while you went on with your life." Her voice faltered as the tears began to fall. She eased away from Linn, who was now in tears too.

"What the hell is going on in here?" A tall, broad-shouldered African-American man asked suddenly, appearing in the classroom doorway. He appeared to be in his early fifties with a thick head of dark hair. Only a few gray sprinkles littered his neat cut. His eyes were dark and assessing as he entered the classroom, going immediately to Linn. On seeing her tears he drew her against him as he stared angrily at Nicole. Unable to see the resemblance between the young woman and Linn due to his concern for his wife, Franklin Walker stood menacingly before Nicole.

Linn tried unsuccessfully to calm her husband. "It's all right, Franklin. Nicole is understandably upset."

"That may be, but it is no reason for her to raise her voice to you," he growled out, locking eyes with Nicole.

Defiant, Nicole returned his heated stare. She wouldn't back down because she was the victim in this drama. "Mr.

Walker, since you don't like my attitude, why don't you take your wife home."

"No Nicole, I can't leave things like this between us," Linn rushed on, pushing out of her husband's grasp. We need to talk. I need to explain."

Nicole crossed her arms defensively. "What you need is forgiveness. Am I right?"

When Linn didn't respond, only stood staring defeated, Nicole knew that was the real reason for this visit.

"You have it. Now you can go home."

Linn took two steps closer. She felt as though she had aged since walking into the classroom. Her heart had ached to find the child she had given up, and she refused to give up on her today. She had to make Nicole understand that she had always been loved.

"Nicole, the day I left you at that church, I left a part of my heart. I loved you from the moment I discovered I was pregnant You have always been in my heart. You are my oldest daughter. You have two sisters," she added as an afterthought.

Up until that last sentence Linn had been making progress. Nicole had truly been listening to her words and hearing the heartache. The ice around her heart was beginning to melt. However, the mention of two other children, who no doubt grew up with a mother's love, reversed the meltdown. Anger and an indescribable pain consumed her. She wanted to make this woman hurt as much as she did.

"You raised them."

"Yes, their father and I did."

Nicole glanced at Mr. Walker, knowing that he was the father. She hurt so badly she was afraid her chest would explode with the pain. Her mother had two other children that she had kept and loved. Nicole had been the only one she abandoned.

"Go away and leave me alone," Nicole mumbled in an exhausted whisper.

"No! I can't do that. I love you, Nicole. Everything that I did was because I loved you." Linn spoke hurriedly, sensing finality to her attempt at a relationship with her daughter.

Those words ignited Nicole's simmering anger. With the last "I love you," Nicole exploded.

"Love! You loved me. Well, let me tell you about your love, Mother. Because of *your love* I was shuffled from one foster home to another before ending up with a woman who didn't like anything about me. Because of *your love,* I grew up without a proper family. Because of *your love* I have been ostracized and ridiculed. And finally because of *your love,* I had the parents of a man I loved tell me that I was unacceptable for their son. And just like you Mother, he left me too." With that said, Nicole turned her back on the crying woman and the shocked man. She wanted to be left alone with her anguish. "Just go."

Linn's heart ached for her daughter. In her attempt to protect Nicole, she had actually hurt her in the most detrimental way. She had destroyed her daughter's belief in love. Crying heavily now, Linn allowed Franklin to comfort her. She wanted to comfort her daughter, but knew now was not the time. With any luck they would have another opportunity for a relationship. She withdrew one of her business cards, scribbling down her home address and telephone number. Placing it on top of Nicole's desk she left the classroom with Franklin. At the doorway, she turned back around, noticing Nicole's heaving shoulders. Her child was in pain again and she was unable to soothe the hurt. With a heavy heart she once again walked away from her firstborn.

Nicole listened to the footsteps recede before finally collapsing into the nearest chair. She doubled over in pain. Racking sobs escaped one after the other as she purged her system of a lifetime of suffering. What hurt most of all was the fact that she had two sisters who grew up being loved by her mother. Why couldn't Linn have loved her too? Why couldn't Xavier love her? The questions continued to come, as did the tears. it was a full hour before Nicole felt capable of driving herself home. While walking to her desk for a tissue, she spotted the deposited card lying on the desk. A floral design decorated the business card, advertising Linn's Flower Shop. Her initial response was to tear it into a million little pieces, but the abandoned child in her held on to it as the last remaining connection to her mother. She slipped the card into her address book. She took a tissue from the box and dried her eyes and face as best she could. With a deep breath she opened the drawer, grabbed her purse and left for home.

Something was wrong. Xavier wasn't sure who was in trouble, but he knew it was someone close to him. He called home to check on Ryan. Rosa answered immediately and assured him that all was in order. Relieved to know that his son was safe, his thoughts instantly shifted to Nicole. The feeling wouldn't subside. If anything, it was getting stronger.

His class was officially over. Checking the clock and noting that the time was nearing six in the evening, Xavier knew he could be home by nine-thirty. His bags were packed and ready to go. So as the feeling of unease intensified, Xavier made the decision to drive back tonight. After another call to Rosa, he checked out of billeting, and headed for Interstate 65 South.

Three and half-hours later, Xavier pulled into Nicole's driveway. He parked behind her car. As he glanced at Nicole's home he noticed it was completely dark. Nicole was a night owl and for her house to be dark at this hour was out of the norm. That feeling of unease he had been traveling with now tightened inside his chest.

Xavier climbed out of the vehicle, running up the walkway to the front door. He rang the bell and waited anxiously for Nicole to answer. He rang the belt a second time after no initial response. He was getting scared now, because Nicole's car was parked out front, and yet she wasn't answering the door. Thinking Gina would know where she was, he was about to leave when the front door slowly opened. He could barely make out Nicole's face, but what he did manage to see confirmed his fears.

"Baby, what's the matter?" he asked as he pushed his way into the house, closing the door behind him. Finding the lamp on the table beside the door and turning its switch, Xavier illuminated the living room.

Nicole's hand came up reflexively, shielding her eyes from the intrusive light. Her eyes were swollen from crying and light sensitive after hours of sitting in the dark. Slowly getting her bearings, she glanced at Xavier. At any other time his appearance would be a welcomed sight, but not tonight. Her emotions were too jumbled and raw to deal with him.

"What are you doing here?" Nicole's voice cracked in a raspy whisper. The hours of crying had taken a toll on her voice as well as her eyes.

Xavier ignored her question. He scooped Nicole up into his arms as he made his way into the kitchen.

"Put me down this instant!" Nicole rasped, struggling to free herself.

Xavier held on tighter. He hit the light switch with his elbow on entering the kitchen, then took a seat at the table, their table. With gentle hands he swept the disheveled hair away from her face.

"Talk to me, Nicole. Tell me what's going on."

"Look Xavier, I'm in no mood to deal with you tonight. Go home please before I say or do something that I'll be sorry for later."

"Not a chance. You say and do whatever you want, but tell me what is causing you so much pain."

Nicole drew back to get a better look at his face. She noted the concern in his gray eyes, and the worry lines across his forehead. A part of her wanted to soothe his concerns, but the other wanted to lash out and wound.

"Please go home, Xavier. I'm trying desperately not to hurt you."

"I'm not leaving until you tell me why you're so upset," he persisted.

Annoyed, Nicole's voice screeched as she tried to raise it. "Why do you care? Aren't you the same person who wanted a no strings agreement?"

"I am, but you haven't answered my question."

"You haven't answered mine either," Nicole threw out as she tried to stand up, but was halted by Xavier's strong grip.

I'm here because I care about you, Nicole, and I sensed something was wrong. I know you don't completely understand my reasons for not wanting a committed relationship. But I assure you I'm doing what is best for us."

There it was again. Someone doing what they felt was best for her. If people were so concerned about her feelings, why did their action appease only them? She lost control of her emotions. The anger she had been trying to rein in poured out.

"How dare people keep justifying their actions by saying they did it for me. You're all liars. Just be honest and admit that you're cowards," she shouted and extracted herself from his grasp.

Xavier knew what he had done, but who was the other party Nicole kept referring to. "Who, Nicole? Who else is a coward?"

"My mother, Xavier—she's a coward just like you." Noticing the confused expression on his face, Nicole realized that he didn't understand. "My mother came to visit me today. She was looking for forgiveness, but I didn't have it to give. And just like you, she claims her abandoning me was in my best interest."

The tears once again flowed as she ranted and paced, recounting her visit with her mother. By the time the story was relayed, Nicole could cry no more, and her voice was nearly gone. When exhaustion finally set in, Xavier scooped her up into his arms once more. This time he placed her in bed before returning to the kitchen. There he prepared Nicole a cup of chamomile tea. He returned to the bedroom and placed the tea on the nightstand. Then he removed his shirt and shoes. He climbed into bed beside her with his slacks on.

"You'll find a pair of new pajama pants in the top, right drawer of the dresser in the guest bedroom," Nicole directed.

Completely surprised, not by the offer, but the implication, Xavier stared coldly at Nicole. Obviously his earlier assessment of her sexual experience was premature. "No thanks. I don't wear other men's clothing."

Rolling her eyes, annoyed, Nicole didn't have the energy to give him the dressing down that he deserved. "They were purchased for Jon when he visits. He never seems to remember to pack pajamas."

"Oh! Well...in that case I would be more comfortable." He got up from the bed to retrieve them. At the doorway he turned. "Sorry for assuming."

Now that the anger had been expelled from her body Nicole was happy to see him. She recalled her hateful words, feeling suddenly ashamed. Xavier hadn't gotten angry with her. He instead had sat quietly by as she spewed venom until she exhausted herself. Then in that special caring way of his, he had taken her into his arms and placed her safely in bed. The cup of tea was to soothe and relax her, as well as help her raw throat She wanted to tell him that all she needed to feel better was his love, but she hadn't. Instead she had accepted the tea with a thank you.

As he entered the bedroom, the sip she was about to take remained in the cup poised at her lips. Her hungry eyes devoured Xavier's male beauty. Her heart beat so rapidly against her chest, she was sure Xavier could hear it. His broad muscular chest was bare except for the fine dusting of hair covering it. The wintergreen drawstring pajama pants rode low on his hips in that sexy way men wore them. His large feet were also bare and the total picture caused sensual thoughts to trip across her mind. Lord, how was she supposed to sleep with this much man lying beside her?

"Drink your tea," Xavier ordered, climbing into bed beside her. He was unaware of Nicole's distress. "It's good for your throat."

Silently Nicole drank her tea under the watchful eye of Xavier. They hadn't discussed the scene in the kitchen or his presence in her bed. He hadn't attempted to touch her, just sat quietly by offering his support. Nicole finished the tea and placed the empty cup onto the nightstand beside her. As she turned to face Xavier, he opened his arms and his heart to her. Nicole didn't need to be asked twice. She slipped into them, taking comfort against his solid chest. She closed her eyes, inhaling his familiar scent and absorbing his warmth. At that very moment she decided to accept his presence in her life on his terms. She would honor their agreement and stop wishing for something that wasn't going to happen. It was enough that he cared.

"I'm sorry about what I said. I took my anger out on you." Xavier tilted Nicole's chin up so that he could look into her eyes. He had dreamed of looking into their golden hue for days now. It hurt him deeply to see their red, swollen condition.

"You were right about me being a coward, Nic. I'm so afraid of the emotions you stir inside of me."

Nicole was finally able to smile. She stroked Xavier's clean-shaven jaw. "You're not a coward. You're just a man who has been hurt by a failed marriage. You have fears and doubts, and only a fool would ignore them. I understand now."

"Do you really understand?"

"Yes, I do. I just know that I've missed your closeness so much."

"Me too, baby," Xavier agreed, drawing Nicole close. "So *really* tell me about meeting your mother."

Nicole confided her initial joy at finally meeting the woman she had dreamed of as a child. She also informed him of the all—consuming anger that overtook her on discovering that her mother had raised two other children. As she recounted their meeting, pain laced each word as it was purged from her system.

"It hurts, Xavier, to know that while I was being handed from house to house, my mother was raising two other daughters. I don't understand what made them so special and me so easy to throw away."

Xavier thought about trying to clarify Linn's decision, but he knew that in Nicole's frame of mind she would only resent his explanation. This was her life and her pain. No one could truly understand another's experience, and he wasn't foolish enough to try.

"I know it hurts, baby, but look at your meeting as a chance to get to know your mother. Aren't you a little curious about your sisters?"

"I don't have sisters, Xavier. My mother has other children. I can't allow myself to think of these people as family. It wouldn't work. I would never be able to fit into their perfect middle class life. Besides, I don't think Franklin Walker likes me."

"He doesn't know you, Nic. All he knows is that you're an angry daughter who was attacking his wife. I'm sure he loves her and was trying to shield her from being hurt."

Nicole stiffened as she sat up slowly and faced him. Her face was void of emotion, but her eyes spoke volumes. "Who was there to shield me from the pain and hurt of life in the system? Does anyone understand that while my mother's life went on, I was living a life of misery? Or do my feelings not matter?"

With each word Nicole managed to speak with her raw voice, Xavier's heart ached for the young woman he cared deeply for. He did understand Nicole's feelings, well, as much as anyone who didn't share the experience could, but what he wanted Nicole to realize was that she had survived the ordeal.

Taking Nicole's face within his hands, Xavier stared into her questioning eyes. "Nicole, I understand where you're coming from, but rehashing it isn't going to change the past. Baby, what I'm suggesting is that you look to the future. It's not your cross to bear. It's your mother's. You're making yourself ill with all this festering anger. Now I'm not telling you to rush to her with open arms, but what I am suggesting is that you listen to what she has to say. It just may change your opinion of her."

Nicole's body sagged as the anger diminished. She returned to her resting place beside him. "I'm afraid to hear what she has to say," Nicole blurted out after a while. "I'm afraid I might understand her reasoning and want to forgive her, and then where will I be without the rage that fortifies me?"

Xavier was speechless as he digested Nicole's words. Never had he given consideration to the fact that Nicole's strength was derived from the anger of her abandonment. Her words revealed a fear of being weak and susceptible to life's obstacles.

"A parent's love can fortify you, Nicole. Shall we give it a try tomorrow?"

After a considerable moment of silence, Nicole finally responded. "Yeah, I think it's time."

CHAPTER 14

Nicole was the first to awaken the next morning. She eased from bed, trying not to disturb Xavier who slept soundly on the other side. She smiled as she recalled how he had arrived last night like a knight in shining armor. He had held her all through the night, reminding her that she wasn't alone. Not once had he tried to take advantage of the situation. Nicole wasn't completely sure how she felt about that now in the light of day. It was the first time she had lain beside a man in bed and he hadn't even kissed her. Was she that unappealing, or Xavier that strong willed? Maybe the cotton pajamas were a turn off. Anyway, it felt wonderful to have him beside her during the night. His warmth and words of encouragement eased her doubts and fears about today.

If Nicole had known the agony Xavier had suffered through the night, she would have known just how much she appealed to him. Her soft warm bottom had nestled against his crotch most of the night, making sleep virtually impossible for him. Every time he moved allowing space between them, she some how managed to wiggle her sweet little rump back into place against him. He was agonizingly hard most of the night. But he didn't think of trying to appease his desire. Nicole's emotions were too raw and vulnerable. He would be a poor excuse for a man if he took advantage of her vulnerability for the sake of his lust. When Nicole gave herself to him, it would be because of mutual need and desire.

Nicole walked into the kitchen and placed a call to her assistant at the community center. She was confident the assistant could handle the class. So with that thought in mind, she cited an emergency for her absence. She quickly outlined today's activities before ending the call.

In the bathroom she stared at her reflection in the mirror. It wasn't pretty, but at least the swelling of her eyes had gone down. A drop of Visine could aid the redness. The rest she decided, makeup would have to hide.

After brushing her teeth and applying eye drops, she removed her pajamas, stepping into the steaming spray of the shower The invigorating water rejuvenated her body. The tension in her neck and shoulders eased. Lathering from head to toe, she tried to think positive thoughts, and rinse the negative ones down the drain. By the time she stepped from the shower she felt rejuvenated and ready to face the day.

Nicole walked out of the bathroom wrapped in a floral silk robe and encountered Xavier's heated gaze. It traveled the full length of her body before resting on her face. Its intensity left her body tingling and wishing for far more. Tightening the belt at her waist, she went to stand before the dresser mirror. She squirted a dab of lotion into her hands and rubbed it in. Then she picked up her hairbrush and began attacking the tangles from her shower. Through the mirror she observed Xavier stretch lazily like a powerful black panther. Flashing his roguish smile, he jump-started her heart and fired her engines. Her pulse rate increased as she continued to watch him laid out before her like a feast. Licking her lips, she devoured the sight of his muscled chest and powerful arms. The white sheet draped precariously across his male hips tantalized her appetite. His powerful masculine legs lay outstretched in invitation to his worldly delights which the sheet did very little to hide. Here before her was her very own Moorish chief, and God, he was magnificent.

Xavier was already on edge and the naked hunger in Nicole's eyes did nothing to calm his senses. Feeling his desire stir as her eyes journeyed across his body, he gritted his teeth. She was on dangerous ground and he had to warn her.

"Baby, unless you intend to spend the entire day on your back, I suggest you stop looking at me like I'm your favorite chocolate bar." He returned her smoldering stare through the mirror.

Meeting his dark fiery eyes, Nicole realized Xavier was quite serious. He had the look of a man barely hanging on to his self control. For a fleeting moment hot untamed images flashed through her mind. With a heaving chest and escalating pulse, she headed for the safety of the door, knowing now was not the time for them.

Xavier joined Nicole in the kitchen after taking a much needed cold shower and speaking to Ryan on the telephone. He had informed his son that he would be home later to take him to dinner. It had been some time since he and his boy had spent some quality time together alone, and he was thoroughly looking forward to the afternoon.

"How's Ryan this morning?" Nicole asked, handing Xavier a cup of coffee. It felt so natural for the two of them to awaken together and share their morning meal.

Overwhelmed by the abundance of happiness surging through her body due to his presence, Nicole focused her attention on the breakfast she was preparing, not wanting Xavier to recognize her vulnerability.

But, he did glimpse the unconditional love shimmering in her eyes. The purity of her love was beautiful and to be cherished. "Come here, baby," Xavier cooed, drawing Nicole into his arms. He squeezed her affectionately, then stroked her back, savoring the rightness of the moment.

"Ryan told me to tell you that he misses you."

"Tell him I miss him too, and on second thought, maybe you should spend the day with him. He missed you so much while you were away."

"You know that's what I like about you. You're always thinking about my son or me. You're right, I know the last month has been difficult on him as well. That's why tomorrow I'm spending the entire day with my boy. I thought we could do a movie, then go to the fun center that he loves so much."

"He's going to enjoy that. You're a good father."

The compliment caused him to smile with pride. Nicole possessed the ability to make him feel confident and sure. "Thanks, it's nice to hear. You know, sometimes I consider giving my career up so that I can spend more time with Ryan. I feel so guilty about the temporary duties and deployments. I'm missing so much of his childhood."

"True, but when the two of you are together it's quality time that you're sharing. Besides, Ryan is so proud to say his father is in the Air Force. You're his hero, Xavier."

"Yeah? He actually says that?"

Nicole could hear the doubt flee as his son's pride took center stage. "Yes, he does."

"Nic?"

"Yeah?"

"Thanks for the words of encouragement. Sometimes I just need to hear that I'm doing okay by my son."

"You're doing better than okay."

"It's been easier with your help. I really appreciate your spending time with Ryan. It made my job easier. I knew he had you and Rosa loving him." Xavier was truly pleased with Nicole's devotion to Ryan. It was nice to have a support system. "Why don't the three of us have dinner tonight? Ryan would love to see you."

Feeling more composed, Nicole withdrew from his embrace, but maintained her hold on his waist. "Sounds like a plan."

Over breakfast Xavier and Nicole finalized their dinner arrangement. It was agreed upon that Xavier would accompany her to the Walkers. After that he would return home to spend some time with his son before picking her up for dinner later. It was also decided that Ryan would have the honor of selecting the restaurant. Xavier volunteered to clean up the kitchen while Nicole dressed for her meeting with her mother. He had retrieved his luggage earlier, and would change himself once he finished the dishes.

On entering the bedroom several minutes later with luggage in hand, Xavier was surprised to find Nicole curled up in the chair still dressed in her robe. She was in a trance-like state. The far-away expression masking her face made her look like a frightened little girl.

"Why aren't you dressed?"

"I'm afraid, Xavier."

"Of what, Nicole?"

"Not measuring up to her other daughters."

With those few words, Xavier truly realized how the brief meeting with Linn Walker had affected Nicole. Her angry behavior of yesterday was a smoke screen to camouflage the fear she was experiencing.

"I know, baby, but there is no need to be. You're a wonderful woman, Nicole."

"But is it enough?"

He could only imagine how frightened she was of being rejected and abandoned again. It was so clear to him now that he didn't understand why he hadn't seen it before—this sense of not being worthy of love. Nicole had never known unconditional love and didn't believe it was hers to have, so she hid her feelings behind this wall of anger, preparing for the worst. He prayed Linn Walker was sincere in her attempt at reconciliation with her daughter. He wasn't sure Nicole would survive abandonment a second time.

He deposited his luggage on the floor near the bed. Approaching Nicole who remained in the trance-like state, Xavier kneeled before her, placing a hand on her knee. When Nicole's eyes met his, he caught a glimpse of the little girl Nicole once was. In her eyes he saw the need to be loved.

"What if they don't like me? It's not like I made the most glowing impression yesterday."

"You of all people have a reason to be angry. Your mother understands that, Nicole. As a parent I know she understands."

"I hope you're right."

"Trust me, I am. Now change your clothes and meet me in the living room."

Xavier parked the Lincoln in front of the two-story white brick home. The meticulous yard indicated a true gardener lived here. Nicole instinctively knew that the gardener was her mother, for she too had a green thumb. A border of evergreen shrubs lined the front of the house. An assortment of summer annuals added a splash of color. The rich green, healthy lawn was freshly mowed and edged to perfection. The symmetrical pear tree placed just left of the yard stood straight and strong, shading the large front porch. A green wrought iron glider sat idle on the porch. More flowers were blooming in pots and baskets decorating the seating area. The feel of the home was strong and welcoming. Nicole sensed love and pride emanating from its foundation.

"Ready to go in?" Xavier asked from beside Nicole, who sat absorbing the beauty of her mother's home.

"She was so close, Xavier. We could have easily met each other on the street."

"I know, baby."

Nicole smiled weakly at him. He would never know how much she truly appreciated his being with her today. "I'm ready now."

Just as Nicole and Xavier exited the vehicle, the front door opened and out walked Linn and Franklin Walker.

They both wore wide, welcoming smiles. Once more Nicole realized that her mother was shorter than she was, yet held a striking resemblance to herself. As Xavier made his way to her side of the vehicle, he clasped her cold hand and walked beside her up the driveway and onto the sidewalk. Just as they neared Linn and her husband, the door behind them opened once more. This time two young women emerged onto the front porch. The shocking resemblance between them and Nicole caused Nicole and Xavier to halt in their tracks. They exchanged glances as they turned to study the two women once more.

Linn Walker interrupted their musing. "Welcome! I'm so glad you called, Nicole." She smiled through the veil of tears shimmering in her eyes. Her heart was full with the love for the daughter she'd feared she would never see again. Her shattered world was now whole. Nicole had returned to her finally. On instinct she opened her arms to her daughter.

Nicole hesitated, not prepared for such closeness. Instead, she extended her hand. Linn followed her lead, though she would have much preferred to embrace her lost child.

"Me too. I had to call you. I need answers."

"I know you do and I promise to answer them all if I can." Still holding Nicole's hand, Linn stroked it lovingly.

Nicole extracted her hand as delicately as possible. The affectionate display and growing audience made her uncomfortable. She felt as though she was under a microscope. She had thought she would be meeting with her mother and Mr. Walker alone.

"I didn't realize they would be here."

"They! We're not they, Nicole." This came from the older sister who resembled Nicole the most. "We're her daughters and this is *our* home," she spat, making her position known.

Nicole visibly flinched as the words hit her like a blow to the gut. Clutching Xavier's arm in desperation, she stood rooted in place. She wasn't as welcome as Linn tried to imply.

"Be quiet, Frances," Linn scolded her daughter. "Nicole is my baby girl as well."

I shouldn't be here...I shouldn't be here." Nicole all but wept, shaking her head from side to side. She turned around heading down the walkway with Xavier beside her. Then the anger took over. She stopped so abruptly that Xavier didn't realize she wasn't beside him anymore. Meeting the young woman's resentful eyes, Nicole unleashed that anger.

"You're welcome to your mother, Frances, because I don't need her. I don't need any of you. I've made it this far on my own, and I'll make it the rest of the way as well." To Linn who was visibly upset by the exchange between her daughters, Nicole commented. "Thank you for leaving me on that church porch. Otherwise I could have grown up to be like your mean spirited daughter there." She indicated Frances with the jut of her chin. "And by the way, your baby girl is an adult and doesn't need you, so get on with your life and leave me alone." Franklin Walker spoke for the first time. "Now that's uncalled for, young lady."

Xavier came to Nicole's defense. "Mr. Walker, I think you should be reprimanding your daughter there. Her words were cruel and insensitive."

"He's right Dad," the younger sister spoke up. She ran off the porch and came to stand in front of Nicole. I apologize for my sister's behavior. I think she's just a little upset about not being the eldest sister anymore. You know, the inherent right to boss me around and give unwanted advice." She smiled sweetly. "I'm Jan, your sister, and I would like for us to be friends." She spoke with heartfelt sincerity.

Nicole silently studied the young woman who possessed the strongest Asian features of the three sisters. in her beautiful dark eyes, Nicole recognized her genuine goodness. There wasn't a hint of resentment to be found. She returned her warm smile.

"I'd like for us to be friends as well, Jan. But I think it's going to take us all some time before we get used to the idea of each other."

"There's nothing to get used to. We've known about you since we were little."

"You have?" Nicole searched Jan's face first, then Linn's. "Why?"

Linn walked to where Jan stood and placed her arm around her youngest daughter. It appeared she would be the one to break through Nicole's defenses. She had always known that her daughter possessed a good heart, but she'd had it confirmed here today. "You have always been a part of this family, Nicole. Even though you weren't with me physically, you were here in my heart," Linn replied, covering her heart with her right hand.

Not quite knowing how to respond, Nicole simply didn't say anything. Instead she nodded her head. "I should

be going now. I apologize for upsetting your household."
Sensing Xavier's closeness, she held out her hand and was
relieved when he grasped it so sure and strong. She took
comfort in that strength and headed back down the sidewalk, exuding more strength than she truly possessed.

"Can we try again?" Linn called from behind her.

Nicole stopped just long enough to respond. "Sure, I'll
call you."

Despite her assurance to Linn that she would contact
her, it had actually taken Nicole several days to do so. It had
been Jan's prompting which finally made her place the call.

Jan had shown up to her summer program and stood
outside the door as Mrs. Nguyen spoke to the class.
Catching sight of her sister, Nicole beckoned her inside,
then made her way to the rear of the room.

"Hi. What are you doing here?"

"I hope you don't mind, but I wanted to see you." She
smiled uneasily.

"I don't mind. I've actually thought about you often,"
Nicole told the nineteen year-old, putting her at ease.
Together they stood in the back of the classroom listening to
the speaker's presentation.

"Let's give Mrs. Nguyen another round of applause,"
Nicole instructed her class. "This presentation was
extremely important to me personally because my birth
mother is Vietnamese, and the presentation represents a part
of my heritage."

"Our heritage," Jan supplied, walking to the front of the room. She took Nicole's hand then turned facing the class.

"Is she your sister, Ms. Edwards?" one of the children yelled out.

Nicole answered from the heart as she glanced at the young woman beside her. "Yes, she is. Her name is Jan."

"And our mother is from a small village in Vietnam called..." Jan continued speaking to the class. She recounted their mother's history. Unlike Nicole, they didn't realize this little presentation was for her benefit as well as theirs, and were riveted to Jan's dramatic recitation. Taking a seat, Nicole listened as her sister introduced her to Linn Walker, her mother.

So after several rough starts, Nicole and Linn gradually constructed a relationship. They shared lengthy lunches together, simply getting to know each other. It wasn't the mother/daughter relationship Linn wanted, but for now it was satisfying. They were at least able to talk to each other without getting angry. The more time they spent together, the more they discovered what they shared in common. So when Linn invited Nicole and Xavier back to her home for a family visit, Nicole readily accepted.

"Welcome home." Linn extended the warm greeting to Nicole on her second visit.

Still uncomfortable about being there, Nicole didn't respond verbally. Her emotions were too jumbled, as she wasn't accustomed to this type of affection. So in response to her mother's greeting, she merely smiled.

Franklin Walker stepped forward from behind his wife and offered his hand in friendship to Xavier. "Welcome, young man," his rich masculine voice boomed.

On hearing her husband's words, Linn glanced at her husband and Nicole's young man shaking hands. He was tall and strongly built like her Franklin. His presence here today, and at their first meeting indicated that he was someone special in Nicole's life.

"And who is the handsome young man?" Linn asked of Nicole while glancing at Xavier.

Nicole clasped Xavier's hand, suddenly remembering her manners. "I'm sorry, I'd like you both to meet Major Xavier Ramón. Xavier, my birth mother, Linn and her husband Franklin Walker."

"It's a pleasure to meet you both." Xavier greeted Linn with a nod. He and Mr. Walker exchanged firm handshakes.

It didn't escape Linn's attention that Nicole hadn't called Xavier her boyfriend, fiancé, or friend. The formal introduction indicated her daughter's uncertainty of their relationship, even though her eyes conveyed her love for the man. Somehow Linn knew this reluctance to place a label on her love was related to her abandoning Nicole twenty-five years ago. She had warped her daughter's view of love and ruined her sense of worthiness. It was therefore her responsibility to rectify the situation.

"Major Ramón seems too formal for the man in my daughter's life. May I call you Xavier?" she asked, smiling mischievously up into his handsome face. Ah, her daughter had inherited her taste in good-looking men.

Xavier returned Linn's brilliant smile, recognizing a kindred spirit. He immediately recalled that which he knew of her life as told to him by Nicole. She, too, had been abandoned by the person who had vowed to love her. In her eyes he saw himself and the loss he had experienced when Monique walked away. But also in her eyes he saw the effects of a second chance at love. Nicole was his second chance and he didn't plan to ruin the opportunity.

"Xavier is fine, Mrs. Walker."

"Only if you call me Linn."

"Linn it is," he conceded.

Linn and Nicole walked ahead of him and Franklin. The men also had agreed upon the use of their first names. He quickly learned that Franklin was retired Air Force. He too had been stationed at the base early on in his career. He had met Linn there and upon learning her secret had promised to return to the Biloxi area. Xavier liked the forthright man.

Once inside the neat home Linn shared with her family, Nicole felt oddly out of place. This wasn't her childhood home and it contained no memories. Only photographs of her sisters decorated the mantle during various stages of their lives. She slowly examined each one of them before her attention was drawn to a small Polaroid fitted into a frame. It was a younger picture of her mother holding a baby. Her mother was smiling brightly and staring adoringly at the small bundle she held. Instinctively Nicole reached out taking the frame in her trembling hands before turning towards her mother.

"This is me, isn't it?"

Linn Walker approached her daughter and placed an arm around her waist. She leaned her head against Nicole's shoulder, looking at the picture she held. So many memories came flooding back to her mind. "Yes, it is. You were a week old."

Noticing once again the loving smile plastered on Linn's face, Nicole discovered the answer to her lifelong question. "You realty did love me."

"I've always loved you," Linn replied with deep emotion.

An hour later as the two couples sat around the kitchen table talking and sharing, Linn recounted for Xavier the details which prompted her to abandon Nicole. She had explained all of this to Nicole at their first meeting alone, over lunch. Neither had eaten anything, but much had been discussed. Not all of it was pretty, yet it had to be said. And so recognizing Xavier's place in her daughter's life, she felt it was best he heard the truth from her.

According to Linn, she and Nicole's father, Nicholas, a young airman, met and fell in love while he was serving in Vietnam. Nicholas married Linn, promising a better life in America. Then she became pregnant just prior to his discharge from service. Without a job and place for them to live, they moved in with his mother. They listened to her criticism for three months in Jackson. The better life never came, for her mother-in-law immediately and intensely disliked her. Nicholas' mother didn't understand why her son had married a foreigner. She repeatedly reprimanded him in front of Linn, saying that he should have married one of his own. Nicholas eventually found a job and got them a place of their own. About a month after they moved into their apartment, Nicholas began staying out late. Linn was left alone in the apartment, barely able to speak English. The only person she could call a friend was the elderly nurse next door. She began taking English lessons from her neighbor in an attempt to better herself. By the time her baby was born, Nicholas was gone. He did leave two months' rent money and a little spending change, but no note or clue as to where he had gone.

The elderly nurse from next door had heard Linn's labor-induced screams and come running. Rushing to the apartment, she was relived to discover the front door unlocked. She ran into the bedroom where she found Linn in full labor. It took the woman only a moment to prepare for the impending birth. Linn had delivered Nicole with no complications, thanks to her neighbor. She had been taken to a local hospital by ambulance, but not having any money she'd fled while they searched for an interpreter.

That same neighbor had taken the photograph a week later. The day after, Linn left Jackson with one month's rent money in her pocket, Nicole in her arms, and a bus ticket for Biloxi in her hand. More and more Vietnamese were arriving in the states and settling along the coastal waters, so Linn decided to do likewise. Back in Vietnam she had worked on her father's fishing boat. So with that in mind she was hoping to make a living doing the same type of work on the coast. After being greeted by prejudice and unable to find employment, she'd made the heart-wrenching decision to leave Nicole at the Catholic church. Her child deserved a better life than she could provide.

Nicole didn't necessarily forgive her mother, but realized that her abandonment had been an act of love by a desperate woman. As she listened once again, she accepted that fact and allowed that love to settle over her. Nicole caught Xavier watching her. In his dark gray eyes she saw an understanding of what was transpiring inside her heart. He winked, then smiled. The simple act went straight to her heart.

Moments later Xavier excused himself from the table to check on Ryan. While he was on the telephone, Linn took the opportunity to question Nicole about their relationship.

"You're in love with Xavier, aren't you?" her mother asked from across the table.

For a brief moment Nicole didn't comment. She lowered her head as she studied her nails, trying to decide how to respond. Finally she met her mother's knowing eyes and nodded her head in affirmation. She didn't dare attempt to speak.

"Why do you look so sad about loving him, Nicole?"

"I'm not sad because I love him. It's just that if you saw it, then Xavier must surely know, and I don't want that."

"Am I missing something here?" Jan blurted out. "Why doesn't your man know that you love him?"

Nicole shifted in her seat, searching for a more comfortable position. Sighing, she finally answered, "Xavier's been married before and it ended badly. His wife left him and their three-day-old son." Her eyes met her mother's who understood his anguish. "He doesn't want to marry again, and he refuses to love me. He cares about me and treats me well, but...he doesn't love me. And I'm afraid if he discovers that I love him, he might end what we have."

"What do you have?" Franklin interjected. "He seems like a nice enough man, but you can't waste your love on someone who doesn't want to be loved. You deserve a man who will love you and give you the family you want."

"Franklin, you're wrong," Linn replied. "You didn't give up on me when I attempted to refuse your love. You persisted and made it so that I needed your love to exist. That's what Nicole must do. Become a part of him, Nicole. Share as much of his life as you can. Make him want only what you can give him. He'll realize that his life is with you. I did." She smiled over at her husband. "And besides, Xavier *is* in love with you. He may not say it, but it's in his eyes, the subtle touches he gives you. Nicole, sometimes people are unable for whatever reason to say the words. Watch their actions. In them you will discover the truth."

Alone at home Nicole pondered her mother's words, understanding their meaning. Xavier's gallant return the night of her distress and his gentle handling of her fragile emotions that next morning could constitute love. His concern when she lost her job could constitute love. His agitation when she mentioned moving to Atlanta could constitute love. Was it possible that he loved her despite his denial? Deciding to take her mother's advice, Nicole planned to keep her eyes open. If Xavier Ramón was demonstrating his love she didn't want to miss one thing.

CHAPTER 15

Nicole found herself unprepared as the new school year resumed. Her life was in such chaos that she felt as though she was performing a delicate balancing act. Between the needs of her students, her relationship with Xavier, and now her mother and siblings, Nicole was a bundle of nerves. The last couple of weeks had been trying and a drain on her spirits. The relationship with her mother and siblings was gradually taking shape, but it was more work than Nicole could ever have imagined. And through it all, Xavier had been right by her side offering his support and wisdom. She had found great comfort in his presence and relied on his support greatly. Yet through it all, they had found very little time simply to focus on themselves and their relationship.

Across town Xavier was missing Nicole like crazy. He missed their times together taking in a movie or simply talking over coffee. Neither of their schedules allowed for much free time, and with school resuming and her newfound family, Nicole's emotions were stretched to the limit. He had tried to be patient and considerate of this new relationship, but being a constant at her side during this ordeal and watching the emotional toll it was taking on her state of mind, he knew he had to do something. Deciding she needed a night out on the town where she focused on no one but Nicole, Xavier made the necessary arrangements. He called Nicole to inform her of the special evening he was planning.

"Hi, sweetheart."

"Hi," Nicole greeted him drowsily.

"Were you sleep?"

Smiling wickedly to herself as she thought about the erotic dream she had awakened from, she responded, "Catnapping."

"Are you sure? You sound...distracted."

Nicole laughed in that sultry alto resonance which fired Xavier's blood. She was unaware of the firestorm she was causing on the other end of the telephone line. "Maybe a little. I was having a dream about you, or rather us." She didn't elaborate on purpose.

"From the sound of things it must have been one hell of a dream."

Intentionally not revealing any more details, Nicole steered the conversation away from her dream. "Did you call for something specific?"

"Okay, I get the hint," he laughed. "As a matter of fact I did. Tomorrow night at seven o'clock, I'm going to whisk you away for an evening of magic, so wear something pretty."

"What's your favorite color?" Nicole asked seductively, still in the throes of her dream.

Xavier laughed, delighted that she would want to please him. "My favorite color is blue, but on you I like red, that incredible gold you wore the first time we met, and lavender. The more I think about it, I think I prefer lavender."

Nicole was charmed by his attention to her wardrobe color scheme, and amazed that he actually knew the difference between lavender and purple. She had never met a man quite like him. Thinking about his choices she knew immediately what she would wear. "Great, I'll see you tomorrow night."

"I can't wait. Goodnight."

Friday night Nicole stood before the mirror closely examining herself. She wore her dark tresses loosely curled and free. Dressed in a lavender shimmering, stretch lace, empire dress with spaghetti straps, and deep V-neck, she tugged at the hem of the dress stopping above her knees. Correction, high on her thighs to be exact. The ultra sheer brown hose enhanced the beauty of her legs as did the lavender ankle strap slings she wore. Examining herself, she decided the shoes were worth every penny for the full effect. Tonight she wanted to throw her doubts and fears away. She wanted to rejoice in being a woman, and feel and look feminine, and in the process if she reminded Xavier of what he had been missing, so be it.

Inside the dark interior of the Navigator, Xavier was quite hopeful for the evening. Nicole had been on his mind all week. The evening he had planned for them would be special, one he hoped she would treasure for years to come.

Punctually at seven o'clock he rang the bell to Nicole's home. As the door opened, Xavier was stunned by Nicole's beauty. He allowed his starving eyes to feast on her loveliness, registering the color of her dress. It was lavender and she had worn it just for him. Despite her petite size, she was more woman than he had encountered in years. Their ten-year age difference was of no significance. She was all the woman he needed.

Tonight she was a study in refinement. She made a man believe he could look all day long, but question whether he could actually touch. Moving past her as he crossed the threshold, he caught a whiff of her perfume. It was soft and alluring, yet not overpowering. Much like the woman wearing it.

When Nicole closed the door and turned back to face him, he presented her with a bouquet of lavender roses.

"Xavier, they're beautiful," Nicole exclaimed in awe. "Where in the world did you find lavender roses?"

"They're called Blue Girl, and a friend's wife grows them. I thought it was a real possibility that you would be wearing something in the shade."

"You didn't have to do this." She spoke with excitement as she accepted the bouquet, taking a whiff of their fragrance. It was a special little treat which went a long way.

Still under her spell as he watched her inhale the fragrant blossoms and offer her thanks, Xavier was truly humbled. Such a simple gift had made her happy. She had no idea of the effect she was having on him. She looked angelic as she stood quietly returning his smile.

"You look stunning, baby."

"Thank you," she whispered, slightly embarrassed by the attention. "You're quite handsome yourself, Major. I compliment your taste in clothing tonight" She smiled admiringly at his well-dressed figure. He wore a black Armani suit with a purple shirt. The purple, yellow, and white silk tie with intricate black designs completed the look. His now familiar cologne caused her stomach to flutter with excitement.

Xavier flashed that roguish grin. "A man likes to complement his lady."

Nicole's eyebrows shot up on hearing those words. She liked the sound of them, but did she dare hope for more? "Am I your lady, Major?" The piercing look she gave Xavier was hot and potentially dangerous.

Xavier liked the fire he saw smoldering within the golden brown eyes. Wrapping an arm around Nicole's narrow waist, he drew her close to his hard body. He placed feather soft kisses down the column of her exposed neck as he inhaled her delicate scent. At her diamond-studded ear he whispered, "Your body says yes."

And he wasn't lying. Her body had gone all soft and pliant against him. Her nipples were the only hard points on her body and they saluted his declaration.

When she pulled her head slightly away so that she could meet his eyes, Xavier claimed her warm lips. Finally breaking the kiss because they both required air, he confessed. "I've wanted you since the first night we met. I knew I had to have you."

His words, though meant as a compliment, left Nicole a little let down. She snuggled closer within the warmth of his arms. She wanted more than anything to belong to this man. She wanted to carry his name as well as his babies. With that thought her heart did a quick palpitation before finding its normal rhythm. She eased out of his arms and looked lovingly into his caramel brown face.

"I better put my roses in a vase. I'll be right back," she called over her shoulder, rushing to place distance between them.

In the kitchen she went immediately to the cabinet beneath the sink. She retrieved a crystal vase filling it with water. She allowed her mind to wander. The man made her feel so much. He made her wish for things that she had always thought were impossible to have. She was suddenly overcome with fear and doubt What if Xavier never said he loved her? He had only recently confessed to deeper feelings. There was a dramatic difference between the two, she silently acknowledged. Just as she turned off the water and spun around to arrange the roses, she spotted Xavier lounging in the doorway silently observing her. She met his eyes. Time stretched on without either one of them saying a word.

"Why do you do that?"

"Do what?"

"Watch me so intensely that I swear I can feel each stroke of your eyes." She turned to face him head-on.

Xavier walked to stand mere inches from her. Looking down into the open expression of her face, he realized that he could tell only the truth. "Because what I feel for you, is that intense," he whispered, fingering the silky texture of her hair.

Nicole exhaled a nervous breath as she digested his words. When she turned her attention back to arranging the roses, she could feel Xavier to her back. The heat from his body warmed the goose-bumped flesh of her arms. He possessed magnetism unlike any she had ever encountered before. Was its strength due to the recent absence of his presence, or the sudden desire to weaken to its force?

"We should be going," she commented, completing her task.

Cloaked within the intimacy of the dark vehicle, Nicole sat quietly in the passenger seat, trying to determine their destination. They were now on I-10 headed west. From the driver's seat Xavier was quite aware of the frustrated expression marring Nicole's lovely face. He could visualize the wheels turning inside her intelligent mind trying to guess where they were spending the evening. He wondered how long it would be before she gave in and asked.

Xavier didn't have to wait long. As they crossed the state line into Louisiana, Nicole couldn't take the suspense any longer. "Xavier, where exactly are we going for dinner?"

"We're doing more than having a mere dinner. I promised you an evening to remember, and my hometown of New Orleans is just the city for such a feat."

Nicole was astonished by what she was hearing. She turned in her seat staring wide-eyed at Xavier. "New Orleans? Are you serious? Xavier, you offered dinner, but I never expected anything on this scale."

"That's good isn't it? It makes my surprise that much more special. Any man could take you to dinner, baby, but I wanted to create magic this evening, and New Orleans is known for its mystical wonders."

He took her small hand within his and brought it to his lips. He nibbled on her knuckles before applying a light kiss. Her hand was warm and soft. He was overwhelmed by the strong desire to shelter and protect this woman.

As Xavier exited the interstate, Nicole took in all the sights of New Orleans' nightlife. He maneuvered the large vehicle through the narrow streets of the French Quarter, turning into a private drive off Royal Street, then switched off the ignition. Quickly exiting the car, he came around the front of the vehicle to assist Nicole in getting out. She grabbed her satin handbag and accepted his assistance. He threaded her arm through his as he led the way along the sidewalk to a private entrance of Claude's. Just inside, a well-dressed Creole man in his early forties greeted them. It was obvious by the exchange of greetings that this man who was introduced as Claude Renault was a close friend of Xavier's. Smiling pleasantly as she was introduced, Nicole felt suddenly undressed as Claude turned his provocative gaze upon her. He possessed as strong and confident a demeanor as Xavier. There was a hint of raw power and lethalness underneath his fine clothing. She ventured a guess that he too had served time in the military.

"It's a pleasure to meet you, Mr. Renault."

"The pleasure is all mine, mademoiselle." His dark roving eyes roamed the length of her body. "Xavier always did have excellent taste in women." This statement was directed at Nicole. And to Xavier he commented, "And this time my friend, you have outdone yourself. She's exquisite. Treasure the love I see within her eyes, and she will never let you down."

The men exchanged knowing glances between them. Xavier hoped Renault's predictions were correct. He professed to possess his grandmother's second-sight ability. Thinking back on the night that he met Monique, it had been Renault who wasn't impressed by her beauty. He kept speaking of *looking into the soul*. Xavier had taken it for gibberish. If only he had listened.

Uncomfortable with the disclosure of her emotions by this friend of Xavier's, Nicole lowered her lashes. When she looked into his extremely dark eyes she sensed a power searching her soul. It was a strange, unusual feeling, and the intelligent side of her chalked it up to being in the mystical city. Feeling Xavier's hand stroking the arm laced with his, she glanced up, meeting his eyes. They seemed to know exactly what she was experiencing. Looking back at Mr. Renault who stood calmly watching her wrestling with the notion of his talent, she suddenly relaxed. She recognized him as a friend, to which he responded with a nod.

Xavier grew annoyed as his friend's gaze continued to linger on Nicole. "I have no intention of allowing this woman to get away, or to be wooed away by some other man." His deep baritone voice warned Claude to back off. If it weren't for the amusement lighting his eyes, Nicole would have thought he was seriously angry. However, the sound of Claude's robust laughter implied that these two were used to these masculine games.

Claude took the hint and directed them upstairs to a secluded table in the corner of the wrought iron enclosed balcony. White linen draped tables overlooked the lively streets of the French Quarter. Fine china and crystal shimmered on the candlelit tables. Accepting the chair Claude pulled out for her, Nicole felt as though she had stepped into a fairy tale, and Xavier was her prince.

"Does this meet with your approval, my friend?" Claude asked as Xavier took his seat opposite Nicole.

"Excellent as usual, thanks."

"Tonight I have prepared a special feast for you both. I'll have your chilled ginger ale and salad delivered. Then I will personally bring out your meal." With that said he quickly disappeared inside the restaurant.

"Claude knows that you don't partake of spirits."

"Outside of Keith, Claude is my closest friend. We served together."

"I knew he was prior military. He has this lethalness about him," she said with an exuberance Xavier found charming.

"You're very observant. He was a member of special operations. Most women either find him irresistible or intimidating. Do I dare guess which one you found him to be?"

Nicole smiled coyly while she pretended to ponder the question. "At first I found him to be intimidating. I experienced this weird sensation of having my soul searched. Then I got the impression that you were telling me that he's some sort of mind reader."

"I was. He claims to be. He says his grandmother possessed the ability of second sight."

"Do you believe him?"

"Was his observation of you correct?" Xavier challenged Nicole. His eyes twinkled with mischief. He was enjoying watching her squirm.

Not to be outdone, Nicole smiled sweetly, then responded. "Now is a very good time to plead the fifth."

"Oh no, not that amendment!"

They shared a moment of companionable laughter while they waited for their drinks. There were only four couples dining on the balcony tonight. The green plants and ferns gracing the balcony and ceiling offered each table a sense of privacy. Meeting Xavier's expectant expression, she smiled excitedly. He had definitely made this evening one she wouldn't forget.

"This is more than I ever expected, Xavier. I've only dreamed of places like this. Thank you for keeping your word. Tonight truly is special."

Their salads and drinks were brought out as promised. Then later Claude served their special entree. A mouth watering shrimp Creole was placed before them. Claude described the dish of Gulf shrimp simmered in a spicy tomato sauce with Creole vegetables served over rice. The required basket of crusty French bread was also placed on the table. Their glasses were topped off before he disappeared once more.

"My goodness, everything smells and looks so wonderful, I almost hate to ruin it."

"Eat up, sweetheart. This is the best shrimp Creole in the Quarter."

Following his lead, Nicole took her first forkful, savoring the spices. Between the good conversation and romantic atmosphere, she soon discovered that she had eaten every tantalizing morsel. She declined Claude's offer of dessert, instead opting for coffee. She glanced across the table into Xavier's warm eyes and got the distinct impression that she was on the dessert menu. Only Claude's knowing laughter caused them to glance away.

"Xavier! I thought it was you," a rapid-fire feminine voice spoke from behind Nicole.

"Hi Michele, Walter." Xavier stood, embracing the tall curvaceous woman. He shook hands with the thick muscular man accompanying her. "Hey, you two, have a seat," he commanded.

"Only if your date doesn't mind our intruding?" The woman turned her inquisitive gaze on Nicole.

"Please join us." Nicole extended the invitation aware that the woman named Michele was taking a keen interest in her. Reciprocating, she examined the woman holding Xavier's hand possessively. She was a pretty woman in her late thirties with shoulder-length hair. Her smile was open and friendly, but Nicole felt her interest was much too intense.

"Nicole Edwards, I'd like to introduce my sister Michele, and my brother-in-law Walter Harrison."

So that accounted for the woman's interest. She was Xavier's sister and no doubt curious about the woman her brother was dating. "It's a pleasure to meet you both," Nicole responded. She was genuinely pleased to meet them and smiled warmly. She stole a quick glance in Xavier's direction and noticed his broad smile.

Michele noticed her younger brother's smile as well. It was obvious from the heated intensity that something more than dinner was happening between him and this woman. Good for him. It was about time he got over that selfish witch. She focused her attention on Nicole, taking in her exotic features. She was a striking young woman. Feeding her curiosity and following the family trait of directness, she began firing one question after the other.

Laughing because he could see the wheels turning inside his wife's head, Walter called a halt to the bombardment. "Whoa baby, allow the people to answer."

"I'm sorry, but it's just wonderful to see my brother dating again." Michele spoke sincerely from the heart. "So what do you do for a living, Nicole? Are you in the military too?"

"No, I'm not. I'm actually an elementary school teacher."

"A teacher," Michele replied, surprised. The woman's looks were too glamorous for a mere teacher. "You're joking right? No teacher I ever had looked like you."

"That's exactly what I told her." Xavier nodded his head in Nicole's direction to make his point.

"Xavier, that was a long time ago. Things have changed considerably since those days." Nicole smiled impishly, completely relaxed in the company of his family.

"You'll pay for that later," Xavier declared, then burst out laughing. His rich baritone engulfed the table and its occupants.

Michele absorbed the harmonious exchange between the two, noticing how comfortable they were with the obvious age difference. She had so many questions wandering around inside her head she didn't know which to ask first.

So, she simply jumped in and fired off another question. "So how did the two of you meet?" She noticed the look Nicole exchanged with Xavier. These two obviously had been seeing each other long enough to develop the silent communication lovers shared. This was getting more interesting by the moment, she thought.

"Our best friends, Keith and Gina Thibodeaux, introduced us."

"Keith did this? Just wait until I see him. It's so romantic," she squealed with delight. "Obviously it worked." Michele smiled brightly, pleased by the fact. Her brother hadn't been seriously involved with a woman since that Monique. She was sure he had romantic liaisons like most men, but it was nice to see him truly involved with a woman. Observing Nicole closely, she couldn't determine her age. From appearance she knew the lady was young, but her demeanor suggested maturity. "Nicole, how old are you?"

Xavier and Walter sat back and enjoyed the excitement they saw infuse Michele. She had always been the inquisitive one. Maybe that contributed to her success as a lawyer. Xavier knew she was surprised to see him out on the town with someone. It wasn't his usual behavior since his disastrous marriage had ended. No doubt the moment she got home this evening she would be on the telephone informing their mother of tonight's events.

"I don't believe *Miss-I'm-Never-Telling-My-Age,* is actually asking such a personal question," Xavier threw in.

"Oh shut up Xavier, this is between Nicole and me. And by the way, you know I'm thirty-seven." She stuck out her tongue playfully.

Nicole had never laughed as much as she did this night. It was delightful to watch the interplay between brother and sister. It was obvious they loved each other, and it was also obvious that Walter loved his wife. He and Xavier appeared to have a close relationship as well. Nicole couldn't help wondering how she would fit in with his family.

"I'm twenty-five and quite legal." Nicole flashed Xavier a knowing smile, recalling the night she had stated those exact words to him.

They had tuned the others out. Xavier was returning Nicole's smoldering stare. They were in that special place that they had only recently discovered since the picnic. In it only they existed.

Michele loved the vibes she was receiving from these two. There was magic between them and she couldn't wait to inform their mother. "Does Mom know you're in town?"

"No, she doesn't. We came over for dinner and a romantic evening *alone.*"

Throwing her hands up, Michele pushed back her chair and stood. "Hey little brother, I can take a hint." She smiled over at Xavier who also stood. "Come on, honey, let's leave the love birds alone."

Nicole now stood as well. "It was a pleasure meeting you both," she stated sincerely as she met Michele's eyes.

"It was a pleasure meeting you too, Nicole." On second thought, she drew Nicole into a warm embrace. "Oh, come here. Be good to my brother," she whispered so only Nicole could hear.

"I will," Nicole whispered back.

CHAPTER 16

Xavier took care of the bill after Michele and Walter said their good-byes. Then he escorted Nicole out the way they had entered. But instead of going back to the vehicle as she expected, he led her to a waiting authentic mule-drawn carriage. There he assisted her into the carriage and then took a seat beside her. He drew her body close, with an arm around her shoulders. As the mule-drawn carriage slowly took to the streets of the French Quarter, Xavier gave Nicole a personal tour of the historic area. His warm breath caressed her ear as he snuggled close, pointing out the jazz haunts, museums, and famous buildings. At one point during the ride Xavier and Nicole shared a passionate kiss.

They had been snuggled so closely together, that when they turned their heads simultaneously to look at the other, their mouths were mere inches apart. The words being spoken were no longer of importance. Xavier took Nicole's cleft chin within his thumb and finger, lifting it ever so slightly. Then he lowered his thirsty lips to her moist mouth. The kiss began as a feather-light brush but grew into something more profound. Tasting the remnants of coffee on Nicole's lips, Xavier craved more of her. He requested entry with a sweep of his tongue and was rewarded by the parting of lips. The world around them was forgotten. Only what they were sharing and experiencing existed. Finally breaking the kiss as the carriage brought them back to their starting point, Xavier and Nicole slowly separated. She smiled shyly as Xavier assisted her down with an arm around her waist. As they walked back toward the car she laid her head against his shoulder, savoring the evening. Tonight had indeed been an evening to remember.

Back inside the vehicle Xavier and Nicole fastened their seat belts, then shared a brief kiss before he pulled back into traffic. He drove them in the opposite direction of the interstate. He headed to the outskirts of New Orleans. The city lights were gradually being left behind as they drove along the tree-shrouded highway. The homes they passed sat a great distance from the road. They became fewer in number, and in some instances could barely be seen. Nicole rode silently, trying to make out the scenery in the dark. She wondered where Xavier was taking her now.

As he turned off the main highway onto a single lane road, she just barely made out the wooden sign at the corner, which read Willow Bayou. He continued to drive further into the dark, heavily wooded area, which seemed to go on forever. Nicole grew slightly anxious. She wasn't worried that he would do her harm, but being so far back in the middle of nowhere at night was unsettling. She couldn't help asking if he knew where he was going.

"Relax, we aren't lost." Xavier chuckled softly and took hold of Nicole's hand.

So she sat back and did as instructed, continuing to watch the trees pass by. Then within ten minutes of asking her question she spotted lights just up ahead. As they rounded a bend in the road the trees gradually receded and a beautiful French Creole style home stood guard. Spotlighted in the glow of floodlights, a large, two-story white wood frame house loomed as testament to a bygone era. It sat in the middle of a lush green lawn flanked by live oaks. Wooden wraparound verandahs encompassed both floors of the house. Two chimney stacks could be seen on opposite sides of the house. Its graceful beauty conjured up memories of old movies. Nicole eased forward in her seat and took in the majestic view. It was truly magnificent.

Xavier sat in the driver's seat enjoying Nicole's response to his home. Somehow he had instinctively known that she would appreciate its beauty. Her golden brown eyes danced like those of a child on Christmas morning. He was pleased with his decision to share it with her. As he unfastened his seat belt, it was all he could do to keep Nicole from running off without him. By the time he exited the vehicle she was already standing in front of the Navigator. He joined her and enjoyed the view himself. It was one he never grew tired of.

"Whose home is this?" Nicole asked in a whisper, as though afraid to wake the past.

"It's mine. My grandmother left it to me," he replied in the same hushed tone.

"It's beautiful, Xavier." Those were the only words she could think of to describe it at the moment. From Carmen she had learned about his privileged life, but nothing had prepared her for this.

"Willow Bayou has been in the family for generations. My grandmother knew how much I loved coming here as a child and later as an adult. It was a wonderful gift."

Nicole glanced over at the man speaking with so much love and tenderness in his voice, realizing that she had yet again discovered another side of his multifaceted personality.

She threaded her fingers through his, squeezing gently. "Your grandmother obviously loved you a great deal."

He smiled, remembering the barely five-foot woman everyone called Miss Willow. "She loved us all. But you know I think she knew I loved this place as much as she did."

"I can see why."

With a light tug to her hand, Xavier led the way to the front door.

"Come on, let's go inside."

Xavier fitted the key into the heavy wooden door. The alarm warning beeped as he opened the door. He swiftly entered the code to silence the alarm. With a sweep of his hand to the right, he flipped the overhead light switch on, then quickly stepped aside to allow Nicole to enter.

Following Xavier through the doorway, Nicole was overcome by the simple beauty of the place. Cherrywood French Provincial furniture decorated the living and dining room. The upholstery was in a rich gold and ivory paisley pattern. Heavy gold cascading drapes covered the four windows in the room. The crystal light fixture in the center of the room sparkled brightly from six teardrop sconces. The walls were painted antique white and displayed several murals depicting Louisiana scenes with African-American subjects. The high gloss hardwood floors had been left bare, allowing their natural beauty to shine through.

As they walked throughout the house Xavier explained the extensive restoration work he had accomplished after inheriting it from his grandmother. He also informed her of the modern conveniences he'd had installed in the home to make it livable by today's standards. And true to his words, the kitchen housed all the modern appliances. Central heat and air had been installed as well. They took the stairs to the second landing and entered a narrow hallway. Two spacious rooms sat on each side, and a bathroom sat just opposite the staircase.

Xavier explained that two of the rooms had yet to be decorated. He had instead focused his attention on the master suite and Ryan's room. Nicole followed him into the first room to the right. He opened the door to reveal a child's wonderland. Cars, trains, blocks, and more toys than she had ever seen in one child's room were stored on a wooden bookcase. An assortment of model planes hung from the ceiling. The room contained twin beds covered in an aviation theme. A great deal of love had been poured into decorating this room, and even without asking she knew Xavier had done it himself.

Xavier opened the door to the master suite across the hall. Nicole knew that this was his room, and a sudden tingling sensation danced down her spine. Stepping inside, the first thing that caught her attention was the queen size sleigh bed in a rich mahogany finish. It was covered with a simple checkered navy blue and white comforter and pillow shams. On the floor beside the bed was a blue braided rug. A leather recliner in blue as well sat by the large double windows overlooking the side of the property. Layers and layers of white gauzy sheers shielded the windows. French doors opposite the bed led out onto the upstairs verandah, and they too were covered in the gauzy fabric. Xavier explained that during the early period the doors would be left open in the summer for ventilation. Each bedroom, he explained, opened out onto the verandah for this reason. A ceiling fan made of traditional cane blades assisted in cooling the room as well. A huge palm plant occupied a corner of the room. The look was one of simplicity and comfort.

Xavier unlocked the French doors and walked out onto the verandah. Nicole quietly followed behind him to stand on his right overlooking the grounds, which were bathed in moonlight. She heard the sound of rushing water in the distance.

"How close are you to the water?"

"The bayou runs just at the edge of the grounds. The aged oaks shroud it at night, but during the daytime you can see it clearly. The view is awesome and the sound of the rushing water is soothing and relaxing."

They stood in the dark of night absorbing the night sounds of crickets and frogs performing a late night sere-nade. Xavier slid behind Nicole, wrapping her within his comforting arms. She snuggled closer seeking his warmth. It felt so right, the two them in this enchanted place alone with only their blossoming feelings. After quiet minutes slipped away, Xavier placed a brief kiss in the bend of Nicole's perfumed neck. He inhaled the delicate fragrance he now associated with her. She sighed from his touch and tilted her head further to the left giving him better access to her neck. Xavier heeded the invitation and planted a succes-sion of kisses along the length of her neck and shoulder. His hands caressed the flat planes of Nicole's stomach as she leaned back against him.

The warmth from his lips and hands were causing the butterflies to take flight within Nicole's stomach. She knew she should pull away from the arousing heat his body was emitting, yet she couldn't. Helplessly, she melted with each magical touch of his hands as they swirled and dipped along her abdomen. She found herself trying to anticipate their next movement, so that she could have her most sensitive flesh present for the caress. As she responded to his sensual torture, her hips brushed and caressed against Xavier. It wasn't long before she discovered his excitement. She was pleased to know that she wasn't the only one being affected by their closeness.

Xavier grilled his teeth, with each sway of Nicole's sweet backside against his now engorged flesh. He was aching to satisfy his hunger. As he allowed his hands to stray higher, closer to Nicole's breasts, he listened to the increase in her breathing. She was burning with desire and he knew instinctively that they would be combustible when they came together. He glided a large hand from the underside of her abdomen to the peak of her breast, and experienced the hardening of her nipple beneath his caress. And at the moment of contact Nicole gasped his name.

"Tell me to stop," Xavier dared her to respond with a nibble on her sensitive earlobe. The touch of his mouth almost caused her to crumple.

"I can't" Nicole's voice was just a breath.

That was all the encouragement Xavier needed. His skilled hands searched and explored more of her lush body. A large hand skimmed her abdomen, then went lower. Nicole would have collapsed that time for sure if it hadn't been for his supporting arm around her waist. Her response to his touch was incredible and so inspiring. And so they stood in the dark of night on the verandah.

Nicole was on fire. Every touch of Xavier's large hands were a sweet torture. He taunted with a caress here and there while his skilled mouth worshipped her ear, neck, and shoulders. She ached for his touch, but was too shy to ask for what she really wanted. As his hands explored more, she prayed that it would lead to fulfilling her wish. But it didn't. Xavier just continued with his torturous touch and she purred and withered from it. She had never known such wonders of the human hand before. She needed to touch him as he was touching her, but she didn't dare move from this position. So instead she reached behind her to stroke his muscled thighs. He jumped from the initial contact, surprised by the sudden caress.

He groaned. "Don't do that, baby." His words came out in a rush.

"I want to touch you as well," she boldly said, reaching for another caress. This time she found her mark and Xavier's knees buckled. She too possessed the power to weaken knees. A tiny ripple surged through her body at this newfound knowledge.

"Nic...sweetheart...you've got to stop," he croaked, but didn't move away from her stimulating touch.

Nicole's confidence grew with each touch and subsequent moan. Then she sensed a change.

She had pushed him far enough. He would burst or die; he wasn't sure which first, if he didn't make love to her. Grasping her shoulders he spun her around, then claimed her mouth for a thorough kiss. Her shocked breath was inhaled by his as he claimed her sweet lips. His hands busily mapped her round hips before drawing her hard against him. He knew there would be no turning back for them tonight.

With little effort Xavier had Nicole up in his arms with her legs wrapped around his waist A hand was buried in the thickness of her now mussed hair as he kissed her feverishly. Seating her on the railing of the verandah, he kissed his way down the length of her neck, then pushed the thin straps of her dress aside and down. He took a moment to enjoy the view of her dark chocolate breasts. He noticed she had a dark tantalizing mole on her left breast, and that her nipples were puckered and pebbled. She was a nice handful despite her petite size. To confirm his thought, he squeezed her lushness gently, drawing forth a small whimper from Nicole.

"Liked that, did you?" He claimed a chocolate nipple as though it was his only source of nourishment He nipped, licked, sucked, and tugged the dark peak. All the while Nicole pressed his head closer to her breast.

She had never experienced anything so sweet and painful all at the same time before. With each assault of his mouth, Nicole let loose a moan as pleasure rippled through her body. She was so lost in the haze of passion that it took her a moment to realize that Xavier was lifting her once more. This time he carried her back through the French doors and toward the bed. Searching Nicole's now passion-dark eyes, Xavier wanted Nicole in the worst possible way. Every touch and response said that she wanted him too, but he had to hear her say the words. He looked into her eyes as his hand caressed the side of her face. He demanded an answer.

"Tell me what you want."

At first Nicole had thought he was going to stop, and her heart cried out *no*. But now on hearing his request she knew what he needed. Returning his heated gaze, she tightened her legs ever so slightly around his waist, and was rewarded by a low, pleasurable moan.

"Make love to me."

No spoken words had ever been sweeter to his ears. Xavier kissed Nicole playfully. He slid his tongue across her lips, but held back each time she tried to draw him into her mouth. He taunted the corners of her mouth. Flicked in and out without being captured. Then he grew hungry for a taste of her. He grasped the back of her head and fitted his mouth to hers, kissing her deeply. Finally separating, he then proceeded to lay Nicole across the bed.

She stretched like a contented feline, boldly watching as Xavier tore away his jacket, then removed his tie and shirt. He revealed that broad muscled chest she still had fantasies about. His washboard abs gave way to narrow, masculine hips. She reached out to touch him and marveled at the heat and firmness of his body. As she continued to lie there watching him undress, Xavier removed his shoes and socks, then confidently stripped away the remainder of his clothing. On powerful muscled legs he stood before her proud and nude. A flash of heat swept through her body as she allowed her eyes to admire his bountiful maleness.

Xavier closely watched as Nicole examined his body. He wanted her to become comfortable with the male form, especially suspecting that this was all new to her. Looking deeply into her eyes he sensed apprehension, but eagerness as well. Both were normal responses and so he relaxed as she continued to admire his body.

Nicole knew what Xavier was doing and she appreciated it more than he could know. Even in his highly aroused state, he thought of her well being. She wasn't afraid of him, but witnessing his cautiousness, she decided she would have to show him. Easing off the bed she met his eyes, which watched her every movement. She stepped out of her shoes boldly. Then she reached under the hem of her dress and located the lace trimmed top of her thigh high. The sheer covering was removed with slow and deliberate hip action. She held it before her and then dramatically allowed it to billow to the floor. Reaching for the second one, she eased down onto the edge of the bed and raised her shapely leg before him. She arched it just so. Gently, she pulled down the second sheer nylon. It too billowed to the floor. Nicole rose from the bed and continued her little strip tease. Her smile was wicked and sultry as she began shimmying out of the lace dress. She stood before him clad in lilac lace panties and nothing else. She hadn't worn a bra. Growing more confident, she fingered the rim of her panties, watching as Xavier's passion-glazed eyes followed along. She was as hot and bothered as he.

No more! He couldn't take another moment of this sweet torture. His engorged flesh was saluting Nicole's efforts but demanding relief as well. With lightening speed he swept her hands aside, then stripped the flimsy garment away from her body. And what he saw nearly pushed him over the edge. He had known she was beautiful with a body to please. However, what he didn't know was that she was the epitome of perfection, and designed to make a man weak with desire.

"You're gorgeous." Those were the only words he could think of to describe her feminine beauty.

His words humbled her, and she suddenly felt shy under his heated gaze. They came together naturally, continuing to entice and stimulate the other. Xavier discovered where and how Nicole liked to be caressed and taught her his own pleasure zones. He paused to protect them before laying claim to her. The union was passionate and tender as Xavier took his time loving her. She was small and inexperienced so he gentled his touch until she was accepting, then they moved as one to the age-old rhythm of lovers. Higher and higher they climbed. And when they reached the pinnacle it was Nicole who screamed and slowly descended from heaven. But it was Xavier who fell fast and hard into hell.

He held Nicole afterwards, shaken by what they had just shared. Sex had never been like that, and then he thought maybe that was because what he and Nicole shared wasn't just sex. She had asked him to make love to her and he knew now that he had, with all that he was physically and spiritually. And for the first time in his life he was scared to death. He wanted to run, but knew he couldn't because he *did* love her. It was actually the first time he had allowed himself to use the words. He knew he had to slow things down. When he made a decision about their future, he had to be thinking clearly.

Nicole lay curled beside Xavier. She was aware of the turmoil inside of him and squeezed her eyes shut, blocking out his confusion. She wanted to bask in the joy and pleasure she had found within his arms. It had been all that she could do not to scream out her love for him. She was glad that she hadn't, because she now knew for sure that he didn't reciprocate her feelings. Maybe he hadn't enjoyed it. Maybe she was a failure at making love. *Making love,* those had been her words. To Xavier she suspected it was only sex. He hadn't claimed to love her she reminded herself. He had only said he cared. At this point she wasn't even sure of that any more. As he left the bed and went out onto the verandah, Nicole curled up in a fetal position. Maybe this had happened too soon. She drifted to sleep worrying about what tomorrow would bring.

Xavier stood just outside the door on the verandah. He inhaled the fragrant scent of honeysuckle, finding peace in the familiar perfume. He could hear Nicole's soft snore. It too gave him pleasure, as well as heartache, because he knew that he had done her a disservice. She had lain against him, waiting for some sign of encouragement that the experience had pleased him. He had said nothing. He had been too caught up in his own insecurities to pay attention to Nicole's.

Xavier returned to the bedroom and slid in bed beside Nicole. He observed her in sleep. She loved him. She hadn't said the words, but it was in her eyes and her loving response to his touch. Could he trust her love? Could he trust his own for her? He didn't have the answers readily available, and so he too drifted off to sleep.

The next morning Xavier awakened before Nicole. He wasn't ready to face her just yet. He had spent the majority of the night contemplating his feelings. There was no denying that last night had exceeded his every expectation. He and Nicole had fit so perfectly together. She had been all he desired within his arms, but could he trust his feelings?

He stood over her sleeping form admiring the tantalizing image of her pillow-sprawled hair. He wanted to crawl back into bed beside her and lose himself within her body once more. But he didn't. He instead tiptoed out of the bedroom to use the bathroom in the hallway, because he was afraid that the sound of the shower in the master bedroom would awaken Nicole. He wasn't quite ready to face her. He needed a couple of minutes alone.

Under the warm spray of the shower his body rose ready as memories of last night flashed across his mind. Nicole had been so responsive to his touch and in synch with his needs. She had held nothing back during their lovemaking and it frightened him, because he too had given his all. The rewards had been bountiful. His climax had been instant and earth shattering. He had responded like an inexperienced lover, going up in flames like dry brittle leaves.

He turned off the shower and toweled himself dry. Wrapping the towel around his hips, he left the bathroom. In the empty room beside the master suite he stored boxes of clothing. Rummaging through a box marked dresser, he found jeans and a T-shirt. Within minutes he was dressed and headed downstairs. He entered the kitchen craving a cup of coffee. While he waited for the coffee maker to brew, he drew the kitchen curtain back, admiring the bright sunny morning. All should be clearer in the light of day, but it wasn't. He released the curtain with a sigh and began taking inventory of the freezer and cabinets. The caretaker made sure to keep both well stocked. The refrigerator held the necessary essentials. So while the coffee brewed, Xavier began preparing breakfast.

Xavier contemplated his next move while sitting upstairs out on the balcony. He required time away from Nicole to sort out his feelings. He knew he was definitely not harboring any feelings for Monique, yet he was still allowing her devious actions to make him question his judgment. Looking out over the lush green lawn and further to the flowing bayou, he began to relax as an idea came to mind. He would return here to the house alone during the Labor Day weekend and sort out the direction of his life. It was close enough to come home in case of an emergency with Ryan, yet far enough away from Nicole. He decided that the moment he got back to work on Monday he would clear his schedule with anticipation of returning.

He glanced back at the bed where Nicole lay asleep. He felt guilty about last night, but it was too late to change things now. She didn't deserve the cold shoulder that she'd received. When she awakened, he would apologize and try to explain his feelings. He only hoped she was willing to listen and willing to wait until he sorted himself out. He ran his hands over his troubled head. He was tired of thinking. He wanted to go with his emotions, but it just wasn't his life involved in this relationship. It was Ryan's as well and he had to be sure.

Nicole lay in bed watching Xavier's struggle. She had been awake when he eased out of bed earlier, yet said nothing as she sensed his need for privacy. She too had needed to be alone. Last night kept replaying within her mind, and she couldn't figure out what had gone wrong. One moment Xavier had been loving her with a burning passion, then poof—he had shut down. It hurt so badly, yet she was unable to go home where she could allow the tears to flow.

It was her fault, she scolded herself. Why had she allowed herself to believe this man could love her? Because she wanted his love like nothing before, came the swift reply. If she closed her eyes she could capture their essences on the sheets. The exercise brought her agony instead of the pleasure it should have. She felt stupid. She felt hurt. She felt rejected.

Finally unable to lie in bed any longer, she moved to get up, but was halted by the soreness in her limbs. Gingerly she threw her legs over the side of the bed as she searched for her discarded clothes. She found them heaped in the recliner. She hated to put them back on. The thought of returning home in evening clothes made her feel cheap. Or maybe it was Xavier's response to her that made her feel less than worthy.

Nicole was disgusted with her self-pity. She scolded herself. *You have done nothing wrong, except given your heart and body to a man incapable of loving you. Hold your head up and square your shoulders. Never let them see you cry.* She chanted the mantra repeatedly until her spirit was bolstered. Pulling the top sheet free from the bed, she wrapped it around her nude form. She would have to pass by the open balcony doors to collect her clothing from the chair and enter the bathroom. Finally wrapped securely within the sheet, she padded across the floor with the bathroom as her destination. She needed a shower desperately.

Xavier turned as she approached the open doorway. For a moment they said nothing, just stared. Nicole finally managed a weak good morning before continuing to the chair and towards the bathroom. Just as she made it to the bathroom door, Xavier entered the bedroom, stopping just inside the doorway.

I found a shirt and a pair of drawstring shorts I think you should be able to wear. You'll find them folded on the counter in the bathroom."

Nicole looked at him with a blank expression, then glanced in the bathroom, noticing the bundle. "Thanks." She closed the door, leaving him standing in the bedroom.

What did he expect? Xavier chided himself. He had treated her awful last night. As the sound of the shower echoed in the room, his mind was filled with images of Nicole's sweet body dripping wet Tightness in his lower region made him run for the balcony door. Back outside on the verandah, he inhaled deeply, clearing his mind. He returned to the table taking a seat. He glanced at the covered tray, which contained their breakfast of English muffins, scrambled eggs, and ham slices. Orange juice and coffee completed the meal. He hadn't eaten without her. He didn't want to. He wanted to share breakfast and the morning's beauty with Nicole. He wanted to share his life, for that matter, but was too damn scared to do so.

Damn, he was disgusted with himself. He commanded a unit and would lead the men and women of his squadron into any battle courageously, but one petite woman had him scared to death.

In the bathroom Nicole used the toiletries Xavier had placed on the bundle of clothes. It was a thoughtful act, yet she wasn't sure how she was supposed to respond in the light of day. She knew there was no point in thinking about all that they had shared last night. So with her courage and pride in place she left the bathroom. She glanced at the rumpled bed, recalling how it had gotten into that state. Determined to put last night in the past, she walked over, ripping the remaining linen off the bed. She deposited it into the hamper in the bathroom. Then expelling a breath, she slid her expressionless face from childhood into place. Her talent for pretending as though nothing fazed her would be put to the test this morning.

Xavier looked up as Nicole stepped out onto the balcony. She went to stand at the railing taking in the view. It was the same spot he had initiated their love making the night before. She was beautiful. Even in his old button down shirt and baggy shorts, she was gorgeous. Her dark mane was wet from her shower and hung over her left shoulder. He wanted to run his fingers through its thickness.

"Come eat while breakfast is still warm."

"You cooked?" She eyed him suspiciously as she took a seat.

"Yeah, and I even wore an apron." He smiled timidly.

Nicole didn't return the smile or acknowledge the joke. "I didn't notice the table and chairs last night," she said instead, drawing her bare feet up into the chair as she sat down.

"They were here," he responded, remembering what had held their attention last night.

Nicole remembered too but didn't show it. She could sense Xavier watching her closely, searching for something. If he expected her to bring up their lovemaking, he would have a long wait. If it didn't matter to him, she would pretend it didn't matter to her either. She removed the lid covering her plate. "It looks good," she said, digging into her food. She was starving.

Xavier watched as Nicole ate leisurely and never once showed any hint of hurt or anger about his behavior last night. Maybe the night hadn't meant as much to her as it had him. Then he got angry with himself, because he realized what she was doing. When they'd first met she had camouflaged her emotions skillfully, like now. She had strength and pride. He knew she would never admit that she was hurting, and the knowledge made him feel ten times worse.

"Nicole, about last night," he began, but didn't get the chance to finish.

"Maybe we make better friends than lovers. I think we should just forget this ever happened." She looked strong and sure of each word.

Reaching across the table he clasped Nicole's hand, only to watch her slowly withdraw it. "Nic, we *are* lovers and there is no way in hell I can pretend last night didn't happen. It was more than I ever imagined," he stated truthfully. "It couldn't get any better."

Nicole thought how to respond and then decided to approach the situation directly. if that's true, do you care to tell me what's going on inside your head? I know you're itching to get away from me."

He started to deny it, but then thought better of it because he knew Nicole would see the truth. So he said nothing.

Receiving only silence, Nicole looked out over the back lawn, gathering her strength for the answer to the question she had to ask. "You really don't want to feel anything for me do you?"

"No."

"But you do and that bothers you."

Shaking his head from side to side, Xavier released a pent up breath. "Yes."

Exasperated because she was getting no help from Xavier in understanding his emotions, she shouted, "Damn it, tell me what you're feeling." Her fork hit the plate with a clatter.

Xavier took note of Nicole's agitated state. He had witnessed most of her moods, but this was different. She was trying to pull something from him that wasn't ready to be set free, and he resented her. "I'm not ready to talk about it," he shouted.

"Well, that's just too bad Xavier, because I want to discuss it *Now.*" Nicole glared across the table at him. She was beyond angry. She had given her heart to this man, and he refused to share his with her. She knew it would all boil down to Monique in the end. Taking a deep calming breath she asked her next question. "Does your desire to ignore these feelings have anything to do with Monique or is it just me—who I am, where I come from, or something I've done?" Her voice trembled, breaking his heart.

"No, Nicole, none of those things." He shook his head emphasizing the point. "It has to do with me." Even as he voiced the words his mind drifted back to those days with his ex-wife.

"And Monique," Nicole supplied. She watched as the truth was revealed within his eyes. She had been right. She felt like such a fool. Last night she had given herself to him while he still carried feelings for his ex-wife. "Was it Monique or me you had sex with last night?"

"We made love!!! *You* and me, Nicole." He didn't like the sound of what she suggested or the fact that she called what they'd shared sex. It was too special for such a fundamental word. He knew the difference between sex and making love and what they'd shared had definitely been love. He thought to himself that if this were true, why was he running? Then he answered his own question. *Because you're afraid that your judgment isn't what it should be. Your confidence has been shaken.*

"No, we had sex. You have to be in love to make love," she stated with a strength she didn't know she possessed. "Are you *in love* with me?"

A part of him wanted to shout yes and seal it with a kiss. But the cautious side of him wouldn't allow him to confess his true feelings. So he said instead, "Do *you* love me, Nicole?"

Laughing dryly, she shook her head as she noted Xavier hadn't answered her question. "What a joke," Nicole snorted. "What do I know about love, Xavier? You forget the State of Mississippi raised me."

Xavier flinched as though slapped. Nicole's words had hit him hard. "Baby, you know a great deal about love. You give it to my son every day. And last night you shared your love with me." He reached for her.

Pushing away from the table, Nicole rose to her feet and looked down on him. This was truly the last time she would allow someone to toss her love back into her face. However, because she did love him, she would adhere to the boundaries of their agreement and bury her love deep. That too caught her attention. It had been months since they'd decided there was more going on than an agreement, and now here they were back where they'd started. She wanted to go home.

"As I recall, our agreement didn't call for love. So what we shared last night was sex. We really should be getting back home."

Xavier knew she was lying about her feelings for him and was about to say so when they heard car doors. They both looked up, making eye contact. Xavier knew immediately who it was at his front door. Once his mother talked to Michele, who had no doubt informed her of Nicole, she had come over first thing in the morning to investigate for herself. Now was not the best of times. Things were unsettled between him and Nicole. He didn't want outside influences to push her further away from him than he had already done.

"Who can that be?" Nicole asked.

"My guess is my parents. Mom no doubt has talked to Michele and now she has dragged my poor Dad out here to see you for herself."

"But we hadn't made plans to spend the night here."

"That's true, but my mother would take the chance of coming out on the hope of our being here. She got lucky."

"I can't meet your parents looking like I just crawled out of your bed." Nicole looked down at her borrowed clothes with disgust.

"You can, and you did," he stated proudly. He was proud because in Nicole he had found something wonderful. His doubt was within himself, and that's what he had to make Nicole understand.

"Xavier, you're sending mixed signals here," she said angrily.

He got up from the table, then placed a brief kiss on Nicole's pouting lips. "We'll talk later, and by the way, you look adorable. Come on." He took her hand, leading her downstairs.

"I hope your mother thinks I look adorable," she mumbled down the stairs behind him.

CHAPTER 17

Nicole stood on the front verandah beside Xavier as his parents made their way up the long walkway. She took the opportunity to scrutinize Helena Ramón. She was a tall woman, close to five-ten, and regal in stature. She walked proudly with her head high and her shoulders back. She wasn't large in body size, but generously curved and quite appealing for a woman of age. She obviously took very good care of herself. From the porch Nicole recognized the quality of her clothing. A basic Donna Karen soft gray dress graced her body. Black patent leather pumps with medium heels accentuated her shapely, caramel brown legs. Nicole immediately liked her short sculptured hair cut which highlighted the gray peppering her dark auburn hair. From her place on the verandah she was well aware that she too was being scrutinized.

Helena Ramón's gaze zeroed in on the petite sable brown woman standing beside her son. The first thing that she noticed was that she wasn't Xavier's usual tall and leggy type. She didn't even reach his shoulder, but fell somewhere mid-chest. The next detail which caught her attention, was the dark mass of hair hanging over her left shoulder. It was longer than Michele had mentioned. She wondered briefly if that's what had attracted Xavier. He had an eye for beautiful women and Nicole was stunning. Even in her bare feet and oversized man's shirt her beauty could not be diminished. And that's what caused her to worry. Monique had been a beautiful woman as well, but with a heart of stone. As she approached the verandah, she hoped this woman's beauty didn't camouflage a similar heart. Xavier deserved better and she as his mother would see to it that he got it.

Nicole was obviously nervous as she stood beside Xavier clutching his hand, Helena thought to herself. She no doubt knew that it would be difficult to pull the wool over her eyes. This woman, if you could call her that, would no doubt cause her son more pain and grief. Oh, she knew what Michele thought of Nicole, but she, like Xavier, hadn't lived long enough to recognize trouble when it came wrapped within pretty packaging.

They obviously had spent the night together and were surprised to see them so early. But Helena had no plans of missing the opportunity to meet the woman in Xavier's life. Michele believed that there was something serious between the two of them. If that were true, she wanted to see it with her own eyes and make sure the woman was worthy of her son.

As his parents walked up onto the verandah, Xavier embraced them both. First his mother then his father. He was a man unashamed of expressing his feelings for his parents.

"It's good to see you both," Xavier greeted his parents warmly, stepping out of their loving arms.

"Hi baby," Helena Ramón spoke to Xavier, but made eye contact with Nicole. "Hello, you must be Nicole." She extended her manicured hand while her eyes drifted to the uniqueness of Nicole's almond-shaped eyes.

Nicole followed suit. "Yes, I am. It's a pleasure to meet you."

The handshake was surprisingly firm. Their eyes connected and Nicole immediately realized that she was being sized up. Would she be comparing her to Monique? Nicole hoped not. It was bad enough that she had to deal with Xavier's inability to move forward in his life. She prayed his parents would give her an honest chance.

"Good morning son, young lady." Raymond Ramón spoke cheerfully in a rich baritone. He followed his wife of thirty-eight years onto the porch.

"Let me guess. Michele called you last night and told you that she saw us." Xavier initiated the conversation still without formally introducing Nicole. "And you decided that you had to meet the mystery lady for yourself." His eyes danced mischievously as he threw an arm around his mother, drawing her close.

"Don't be a smart mouth, Xavier. Can't a mother visit her son?"

"Oh, is that what you're doing?" He laughed deeply, winking at Nicole who remained silent. "Allow me to do the honors. Mom and Dad, I'd like to introduce Miss Nicole Edwards. Nicole, my parents, Helena and Raymond Ramón."

Nicole had stood on the sidelines watching the exchange between Xavier and his parents. It was obvious that they shared a loving relationship. She also noticed that Xavier was the spitting image of his handsome father, all except for the color of his eyes. The charcoal gray magnetic eyes were inherited from his striking mother.

Raymond Ramón seemed the strong, silent type. In his eyes you could see his love for his wife and son. He felt uncomfortable being there so early in the morning, but no doubt to please his wife he had tagged along. Nicole especially liked the manner in which the men greeted each other. They had embraced without reservations. Nicole knew many men who wouldn't be caught dead embracing their fathers. She never would understand that machismo mindset. When a man could openly express his love for his parents, that made him a special man in her book.

"It's a pleasure to meet you both. Xavier and I were having coffee on the verandah. May I offer you both a cup?"

"That sounds wonderful, Nicole. Why don't I help you in the kitchen?" Helena Ramón seized the opportunity to be alone with her son's friend.

Nicole led the way to the kitchen, acutely aware of Helena Ramón on her left. She felt dowdy dressed as she was in shorts and shirt. This was definitely not the impression she wanted to make on Xavier's parents. She sensed that Mrs. Ramón was protective of her son and was on a mission to discover whether or not she was worthy. Nicole found the situation almost comical because at the moment she wasn't even sure Xavier wanted her.

Nicole entered the kitchen and went immediately to the coffeemaker. She changed the filter, added coffee, then poured water into the reservoir. While she waited for it to brew, she began assembling a tray. She was thankful for Xavier's guided tour last night; otherwise she would be searching blindly for items in front of his mother, prolonging their time together unnecessarily. Cups, saucers, napkins and utensils were arranged. The leftover English muffins and strawberry jam from their breakfast was added to the tray. Once the coffee was ready, she removed the creamer from the refrigerator, adding it and the sugar container. Picking up the tray, she turned to find Mrs. Ramón watching her closely.

Helena Ramón had taken a seat at the kitchen table and silently watched the efficiency of Nicole's movements in the kitchen. It was a definite improvement over Monique, she mused. That woman barely knew the way to the kitchen, let alone what to do once inside, but not Nicole. She appeared quite comfortable performing domestic tasks. As Nicole turned facing her, carrying the tray, she decided now was just as good a time as any to have a little talk with the woman.

"Nicole, I'm not the type to beat around the bush. As you may have noticed, my children have inherited my direct approach. I hope I don't offend you."

"No, ma'am, you're not. I actually prefer that you be direct. According to Xavier it keeps down confusion." She smiled briefly. The tray was returned to the counter. She joined Mrs. Ramón at the table.

"Nicole, I'm concerned by the age difference between you and Xavier. You're a beautiful woman and could have any young man."

"And you want to know why Xavier?" Nicole asked knowingly.

Helena Ramón nodded her head while she waited for an answer.

"Whether I could have any young man is irrelevant. The Thibodeauxs introduced Xavier and me over dinner.

There was an instant attraction, but it was the feeling of having known one another which drew us together."

"But you're so young. I can't imagine what you two would have in common.

Nicole smiled thoughtfully, remembering the first night they'd met. She had revealed her history to Xavier within hours of meeting him, feeling safe and comfortable in his presence.

"Loneliness, heartache, happiness, and love know no age. In each other we have found a safe haven where we can be ourselves. He makes me feel cherished and important I try to reciprocate those feelings. It's difficult to explain, but we work, or at least I hope we do."

In those brief words Helena recognized a woman in love. She also recognized a woman not sure of whether she was loved in return. Helena found Nicole's innocence to be refreshing and just what her son needed.

"Nicole, my son has never before brought a woman to this house as far as I know."

Nicole was stunned by those words. Was Helena Ramón trying to encourage her about their relationship? "I know. He confided that much to me."

"I take it that you know about Monique as well."

"Only what he has willingly shared. There's so much bottled up inside of him that I have serious doubts whether there's a chance for me."

Helena Ramón patted Nicole's hand with her own. She had misjudged this woman based on her external beauty. What she saw in her golden eyes convinced her that Nicole was just as beautiful inside as outside. Xavier couldn't let this young lady get away. "You love my son." It was a statement of fact not a question.

Through a blur of tears Nicole stared back at Xavier's mother. In her she recognized a friend. It was comforting. "With all that I am. But Monique stands between us."

Out back Xavier and his father strolled around the grounds talking about nothing in particular. Raymond sensed confusion within his son and waited for him to approach the subject. He recalled Xavier as a child mulling over some dilemma. No matter how much prodding one did, Xavier would discuss a problem only when he was ready. And so he waited.

Standing close to the bank of Willow Bayou, Xavier glanced back at the upstairs balcony, remembering last night. It had brought him so much pleasure and so much aggravation as well. He wanted Nicole for sure, but had yet to convince himself that it was a wise decision.

He began to speak, drawing his father's attention. "I hurt Nicole last night"

Knowing his son didn't mean physically, Raymond Ramón replied, "How?"

Xavier didn't face his father because he was ashamed of his actions. He found peace in watching the slow-moving bayou instead. "We made love last night." There was no subject this father and son couldn't discuss. "It was more than I could ever have imagined. It was Nicole's first time."

"So what's the problem?"

"Afterwards I wanted to run as fast as I could in the opposite direction. I felt so much and so deeply for her that it frightened me." He turned to his father with a sad smile. "Do you know how it makes me feel as a man to admit that a petite woman scares the hell out of me?"

"Son, most men are frightened when they realize that they have gone and done the one thing they swore they would never do. You've fallen in love."

"Yes, I have, but I don't know if I can trust what I feel."

"You're talking about Monique now, son." Raymond slipped his hands deep within his pockets to keep from hugging his son as he had when he was a troubled little boy. "Does Nicole remind you of Monique? Do you see similarities between them?"

"No—not at all. Nicole is warm, loving, and giving to a fault. She tries to pretend to be strong, and in some respects she is the strongest person I know. But with her heart she's giving and quite vulnerable."

Raymond Ramón watched the play of emotions on his son's face. It was obvious that he loved the lady, but there were still issues from his marriage to be dealt with. "You love her, but the relationship has moved too suddenly. Is that what you're feeling?"

"I'm not sure if it moved too suddenly or we seem to fit too perfectly, which scares me. But I do want to step back and examine my feelings?

"Have you told Nicole how you feel?"

Xavier shook his head, meeting his father's concerned eyes. "Not exactly. I became aloof last night, and this morning I tried ignoring the situation, but Nicole wouldn't let it rest. She confronted me head-on. It's amazing how well she can read me. Monique never understood who I was."

"Xavier, please don't take this as criticism, but you have to let go of Monique. You made a bad choice. You're not the first person to do that, man or woman. You can't keep comparing Nicole or your relationship to Monique."

"I don't compare Nicole to Monique," he defended himself, then thought back to this morning when Nicole too had mentioned his ex-wife. "Nicole accused me of making love to Monique last night."

"Did you?"

"No!" Xavier was horrified that his father even asked the question. "Why do you believe I'm in love with Monique? Don't you know that woman ripped out my heart? She shook my sense of decency and completely destroyed my self-confidence." Then it hit him. He was approaching this relationship with his failed marriage in the forefront of his mind. He didn't compare Nicole to Monique, but he did their relationship. He based each action in this relationship on those he'd made in his failed marriage. No wonder he couldn't seem to go forward with Nicole. He was stuck analyzing and trying to correct the past.

"Dad, I love Nicole. This I'm sure about. But it's not just me involved in this relationship with her. I have to consider Ryan as well."

"I agree with you," Raymond Ramón commented. "May I offer a suggestion?"

"Sure."

"Tell Nicole what you just told me. If she loves you, she will understand and appreciate your honesty."

He knew his father was right for it had just been about thirty minutes ago when she had asked this very thing of him. "You're right, I will."

"So tell me about this pretty young woman of yours." Raymond Ramón encouraged Xavier to discuss Nicole in hope of him seeing her clearly.

Xavier began with their initial meeting and his instant attraction to her. He spoke of her great cooking ability and her love of home. He confided in his father about Nicole's abandonment and her special connection with his son, how he'd discovered the genuine love which he possessed for her and the belief that what they shared was for keeps. But what he needed most at the moment, he said, was time alone to deal with his past mistakes. Before he could go to Nicole with his love, he had to deal with the past. He would follow his father's advice and pray she would understand.

Back in the kitchen Nicole too had confided her past. She had initially been leery of confessing her parentless childhood, but was now happy that she had done it. The secret was no longer a ticking time bomb waiting to explode. She didn't have to wonder any more about how his parents would receive her, because Mrs. Ramón had opened her arms wide.

That's just how Xavier found them when he stuck his head into the kitchen doorway. He didn't interrupt the women, but remained silent watching the exchange and loving his mother even more. Her softly whispered words of "You're not alone any more, young lady," warmed his heart. He had instinctively known that his mother would like and accept Nicole. He entered the kitchen as the women parted. His eyes briefly held Nicole's, then his mother's. They were both strong African-American women and he loved them dearly.

"What's keeping that coffee?"

"Coming right up." Nicole grabbed the tray once again. She lead the way out onto the verandah.

The foursome spent the better part of the morning hours sitting companionably on the verandah enjoying the beauty of the day. Conversation was easy and quite enjoyable, punctuated with humor and laughter. Raymond and Helena Ramón sat in the matching wicker chairs with the table between them. Xavier and Nicole sat closely on the wicker bench across from them. Xavier sat with his right arm stretched out behind Nicole, and ever so often he would allow his hand to stroke her drying hair or caress her slender neck. His subtle touches weren't lost on his parents. Several times they shared knowing glances. The sight of the young couple pleased them, and their son's sweet caresses only confirmed what they both knew to be the truth. A loving couple sat before them.

Nicole, however, didn't know what to make of Xavier's attentiveness. He was making her nervous and angry all at the same time. She wanted to enjoy the attention he was bestowing upon her, but the events of last night wouldn't allow her to enjoy the moment. So she chalked his attention up to putting on appearances for his parents. She played along and smiled sweetly in return, but soon realized she was no longer pretending. She was enjoying his parents' company and his soft caresses as well. Several times she tried to capture his attention with her eyes in an attempt to guess at his game, but he only smiled in that roguish manner which made her forget her thoughts. Frustrated, she tried focusing on the conversation, but once again found her thoughts straying to Xavier. Why was he toying with her? Didn't he know how susceptible she was to his charm? Sure he did. Last night had been all the proof he needed, and what had he done? The memory caused her a brief moment of sadness. It must have been reflected on her face for it drew a comment from Mrs. Ramón.

"Nicole, is everything all right dear?"

Quickly raising her head Nicole glanced first at Xavier, then at his mother. The woman was truly concerned about her. The realization made her smile.

"Yes ma'am, I was only listening," she lied.

There was no way she was going to allow anyone to know that she had given her love to this man and it had been rejected. The simple knowledge brought her enough shame without others knowing.

Xavier too had caught the sudden sadness in Nicole's eyes and knew he was the source. Although he had enjoyed the morning with his parents and Nicole, he was anxious to speak to Nicole alone. The longer he allowed her to specu-late about their relationship, the more pain she inflicted on herself. She found it so easy to believe that he could actu-ally reject her. She was such a treasure, and yet she didn't see herself that way. And of course his actions last night hadn't helped.

Raymond and Helena sensed their son's anxiousness to be alone with Nicole. They had accomplished what they had set out to do. They had met Xavier's young lady and both felt he had made a wise selection this time around. The couple began gathering their belongings. Standing, they announced their departure.

"Nicole, it was a pleasure to meet you, and I know we'll be seeing you again." Mrs. Ramón spoke for them both.

Nicole returned the older woman's warm smile as she stood before her, doubtful of her last comment. "It was a pleasure meeting you both as well, Mrs. Ramón."

She stood on the verandah watching as Xavier walked with his parents to their car. He kissed his mother before opening the door for her, then walked around to the driver's side of the vehicle and embraced his father. They shared a few words before Mr. Ramón patted his son on the back. Then he too climbed into the vehicle. A few more words were exchanged between him and Xavier before he closed his car door. During the exchange, Xavier glanced up onto the porch and observed Nicole thoughtfully. It unsettled Nicole because she didn't know how to interpret its meaning. Confused, she walked back into the house and headed for the upstairs bedroom. She would gather her things and be ready to head home as soon as he came inside.

Xavier registered the confusion on Nicole's face. He knew that he was completely responsible for her pain. He stepped back from his parents' car and watched as his father drove off with the love of his life by his side. He wanted that too. More than he ever really realized. He could have that with Nicole, he was sure, but when he put words to his emotions he wanted them to come from the heart unencumbered. Deciding that this was just as good a time as any to speak with Nicole, he returned to the house. In the master bedroom he found her folding the dress she'd worn last night. Her back was to him as he walked into the room.

"Nic," he called, walking up behind her.

Nicole knew he stood in the doorway watching her, yet she ignored him. She didn't turn around because she was afraid of letting him see the pain she was in. All she wanted was to go home and forget that last night had ever happened. But Xavier wouldn't allow it. He grabbed her hand, halting her movements. At his touch she was forced to look up at him.

"We should be getting home," she replied, trying to extricate her hand from his grasp.

Drawing Nicole before him he murmured, "We need to talk, baby. This can't wait." He tried unsuccessfully to capture her eyes.

"We've talked," Nicole mumbled, trying to pull away.

Her avoidance hurt. He didn't want to see what they shared disappear before it was allowed to truly flourish. Without a word he drew Nicole flush against him and captured her surprised lips in a heated kiss. He wasn't gentle as he explored her mouth. He wanted her to experience the desperation he felt. As she tried to move away to avoid his kiss, Xavier captured the back of her head, bringing her mouth back to his.

She was losing the battle. Her brain warned her to resist the feeling, but her body demanded more of the fiery embrace. She gave up that fight when Xavier sucked hungrily on her tongue. Her knees buckled, then she began returning his kiss with just as much fervor. Their tongues danced and mated as their bodies sought to do the same. Lost in the euphoria, Nicole failed to realize that she was now back in bed. Xavier's hands were stroking and caressing all of her sensitive points masterfully. By the time her clothes where eventually removed and he buried deep, she was beyond thinking. She could only feel and love this man she held within her body. Her heart cried out her love, but she never truly voiced the words. She allowed her body to do the speaking for her.

Xavier couldn't get close enough, or deep enough. He wanted all Nicole had to give and he knew he had no right to demand this of her. But he did, with every stroke, every caress, and every kiss. She was his and he wanted her to accept that fact. He touched her just so, making her purr like a kitten as they rode higher together. He loved her with the intention of making her crave his touch in the dark of night. She would wait for him to sort out his life because only he would be able to satisfy her hunger.

They moved together in that age-old rhythm. The only sound to be heard was the beating of their hearts. The heat was incredible and almost unbearable as they danced the lover's dance. The rhythm escalated to a sultry frenzy beat as the end neared. With sweat-dampened bodies they executed the final masterful steps before catapulting over the edge together.

Nicole listened to Xavier's labored breathing so like her own. This wasn't supposed to happen, and yet she couldn't stop herself from rejoicing in their union. He still held her in place beneath him. She wanted to open her eyes and see what expression he wore after their fierce love making, but she didn't, for fear of seeing the same rejection as last night. So she waited.

Xavier could barely move after the loving they'd shared. He had been trying to imprint himself onto Nicole, but she had instead left her mark on him. He wouldn't be able to sleep at night without her beside him, beneath him. There was no other woman for him and he accepted that fact, but he still had work to do on himself. The time when he would be separated from the woman he loved would be difficult, but for their future it had to be.

Xavier eased his chest off Nicole's body. He called her name with all the love he felt inside. "Nicole, look at me, baby."

Slowly she responded, opening her closed lids to reveal troubled brown eyes. She didn't say a word, just watched him closely.

He smiled lovingly as he kissed her lips briefly. He could see her fear and wanted to erase it. "Give me your hand," he demanded and was pleased when she capitulated. He placed it over his rapidly beating heart. "Do you feel what you do to me?"

Nicole stared up into Xavier's handsome face. She wanted to say he did the same to her, but she didn't. She wouldn't lend voice to what she felt. She wouldn't give him the opportunity to throw her feelings back into her face, and so she silently stared into his searching gray eyes. Her hand absorbed the thunderous beats of his heart while her soul begged him to say he loved her.

Instead, Xavier covered her small hand with his. When he finally gathered the strength to speak, it wasn't the words she wanted to hear.

"Nicole, you mean more to me than any woman I've known, and that includes Monique. I made love to *you* last night and today. I'm not confused about who's in my bed. It's you I want."

"You want me." Disappointed, Nicole abruptly removed her hand and tried to dislodge him from her body. She didn't want to hear his attempt at explaining why he couldn't love her. She wasn't strong enough to listen to his explanation twice in one day. So she pushed against his chest trying to free herself.

"No baby, don't fight me. Listen to what I'm trying to say. If you love me, if only a little, please listen." His eyes begged for understanding.

Nicole sagged back into the mattress, defeated, because she did love him. "Say whatever you have to say and then take me home." She was rude and behaving childishly, but she didn't care.

Xavier knew Nicole was in pain but was helpless to say those words she longed to hear. He could only pray that she would listen and understand the importance of what he was doing. "Nic, there are details about my marriage that no one knows. Things that I'm ashamed to admit. I have to deal with those issues before I can come to you with my feelings."

"Are you still in love with her?"

Xavier stroked her kiss-swollen lips with his index finger, loving the way they trembled under his touch. He wasn't in love with Monique, but he acknowledged that she still evoked strong emotions within him. "No, baby I'm not."

Nicole saw the brief play of emotion flash across his face. She glanced away as a lone tear tracked down her face, alerting Xavier to her greatest fear.

In that moment he realized how attuned Nicole was to his emotions. She confused his acknowledgment of Monique's grasp on him as love. She had to know how wrong she was. "Nicole, do you honestly believe I'm in love with my ex-wife?" His voice sounded desperate.

She met his questioning gray eyes unwaveringly. "Yes. She occupies a place inside of you that I can't reach, and you're unwilling to share. I refuse to even try any more. Agreement or not, I'm through. I can't do this to myself."

Flabbergasted, he thought back to his conversation with his father. His father too had had doubts about his feelings for Monique. He was angry now because he didn't know how to convince Nicole. "Listen to me good, Nicole, because I'm only going to say this once. I'm not in love with Monique," he growled out, then fell silent. I'm in love with *you.*" The words came out whispery soft and resigned. "Do you hear me? I love you, Nicole, but I'm not ready to make a commitment. I'm not sure at this point if I ever will be. There are issues from my marriage which can no longer be ignored. Issues that could resurface if they're not dealt with now. I don't want that."

Nicole started to speak, but Xavier silenced her with a finger to the lips, just listen, please. Nicole, when I married Monique I believed it was forever. She destroyed not only our marriage with her manipulation and lies, but also my self-confidence. She caused me to question my judgment. I'm afraid to open myself completely to another woman because I don't know if I'll survive that kind of betrayal again."

"So what do you propose?"

"First thing Monday morning I'm going to work and clear up a few loose ends, then I'm coming back here alone. I have some leave time coming, so I'm thinking of taking two or three weeks. The time away should help me focus on those issues and take stock of what we have. I can't make promises, because it just isn't my life affected by my decision. I have to consider what's best for Ryan as well."

Xavier would be leaving for weeks with no guarantee that he would be returning to her. Her heart beat rapidly at the prospect of losing him. She wouldn't cry, because she had spent so much of her life crying for what could have been. Instead she summoned her inner strength as she shut off her emotions. As long as she kept the barrier in place he couldn't hurt her. It had worked as a child; she could only hope it would work now when she needed the protection the most.

"Do what you have to do, Xavier, because I'm quite familiar with this brand of love. It seems to be the only type I receive. First my mother...now you." Her facial expression was blank and closed off to him.

The meaning of her words cut him to the core. "Wait a minute, Nicole. Are you listening to what I'm saying?"

She turned lifeless dark brown eyes on him, and with an empty smile replied, "My hearing is perfect." She pushed against his shoulder and this time he allowed her to move. "I need a shower before we head home."

Xavier was fuming as he turned off the ignition to the Navigator. They were parked in Nicole's driveway. Not a word had been spoken since leaving New Orleans. "Nic, why can't you understand how I feel? I simply need this time alone to work out my problems." He paused hoping she would say something. When she didn't he continued, "Is it that easy for you to place me out of your life?" On that thought he studied her profile, wondering whether she loved him at all. She hadn't spoken the words, he reminded himself.

Nicole had had enough of this drama. How dare Xavier try to turn this around on her. She grabbed her bundle of clothing as she unlocked the door. But before she opened it, she spun back around facing him. "If you want to be alone, so be it. I won't bother you ever again. You can go anywhere you choose," she yelled, building up steam. "You can spend the rest of your life pining away over Monique. I'm through giving my heart to a man who doesn't want it. I was a fool to believe that a normal life was possible for someone like me anyway." With that said she threw open the door. "Thanks for dinner and have a safe trip," she mumbled as she closed the door in his stunned face.

Unable to contain his anger, Xavier bounded out the driver's side door stalking towards Nicole as she made her escape up the walkway. He grabbed her by the arm and spun her around to face his wrath.

"Thanks for dinner and have a safe trip? Who do you think you're dealing with, Nicole? I'm not one of these young pups you can play with for a while then send him on his way. I'm a man, damn it. I'm the man you crawled into bed with not once, but twice." He held up two fingers to emphasize his point. "You don't send me home with a pat on the head and a thanks for dinner," he roared, grabbing her by both arms and drawing her forward against him for a kiss. He claimed her mouth, savagely drawing forth a weak moan, then slowly gentled before finally releasing her. Gazing into her blazing eyes he smiled roguishly, pleased with himself. She wasn't immune to his touch after all.

"I'll call you."

And with that he walked back to his vehicle. Starting the ignition he reversed out the driveway, then pulled off without *a* glance in her direction. He turned at the corner then disappeared from sight. Nicole remained on the porch reeling from their confrontation.

CHAPTER 18

A week later Nicole was handling Xavier's sudden departure from her life no better. Over the course of the week she had experienced a wide range of emotions. On Sunday she battled a cloud of depression which threatened to envelop her.

By Wednesday she was angry with herself for allowing him into her life. Then Friday night she felt weepy and alone. Now this morning she wandered through her home aimlessly in a numb state. She missed the comfort of simply knowing he was close by and that he cared.

Nicole stared out of the window. She failed to see the beauty of the day. The sun was shining bright, and it was going to be a glorious day on the Mississippi Gulf Coast, but to Nicole it was as bleak as a winter's day in Montana. She wondered whether he was missing her as much as she was missing him. But considering he hadn't called as he said he would, she guessed she had her answer. Well, so be it. She didn't need him. There was a time when she hadn't even known he existed. Telling herself that she would put him out of her mind, she headed to the kitchen for breakfast. She withdrew eggs and bacon from the refrigerator, but never made it to the stove. As she closed the refrigerator door she was assailed by the memories of their passionate escapade in this very room. The kitchen table especially held heated memories. She couldn't eat there this morning. She returned the items to the refrigerator, no longer hungry, then ran out of the kitchen as though hounds were chasing her.

She managed to find a semblance of peace out on the back patio. Lying in the hammock she studied the clouds overhead as she had when a child. The big white, fluffy cloud to the right was shaped like a heart. The one over from it resembled a person smiling. The smaller cloud to the left was a couple embracing. That one looked like Xavier. *What in the world am I doing?* Fed up with the game after realizing that everything, even the stupid clouds, was reminding her of Xavier, Nicole screamed, closing her eyes to the world. She chanted repeatedly to herself that she didn't need him. Didn't want him. Didn't love him.

That was a lie and she knew it. Defeated, she came to the conclusion that a change in scenery was needed and rose from the hammock. Labor day was Monday after next and she had planned to fly out to Atlanta Wednesday evening. However, there was no reason she couldn't change her flight. She had a capable substitute who could handle her class in her absence. Returning to the house, she grabbed the phone with that purpose in mind. Within minutes she had rescheduled her flight for tomorrow morning at nine and called to inform Jon of her change in plans. To her delight he was ecstatic with the change. The additional days would give them a lengthy visit. Feeling rejuvenated, Nicole ran off to her bedroom to begin packing. She made a vow as she folded clothes and placed them into her luggage to enjoy this time with Jon and leave all thoughts of Xavier in Biloxi.

"Nicole, you can't leave with things between you and Xavier unresolved," Gina tried to convince her stubborn friend. She was driving Nicole to the airport for her nine o'clock flight

"It's resolved. Xavier wanted time alone, and that's exactly what he's got."

Rolling her eyes, Gina didn't know the details of the breakup, but she knew Nicole well enough to know that her friend was hurting. "Did you at least let him know you would be in Atlanta?"

"If Xavier was concerned about my whereabouts, he would have called me like he said he would." Turning in her seat to face Gina, Nicole spelled it out. "Look Gina, I know you and Keith were hoping things would work out between Xavier and myself, but they didn't and so now it's over."

Gina took her eyes off the road briefly. She caught a glimpse of the hurt in Nicole's eyes. It was obvious that she was putting up a valiant effort to appear in control when she was actually hanging by a delicate thread. "Nicole, I'm a pretty good judge of character, and I know Xavier has strong feelings for you. I would even venture to say he's in love with you."

Shaking her head at the absurdity of the situation, Nicole didn't know how to reply. "Gina, the man doesn't want to feel anything for me, let alone love me."

"The heck with what he wants. If you want that man, go after him with everything you have. Anyway, when have you known a man to know what's best for him? Keith sure didn't. Listen, this is what you do."

Nicole laughed as her friend outlined one outrageous seduction scene after the other. By the time they arrived at the airport they were both in tears from laughing so hard. A Nicole settled into her seat for the flight ahead, she allowed her mind to play out one of those scenes with her and Xavier cast in the leading roles.

Xavier had tried to leave Nicole in Biloxi, but to no avail. She was constantly on his mind. He didn't feel comfortable with the situation as it stood. He knew within his heart that he was doing what was best for all three of them in the long run, but here in the present he wasn't so sure. In his attempt to protect himself, he had hurt Nicole. The thought pained him tremendously because she'd only tried to bolster his confidence, whether it was pertaining to his being a single parent, his failed marriage, or his career. Not once had she made him feel less a man because of the events in his life. And yet, he did feel less than a man, because he was afraid to venture into the future with Nicole. He loved her. There was no doubt in his mind about his feelings; however, he couldn't begin to make plans for the future until he had purged the effects of his failed marriage from his system.

Lying across his bed, he allowed his thoughts to wander back in time. He allowed his mind's eye to see Monique as she truly was. She had been a beautiful woman capable of making heads turn and she'd known it. He realized now that she used her beauty to achieve her goals and he had been one of them. From the time he'd approached her on the dance floor, she had made it perfectly clear that to be with her was an honor, for she could have her pick of any man. And like a young pup he had truly been honored. So much so he had swallowed her well-contrived innocent routine all the way to the courthouse. *How could I have been so stupid?* He had never once doubted her word or her motives. Not even the night when she announced that she was carrying his child.

"I won't have this baby if I have to stay here in this godforsaken town with my father, Xavier. There's no future for me here without you, and our baby would have no future amongst these farmers. With you we would both have a bright future."

She had looked so sincere and frightened. He recalled how she hated the North Dakota town her father had retired in. She dreamed of a life in the big city with all its trappings. He knew that with his family's name behind him he could lay the world at Monique's feet. She was perfect in his opinion, and would complement his career well. She was a military brat who understood the workings of the military, and therefore could only prove to be an asset. Besides, he was hopelessly in love with her. She was more than beautiful. She was a sensuous woman who exuded passion and a zest for life. He had never known such a woman before. There was no way he wasn't going to marry the woman he loved and provide a home for their child.

"Your future is with me, Monique. You and our child belong beside me. We'll get married and see the world together. Will that make you happy?"

And so he had fulfilled his promise and married her within the week to the dismay of both their families. He was a man in love and didn't care what anyone thought about his sudden marriage. Monique was the woman for him and now they had a child on the way. But the dream had been shattered while he was on temporary duty to San Antonio. He had received a telephone call from Monique claiming to miscarry. He had flown home on emergency leave to be with his stricken wife. Later, several months later, he would discover that there had been no baby. His loving wife had lied to force him to marry her.

"How could you have lied about a baby, Monique?" Xavier had bellowed angrily.

"I wanted you, Xavier. I just wanted you to love me. I was afraid you would take the assignment and forget about me. I did it for us." She had lied skillfully once again. And once again he had fallen for her well-placed lies.

Xavier tossed on the bed while trying to analyze the reason for his gullibility. He concluded simply that he had been young and arrogant. Because of his deep and abiding love for her, he automatically thought that it was reciprocated. He was accustomed to women's attention and therefore thought he knew his way around them all. He was a big city man from a prominent family who had attracted and dispelled women's attention since high school. There was no way a little small town girl could dupe him. She had to be in love with him as well.

"What a joke," he voiced out loud. He got up from the bed and began pacing the room. He needed to see Nicole. It had been two full weeks since their night in this very bed.

He had promised to call but hadn't because nothing had really changed. Going to the telephone he dialed her number and received a busy signal.

Dejected, Xavier returned the phone to its cradle. He sat at the foot of the bed and rested his forearms on his thighs, tilting his head forward. This time when he drifted off down memory lane it was with Nicole. She was so vastly different from Monique. Where Monique measured her self-worth by her appearance, Nicole placed no value in hers at all. She didn't use her beauty to attract and manipulate men. To the contrary, she was always trying to tone down her looks, as if that were possible. Just the idea caused him to smile.

Xavier found himself smiling quite a lot when he thought of Nicole. Her incredible strength, loyalty, and determination were just the tip of the iceberg when it came to her character. He loved the way she pampered him and thought of his son first and foremost. Sometimes he found himself jealous of the attention she showered on Ryan, and then his pettiness would dissolve into love. He liked the fact that she didn't play coquettish games. She said and did exactly as she felt. There had been no pretense when she had shared herself with him. He recognized the truth and beauty in her passion. Her love had been bountiful and without motive.

His heart constricted with the knowledge of just how deeply he had hurt Nicole. He had made love to her just as passionately with his entire self, and she had welcomed him. He had sent mixed messages as she accused him of doing. He had loved her completely with his body, but not with his heart. With Nicole it was all or nothing, and she deserved no less.

Then realization dawned. He finally recognized what had caused him to doubt his relationship with Nicole. It was too easy—uncomplicated. He didn't have to weigh her words for the truth. He didn't have to question whether or not this was another scheme to have her way. When she gave her word he accepted it without a moment's doubt. This was true love.

His parents shared it. And so did Michele and Walter. He never once heard or saw doubt in their partner's eyes. When one was out of sight, they didn't worry whether their spouse was being loyal; they knew they were because they were their other half. He felt that way about Nicole. Her love wasn't fickle. For such a young woman she was mature beyond her years and he admired the quality.

He and Monique had simply been wrong for each other to begin with. His father was right; he had made a poor choice. Unfortunately, he had believed that adage about marriage taking work. He didn't anymore. When two people were right for each other it wasn't work which held them together, but friendship and respect. He knew he and Monique had never been friends. He also had to accept his share of the responsibility for their failed marriage. He had fallen in love with the package, as Nicole would put it, and never once stopped to see the real person. But that wasn't true with Nicole. With her he had moved past her physical beauty to discover the woman within.

And in doing so he'd found a woman he could respect and love. A woman that was just as beautiful internally as externally. A woman who placed value on her word and deed, and not her physical appearance. He had discovered a treasure.

He decided to spend the Labor Day weekend with Nicole and Ryan instead of remaining in New Orleans alone. He had some apologizing to do. But first he had to trust her with his past. They couldn't move forward as a couple until he dealt with those issues. He wanted a future with Nicole and intended to have it.

Nicole deplaned and followed the throng of passengers down the concourse into the waiting area. She was in Atlanta and planned to make the most of this week with her brother. Dressed in a white linen pantsuit, which complemented her petite figure, she looked fashionable. Her dark mass of hair was worn lose and enhanced the exotic mystique surrounding her. As she emerged into the waiting area heads turned as she passed. Curious onlookers tried to guess who she was meeting.

"Nicky," Jon called to her from the back of the milling crowd as he waved an arm.

Nicole spotted him immediately. He looked great as always dressed in his standard khakis and chambray shirt. Standing at six-one, he was easy to spot. Nicole admired his handsomeness. His thick dark head of hair was parted naturally to the right and hung just below the collar of his shirt. His piercing blue eyes reflected his happiness in seeing her, as did the brilliance of his white smile. His natural olive complexion was darker from the summer sun.

Nicole smiled and returned his wave as she forced her way through the milling crowd. She was effortlessly swept up into his loving arms for a hug.

"Love must agree with you," Nicole beamed. She returned his smile as she was placed back on the floor. "You look great."

"Thank you and it does." He kissed her forehead as he had when she was a little girl. "You look good yourself. I can't remember the last time I saw you with your hair free," Jon commented.

"Yeah well, things change; people change."

"Or maybe Xavier is responsible for this change in you."

Halting in her tracks, Nicole turned on Jon. Her pained brown eyes stopped him dead in his tracks. "Look, for the next week don't mention that name to me, okay?"

Jon didn't comment right away, but recognized the hurt in her eyes. He knew Nicole was the type to allow her emotions to fester, thereby creating an even greater problem than what actually existed. He would have to force her to talk before she headed back home. "No can do. Something is bothering you and we'll talk about it before you leave, but for now we'll drop the subject."

They collected Nicole's luggage and strolled side by side out into the parking area. Tossing the bags onto the back seat of his Jeep Cherokee, Jon climbed in beside Nicole. They talked non-stop all the way to his home. He brought her up to date on his latest book, which would be released next year. He discussed everything except what Nicole was dying to hear about.

Nicole turned in her seat to face him. She had had enough of this frivolous conversation. She wanted to hear about his recent engagement. "Okay, enough about work. I'm extremely proud of your writing abilities, but I didn't come all this way to discuss your book."

"No? What did you come all this way to discuss?" he asked innocently, keeping his eyes on the heavy city traffic.

"Kimberly, what else?" She laughed as he made an exaggerated face.

"Oh, her!"

"Jon, don't make me hurt you. I need details, brother dear!"

Jon sneaked a peek at his sister. He was delighted to have Nicole with him. As odd as their union might seem to the outside world, it was a typical brother and sister relationship. From the time Lillian and Ronald had brought Nicole home, Jon had been hooked on the golden-eyed beauty. He liked being a brother and took his responsibilities seriously even until this day. Nicole thought she was there to get the low down on Kimberly; well, he had news for her because he intended to do the same for Xavier.

"Okay Nicole, you never were a patient child," he remarked laughing.

"So tell me, what is she like?"

A large smile, which could only be described as goofy, brightened his face as he thought of his lady. "I really got lucky with Kimberly. For a while there I wasn't so sure we would make it, but I knew what I wanted and was determined to have it. She's wonderful, Nicole. From the day I laid eyes on her, I knew she was the one. This feeling I can't explain came over me, and my heart rate sped up, and when we touched I could swear there were sparks. Do you know what I mean?"

Nicole understood exactly what Jon was describing. She rested her head against the seat lost in thought. She recalled her initial meeting with Xavier and the electrical current which had run up her arm. Yeah, she knew exactly what he meant. "Yes, I do."

Jon heard something special in Nicole's voice and glanced over at her. He recognized the far-away expression. "You and Xavier huh?"

"I thought I told you not to mention that name."

Jon reached over, clasping Nicole's hand with his own as he drove along. "It's not as hopeless as you think."

"How would you know? You're in love with Ms. Wonderful," Nicole said with a smile.

"I know because for awhile there I didn't think we would make it. There were obstacles and issues to be dealt with. It seemed easier to walk away than fight for the woman I loved."

"But you did fight because you *loved* her."

"What are you saying, Nicole? Xavier broke it off with you?"

Nicole closed her eyes. She wasn't up to discussing this right now, but Jon as always was determined to make her talk about her feelings.

"To be honest, Jon, I don't know where we stand at the moment. One moment he's loving me so tenderly and then the next he can't get away fast enough. He says he loves me, but then he insists he needs time alone. Then I make a decision to end the relationship and he gets bent out of shape. I don't know what to make of it."

"He sounds like a frightened man."

"Humph! Xavier frightened? I don't think so. This man is the commander of a military police squadron. He's not afraid of anything."

"Only a five—foot-four-inch woman, who has probably gotten closer to him than anyone before."

"You're crazy. Why would that cause him to be afraid?"

"Because he's in love and trying to fight the feeling, sweetheart."

Nicole could only shake her head in response to Jon's comment There was no way Xavier was in love with her. Sure he said the words, but only because that's what he thought she wanted to hear. She recalled the expression plastered on his face when she'd asked whether he was still in love with Monique. He had denied it, but that something in his eyes said she still maintained a hold on him.

"No, you're wrong this time, brother dear. I know the writer in you believes you're an expert on human nature, but this time you're wrong."

"Why am I wrong, Nicole? Because you can't accept the fact that you're worthy of being loved?"

A knot formed in the pit of Nicole's stomach as she heard the truth in Jon's words. Only now noticing that they sat in front of his home, she breathed deeply, trying to ease the tightness. Jon awaited her response.

"Look, let's not get into this discussion right now. We've had it before and nothing has changed."

Jon threw his right arm over the back of the seat as he turned to face Nicole. "Nicky, something has changed this time. You made love with a military man. You wouldn't have done that if he didn't make you feel safe. He made you trust him, love him."

"Jon, women sleep with men all the time."

"True, but you're not most women. Unless things have changed, you went to Xavier untouched. He could get sex anywhere, but with you he obviously wanted something more. Believe me, he wouldn't have waited around for you unless he cared about you. There are too many other women out there willing."

"Spoken like a true man."

"I'm simply stating fact."

Nicole was tired of this discussion and wanted to put it to rest. "I'll think about what you've said, but for now can we please drop the subject?"

"Sure. Come on, let's get you settled inside.

The day progressed with the two of them sharing lunch at a local eatery while catching up. Back at his home they curled up on the sofa like children, each on opposite ends talking and laughing joyously. Jon possessed the talent to make her smile and forget about her troubles. During this time together it felt as though they had never been apart. Their conversation and conduct was easy and natural. Nicole missed days like this. With Jon she didn't have to be on guard with her emotions or her past. With him she could simply be Nicky the girt who loved to read, cook, and sing off-key.

As they lay on the sofa enjoying the lull in conversation, Nicole noted that this would probably be the last time that she and Jon would share a moment like this. He would no longer be hers only. In a couple of months he would belong to Kimberly. Glancing down to where he lay, she was surprised to find him watching her.

"Why are you staring at me?"

"Just now, you looked so sad. I know you said you didn't want to talk about Xavier, but maybe..."

"I wasn't thinking about Xavier for a change," Nicole replied, barely smiling. "I was actually thinking about you, or rather us. Have you realized that this wilt probably be the last time we share a sofa like this?"

"I'm getting married Nicole, not disappearing from your life."

I know that, but things will change, as they should. I'll just miss this," she commented with a slight shake of her head.

"Nicole, what you and I share is for life. No one can take your place."

With love in her eyes she smiled brightly. "Thanks, big brother, I needed to hear that"

The following day Jon announced that Kimberly was due over at noon. They would all go out to lunch together, giving the women a chance to get to know each other. Jon was anxious for his two favorite ladies to meet. He knew they would like each other and form a sisterhood of their own.

Jon was on the telephone talking with his publisher when the doorbell chimed exactly at noon. From the kitchen he asked Nicole to answer the door.

"That should be Kimberly," he whispered with his hand over the mouthpiece.

Nicole couldn't wait to meet her brother's lady. Jon had informed her that Kimberly was a professional researcher. She did contract work for writers, directors, and reporters. His publisher had referred him to Kimberly for work on his latest book. She too was twenty-nine. From all he had revealed she appeared to be a wonderful lady. When Nicole had asked for a description, he had laughed and told her he would let that be a surprise. At the time Nicole didn't understand the secrecy, but as she opened the door it became quite clear.

"Hello, you must be Nicole."

"Yes, I am." Nicole was stunned.

"Jon didn't tell you," the tall, willowy five-nine, nut-brown woman supplied.

"No, he didn't, but it's a pleasure to meet you, Kimberly." Nicole extended her hand, then stepped aside to allow the woman to enter.

"I prefer to be called Kim. However, your brother insists upon calling me Kimberly. I think he does it to annoy me." She smiled lovingly in his direction and show-cased her dimples.

Nicole laughed good-naturedly along with Kim. She took an immediate liking to the attractive woman who wore her hair in braids. She especially liked the love she saw reflected in her eyes as she blew a kiss to Jon. There was definitely chemistry between these two. It consumed the room and drew one into their happy world of love. Nicole felt like a voyeur watching these two exchange such heated glances.

Jon disconnected from his phone call and approached the women standing in front of the sofa. He placed his arms around Kim's waist, drawing her back against him as he deposited a kiss to her cheek. He glanced at Nicole smiling. "I told you she was wonderful."

Nicole could only laugh. She had never seen this side of Jon before. Sure, she knew of his love and tenderness from a sister's perspective, but this consuming happiness was new. She was happy for him and little bit jealous. "Yes, you did, but you didn't tell me we had more in common than you."

Understanding the meaning Jon laughed deeply. I didn't feel it was necessary to say. Besides, the only women who mattered in my life were you and Lillian. I don't remember my mother, and Patsy barely accepted me, so the qualities I admire in women are those I saw in you both. I found them in *Kim.*"

Nicole focused on the couple before her. She watched as they exchanged loving glances. They appeared to be perfect for each other. "I wish you both a lifetime of happiness."

Over a light lunch of grilled chicken salads, Kim and Jon discussed their wedding plans with Nicole. They were setting a date for spring when both their schedules would be free. It would be a small, intimate wedding with family and close friends. Nicole discovered during the course of the meal that it was Kim's second marriage and she wanted something small this time. Nicole silently wondered how Jon felt about Kim's previous marriage. She knew she felt as though she was competing with Xavier's ex-wife.

"The only people you have to please are yourselves," Nicole offered. "Just notify me of the definite date and I'm there."

Kim looked at Jon, then Nicole, before putting her thoughts to words. "I wasn't sure I wanted to meet you."

Nicole glanced sharply at Kim. "Why?"

Taking Jon's hand while she gathered her thoughts, she threaded her fingers through his, then glanced back at Nicole. "I didn't believe it was possible for the two of you to simply be brother and sister. I kept trying to detect something more intimate in your relationship. The first time I spent the night at Jon's I saw the picture of you on his shoulders. You know, Jon, the one at the beach."

"Yeah, but I told you it was my sister."

"I know what you said, but my insecurities wouldn't accept it. And you have to admit it's a little difficult accepting the fact that a black woman and a white guy consider themselves siblings. I stared at the two of you in that photograph and could see only the love you shared. Nicole was gorgeous in that *little* bikini and you seemed so happy to be with her. I was jealous and conjured up this image of her. But you're not at all what I was expecting." She smiled nervously, wanting Nicole to understand.

Nicole didn't know what to say, but she did understand insecurities. "I'm just glad we got the chance to meet before the wedding. I would have hated for the two of you to marry with this doubt hanging between you. Jon loves you

Kim and I would never do anything to come between you. I would like to think of us as friends."

"That you may, Nicole." Kim smiled brightly and reached over to embrace the other woman.

Nicole returned the spontaneous gesture, glad to have the matter resolved. As she watched Jon press a tender kiss to Kim's lips, she suddenly felt lonesome and homesick. She missed Xavier. No matter how she tried to push thoughts of him from her mind, he was always on the periphery of her thoughts. She wanted what Jon and Kim had. She wanted to know she was loved completely by the man she loved.

"So tell me you two, was it love at first sight?" Nicole asked trying to lighten her spirits.

"According to Jon it was for him, but I was terrified," Kim responded. "I was divorced and suspicious of all men. I never thought I'd be in an interracial relationship. Then Jon and I began working together and we seemed to have so much in common. A part of me wanted to get close, and then the next day I would take two steps back. I drove him crazy."

Nicole shared the couple's laughter as they took her down memory lane. Then Kim began explaining the fear she had about becoming involved in a new relationship, and her words held special meaning for Nicole. In them she gained insight into her relationship with Xavier.

"I had been hurt by a black man Nicole, and so when this white man approached me I was scared. I didn't know if I could trust him, or if he was some white guy experimenting. Jon was patient and loving despite my aloofness. But then I noticed the light missing from his eyes, and I recognized it as pain. I was so busy protecting myself that I didn't realize I was hurting Jon and our friendship. But it's difficult trusting someone with your most intimate feelings once you've been betrayed. You find yourself questioning your actions and comparing them to your previous relationship. Am I repeating the same mistakes? Is this what I did wrong the first time? Will he be there when I need him?" Kim covered Jon's hand as she looked into his eyes. She loved him and was sure of their future. "You know what? I decided to give us a chance, and I'm glad that I did because we are great together."

Nicole was silent for a moment, lost in thought. She processed Kim's words and applied them to Xavier. Was it possible that he was frightened of making the same mistakes with her that he had with Monique? The future suddenly looked brighter, yet she reminded herself that she could be wrong.

"You're thinking about Xavier," Jon commented drawing her attention.

"Yes, I am."

"What Kim said sounds familiar?"

Nodding her head yes, Nicole informed Kim of their relationship and their last encounter. She felt comfortable discussing the matter with her future sister-in-law.

"He's scared just like I was, Nicole. Don't give up on him if you really love him," Kim offered wisely. "Give him the distance he needs to really observe you. If he feels pressured, he'll only pull further away. He sounds like a man in love. The suddenness of your relationship has him frightened. We all somehow believe love should take a long time, but it doesn't. I believe whether we acknowledge it at the time or not, it can happen in a split second."

"You believe that?" Nicole looked skeptical.

Nodding her head vigorously, Kim replied, "I most definitely do. I remember the details of our first meeting." She was speaking of Jon. "I can recite the time of day, where we were, the chairs we sat in, what he was wearing, the cologne he wore..."

Throwing up her hand like a stop sign, Nicole interrupted Kim's recital. "Okay, I get your point. And, yes, I can do the same for me and Xavier, but love? I'm not sure."

"But you did feel something at that moment didn't you?"

A knowing smile spread across Nicole's face as she recalled the feeling. "Electricity."

"Nah—Cupid's arrow," Kim supplied with a wink.

Nicole had laughed joyously at Kim's words. They were so romantic and filled with hope.

Now on the airplane headed home she found herself laughing once more, because they had filled her with hope as well.

Xavier returned to Willow Bayou late Monday night disappointed that he didn't get to see Nicole. He had gone home for the holiday with the hope of clearing up their misunderstanding, but Nicole had been out of town. Gina had informed him of her trip to Atlanta. Obviously she wasn't as upset about their argument as he'd thought she would be. Maybe he should just let the matter go. Was he really ready for a committed relationship? For once his heart and his head were in agreement They both shouted yes. He missed Nicole and desperately wanted the opportunity to love her. However, he wasn't stupid enough to go to her with undying love so soon after pushing her away. Nicole would doubt his sincerity in an instant. He decided the best course of action would be to demonstrate his love. In the face of cold hard facts, she would have to accept the words when they were spoken. Now, if only he could get the chance.

"What are you doing here?" Nicole asked Xavier. Her flight from Atlanta had just arrived and she was expecting Gina to meet her.

"I'm here to take you home." Xavier didn't elaborate.

"I could have taken a cab if Gina was unable to collect me. I'm sorry she disturbed you." She was not going to give him an inch.'

Exasperated, Xavier grabbed Nicole by the forearm and dragged her out of the line of traffic. "Look Nic, I asked to pick you up. I didn't believe you would see me any other way. Not after the way we left things."

"Left things?" She raised arched brows in challenge. "I gave you what you wanted."

"No, you misunderstood what I said. But enough of that Nicole, I came here today to say that I'm not afraid of my feelings for you anymore. I'm embracing them because what we have is too special to throw away. Now you can stand here and lie to me and yourself and say that you don't have feelings for me, but we would both know that you were lying."

Nicole dropped her eyes to study the parquet floor of the terminal. There was truth in his words. Raising her eyes back to his anxious face, she commented, "This isn't about my feelings and what I want. This is about you not being able to get over your wife and allowing yourself to really feel again. In here," she pointed to his heart.

Xavier enclosed the hand which pointed to his chest. He caressed it lovingly with his thumb. Her skin was always dewy soft, and since that night in New Orleans, he knew it was this soft all over. "Monique is my ex-wife and my past. You, Nicole Edwards, are my heart and my future."

It took Nicole less than a second to process his words. Their meaning was clear and welcomed. The tears were instantaneous as she flew into his open arms. She wrapped herself tightly around him, familiarizing herself with the feel and scent of him. Who knows she just might get the chance to put one of Gina's little seduction scenes into action.

CHAPTER 19

Joyous laughter filled the interior of Nicole's kitchen as Xavier and Ryan stole yet another chocolate chip cookie from the cookie jar. Nicole's wildly thrown potholder went wide missing them by a mile. The comical action caused them to release another round of laughter as she stood with her hip propped against the cabinet shaking her head. A smile illuminated her face as she joined the men in her life in laughter. It had been a year since that confession in the airport, and since that time they had become a couple sharing and growing. However, Nicole still prayed for more. She wanted to be Xavier's wife and a mother to Ryan, but she had taught herself to not allow the need to overshadow the time they shared.

Over the past several months they'd spent all their available time together. They attended Ryan's school and sporting events as a couple. Nicole baked and worked right alongside the mothers. She accompanied Xavier to squadron functions and private dinners. She became as much a part of their lives as they allowed. And they allowed her to experience almost all of it. In turn, Xavier was always present beside her as well. They shared the holidays together, and he accompanied Nicole to her mother's surprise anniversary party in June. To the outside world they appeared to be a real family, but to Nicole she was on borrowed time and intended to make the most of it.

"Not another cookie you two. You'll ruin your appetites."

Xavier got up from the table and walked toward Nicole. He wrapped his arms around her waist while looking down into her beautiful golden eyes. Wanting to share his love the only way the moment allowed, he lowered his mouth to hers. His son's childish giggles were ignored, as he slipped his tongue between Nicole's lips, tasting her own recently eaten chocolate chip cookie. She was sweet and so responsive to his touch. He loved this woman more and more each day.

"You are so good to us," he whispered while his hand stroked the side of her face.

Nicole turned her head to kiss his palm as it caressed her cheek. "We're good to each other."

"That we are. You do realize that you have cooked enough food to feed an army here," Xavier indicated the dishes lining the counter tops.

Nicole followed his gaze and conceded that maybe she *had* gone overboard.

"Maybe I did prepare too much, but my mother said there would be a lot of people at her Labor Day cookout, and I just wanted to make sure there was plenty.

Kissing her nose playfully he replied, "Trust me there's plenty. By the way it's wonderful to hear you call Linn *mother.*"

"It feels pretty good to be able to. It hasn't been easy, though. There were some days I felt extremely close to her and then others when I was consumed with anger, but she didn't give up on me. She listened and really tried to understand my feelings. For that I can only respect her." Nicole shrugged her shoulders. "I don't know if it's normal these feeling I have, but I'm tired of being angry and on guard all the time. They have truly embraced me as a part of the family, and I can't refuse the offer. I don't want to refuse. I need the love of a family."

Xavier heard and understood Nicole's meaning. He knew their relationship couldn't continue like this much longer.

Nicole and Xavier strolled across the lush green lawn of the Walkers' backyard. They were stopped numerous times to join in various conversations. Along the way, they exchanged greetings with Frances, who preferred being called Frankie. Nicole took great joy in the sisterly relationship they were forging. She and Jan would always be closer, but she and Frankie now behaved like siblings as well. As they talked, the wind gust increased kicking up the red, white, and blue tablecloths. The sun was bright, and the sky remained clear, yet with each gust the wind became stronger. It was a reminder of the hurricane that churned indecisively out in the Gulf of Mexico. Everyone along the Gulf Coast was aware of the looming storm, tracking its erratic path. While they hastily chased the windblown napkins and paper plates, Xavier's beeper went off. Checking the readout, he headed inside to use the telephone. The call was from the squadron.

"I'll be right back. I have to check in with the desk," he called to Nicole in passing.

Nicole joined her mother who sat on the glider conversing with friends. She half-listened to their conversation. Her attention was focused on her mother's hand lying next to hers, and its similarity to her own with its delicate bones and slender fingers. As though sensing her daughter's thoughts, Linn reached out and took Nicole's hand within her own. It was such a simple gesture, but it went a long way in bridging the past. As the other women excused themselves, Linn turned to face her firstborn.

"Are you having a good time?"

"Yes, I am. It's been a wonderful day." Nicole looked across the lawn to where Ryan tossed a baseball with another boy. "Ryan's had a good time as well. He appears happiest when he's around family." Catching herself and realizing what she had said, Nicole tried to clarify herself. "I mean..."

"I know what you mean, dear. I'm just wondering when you and Xavier are going to stop wasting precious time and make a commitment to each other."

"Mother, I don't know," Nicole whispered with frustration. "Xavier hasn't mentioned marriage. He appears perfectly happy with things the way they are."

"And what about you? Are you content with the current situation, Nicole?"

Nicole knew that she wasn't, but she couldn't tell her mother the truth. "For now I am. This level of involvement is new for me and I'm still settling into it."

Linn didn't believe one word. "Settling in huh? Is that what you call it? Nicole, you love that man and his son with all your heart."

"I'm not denying my love for them."

"No, you're not, but you are trying to convince me that you don't want to be Xavier's wife." Linn's expression dared Nicole to deny the truth.

Nicole couldn't and therefore allowed the subject to drop as Xavier emerged from the back door.

Xavier approached both women unaware that he was the topic of conversation. His thoughts were on the information he had received. He wanted to put on a pleasant face, but was no longer able to maintain the smile as he thought about the news he had to deliver.

"Excuse me, ladies, but I'm afraid I've got some pretty bad news to report. Searching around the yard for Franklin, he finally spotted the man and waved him over. As Franklin pulled up alongside, Xavier delivered his news.

"Franklin, I wanted you to hear the latest on the storm. Hurricane Isobel has been upgraded to a Category 3 with the possibility of strengthening. She has also made a dramatic turn straight for us. The wind speed has increased and the barometric pressure has dropped within the hour. The civil defense will be making voluntary evacuation requests probably in the morning."

"Then I guess its time to end this party and start making final preparations," Franklin voiced. "Linn, it appears those storm shutters were worth the investment after all."

"It appears that way, honey." Linn faced Nicole and took her hand. "Will you be bunking with us during the storm?"

Nicole was touched by the request, but she shook her head no. "I have my home to secure."

Xavier's eyes widened as Nicole spoke up. "Are you crazy? There is no way I'm allowing you to remain in your home alone during this storm. Nic, I'll secure your home. You stay here with your folks or with Rosa and Ryan in the shelter."

"I've stayed by myself before, Xavier. You forget I was raised on hurricanes."

"That may be true, but you won't be staying this time. I have to report to the base, and the last thing I want to do is worry about your safety. Do this for me please, Nic."

She could refuse him nothing when he called her Nic and looked genuinely concerned for her well being. "Okay, I'll stay with Rosa and Ryan because this is probably their first hurricane. But I'll secure my own home and gather some personal items."

"You're right, it is, and I would feel much better having all of my loved ones together," Xavier admitted.

Nicole leaned over and placed a kiss on her mother's cheek. "I'll call you."

The couple collected Ryan as Franklin made an announcement concerning the changing weather. The crowded backyard of a moment ago was soon empty.

Xavier dropped Nicole off at home with the promise to return for her later. While he was away, she went through the standard hurricane preparations. She turned the freezer up to its highest selling because rock-hard food would keep longer in the event they lost power during the storm. She had gathered sufficient canned goods and a stash of batteries for the flashlight and camping light. Important papers she sealed in waterproof plastic bags. She stored and secured loose items, and from the shed out back, she pulled out the precut plywood used to board up the windows. Finally she charged up her cell phone.

At home Xavier went through similar preparations before returning to the base. There, too, preparations were taking place. Government buildings were swiftly boarded up, and the city within a city was beginning to look like a ghost town. At the squadron he noticed that the building's front doors and windows had all been boarded as well. The patrol cars were being gassed up, and loose items were being brought in for storage. The last thing anyone needed was for a loose item to be used as a projectile by damaging winds. As he walked the halls of his squadron, he saw his people continuing preparations for what would be several long tedious days and nights of monitoring and patrolling.

The base shelters were ready, as were the teams to monitor their safety. A schedule of personnel to patrol the housing areas for looters if evacuation became necessary was established. All contingencies were outlined and discussed. His people were well trained and up to the challenge of protecting and securing the installation. All they could do now was sit and wait for the latest update on the storm from the Hurricane Hunters. Their data would be provided to The Weather Channel and the base's commanding officers.

When the report came that the storm was indeed heading their way and intensifying, yet still a Category 3, Xavier began releasing his people in shifts to take care of their families. He went to Nicole's to check on her preparations and was once again impressed by this woman's capable abilities. Her home was secured, and she'd taken care of all necessary preparations. Her television, like that of everyone along the coast, was tuned in to The Weather Channel for the latest update.

"It looks like we're in for a rocky ride," Nicole commented as they sat side by side on the sofa with their eyes glued to the television.

"Hurricane Hunters clocked winds at 120 mph," Xavier informed her. Placing his arm around Nicole's shoulders, he drew her close and kissed her temple. "Are you ready to head over to my place?"

"Yes, I am. Help me load my things into your car and we can be on our way. By the way don't forget to unplug the TV."

As Xavier loaded his vehicle with the necessary evacuation items and food supplies, he acknowledged that Nicole really had been raised on hurricanes. The lady was prepared and well organized. It took them less than fifteen minutes to secure her home and drive over to his place. There they unloaded everything and checked the latest update. Once he was equipped with the latest information, Xavier kissed Nicole and hugged Ryan before returning to the squadron to oversee base security.

When the new morning dawned, the winds and rain along the coast had increased dramatically as Isobel drew near. The winds of the storm were now reported to be 130 mph and increasing. Everyone held their breath and prayed this storm would not make the catastrophic Category 4 or 5. The local civil defense began making pleas for voluntary evacuations. Base residents were awakened by Security Forces personnel and ordered to evacuate the housing area and take shelter on base within the next three hours. Each squadron was assigned a designated sheltering area. The shelters and buildings occupied by security and emergency personnel would be the only buildings with utilities.

Nicole had spent the night in Xavier's home in Xavier's bed. He had not returned home the night before, but had phoned saying that he would spend the night on the sofa in his office. Conditions were rapidly changing and he wanted to be available for his personnel as they prepared for the impending storm.

It had taken Nicole awhile to fall asleep. Last night was the first time that she had actually spent the night in Xavier's base quarters and in this particular bed. When they wanted to be alone, it was at her place or his home in New Orleans. It was no wonder her mind kept conjuring up images of her and Xavier making love in his bed. Then her thoughts ventured toward Monique. She wondered if Monique and Xavier had shared this bed. Had they created their child on this very mattress? The thought made her toss and turn with unease. Eventually she convinced herself that it didn't matter, because Monique no longer slept there. She had finally drifted off to sleep with thoughts of she and Xavier sharing this bed as husband and wife.

Nicole now awaited his return to escort them to the squadron shelter on base. She went through the house making sure all electrical items, but the refrigerator and stove, were unplugged. She gathered items for the hours in the shelter. Dressed in jeans and a long sleeve shirt with T-shirt underneath and Timberland boots, Nicole was prepared for the aftermath of the storm. If they were struck as was predicted, she knew sturdy, dependable clothes and shoes would be needed. The storm would create dangerous hazards out of everyday materials, and the mosquito infestation could be severe. She made sure Rosa and Ryan were dressed similarly.

Xavier bound through the back door with the weight of the world on his shoulders, or so it seemed. The hurricane was barreling straight for them, and it was his responsibility to secure the base while riding out the storm. That's why it was such a relief to have Nicole with Rosa and Ryan. He knew she was capable of getting them through the storm and the hours of sheltering. They made a good team and he didn't take the fact lightly. He knew how important it was for a military man to have the support of his spouse. The thought brought him up short. Nicole wasn't his wife nor had he asked her to marry him. But here he was thinking of her in those terms. Marriage no longer frightened him, and he knew Nicole was responsible for this change. He smiled as his eyes landed on her at the stove.

"Hi, baby." He greeted Nicole with a bear hug. They rocked slowly together as they savored the warmth and closeness of the other. "I missed you last night." His early morning baritone caressed her sensitive ears. He felt a tremor course through her body as he nibbled on a pierced lobe.

Nicole returned his greeting with her own sensual voice. "I missed you too."

That morning purr stirred his blood. He lowered his lips to hers oblivious to everything and everyone. The kiss was intense and scorching. Their tongues performed a mating dance as their bodies pressed close together. Nicole's hands roamed Xavier's muscled back while his hands framed her face for his kiss. As his hands lowered to cup her backside and draw her closer, advancing voices could be heard. Nicole tried to withdraw from the embrace, but Xavier had different ideas. He held her tightly as his mouth continued to drink from hers. He didn't care who knew he loved this woman.

"They're at it again," Ryan whispered to Rosa, yet loud enough for Nicole and Xavier to hear. His childish laughter caused the adults to laugh as well.

"Good morning, you two," Xavier greeted the new arrivals as he finally released Nicole.

Uncomfortable with the little scene Xavier had put on, Nicole busied herself placing breakfast on the dining room table. She didn't meet Rosa's knowing smile as she moved around the kitchen. Finally with nothing left to do but eat, she unplugged the stove and called the others to the table. Forgetting the napkins she dashed back into the kitchen, but before she could leave Xavier entered behind her.

"Hey, wait a minute. Did I embarrass you in here? Ryan has seen us kissing before."

Nicole met his questioning gray eyes and nodded. "I know Ryan has, but what is Rosa going to think about me? I slept in your bed last night, and now she finds us in a lip lock in the kitchen. I don't want her to think I'm a bad influence on Ryan or a loose woman."

Remembering Nicole's high school years and the accusations she'd faced, he understood her concern. "Baby, no one who knows you would consider you a loose woman. And as for Ryan and Rosa, they know what you mean to me. You're mine, Nicole Edwards, and you belong here with us."

There it was again—inclusion. Nicole's stomach did a somersault at the implication. "Breakfast is getting cold." What else could she say? She couldn't say that she wanted to be his wife, because Xavier hadn't brought the subject of marriage up. So she decided against commenting.

An hour later Xavier escorted *his* family into the base shelter. Nicole, Ryan, and Rosa claimed a corner in the rear of the room located on the third floor of the cinder block building. Depositing their sleeping gear on the floor, Nicole instructed Rosa in the art of creating a private haven. She followed Xavier back outside to the car. They gathered several grocery bags and a cooler. On their last trip to the vehicle, Xavier delayed Nicole's return inside. He drew her into the vehicle and closed the doors on the crowded parking lot. The tinted windows of his vehicle offered them a modicum of privacy. No one knew what this hurricane would bring, so Xavier took the time to express his thoughts to Nicole.

"Sweetheart, I'm going to be unavailable for the next several days. You probably won't be able to reach me until this storm has passed," he explained, caressing her hands which were locked within his.

I know you have a job to perform. Don't worry about Ryan and Rosa. I promise to take care of them both."

"Take care of all three of you," Xavier replied softly, then added. "When this is over, there is something you and I need to discuss."

The memory of those softly spoken words reverberated inside Nicole's head. They silenced the crowded hum of the people seeking shelter. As she propped against the cold rear wall of the shelter, she closed her eyes reliving the potent yet chaste kiss they had shared before he escorted her back inside. Absorbed in her thoughts, she failed to hear the winds increase to a low howl. It wasn't until Ryan shook her leg that she returned to the present. Nicole glanced at his almond brown face, realizing she couldn't love him any more than if she had given birth to him herself. She opened her arms in recognition of his fear and cradled him close. She smiled over at Rosa who watched them intently.

After Ryan dozed off to sleep still within Nicole's arms, Rosa allowed her thoughts to wander. Silently she had watched the relationship between Nicole and Xavier develop. In her sometimes invisible capacity she was allowed to view people clearly and undisturbed. She had been with Xavier since Ryan was an infant and knew him as well as she knew her own children. He was a kind, gentle, respectable young man who didn't run around with an assortment of women. He was selective in the women he did date, and never once had he brought them to his home. And as a rule, he never allowed Ryan to become emotionally attached to any of them. So for Xavier to allow Nicole to become a part of their lives, a member of the family, meant she was there to stay.

Stretching out on the egg crate padding Nicole had wisely insisted she bring, Rosa focused on the tender scene across from her. Nicole was stroking Ryan's hair lovingly as he slept. She was a fine young woman and would make both

Xavier and Ryan's life complete. Rosa recalled how reserved Nicole had been when they initially met. She could be with a crowd of people and yet appear to be alone. She hadn't understood the cause for Nicole's isolation until later when Xavier had confided in her about Nicole's abandonment as a child. Her heart had gone out to the lovely woman who gave so much of herself. Now looking at her, Rosa could see the visible changes in her since Nicole had met her mother and gained a family. She smiled now with her eyes as well as with her mouth, as if she'd gained a confidence she hadn't possessed before. But what hadn't changed about her was her obvious love for Xavier. Rosa knew she tried to hide the fact but all one had to do was look into her eyes. Rosa had no doubt that Xavier knew of Nicole's feelings. However, what confused Rosa was Xavier's response to Nicole. He was interested and obviously in love, yet he wasn't doing anything about it.

Finally drifting off to sleep, Rosa vowed to give the young lovers a push in the right direction. After this hurricane passed and the cleanup was complete, she would take Ryan to New Mexico with her for a weekend visit with her son. Ryan always enjoyed visiting Jesse and his family. The children were all close to the same age and played well together. The time away would afford Xavier and Nicole quality time together to discover what they truly possessed. She knew a marriage could possibly be the end of her job, but she loved Xavier and Ryan enough to want to see them happy. And she had no doubt that Nicole was the woman for the job.

CHAPTER 20

Around two o'clock in the morning, their second day in the shelter, Hurricane Isobel blew into the Gulf Coast area. The wind howled outside the building. With each gust it appeared to grow louder and fiercer. A small television was on in the large room and fortunately the local news channel remained on the air. The weather anchor informed the viewers that this wave of storms was just the beginning as the outer bands of the hurricane moved inland. While Rosa and Ryan slept, Nicole listened to the weather report, concerned for Xavier's safety. She prayed he and his people were somewhere safe and dry. Just as a reporter ventured outside to give the viewers a view of the storm, the lights in the shelter blinked. Startled cries went up from the nervous evacuees. When the room settled down, a weary Nicole laid down on her pallet beside Ryan and drew him into her arm. She then drifted off for the night.

Meanwhile Xavier stretched out on the sofa in his office for a couple hours' sleep. For the moment there was nothing anyone could do but wait out Isobel's wrath. The majority of his squadron was bedded down throughout the building. Only a skeleton crew manned the front desk and emergency phones. As he adjusted his large body to a more comfortable position, his thoughts turned to his family secured in the shelter. Simply having Nicole with

Rosa and Ryan helped to ease his mind. Her thorough planning and level-headedness were essential in the making of a military spouse and so far throughout this crisis she had risen to the challenge. And to think he had been reluctant to become involved with her due to their age difference.

In the dark of his office he allowed his mind to drift as the wind's velocity increased. Nicole had looked so at home standing in his kitchen yesterday morning. And when she greeted him with a welcoming kiss, he'd caught a glimpse of his future. Nicole belonged in his life. She had been created just for him and he for her. Before drifting off to sleep he promised himself that before the end of the year, Nicole would agree to become Mrs. Ramón.

The screaming wind outside the boarded window awakened Xavier. He tilted his wrist so he could see the night-gb watch face. Stretching his long body, he slowly rolled into a sitting position and with a twist and a stretch tried to work out the kinks. He walked over to the door and switched on the overhead lights. Shielding his light sensitive eyes, he waited for them to adjust. When they did, he opened the door of his office and walked out to check on the status of the storm. Several minutes later, while he nursed his second cup of coffee, he learned the worst of Isobel was yet to come.

By noon the shelter was an ever-increasing body of motion and noise. The parents were nervous and anxious about their futures, while their children were restless and tired of being cooped inside. A young boy no more than four or five, who had grown bored with the books and games his mother had packed for sheltering, unscrewed a flashlight spilling batteries onto the floor. After his third time of collecting batteries and stuffing them back into the flashlight, for a repeat performance, his father sat him down with a stern reprimand. Five minutes later he was kicking the side of the family cooler.

Nicole had watched the scene and many others just like it from her position in the corner. Repeatedly, parents lost their tempers as their children rushed full steam ahead from one bout of trouble to the next. Unable to sit there any longer watching theses scenes replay themselves, she decided to do something about the situation. Rising, she walked over to the shelter guard, a young, slender airman who was obviously annoyed by the situation. After explaining her idea, Nicole within minutes was marching out a line of school-aged children to another available room down the hallway. Equipped with the supplies and games she had stored for Ryan and other donated items from various shelter families, she and several volunteers set up a makeshift day care center.

By four o'clock the children were returned to their much-rested parents for a meager meal. Nicole and Ryan made their way to their place in the corner where Rosa had assembled a meal of peanut butter and jelly sandwiches and sliced apples. As the three of them ate, Nicole listened to the howling gales of Hurricane Isobel. The sound alone was enough to drive a person mad, let alone being locked in a room with nervous anxious people. With that thought in mind, Nicole surveyed her little party. Rosa's face was marred with worry as well as exhaustion. Waiting out a hurricane affected the mind as well as the body. Ryan, on the other hand, exhibited less signs of stress for which Nicole was grateful.

At eight-thirty that night the eye of Hurricane Isobel slowly moved over the Gulf Coast offering a temporary moment of calm and quiet. Xavier and his men ventured outside for their first glimpse of Isobel's destruction. Standing outside on the walkway of his building Xavier glanced toward the heavens and was struck with awe at the clear, cloudless sky, which was the eye of the storm. Stars twinkled above, and the wind had died down into a gentle breeze. However, when he glanced around the grounds of his facility, he was shocked by the devastation. Numerous trees were down, littering the streets and grounds. Roads were flooded with waist deep water. Rooftops were ripped and torn away from their structures. Windows of local buildings that had been boarded prior to the storm now housed fallen trees. Isobel was clearly wreaking havoc. Ordering his men back inside the shelter, they once again secured the front door as they awaited the most violent winds of Isobel. The backside of the hurricane would do the most damage, and from what he had just witnessed, it would be immense. His thoughts returned to his family locked away in the shelter. He wouldn't breathe easier until they were back in his arms and safe.

Xavier was awakened by the sound of the birds chirping outside his window on the third day. Listening closely, he knew that the rain had finally stopped. Anxious to get a glimpse of the base, he left his office to investigate Isobel's destruction. On entering the foyer he was pleased to see a young airman uncovering the door. Whispering a thank you, he walked past the young man out into the breaking dawn. Speechless, he took in the destruction left behind. Everywhere his eyes booked there were debris and standing water. The once immaculate base known for its abundance of beautiful trees was no more. Isobel had snapped, sheared, or uprooted most trees. The side of the commissary had fallen victim to the oldest tree on the base. Insulation littered the street, and sections of rooftops were peeled backed like lids on a can. It would take several days to make the base barely livable. Finally shaking himself out of his stupor, Xavier began dispensing orders.

He spent the next hour in meetings with the disaster team leaders to lay out the plans for cleanup and recovery. Each member was well aware that it would be several weeks, if not months, before the base and local community were back to normal. It was their job to see to a speedy recovery. As the meeting broke up, Xavier was finally free to go check on his family in the shelter. He looked forward to laying his eyes on the three of them.

The moment Xavier passed through the door of the shelter he was bombarded with questions. Assuring them that everyone was healthy and in one piece, he began enumerating the steps for recovery. He promised the captive audience that all was being done to get them back into their homes. After satisfying the crowd, he went to his family. Xavier's heart picked up speed as he spotted Nicole cradling a sleeping Ryan in her arms.

There he was all in one piece and looking just as good as the last time she saw him. As his eyes connected with hers she experienced a flood of warmth. He looked so handsome and commanding in uniform and had such a professional demeanor as he spoke to the crowd. When he headed in their direction, she ran a hand over her hair. She must look awful after all the hours of being cooped up inside the shelter. When he finally reached them and stooped down before her, she smiled as she examined his handsome face. With her right hand she caressed his now noticeably tired features. There were thin brackets around his mouth and half circles under his eyes, but he was in one piece.

"Hi baby—Rosa," Xavier greeted them as he ran a hand over his son's sleeping head. "How are you ladies holding up?"

"We're doing well, Major, thanks to Nicole here. With her expertise we were well prepared for a long stay. Any smart man would snatch her up," Rosa hinted with a wink.

Xavier couldn't agree more with Rosa's remarks. To Nicole, however, he commented. "How do I thank you for taking care of my family?"

"You just did," she replied. "I love them too."

"Major Ramón," Jennifer Melendez interrupted the small group, "I just wanted to inform you of the jewel you have there." She pointed to Nicole. "That young lady of yours was a Godsend yesterday. The children were restless and the parents on edge; it made for an unpleasant combination. Nicole set up a makeshift day care area in one of the available rooms. The children enjoyed themselves and the parents were able to relax for a couple of hours. She's a special lady, Major. She would make a man an excellent military wife." She patted Xavier's arm as she smiled down at Nicole. "If anyone needs any help after this storm, let me know."

"Yes, I will," Xavier replied as she turned to walk away. "And thanks for the advice."

All the talk about marriage was making Nicole uncomfortable. She didn't want Xavier to feel pressured into saying or doing something he didn't want. Instead of giving him a chance to comment on Jennifer's remarks, Nicole began asking questions.

"How extensive is the damage? Do you have any idea when we will be allowed to return to our homes?"

Xavier wasn't fooled. He knew exactly what she was doing. He would allow her to change the subject for now, but once things returned to normal he was stating his case.

"The destruction is extensive throughout the city. We're estimating that it will take the base at least today and maybe part of tomorrow to be semi-livable. The base utilities were turned off in unoccupied areas as a precautionary measure just prior to the brunt of the storm coming ashore and appear to have weathered the storm without mishap. They should be turned back on sometime later today after civil engineers check the systems more thoroughly. I'm guessing by late morning people will be returning to their quarters."

"What about in the city? Any idea as to when people will be allowed back into the neighborhoods?" Nicole asked, concerned for her home.

Xavier's face looked grim. "It's going to be a long time before electricity, water, or telephone systems are operational. Some areas are completely flooded. Bayous have overflowed, releasing alligators and moccasins into nearby neighborhoods. Highway 90 is covered by sand washed from the beach and uprooted trees block streets."

"Enough! I get the picture," Nicole sighed.

Xavier wished he could reassure Nicole that her home was in one piece, but he couldn't. At the moment he wasn't even sure whether his home had survived the storm. So far there had only been hit and miss damage in the housing area closest to the squadron. They hadn't ventured any further.

He clasped Nicole's hand and caressed it lovingly. "We have to take it one day at a time, love. Everything will work out."

"I know you're right, but I'm anxious. It's the only real home I've had." This was the worst part of going through a hurricane. The terrible wait until the infrastructure of the city was back in some degree of working order.

"Come on, a little fresh air will do you good," Xavier offered, easing his son off Nicole's lap. It amazed him how children could sleep through just about anything.

Nicole followed behind Xavier as he meandered around the congested room. Out in the hallway he took her hand and gave it a reassuring squeeze. Downstairs he held the door open as Nicole stepped through, taking in her first sight of Isobel's aftermath. All around her was destruction in one form or another.

Nicole tilted her head up to the sunlight and closed her eyes. She blocked out the sight and gave herself over to the sun's warmth. It was wonderful to breathe fresh air again. "Thanks, sweetheart, this was exactly what I needed."

"No problem, baby, I aim to please."

Late the next morning the shelter occupants were allowed back into their homes. Xavier was there to pick up his family after surveying his quarters. Except for the yard, all was intact. They talked non-stop all the way back to his home. The stress of being confined in the shelter had taken its toll on them all, and the sudden freedom sparked joyous conversation. Ryan related his experience in the shelter and spoke of new friendships he'd made. He delighted in telling his father about assisting Nicole in setting up the daycare.

"Nicole said I was a big help, Dad. She even let me read to the little kids," he beamed proudly as he informed his father.

Xavier's face was lit with a smile just listening to his son's happiness. He had Nicole to thank for that. Glancing at each other, they shared a smile over Ryan's exuberance.

It had been agreed that as soon as the interstate was reopened, Ryan and Rosa would go stay with his parents until the city returned to normal. School wouldn't be resuming for some time and it was the perfect opportunity for Ryan to visit his grandparents. It would also afford Rosa a much-needed break after spending time in the shelter. So upon arriving home, Xavier placed a call to the squadron desk inquiring about road conditions. As expected, the highway patrol had reopened the interstate. Rosa and Ryan prepared to leave.

Nicole paced the living room while Xavier tended to his family. She was anxious to get home. Turning on the television set, she listened as the reporter announced that local shelter occupants would not be allowed back into the local communities. Power lines littered the neighborhoods. Only the main arteries of the city had been cleared and opened to vehicles. The reporter estimated that it would be several days yet before people would be able to return home. It wasn't the news Nicole wanted to hear. She slapped the power button off.

Xavier had caught the last of the reporter's story. He could only imagine her anxiety. "Nicole, you know that you can stay here with me for as long as it takes."

Nicole had been unaware of Xavier's presence. When she turned around, she read the worry in his face and knew that she was responsible. She walked up to him and slid her arms around his waist, hugging him sweetly. Their closeness made her feel better. "Thank you, but you don't have to worry about me. I'm going to be fine." She tried to smile but failed miserably.

"You don't have to pretend for me, Nicole. I know the news isn't good for the local area, but with God's blessing your home came through the storm just fine."

Nicole smiled as she listened to that spiritual side of Xavier exposing itself again. In her heart she felt that everything was all right.

After Rosa and Ryan left for New Orleans, Nicole and Xavier both took long leisurely showers. The base water system hadn't been contaminated. Feeling rejuvenated they headed outside to tackle the cleanup around the house. Broken branches from the oaks and magnolias littered the ground, and leaves and other debris washed on the waves of flooded streets choked the flower beds. Landscaping timbers lay scattered everywhere.

The couple worked for several hours side by side. It was a simple pleasure to be outdoors and united again. They worked well together, each knowing when the other needed assistance. Xavier raked the lawn free of broken twigs and stripped leaves. He paused to wipe the sweat from his brow. While doing so, he watched Nicole as she cleaned out the flower beds.

She was on her knees, unconcerned for her appearance or her clothing. She worked with gloved hands as she removed debris from the beds, but when she replanted the uprooted vegetation, she removed the gloves and used her bare hands. She was skilled at the task and worked efficiently. The tranquil expression on her face indicated that gardening was a soothing chore. Thoroughly absorbed by the task, she absently swiped at a loose strand of hair, leaving a trail of dirt.

Xavier realized he must look like an idiot just standing there smiling foolishly, but the sight of Nicole warmed his insides. She was so different from Monique. That woman would never be caught dead on her hands and knees digging in a flower bed. And to help with the yard work? Not a chance. He could visualize his future with Nicole. They would share many days and hours like this at Willow Bayou fixing it up together. Their children would be running around the yard laughing as they played. He loved this young woman and was suddenly desperate to claim her. He wondered what she was thinking. Did she feel the magic of the moment?

As always, Nicole knew when Xavier was watching her; it was the pull of his magnetic gray eyes. She didn't dare turn to look at him for fear he would be able to read the joy on her face. She loved being with him like this. It gave her a sense of belonging to him and his space. She wanted desperately to build a home with him at Willow

Bayou. She could envision the garden she would plant and the landscaping they would do themselves. She dreamed of their children romping in the yard under their watchful eyes. She wanted a life with this man.

Finally pleased with the appearance of the flower beds, Nicole straightened and eyed their handiwork. Rubbing her lower back, she found Xavier watching her again. This time she returned his bold stare. There was something different in his eyes today and it caused her to shiver. Something had changed within their relationship and she wasn't sure what it was. Nervously glancing down, she realized how utterly dirty she had become. Stupidly she swiped at her hair trying to right its condition, but only managed to smear more dirt. Now she knew for sure why Xavier was looking at her so strangely. She looked a mess. She'd bet Monique was never caught with a hair out of place.

"I must look a sight." She tried to knock some of the dirt off her jeans.

Xavier watched with amusement as Nicole fussed over her appearance. The woman obviously had no idea how turned on he was by her disheveled state. The idea of rolling around on the ground with her making love ran through his mind. He could never recall seeing Monique any way but pristine. Nicole was the type of woman a man could enjoy exploring all day. He didn't have to worry about her hair, make-up, or clothing. He could wrap his arms around her and truly love her at all times of day and night. And so with that thought in mind he decided to do just that.

"What are you doing?" Nicole asked nervously as Xavier advanced purposefully.

"Just what I've been thinking about all day," he commented, wrapping his arms around her as his lips claimed hers. He kissed her sweetly because the love flowing through his veins at the moment was light and pure. He embedded his fingers in her braided hair, loving the idea of simply being able to do so. "Come on, let's go inside," he said finally as they came up for air.

Overwhelmed, Nicole merely nodded.

Once inside, the dictates of their stomachs took precedence. Nicole took a quick shower before going into the kitchen to prepare an early dinner. By the time Xavier returned from his shower, she had the table set and several sandwiches made. She added chips and fruit. It was the best she could do on short notice.

Neither one cared what they were eating. It was the company they were sharing which truly made the meal. Their conversation was light and sometimes comical. Nicole had never felt so free and relaxed with Xavier before. She felt the way she did when she was with Jon, simply Nicole. That realization was like a splash of cold water on her mood. She knew she was hopelessly in love with this man, and that there would be no recovering from this love.

Xavier immediately noticed the change in Nicole and wondered what had happened. "Is something wrong?"

Wide-eyed, Nicole knew she couldn't tell Xavier the truth, so instead she said, "I realized I don't have anything to sleep in tonight."

A quick retort popped into Xavier's head, but deciding against verbalizing the thought, he said instead, "Is that all? I'll clean up this mess. Check the center drawer of the dresser in my room."

Nicole opened the center drawer as instructed and discovered several T-shirt and a pair of black silk pajamas. She opted for the large pajama top because she knew it would cover her completely. As she reached in to remove it, her finger snagged on something in the bottom of the drawer. She immediately stuck the injured finger into her mouth and with her left hand pushed the other clothes out of the way. The bottom half of a gold picture frame was now visible. Her heart dropped. She knew instinctively whose picture it was. Removing her discovery, she stared into the face of the woman who'd shared Xavier's name. She was beyond pretty. She was gorgeous. Nicole immediately noticed the similarities between this woman and Carmen. She could feel the insecurities returning.

"That's a keepsake for Ryan," Xavier softly said as he came up behind her.

She hadn't heard his approach as she was absorbed in admiring the competition. What did this man want with her? "She's beautiful."

"Only on the outside," Xavier replied, gripping the edge of the picture frame. He gently pulled it from Nicole's hand and replaced it in the bottom of his drawer. "She can't compare to you, Nicole."

"What does that mean?"

"It means that you're beautiful here," he touched her face, "yet also beautiful here." He pointed to her heart. "I'd choose a beautiful heart over a pretty face any day."

His words pleased her. She couldn't help the smile which tugged at the corners of her mouth. "You mean to say, if I looked like Cousin It you would still love me?" Her golden brown eyes danced teasingly.

"I would love you just the same," Xavier voiced reverently. He gently pulled Nicole against him rubbing her back. I will love you, Nicole Edwards, even when I no longer walk this earth."

"Oh, Xavier." His beautiful words caused her eyes to blur with tears. "I love you so much." Nicole returned his embrace. She couldn't seem to get close enough to express how his words affected her. So when his mouth swept down covering hers, she eagerly met his kiss with a passion of her own.

Xavier drank deeply from Nicole's sweet mouth. His inserted tongue flirted and mated with hers until a moan was torn from his lips. He allowed his hands to travel the length of her body. She was soft and supple in his hands. The heat of her body aroused him and he had to get rid of their clothes immediately.

Nicole returned the fire in Xavier's kiss. She brazenly caressed herself against his most sensitive and aroused appendage. She welcomed Xavier's removal of her clothes. Actually, she assisted by unzipping her jeans as he freed her buttons and removed her shirt and bra. She needed his touch.

Xavier swept Nicole's hands aside as he removed her pants, taking her panties along. He wanted her bare before him. Accomplishing his mission, he eased Nicole down on the bed and showered her with kisses. He kissed her eyes, her nose, and her pretty little cleft chin. The tips of her proud erect breasts were next, followed by her belly button. The final kiss was the ultimate and Nicole nearly came off the bed. Xavier couldn't remove his clothes fast enough.

He took the necessary precaution and entered Nicole swiftly and with purpose. He made love to her from head to toe, and missed nothing in between. His heart, his spirit, and his body were one as he buried himself deeply. Their passion was indescribable. He didn't want the magic to end too soon so he tempered his pace as he carried Nicole on a wave of ecstasy. They rode together, their movements synchronized and unhurried. They touched and kissed, and loved each other as though it was the first time. With the cresting waves building, Xavier declared his love repeatedly, then was swept away in a wave of pleasure.

He was too stunned by the experience to move. He wanted to sleep exactly where he was but knew his body was too heavy for Nicole to support. Separating their bodies, he kissed her abdomen reverently, knowing it would nurture their future children.

Nicole lay dazed from the loving they had just shared. It was like nothing she had ever dreamed. It had been loving and tender, yet demanding and insatiable. With each touch Xavier had demanded more of her and she'd given it without hesitance.

Xavier rolled over onto his back and drew Nicole against him. He felt completely free of the past and knew that it was time to share the sordid details of his tragic marriage.

"Nic, I told you that Monique didn't want Ryan."

"I remember," Nicole replied softly.

"What I didn't tell you was that she held our son's life for ransom."

Nicole was too stunned to speak. She knew something extremely painful had taken place in Xavier's marriage, but this was worse than anything she could have imagined.

CHAPTER 21

That nightmarish evening came flooding back to Xavier. He had arrived home with the intention of ending their mistake of a marriage. But what he found was Monique sitting at the kitchen table sipping champagne. She held a photograph in her hand.

"What's going on Monique?"

"I'm celebrating, Xavier," she purred smugly.

Moving to stand before her, he picked up the bottle of champagne she had half consumed. "I didn't realize we had anything to celebrate."

"Oh, we don't, but I sure do!" She took another sip from her glass, swinging her crossed leg.

"Do I have to ask or are you going to tell me?" He was slowly losing his temper.

"I'll tell you all right, but first I have a question for you."

"What now, Monique?"

"Do you think I don't know what you've been doing behind my back?"

"Just what are you accusing me of this time."

"It's not an accusation. It's the truth. You and your family think you're so smart. I know you're planning on divorcing me."

"Don't you think it's about time we put an end to this farce?"

"Actually I agree with you, but just not yet. See, I have something you want."

"Believe me, Monique, you have nothing I want. When I married you, I hoped for a loving marriage, but it didn't happen, and so I'm cutting my losses."

"Not so fast, darling. Look at this," she said, dramatically extending the photograph.

Xavier took the small black and white photograph. He turned it around so that he could get a better look. Examining the light and dark shading, his heart stilled with the realization of what he was looking at. His head shot up as his eyes locked with Monique's. "Is it mine?"

Laughing triumphantly, Monique rose from her seat, swaying her hips as she approached him. "I may be a lot of things dear, but stupid I'm not. This baby is definitely yours," she declared, patting her stomach.

"Why didn't you tell me?"

"I'm telling you now," she smarted off. She reached for her glass of champagne. However, before she could take another sip, Xavier swatted the glass from her hand, sending the contents spilling to the floor and down her spotless peach silk dress.

"How dare you!" she yelled, upset for the first time tonight.

Thumping his chest Xavier bellowed, "I dare because you're carrying my child and I will not have you poisoning it."

Catty, boisterous laughter reverberated throughout the room as Monique swiped at the champagne spotting her dress. "I'll bet you're sorry for that little slip up. Don't be angry. I'm giving you what you want. You do want this baby?"

Something in Monique's voice wasn't right He heard her words, but they sounded more like threats. "Despite the current state of our marriage, you know I want this child."

"How badly do you want the bundle of joy?"

"What?" Xavier studied the woman who carried his name, not recognizing her. Or maybe he was only now seeing her for the person she really was.

"I said, how badly do you want this baby? You see, I have no real desire to watch as my body is stretched out of proportion. One visit to the right doctor could put an end to this problem." She watched intently as awareness dawned on Xavier's face. His gray eyes darkened and steeled as they zeroed in on her. For the briefest of moments Monique considered that maybe she had pushed him too far.

"Are you threatening the life of this child?"

"No, not at all. I'm making an investment in my future. It's like this, darling. I'll carry this child to term. Upon delivery you pay me $100,000 for sole custody and a speedy divorce."

He knew he couldn't be hearing this correctly, so he asked Monique to repeat herself. Without shame she did and demanded a response.

"I'm waiting."

"You're actually holding our child for ransom?" Xavier shouted, not caring who heard. "What type of woman are you, Monique? This is your child too. Don't you feel anything for it?"

"It's a means to an end, Xavier, nothing more, nothing less."

He was disgusted by the proposal. He felt nauseous and angry all at the same time. Collapsing into the nearest chair, he hung his head in shame. How had this marriage gone so wrong? And who was this woman he had married? "Monique, you can't be serious."

"Deadly."

"Yes, damn it, I agree to your terms! Upon delivery and a confirmed blood test I'll pay you the money. However, I have a couple of conditions of my own."

Nicole didn't know what to say. She had never heard anything more scandalous. The woman was the lowest form of motherhood. Thank God she had left Ryan with his father. Nicole would hate to think of her rearing Ryan."

"I'm so sorry for both you and Ryan, sweetheart." Nicole rolled over and kissed him tenderly. She didn't know how to respond or how to ease his pain. She finally decided upon simply holding him. "I love you."

A week after Halloween, Nicole knew she was in deep trouble. Since the hurricane and their night of passion, the three of them had been inseparable. Their lives were more interwoven than before. They were so close and often together that several people mistakenly referred to her as Mrs. Ramón. And each time they did, Nicole's heart bled a little more because it was a reminder that she was on borrowed time. However, none of this seemed to faze

Xavier, and because it didn't, it angered Nicole immensely for she wanted far more from this relationship.

She had actually been expecting Xavier to pop the question after the storm. His mention of a discussion had raised her hopes. However, the discussion had turned out to be intimate details about his failed marriage.

In desperate need of advice, Nicole thought to call Gina who now lived in California where Keith was stationed. But deciding this conversation was a face-to-face one, she instead found herself standing on her mother's doorstep forty minutes later. If even a girl needed a mother's advice it was now. As the door swung open it was Jan who greeted her.

Unable to miss her sister's distress, Jan informed Nicole that their mother was out running errands and should be home anytime. She offered her sister something to drink while she waited. Jan opened the refrigerator and removed the pitcher of iced tea while Nicole retrieved the glasses. They sat now facing one another. Jan couldn't stand this quiet moody Nicole. It was too reminiscent of their earlier days as sisters.

"I'm a good listener, Nicole. I know something is bothering you."

"You're right, but I think this is a little complicated for someone your age."

"I'm not that young. Please talk to me."

Since Gina and Keith's departure, the three sisters had bonded, and it was Jan to whom Nicole was the closest. It felt wonderful to have siblings; however, at the moment she needed her mother. On second thought, maybe Jan could help. She was levelheaded and quite mature for such a young age. Circling the rim of her glass with her index finger, Nicole relieved herself of the burden. She gave her sister the edited version.

"I'm in love with Xavier, and he says he's in love with me."

"So what else is new?" Jan quipped, smiling.

"Am I hearing wedding bells?" Linn exclaimed from the doorway.

Both women's heads whipped around at their mother's excitement. Nicole glanced nervously at her sister, then back at her mother. "No wedding bells, Mother."

"No wedding?" Linn said in a disappointed voice as she placed her one grocery bag on the counter top. "What's going on Nicole? You and Xavier love each other."

"Jan, will you excuse us?"

"I can't believe my own sister is treating me like a child," Jan mumbled to no one in particular as she left the kitchen in a huff.

Despite her mood, Nicole managed to smile at her sister's words. Running a hand nervously through her hair, she avoided looking at her mother. She wanted to tell her she knew Xavier loved her and that everything would work out, but then the frightened little girl in her simply wanted her mother to make it all better. "You were right. I do want to marry Xavier and be his wife."

"Doesn't Xavier want the same thing? Marriage is the natural progression of a relationship."

"I don't think so. I'm not sure anymore."

"Nicole, this goes back to your earlier beliefs that Xavier never wanted to love or marry again, doesn't it?" Linn knew she was on to something.

"Yes."

"But Xavier does love you, and marriage is just the next step for you two."

Nicole wished it were that simple. "Mother, there are details of our relationship that you are unaware of." She closed her eyes briefly as she summoned up her courage. Exhaling, she forged ahead with the details of her agreement with Xavier.

"First of all, Nicole, I can't believe a daughter of mine would be so foolish." The words flooded forth like a slap to the face.

Nicole instantly became defensive and struck back. "*Your daughters* weren't foolish enough to make such an agreement, but considering you taught me firsthand about my worthiness, I took what I could get. And believe me, *Mother,* I have paid the price for it. I'm hopelessly in love with a man who says he loves me, but may not consider me worthy of being his wife. But then, why should I expect Xavier to want me, when my own mother didn't?" Nicole jumped from the stool she was sitting on and grabbed her purse. She didn't need this on top of everything else.

"Nicole, I didn't mean that the way it sounded." Linn rushed to block her escape. I know my abandoning you has left scars, but I love you. And any man would be lucky to have you for his wife. Xavier loves you dearly."

Uncontrollable tears ran down Nicole's face. "It was foolish, Mother. I admit that now, because some part of me knew then that I loved him, and that when it ended I would be the one left with a broken heart."

Linn consoled her daughter by drawing her head down to her shoulder and stroking it lovingly as she had dreamed of doing when Nicole was a child. This was her firstborn, and she was in pain. "Nicole, Xavier loves you, sweetheart."

"Yes, but does he love me enough to make me a permanent part of his life as his wife?" She eased out of her mother's embrace, facing her. "Mother, I need for someone to want me. *Just me.*" Her voice broke with a lifetime of yearning.

No one had to tell Linn that she was responsible for this *need* in her daughter. "This is all my fault, Nicole."

"Not this time, Mother. I created this mess on my own."

"Nicole, if this relationship is causing you pain, you either have to end it or tell Xavier how you feel."

"I don't think I'm strong enough to walk away, Mother. Besides it just isn't Xavier I love. Ryan is like a son to me. I would be abandoning him like his mother did, and I can't do that to him."

Like I did you. "Well, I suggest that you and Xavier sit down and discuss where your relationship is heading, because you aren't going to find any peace until you know."

Nicole knew her mother was right. Slipping the strap of her purse onto her shoulder she kissed her mother and hugged her sister on the way out. "I'll speak to you both later."

Nicole arrived in front of Xavier's base quarters thirty minutes later. As she shut off the ignition, she took a deep breath and released it. She removed the key, grabbed her purse, and stepped out into the warm November weather. At the front door she rang the bell and waited. No one answered, but she could clearly hear voices through the door. Hesitantly she tried the knob and discovered the door unlocked. Letting herself in, she heard loud, angry voices coming from the kitchen. She recognized Xavier's voice instantly, but the feminine voice didn't belong to Rosa. Slowly approaching the kitchen doorway, she halted in her tracks as she recognized the owner of the voice.

There in the middle of the kitchen floor stood Xavier's ex-wife, Monique. Immaculately dressed, she was more beautiful in person. Her red hair was now long. It helped to soften her look. She was tall, about five-eight, and sinfully curved in all the right places, and Nicole immediately regretted crying at her mother's. She prayed her eyes weren't red and puffy.

"Why the hell are you here, Monique? Don't give me that line about wanting to get to know your son."

"I was young and foolish, Xavier. I made a mistake," Monique pleaded.

"You're right, you made a mistake. You should have kept on down the road."

Moving in close to Xavier, Monique laid a manicured hand against the wall of his chest She gave him her most repentant expression. "I want my family back, Xavier. I've finally realized what's important. We can still have the life we used to dream about. Please give us a chance."

Nicole stood glued to the floor as she listened to the exchange. She couldn't believe the nerve of the woman to show up after eight years and believe Xavier would just welcome her back with open arms. Moving into the room, she drew both their attention. She didn't know if what she was doing was right, or how Xavier would react, but she was willing to risk it for the sake of the men she loved.

"Hello Monique, I'm Nicole," she stated confidently as she slid her arm around Xavier's waist possessively. She wanted there to be no doubt that she was laying claim to the man. Meeting Monique's surprised eyes, Nicole relaxed inwardly when she felt Xavier draw her closer to his side.

Monique examined Nicole closely. She had to admit the young woman was stunning with her exotic features, and obviously loved Xavier very much, if the fire in her unusual eyes were any indication. And the way Xavier was holding her close, it was obvious that he too was in love with her. She knew getting back into his life would be difficult, but there wasn't a man alive that she couldn't have.

"Nicole, was it? Xavier and I were having a private conversation."

"Oh, I heard part of that conversation, and there are a couple of flaws with your thinking. For starters, Xavier has to want you back, and I'm sure I heard him say that you should have kept on down the road. And lastly, there is no way I'm going to stand back and allow you to take the man I love. As for Ryan, he's your son, and deserves to know his mother, if you are sincere in wanting a relationship with him. But, I swear to you, if you hurt that child, I'll make you regret the day you came to town."

Xavier was speechless. His brows arched in surprise as he glanced over at Nicole. He couldn't believe this was the same woman he'd cuddled with only two nights ago. The sweet, soft-spoken Nicole was gone. In her place was a lioness marking her territory and protecting her young. If it were possible to love her any more, then he most certainly did. They were a united front ready to meet any challenge Monique threw their way.

"I don't want to hurt *my* son or you, Xavier. I've done enough of that in the past" She paused dramatically. "We were once good together. You loved me something fierce. I remember you couldn't keep your hands off me." She shot Nicole a look which said, *You intruded, so now* take *it like a woman.*

Xavier knew what Monique was up to and wasn't about to allow her to make Nicole doubt his love. "It's truly amazing what you choose to remember. See, I remember your lies and your infidelity. I remember your ransoming the life of our child. And I also remember my infant son crying for a mother that wasn't around."

Monique visibly flinched under Xavier's rebuttal. Nicole considered the possibility the woman was sincerely remorseful for her past behavior. However, chancing a glance at Xavier, she knew he wasn't buying her repentant act for one moment. Nicole had never seen him so angry. She gently caressed his back with long soothing strokes and felt the tense muscles slowly relax.

"I see we aren't going to have a civil conversation, so I think I'll leave. Just think about what I've said, Xavier, and try to remember the good times. We had some." Monique then turned cold, hateful eyes onto Nicole and issued a challenge. "There's nothing I like more than a good fight. I hope you're up to it little girl, because I intend to get exactly what I came for."

Xavier quickly interrupted before she could say more. "My son will be home any moment. Please leave." He wouldn't have Monique attacking Nicole or disrupting the peaceful life he had finally created.

Nicole finally released the breath she had been holding after the door closed behind Monique. Anxiety quickly claimed her as she replayed Monique's words. Unconsciously pacing the length of the living room, she acknowledged that she could lose everything she'd ever wanted. Despite Xavier's claim of not being interested in his ex-wife, they shared a child and a history that could very easily be rekindled if Monique played her cards right

"Stop pacing and talk to me"

Nicole came to an immediate halt and placed her hands on her hips as she turned to face him. He was handsome and everything she wanted in a man, and if Monique had her way, she would lose him.

"Is there a chance I could lose you to her?"

Xavier closed the distance between them. He cupped Nicole's face lovingly. "Not a snowball's chance in hell. I love you, Nicole Edwards," he declared, affirming the declaration with a passionate kiss.

The following weekend while working the concession stand at Ryan's football game, Nicole spotted Monique approaching the bleachers. Overly dressed in a beautiful hunter green pantsuit with matching suede boots, she was a definite head turner, and there was no doubt in Nicole's mind as to whose head she wanted to turn. Glancing down at her own blue jeans, sweatshirt, and sneakers, she felt herself to be no competition for the immaculate Monique. She forced herself to ignore what was going on in the bleachers and concentrated on what she was doing. Xavier loved her and she would trust in that love.

Xavier recognized the floral scent taunting his senses as Monique slid onto the bleacher beside him. It used to be his favorite fragrance on her. Now he resented her wearing it. He didn't want her here. This time was reserved for his family. Annoyed that she would intrude, he shot her a withering glance as she slid in next to him, brushing her leg against his. He moved over perturbed by the action. He didn't want anyone to think this woman was his. He knew what type of person lay beneath the expensive clothes, and he had no intention of giving her the opportunity to destroy him again.

Monique chose to ignore Xavier's foul mood. She'd known this wasn't going to be easy, so she would have to be patient and play her hand just right. From the investigator she'd hired to locate Xavier, she knew Nicole would be working the concession stand and would have a bird's eye view of her and Xavier. So with that thought in mind, she put her plan into action."

"Where is Ryan?" she asked, caressing Xavier's arm.

"Number twenty-four standing by the coach." Xavier removed his arm from her grasp.

Monique quickly located her son and felt her heart flutter. She hadn't expected to feel this connection to the son she'd left behind. He stood with his helmet under his arm as he listened intently to whatever the coach was saying. His little head bobbed up and down taking in the information. He was beautiful. In him she saw so much of herself. Her plan was forgotten as she sat there admiring her child. Only the crowd's cheer drew her attention away from him. Checking the scoreboard, she realized the game was over. As she rose to leave, she caught sight of Ryan rushing into Nicole's arms. They exchanged big smiles as they hugged each other lovingly. Her heart ached with jealousy because Nicole was able to give her child something she wasn't capable of giving.

"She loves him, doesn't she?"

Xavier followed her line of vision. "Yes, she does, and he loves her."

Monique couldn't comment at the moment. Her conscience, or what there was of one, was bothering her. How could she destroy her son's happiness? She rose from the bleachers preparing to leave.

"Where are you going? I thought you wanted to meet your son."

"I'm not prepared to meet him today. I just wanted to see him."

Xavier watched Monique as she walked down the bleachers and out of the ball field. Happy that she was gone, he could only hope that would be the last time he'd see her. He hoped she would get bored with the family scene and return to wherever she'd come from.

But it wasn't to be. Over the next several weeks Monique was in and out of his home for one reason or another. Each time he was unfortunately home alone when she arrived. And each time she visited, she tried another seduction scene, and like a bad dream, it never failed that Nicole showed up to witness the drama. Xavier knew Nicole's patience was wearing thin, but he had to play a hunch. Monique was after more than her family back. His police officer's mind was working all the angles, and her story just didn't add up.

"Jan, the woman is everywhere. Every time I show up at Xavier's place, she's there for a private discussion. Like I believe that. Saturday, she was at the library for children's hour. She sat in the back of the room, but never approached Ryan. Sunday during church service, I spotted her two pews behind us to the right After church she disappeared. I can't stand it. She's like a ghost haunting."

Laughing at her sister's description of Monique, Jan asked, "What does Xavier have to say about it?"

Nicole joined her sister who sat crossed-legged in the middle of her bed. She confessed that she didn't know what to make of Xavier's behavior. "He doesn't say much; he just seems to accommodate her."

"Nicole, you don't honestly believe Xavier is interested in his ex-wife?"

Exhausted by the subject, Nicole fell back on the bed and closed her eyes. She replayed the last couple of days over in her mind and couldn't honestly say that he was. "No, I don't. But Jan, as the saying goes, it's a thin line between love and hate."

"Nicole, if you love Xavier, you have to trust him." Jan covered her sister's hand with her own.

"You're absolutely right, little sister." Rising off the bed, she walked over to the dresser and retrieved a large brown envelope. She returned to the bed and passed it to Jan. As her sister read the return address and opened the envelope to retrieve its contents, Nicole told her basically what the enclosed letter said.

"Mr. Stanley is the director of Walden Preparatory in San Diego. He was here on the coast last year when that article on my summer program ran in the newspaper. He mentioned in the letter that Walden is always looking for new programs to offer its students, and my class caught his attention. He wants me to teach a similar course at Walden. He has enclosed a brochure on Walden and a benefits pamphlet. All arrangements have been made and paid for by Walden. He wants to meet with me during the first week of Christmas break. It would be a great opportunity," Nicole said to her sister who was looking at her as though she had lost her mind.

"You aren't seriously considering taking this position, are you?"

"No, of course not," she shook her head in response. "But it wouldn't hurt to visit I mean, it's a great opportunity, and you never know what the future holds in store for you."

Perceptively Jan commented, "You mean just in case Xavier gets back with Monique."

Squeezing her eyes shut, Nicole tried to banish the thought that had been lingering somewhere in the back of her mind. "I love Xavier, sis, but I want more from our relationship. I want to be his wife, and with Monique around reminding him of his failed marriage, I'm just afraid it will never happen."

"You'll never know if you run away. Stay and see where things lead."

Nicole glanced over at her young sister smiling. Her advice was sound, and appreciated.

The last day of school before the Christmas break was a half day. Nicole arrived at Xavier's office for a scheduled lunch date. Informed by his secretary that he had already left for lunch with Mrs. Ramón, Nicole visibly flinched. The reference to Monique was a stab to the heart. Nicole was hurt and disappointed. How could Xavier stand her up for that woman? Consumed by uncertainty, she decided it was time to take care of herself. For weeks now she had patiently tolerated Monique's presence and believed in Xavier. However, now left alone while he dined with his ex-wife, her survival instincts kicked in. Xavier's time at the base was fast running out, and with it her chance of a future with him. He said he loved her, and she believed him, but she also had to acknowledge that it didn't appear he loved her enough to make her his wife. And now that Monique was on the scene, her chances were starting to look slimmer. Determined not to be the one abandoned this time, she knew what she had to do. Exiting the building, she pulled out her cell phone and the card with Mr. Stanley's telephone number. She punched in the digits and made the first move for a life without Xavier.

CHAPTER 22

Ringing Nicole's doorbell, Xavier knew he had some serious explaining to do. But when Monique had showed up at his office wanting to discuss joint custody of Ryan, he knew that this was a luncheon he couldn't miss.

"Hey, baby," he immediately greeted Nicole as she opened the door.

Nicole didn't reply, just left the door standing open as she walked back towards her bedroom. She heard the door close behind her and knew he was following. Back inside the bedroom she picked up a pair of slacks and continued with her packing.

The first thing Xavier noticed on entering the room was the luggage laid out on the bed. He didn't recall Nicole mentioning a trip. "Going somewhere?"

"California," she supplied, not looking at him.

"California?" He walked towards her and turned her around to face him. "You didn't mention going to visit Gina." His brows were wrinkled with concern.

"I'm not going to see Gina," Nicole informed him, finally meeting his intense gray gaze. "I have an interview at a private school in San Diego."

Taken aback, Xavier felt as though he had been punched in the gut. "An interview? And when were you going to tell me?" His voice was escalating as quickly as his temper.

"To tell you the truth, I hadn't planned on making the interview. But considering every time I turn around you and your ex-wife are together, I thought it was about time I started looking out for myself."

"What the hell do you mean looking out for yourself? For over a year now it has been *us* looking out for each other."

"You're absolutely right, but it appears now that *us* includes Monique," Nicole replied just as heatedly.

Xavier knew Nicole was losing patience with the situation, but he had no idea it had come to this. Taking a calming breath, he tried reasoning with Nicole. "Nic, I had lunch with Monique today because she came in threatening to file for joint custody of Ryan. I had to know what game she was playing."

Angry at the nerve of the woman, Nicole's eyes blazed as she placed her hands on her hips facing him. "I'll tell you the game she's playing. She's using Ryan once again to get what she wants. She doesn't want Ryan, Xavier. She wants you. Have you noticed that she has made no attempt at meeting her son? Sure, she shows up at places where he is, but she has yet to meet him. Each time she makes some excuse, then leaves."

Xavier was once again reminded of Nicole's sharp mind. He smiled with pride. "You're absolutely right, sweetheart. I have noticed and that's part of the reason I went to lunch with her. Things just don't add up."

"Sure they do. She has accomplished exactly what she set out to do. Look at us, Xavier." She paused. "You and I haven't had a conversation that doesn't include Monique in weeks. Every time we're together it seems that we are at odds because of her. Yeah, things do add up. We're drifting apart."

The wind knocked out of his sails, Xavier collapsed into the corner chair. Nicole was absolutely right. And he was allowing it to happen. "Nicole, I have been trying to figure out her scheme and have completely overlooked the obvious. But why try to break us up?"

Exasperated, Nicole threw up her hands. "The woman wants you back, Xavier!"

The explanation didn't fit. He knew Monique, and knew she didn't want him back. He was the same man she'd married and divorced, with the same dreams and career. No, she was here causing trouble for another reason, and he intended to find out why.

Xavier rose from the chair and approached Nicole. He took her hands, drawing her to sit on the bed beside him. As he did so, he couldn't remember the last time he and Nicole had shared a bed. Monique had definitely come between them. He studied Nicole's beautiful golden-brown eyes and was able to see the fear in them, despite her valiant attempt at hiding it. She thought she was losing him, and until he got to the bottom of Monique's game there was nothing he could say at the moment to convince her otherwise.

"Nicole, I love you. If this interview in California is important to you, then I won't stand in your way. Just know that Ryan and I will be here when you return." With that said, Xavier quietly left. He could only hope the time away would allow Nicole to realize what she would be walking away from.

Two days. Nicole had been gone two days and it felt like an eternity. Her sudden absence from his life was thought-provoking. He had taken her presence in his life for granted, and now he realized that he could be losing the woman he loved. They had originally made plans to spend the holiday break together in New Orleans. He had taken leave from work so they could do just that. It hadn't worked out that way and he had Monique to thank for that as well. He had allowed Monique to come between them earlier in their relationship, but he would be damned if he'd allow her to drive Nicole away now. He *would* uncover her scheme.

Late Sunday night the opportunity presented itself. Xavier answered the door to discover Monique on his doorstep. She was dressed for seduction in a curve-hugging red sheath, which left nothing to the imagination. Her long, almond brown legs appeared to go on forever. Moving aside, he allowed her to enter.

"What brings you by so late?" Xavier asked, closing the door behind her. He wore pajama bottoms and no shirt. His feet were bare as well.

Monique walked further into the living room and took her time before answering. Her stride was slow and sensual. Pivoting around, she gave Xavier the full view of her feminine outline. She wore her brightest smile while her brown eyes devoured him. She had to admit the man was handsome. He was obviously one of those men who would get better with age. She recalled what making love with him had been like. It was good. Damn good, and she hoped to experience it again tonight. But then, that had never been their problem. Their problem was that they wanted different things in life.

Xavier, born to wealth and society, desired a simpler life. And she, the daughter of a career military man, wanted glitz and glamour. With his background he could fulfill her desires, and for a while there he had. However, over time it became quite apparent that he wanted a traditional home life, which included a traditional wife and children. And from what she had seen of him and Nicole during her weeks in town, he seemed well on the way to achieving that wish. But not if she succeeded. While she had been plagued by a bout of conscience earlier, she had convinced herself that it would be Xavier and Nicole's fault if their love wasn't strong enough to withstand a little interference,

"Would you believe me if I said you?"

Xavier could see the wheels turning inside her devious little head. "Not for a second."

Moving in close, she ran a red nail down the center of his exposed chest If she could just maneuver him into bed, her mission would be accomplished, because Xavier would either confess his infidelity, and lose the competition, or he would be willing to pay to keep it a secret. Either way she couldn't lose.

"Xavier, I really have changed. I made a great many mistakes, but baby, I want us to try again," she purred while running her hand through the mat of hair covering his chest. "It was good between us. It can be that way again." Her body brushed up against him.

Xavier stared intently into her lying eyes. He recalled how vain Monique was. Her self-worth was based on the men she could seduce and what she could manipulate them to do. She didn't take rejection well, and therefore didn't have female friends because she viewed all women as competition. He knew that was her Achilles heel and set out to attack it. Tangling his hands into her thick red hair he drew her lips to his. He kissed her deeply and was rewarded by a satisfied moan. Suddenly shoving her away, he launched his attack. "Go home, Monique, and I don't mean that hotel you've been living in. I don't want you."

Beyond angry, Monique glared at him. How dare he taunt her. She could have any man she wanted. She remembered how easy it had been to manipulate him to do anything she desired, whether he agreed with it or not. An hour in bed with her and he would agree to anything.

"Your brave act is admirable, but this is me, Xavier, and I know you want me. You always desired me." To prove her point, she reached behind to unzip her dress.

Xavier sensed he was on the right course and continued to push her buttons. "Monique, you can strip butt naked and I wouldn't want you. Nicole is the only woman I want in my bed and in my life. Why would I want you when I have a beautiful twenty-six year old?"

That did it. She was pissed. "That bony little girl could never please you like I did. And how dare you insinuate that I somehow come up short in comparison to that girl. I'll have you know I turn heads every where I go. Far better men than you, Xavier, have courted me." Her face was red with anger as she stormed towards the door. She grasped the knob, then turned to face Xavier with murder in her eyes. "That little witch can have you, because I didn't want anything from you except more money anyway."

"You're slipping lady," Xavier took great pride in informing a bewildered Monique. "You just got a taste of your own medicine."

"And what medicine would that be?"

"Manipulation. You, Monique Knowles, were just man ipulated into revealing your scheme. I didn't buy your little act for one moment."

Only now realizing her mistake, Monique looked uncomfortable. "So you tricked me. What do you expect me to say? That I'm sorry?"

"That's just it, Monique. I learned the hard way not to expect anything of you." Xavier pulled the door open, signaling the end of their conversation.

"About Ryan," Monique spoke up as she stood in the open doorway. It was good seeing him."

Xavier studied the woman who had been his wife. She was telling the truth, probably for the first time in her life, but the truth nonetheless. Tonight he was finally getting closure on that chapter in his life.

CHAPTER 23

Tuesday evening Xavier waited patiently inside Gulfport/Biloxi International Airport for Nicole's plane to arrive. Staring out into the dark night sky, he thought about the last couple of days. So much had taken place in such a short time. There was much for him and Nicole to discuss. But first he had to convince her not to leave him.

"Flight 781 just arriving at Gate 3."

Xavier followed the gathering crowd to the concourse doors. His eyes strained to locate Nicole as the first passengers made their way out He couldn't recall ever being this anxious to see anyone, but then he hadn't been truly in love before either. He prayed it wasn't too late for them. And then there she was searching for him. Maneuvering himself so that he could be seen, he held his breath as their eyes connected.

God, she was beautiful. Wearing a black turtleneck silk cashmere dress which stretched and conformed to her body and black suede boots with a three-inch stacked heel, she looked regal and exotic. Her mane of hair was free and flowing.

He'd come. Nicole hadn't been sure Xavier would be there to meet her flight. Considering the way they'd left things, she wouldn't have been surprised if he hadn't shown. But was she ever relieved to see him. She had missed him fiercely and couldn't wait to be wrapped within his loving arms. She only hoped it was she he wanted in his arms and not Monique.

"Hi," she said, now standing in front of him.

For a moment Xavier said nothing. He searched her golden-brown eyes for answers. And what he saw within them was the love they shared. "Welcome home, baby," he whispered while folding her into his arms. Reluctantly releasing her, he guided them out of the line of traffic to a secluded little corner. He then drew her back into his arms. Her head rested against his chest His heart was beating so hard he was sure Nicole could hear it.

"I was so afraid you wouldn't be here."

"With you is where I belong, Nicole." Xavier released her so that he could look into her eyes.

"What about Monique?"

"Long gone and good riddance." He smiled. "Nicole, if you want the position in San Diego, I can pull a special duty assignment in the area."

Nicole couldn't believe what she was hearing. Xavier was actually contemplating moving with her so they could be together. She searched his gray eyes for sincerity. "That's a great effort to make for a lover."

"A lover yes, but my wife, not at all."

Nicole was speechless. Her eyes glazed over with unshed tears. He had finally asked her to marry him. He did find her worthy of being Mrs. Ramón. They would be a *real* family. "You want to marry me?" Her voice was low and unbelieving.

Standing before him was that frightened little girl who wished to be loved. Xavier thought after the time they had shared, Nicole would have known his love was forever, and that marriage was in their future. But considering her life and the disappointments, he now realized that she didn't place much value in hope.

"More than anything I've ever wanted to do. I love you, Nicole Edwards, and would be honored to have you for my wife."

"I love you so much, Xavier. Yes, I'll marry you," Nicole squealed. She wrapped her arms around his neck as his lips found hers.

EPILOGUE

Nicole sat on the front porch of Willow Bayou soaking up the mild March sunshine. She had just mailed a card to Gina and Keith to thank them for bringing Xavier into her life and giving her a chance at such happiness. It had become an anniversary of sorts, and she owed it to her friends. Their five-year marriage was loving and solid. Built on friendship, cemented with respect, and nurtured by love.

There had been no word from Monique since her sudden departure. So for the moment she was relegated to the past. They knew it was only a matter of time, however, before Ryan's curiosity about his mother would bring Monique back into their lives.

The move to California had been a good one for them all. Initially Nicole had refused the position, but with Xavier's willingness to move, and actually his encouragement for her to accept such a prestigious position, she had accepted. They had learned to rely on each other while away from their families, and the bonds between them strengthened.

Nicole had never once regretted her decision. And how could she when their life together had been filled with blessings. They had returned to Willow Bayou a year ago and worked side by side to restore the remaining section of the house. It had been a labor of love because they were rearing their children in this home. Xavier's military career was behind him, and so he had established his own security and investigation firm. The business was doing well and kept him involved in the career he loved.

Thinking of Xavier, she marveled over the changes in him. He was tenderly loving and free with his emotions. He confided his deepest secrets and thoughts to her. They were closer now than ever, and with the birth of their child their love grew. At forty-two he was still fit and trim and just as appealing as the day she'd laid eyes upon him. And with his gray, magnetic eyes he could still make her tingle all over

Nicole was now enjoying being a mother to their two children. It was a role she had eagerly taken on. Initially she had had doubts about her abilities to be a good mother, but loving Ryan had come naturally. And by the time their daughter had been born, she was quite content in her role. Now she ran a hand across her slightly swollen abdomen as she thought about the child on the way. Her rooms were filled with children and their laughter, just the way she had always dreamed a home should be.

Xavier, who sat on the porch railing, loved watching his wife when she grew quiet and introspective like now. Her facial expressions always gave her thoughts away. When she smiled just so and her eyes twinkled, she was marveling over the children. And when her golden brown eyes glowed radiantly like now, he knew her thoughts were sensual and passionate—definitely about him.

Nicole had come such a long way since their initial meeting. She was self-confident and sure. She was his best friend, his lover, and his wife. But most importantly, she was the mother of his children. She was patient and loving to a fault, she doted and encouraged. She reprimanded and offered guidance, but most of all she loved them for who they were. And they were each so very different. Ryan, who was now fourteen, looked more and more like his father. He and Nicole, whom he now called mother, shared a special bond. He was highly intelligent, yet reserved as he grew into adulthood. Lillian, their daughter, was four. She was a small replica of her mother, all except for the smoky gray eyes. She was her father's heart. Her carefree spirit would no doubt give him hours of concern in the future. Her childish laughter filled the air as she ran around the yard on short skinny legs, chasing her brother.

"Penny for your thoughts," Nicole interrupted Xavier's musing.

Turning his thoughtful gaze onto his radiant wife, Xavier, realized he'd never loved Nicole more. Their ten-year age difference was no longer an issue because despite it, they were definitely compatible. "I was thinking about doing a little cooking," he replied with a wink. "Rosa is out here to watch the children, and our room is nice and quiet."

Nicole sneaked a peak over at Rosa. She wondered if she had heard Xavier's suggestion. Noting she gave no indication of listening, Nicole blushed with wickedness as she nodded yes to his invitation. She eased out the chair clasping his hand an led the way into the house. At the foot of the stairs she release his hand and headed in the direction of the kitchen.

"Where the devil are you going?" Xavier whispered impatiently.

"To get the apron of course."

2007 Publication Schedule

January

Rooms of the Heart
Donna Hill
ISBN-13: 978-1-58571-219-9
ISBN-10: 1-58571-219-1
$6.99

A Dangerous Love
J. M. Jeffries
ISBN-13: 978-1-58571-217-5
ISBN-10: 1-58571-217-5
$6.99

February

Bound By Love
Beverly Clark
ISBN-13: 978-1-58571-232-8
ISBN-10: 1-58571-232-9
$6.99

A Love to Cherish
Beverly Clark
ISBN-13: 978-1-58571-233-5
ISBN-10: 1-58571-233-7
$6.99

March

Best of Friends
Natalie Dunbar
ISBN-13: 978-1-58571-220-5
ISBN-10: 1-58571-220-5
$6.99

Midnight Magic
Gwynne Forster
ISBN-13: 978-1-58571-225-0
ISBN-10: 1-58571-225-6
$6.99

April

Cherish the Flame
Beverly Clark
ISBN-13: 978-1-58571-221-2
ISBN-10: 1-58571-221-3
$6.99

Quiet Storm
Donna Hill
ISBN-13: 978-1-58571-226-7
ISBN-10: 1-58571-226-4
$6.99

May

Sweet Tomorrows
Kimberley White
ISBN-13: 978-1-58571-234-2
ISBN-10: 1-58571-234-5
$6.99

No Commitment Required
Seressia Glass
ISBN-13: 978-1-58571-222-9
ISBN-10: 1-58571-222-1
$6.99

June

A Dangerous Deception
J. M. Jeffries
ISBN-13: 978-1-58571-228-1
ISBN-10: 1-58571-228-0
$6.99

Illusions
Pamela Leigh Starr
ISBN-13: 978-1-58571-229-8
ISBN-10: 1-58571-229-9
$6.99

2007 Publication Schedule (continued)

July

Indiscretions
Donna Hill
ISBN-13: 978-1-58571-230-4
ISBN-10: 1-58571-230-2
$6.99

Whispers in the Night
Dorothy Elizabeth Love
ISBN-13: 978-1-58571-231-1
ISBN-10: 1-58571-231-1
$6.99

August

Bodyguard
Andrea Jackson
ISBN-13: 978-1-58571-235-9
ISBN-10: 1-58571-235-3
$6.99

Crossing Paths, Tempting Memories
Dorothy Elizabeth Love
ISBN-13: 978-1-58571-236-6
ISBN-10: 1-58571-236-1
$6.99

September

Fate
Pamela Leigh Starr
ISBN-13: 978-1-58571-258-8
ISBN-10: 1-58571-258-2
$6.99

Mae's Promise
Melody Walcott
ISBN-13: 978-1-58571-259-5
ISBN-10: 1-58571-259-0
$6.99

October

Magnolia Sunset
Giselle Carmichael
ISBN-13: 978-1-58571-260-1
ISBN-10: 1-58571-260-4
$6.99

Broken
Dar Tomlinson
ISBN-13: 978-1-58571-261-8
ISBN-10: 1-58571-261-2
$6.99

November

Truly Inseparable
Wanda Y. Thomas
ISBN-13: 978-1-58571-262-5
ISBN-10: 1-58571-262-0
$6.99

The Color Line
Lizzette G. Carter
ISBN-13: 978-1-58571-263-2
ISBN-10: 1-58571-263-9
$6.99

December

Love Always
Mildred Riley
ISBN-13: 978-1-58571-264-9
ISBN-10: 1-58571-264-7
$6.99

Pride and Joi
Gay Gunn
ISBN-13: 978-1-58571-265-6
ISBN-10: 1-58571-265-5
$6.99

Other Genesis Press, Inc. Titles

A Dangerous Deception	J.M. Jeffries	$8.95
A Dangerous Love	J.M. Jeffries	$8.95
A Dangerous Obsession	J.M. Jeffries	$8.95
A Drummer's Beat to Mend	Kei Swanson	$9.95
A Happy Life	Charlotte Harris	$9.95
A Heart's Awakening	Veronica Parker	$9.95
A Lark on the Wing	Phyliss Hamilton	$9.95
A Love of Her Own	Cheris F. Hodges	$9.95
A Love to Cherish	Beverly Clark	$8.95
A Risk of Rain	Dar Tomlinson	$8.95
A Twist of Fate	Beverly Clark	$8.95
A Will to Love	Angie Daniels	$9.95
Acquisitions	Kimberley White	$8.95
Across	Carol Payne	$12.95
After the Vows	Leslie Esdaile	$10.95
(Summer Anthology)	T.T. Henderson	
	Jacqueline Thomas	
Again My Love	Kayla Perrin	$10.95
Against the Wind	Gwynne Forster	$8.95
All I Ask	Barbara Keaton	$8.95
Ambrosia	T.T. Henderson	$8.95
An Unfinished Love Affair	Barbara Keaton	$8.95
And Then Came You	Dorothy Elizabeth Love	$8.95
Angel's Paradise	Janice Angelique	$9.95
At Last	Lisa G. Riley	$8.95
Best of Friends	Natalie Dunbar	$8.95
Beyond the Rapture	Beverly Clark	$9.95
Blaze	Barbara Keaton	$9.95
Blood Lust	J. M. Jeffries	$9.95

Other Genesis Press, Inc. Titles (continued)

Bodyguard	Andrea Jackson	$9.95
Boss of Me	Diana Nyad	$8.95
Bound by Love	Beverly Clark	$8.95
Breeze	Robin Hampton Allen	$10.95
Broken	Dar Tomlinson	$24.95
By Design	Barbara Keaton	$8.95
Cajun Heat	Charlene Berry	$8.95
Careless Whispers	Rochelle Alers	$8.95
Cats & Other Tales	Marilyn Wagner	$8.95
Caught in a Trap	Andre Michelle	$8.95
Caught Up In the Rapture	Lisa G. Riley	$9.95
Cautious Heart	Cheris F Hodges	$8.95
Chances	Pamela Leigh Starr	$8.95
Cherish the Flame	Beverly Clark	$8.95
Class Reunion	Irma Jenkins/	
	John Brown	$12.95
Code Name: Diva	J.M. Jeffries	$9.95
Conquering Dr. Wexler's Heart	Kimberley White	$9.95
Crossing Paths,	Dorothy Elizabeth Love	$9.95
Tempting Memories		
Cypress Whisperings	Phyllis Hamilton	$8.95
Dark Embrace	Crystal Wilson Harris	$8.95
Dark Storm Rising	Chinelu Moore	$10.95
Daughter of the Wind	Joan Xian	$8.95
Deadly Sacrifice	Jack Kean	$22.95
Designer Passion	Dar Tomlinson	$8.95
Dreamtective	Liz Swados	$5.95
Ebony Butterfly II	Delilah Dawson	$14.95
Echoes of Yesterday	Beverly Clark	$9.95

Other Genesis Press, Inc. Titles (continued)

Eden's Garden	Elizabeth Rose	$8.95
Everlastin' Love	Gay G. Gunn	$8.95
Everlasting Moments	Dorothy Elizabeth Love	$8.95
Everything and More	Sinclair Lebeau	$8.95
Everything but Love	Natalie Dunbar	$8.95
Eve's Prescription	Edwina Martin Arnold	$8.95
Falling	Natalie Dunbar	$9.95
Fate	Pamela Leigh Starr	$8.95
Finding Isabella	A.J. Garrotto	$8.95
Forbidden Quest	Dar Tomlinson	$10.95
Forever Love	Wanda Y. Thomas	$8.95
From the Ashes	Kathleen Suzanne	$8.95
	Jeanne Sumerix	
Gentle Yearning	Rochelle Alers	$10.95
Glory of Love	Sinclair LeBeau	$10.95
Go Gentle into that Good Night	Malcom Boyd	$12.95
Goldengroove	Mary Beth Craft	$16.95
Groove, Bang, and Jive	Steve Cannon	$8.99
Hand in Glove	Andrea Jackson	$9.95
Hard to Love	Kimberley White	$9.95
Hart & Soul	Angie Daniels	$8.95
Heartbeat	Stephanie Bedwell-Grime	$8.95
Hearts Remember	M. Loui Quezada	$8.95
Hidden Memories	Robin Allen	$10.95
Higher Ground	Leah Latimer	$19.95
Hitler, the War, and the Pope	Ronald Rychiak	$26.95
How to Write a Romance	Kathryn Falk	$18.95
I Married a Reclining Chair	Lisa M. Fuhs	$8.95
Indigo After Dark Vol. I	Nia Dixon/Angelique	$10.95

Other Genesis Press, Inc. Titles (continued)

Indigo After Dark Vol. II	Dolores Bundy/ Cole Riley	$10.95
Indigo After Dark Vol. III	Montana Blue/ Coco Morena	$10.95
Indigo After Dark Vol. IV	Cassandra Colt/ Diana Richeaux	$14.95
Indigo After Dark Vol. V	Delilah Dawson	$14.95
Icie	Pamela Leigh Starr	$8.95
I'll Be Your Shelter	Giselle Carmichael	$8.95
I'll Paint a Sun	A.J. Garrotto	$9.95
Illusions	Pamela Leigh Starr	$8.95
Indiscretions	Donna Hill	$8.95
Intentional Mistakes	Michele Sudler	$9.95
Interlude	Donna Hill	$8.95
Intimate Intentions	Angie Daniels	$8.95
Jolie's Surrender	Edwina Martin-Arnold	$8.95
Kiss or Keep	Debra Phillips	$8.95
Lace	Giselle Carmichael	$9.95
Last Train to Memphis	Elsa Cook	$12.95
Lasting Valor	Ken Olsen	$24.95
Let Us Prey	Hunter Lundy	$25.95
Life Is Never As It Seems	J.J. Michael	$12.95
Lighter Shade of Brown	Vicki Andrews	$8.95
Love Always	Mildred E. Riley	$10.95
Love Doesn't Come Easy	Charlyne Dickerson	$8.95
Love Unveiled	Gloria Greene	$10.95
Love's Deception	Charlene Berry	$10.95
Love's Destiny	M. Loui Quezada	$8.95
Mae's Promise	Melody Walcott	$8.95

Other Genesis Press, Inc. Titles (continued)

Magnolia Sunset	Giselle Carmichael	$8.95
Matters of Life and Death	Lesego Malepe, Ph.D.	$15.95
Meant to Be	Jeanne Sumerix	$8.95
Midnight Clear	Leslie Esdaile	$10.95
(Anthology)	Gwynne Forster	
	Carmen Green	
	Monica Jackson	
Midnight Magic	Gwynne Forster	$8.95
Midnight Peril	Vicki Andrews	$10.95
Misconceptions	Pamela Leigh Starr	$9.95
Montgomery's Children	Richard Perry	$14.95
My Buffalo Soldier	Barbara B. K. Reeves	$8.95
Naked Soul	Gwynne Forster	$8.95
Next to Last Chance	Louisa Dixon	$24.95
No Apologies	Seressia Glass	$8.95
No Commitment Required	Seressia Glass	$8.95
No Regrets	Mildred E. Riley	$8.95
Nowhere to Run	Gay G. Gunn	$10.95
O Bed! O Breakfast!	Rob Kuehnle	$14.95
Object of His Desire	A. C. Arthur	$8.95
Office Policy	A. C. Arthur	$9.95
Once in a Blue Moon	Dorianne Cole	$9.95
One Day at a Time	Bella McFarland	$8.95
Outside Chance	Louisa Dixon	$24.95
Passion	T.T. Henderson	$10.95
Passion's Blood	Cherif Fortin	$22.95
Passion's Journey	Wanda Y. Thomas	$8.95
Past Promises	Jahmel West	$8.95
Path of Fire	T.T. Henderson	$8.95

Other Genesis Press, Inc. Titles (continued)

Path of Thorns	Annetta P. Lee	$9.95
Peace Be Still	Colette Haywood	$12.95
Picture Perfect	Reon Carter	$8.95
Playing for Keeps	Stephanie Salinas	$8.95
Pride & Joi	Gay G. Gunn	$15.95
Pride & Joi	Gay G. Gunn	$8.95
Promises to Keep	Alicia Wiggins	$8.95
Quiet Storm	Donna Hill	$10.95
Reckless Surrender	Rochelle Alers	$6.95
Red Polka Dot in a World of Plaid	Varian Johnson	$12.95
Reluctant Captive	Joyce Jackson	$8.95
Rendezvous with Fate	Jeanne Sumerix	$8.95
Revelations	Cheris F. Hodges	$8.95
Rivers of the Soul	Leslie Esdaile	$8.95
Rocky Mountain Romance	Kathleen Suzanne	$8.95
Rooms of the Heart	Donna Hill	$8.95
Rough on Rats and Tough on Cats	Chris Parker	$12.95
Secret Library Vol. 1	Nina Sheridan	$18.95
Secret Library Vol. 2	Cassandra Colt	$8.95
Shades of Brown	Denise Becker	$8.95
Shades of Desire	Monica White	$8.95
Shadows in the Moonlight	Jeanne Sumerix	$8.95
Sin	Crystal Rhodes	$8.95
So Amazing	Sinclair LeBeau	$8.95
Somebody's Someone	Sinclair LeBeau	$8.95
Someone to Love	Alicia Wiggins	$8.95
Song in the Park	Martin Brant	$15.95

Other Genesis Press, Inc. Titles (continued)

Soul Eyes	Wayne L. Wilson	$12.95
Soul to Soul	Donna Hill	$8.95
Southern Comfort	J.M. Jeffries	$8.95
Still the Storm	Sharon Robinson	$8.95
Still Waters Run Deep	Leslie Esdaile	$8.95
Stories to Excite You	Anna Forrest/Divine	$14.95
Subtle Secrets	Wanda Y. Thomas	$8.95
Suddenly You	Crystal Hubbard	$9.95
Sweet Repercussions	Kimberley White	$9.95
Sweet Tomorrows	Kimberly White	$8.95
Taken by You	Dorothy Elizabeth Love	$9.95
Tattooed Tears	T. T. Henderson	$8.95
The Color Line	Lizzette Grayson Carter	$9.95
The Color of Trouble	Dyanne Davis	$8.95
The Disappearance of Allison Jones	Kayla Perrin	$5.95
The Honey Dipper's Legacy	Pannell-Allen	$14.95
The Joker's Love Tune	Sidney Rickman	$15.95
The Little Pretender	Barbara Cartland	$10.95
The Love We Had	Natalie Dunbar	$8.95
The Man Who Could Fly	Bob & Milana Beamon	$18.95
The Missing Link	Charlyne Dickerson	$8.95
The Price of Love	Sinclair LeBeau	$8.95
The Smoking Life	Ilene Barth	$29.95
The Words of the Pitcher	Kei Swanson	$8.95
Three Wishes	Seressia Glass	$8.95
Ties That Bind	Kathleen Suzanne	$8.95
Tiger Woods	Libby Hughes	$5.95

Time is of the Essence	Angie Daniels	$9.95
Timeless Devotion	Bella McFarland	$9.95
Tomorrow's Promise	Leslie Esdaile	$8.95
Truly Inseparable	Wanda Y. Thomas	$8.95
Unbreak My Heart	Dar Tomlinson	$8.95
Uncommon Prayer	Kenneth Swanson	$9.95
Unconditional	A.C. Arthur	$9.95
Unconditional Love	Alicia Wiggins	$8.95
Until Death Do Us Part	Susan Paul	$8.95
Vows of Passion	Bella McFarland	$9.95
Wedding Gown	Dyanne Davis	$8.95
What's Under Benjamin's Bed	Sandra Schaffer	$8.95
When Dreams Float	Dorothy Elizabeth Love	$8.95
Whispers in the Night	Dorothy Elizabeth Love	$8.95
Whispers in the Sand	LaFlorya Gauthier	$10.95
Wild Ravens	Altonya Washington	$9.95
Yesterday Is Gone	Beverly Clark	$10.95
Yesterday's Dreams, Tomorrow's Promises	Reon Laudat	$8.95
Your Precious Love	Sinclair LeBeau	$8.95

Order Form

Mail to: Genesis Press, Inc.
P.O. Box 101
Columbus, MS 39703

Name _____
Address _____
City/State _____ Zip _____
Telephone _____

Ship to (if different from above)
Name _____
Address _____
City/State _____ Zip _____
Telephone _____

Credit Card Information
Credit Card # _____ ☐ Visa ☐ Mastercard
Expiration Date (mm/yy) _____ ☐ AmEx ☐ Discover

Qty.	Author	Title	Price	Total

Use this order form, or call **1-888-INDIGO-1**	**Total for books** _____
	 Shipping and handling:
	   $5 first two books,
	   $1 each additional book _____
	 Total S & H _____
	 Total amount enclosed _____
	 Mississippi residents add 7% sales tax

Visit www.genesis-press.com for latest releases and excerpts.